MW00714558

Soldier's Gap

by
David Schwinghammer

HATS
OFF™

β

Soldier's Gap

Copyright © 2001 David Schwinghammer

All rights reserved. No part of this book may be
reproduced or retransmitted in any form or by any
means without the written consent of the publisher.

Published by Hats Off BooksTM
601 East 1st Street
Tucson, Arizona 85705
www.HatsOffBooks.com

ISBN: 1-58736-039-x
LCCN: 2001088500

Book and cover design by Jay Carlis

Printed in the United States of America

This work is a work of fiction and solely the product of the author's imagination. Characters, names, events, places and dialogue, found herein, are not intended to and should not be interpreted to recount or to tell of the life of any person, living or dead (excluding public figures). Any such similarity to events, names, persons or dialogue is unintentional and arises from coincidence.

To JoAnn,
my most reliable reader and critic

Chapter 1

Siege Perilous

"If the slayer thinks he slays,
If the slain thinks he is slain,
Both these do not understand:
He slays not, is not slain.
— Katha Upanishad, 2.19

Jerry Egge looked up from tying the laces of his high-top sneakers, then sat back hard on the front step of his house, a stabbing pain wrenching his gut. There, scrawled in four-foot-high, blood-red lettering on the newly-painted water tower across the way, were the words, "Fuck You, Egge."

Damn kids. Why couldn't they be satisfied with overpasses, stop signs and bathroom stalls? He swore some of them saw their high school principal as a two hundred pound, balding lab rat. He could hear them now, bragging over Cokes and hamburgers at Andy's Diner: *How much can the pinhead take before he locks the door to his private washroom and slashes his wrists on his sharpened Wayne Newton belt buckle?*

Jerry thought about going back to bed and burying his head under the covers. Instead, he stood, inhaled deeply, and let it out, his breath visible in the early morning air. What a job. A coal miner had a greater sense of ease. He rolled his neck, hearing it crick once, twice, then trotted on down the steps, tiptoed around the stacks of lumber on his front walk, and set off for the woods on the outskirts of Soldier, where every day he ran a little deeper into the pines. Maybe this would be the day he'd keep on going, run right into Fertile and catch a bus to Chicago. He could get a job selling textbooks or something.

He shuffled along, dodging the refuse left behind when the tons of snow had melted. Dead leaves, dormant sod. It was that depressing time of year, when the green tint of the lawns reminded him of bile and the melting snow looked like dirty laundry.

1

Through the early morning haze, he could see a group of runners approaching at a rapid rate, blue uniforms bouncing up and down, the flap, flap, flap of their sneakers arriving before he could make out their faces. The Commando track team, out for a morning workout. As the lead runners passed, some of them snickered. For a moment, he thought they'd seen the graffiti on the water tower, but from this vantage point, the tower was blocked by the trees. It must just be him. Stoop-shouldered, gangly, long legs with a short torso—he looked weird enough in his principal's coat and tie. In sweats and a Minnesota Gopher baseball cap, he must look like a damn cartoon.

Jerry plodded on down Wheat Field Lane, ignoring the good mornings of the trailing runners, chewing over what he'd do to the kid who'd painted that obscenity on the tower.

He slowed somewhat as he approached Veteran's Park, where the statue of Colonel Colvill, leader of the First Minnesota at Gettysburg, held court, waving his sabre menacingly. Colvill and his infantry troops had saved the Union's butt on the second day of the battle, filling in the breach when General Sickles disobeyed orders and attacked rather than hold his position.

Eighty-three percent fatality rate. At least they'd died repelling foreign invaders. What Jerry wouldn't give to have been there among the 262 men staring death in the face in a bayonet charge against Longstreet's 1600 Alabamans. Jerry was so absorbed he could hear a volley of the muzzle-loaders the troops had used at Gettysburg. No, just hammering coming from the holy roller church at the end of Wheat Field Lane.

Jerry saluted. There seemed to be a hint of a smile on the Colonel's greenish-bronze face. Never noticed that before.

He pounded on, panting, feeling as though he were running in place. Glancing to his left, he noticed flashing lights, one of those rental signs in front of Audette's Monuments. *Plan ahead! Special discount for you and your spouse.*

Grave stones. Jerry had a donor card in his wallet. What would the doctors do with the rest of him after they'd mined his organs? Cremation? Sue would flush him down the bowl. They weren't exactly a poster couple for nuptial bliss. If he stayed with her, it wouldn't be long before the knives came out of the drawer.

Last night he'd talked to Sue for the first time about divorce.

"Do you know what sort of man your lover is?" he'd said. "How can you expect me to hand over my paycheck every two weeks when you're sleeping with him?"

"Say you love me," she said. She always knew how to burst his bubble.

As he approached the holy roller church, the hammering and the crying noise nails make when yanked from wood caused his teeth to clench. Twenty or thirty men were roofing the church, which, until a couple of months ago, had resided in Fertile and had blocked traffic for hours as it made its way, on a flatbed truck, to Soldier. Over, under, and through the hammering, he could hear music: "Shall We Gather at the River?"

Jerry'd heard that attendance was down at Immaculate Conception. Father Mischke's polka masses couldn't compete with the unbridled abandon a parishioner could experience in the holy roller church. Since the fundamentalists had arrived, their Sunday morning service—and Sunday evening and Wednesday evening—made such a racket that the neighbors had petitioned Sheriff Kline to invoke the noise ordinance.

Some of the men stopped hammering and looked down at him running past. He waved. None of them waved back.

Jerry tramped over the bridge crossing Plum Creek, a tributary of the north-flowing Red River. Only a block or so and he'd be clear of houses and headed into the country. He could already smell the manure in the outlying fields.

He scooped up some slush, formed an iceball, and whipped it at a signpost, trying to visualize the homely face of Sue's lover. He missed badly. He slapped the snow off his hands, wiped his hands on his pant legs, and ran on.

The houses disappeared and he was in the woods, which, for some reason, made him feel disoriented. When he came to a fork in the trail, he was unsure of which of the two paths to take. He chose the one on the right. Back in town, a train whistle blasted the air. A morning freight, clattering along over the trestle crossing Plum Creek. The engineer, frustrated jazzman that he was, played variations on the usual jarring toot. A long, a languid short, followed by a blare of grand proportion. Sounded like *Nooo, don't gooowww* to Jerry.

But he kept on going, needed to sweat the poison out of his system. He came to a stretch where the path wound slightly downhill through a canopy of trees, his feet making an echoing sound as he galloped along. A gust of wind whistled in the pines, roiled last autumn's fallen leaves, and swiped his Minnesota Gopher hat. It blew into the woods and snagged on a tree branch; then, just as he was about to grab it, an updraft took it and tossed it higher into the trees, out of reach. He finally managed to retrieve it with the aid of a fallen branch, tightened the one-size-fits-all band in the back, and got moving again.

Off in the woods somewhere, he could hear shouting, laughter. Damn, must be those splatballers, oddballs acting out some sort of mercenary fantasy with paint-pellet guns. Just another form of vandalism in his mind.

Turn around now, sprint back to your house, and lock all the doors, he told himself. Why did he feel so uneasy this morning? He'd set a goal, though—principals were good at setting goals—and if he didn't beat yesterday's distance, he'd be nagging himself all day.

His side was beginning to ache. He'd run up to that bare oak in the distance, well beyond yesterday's mark, then call it a day. The bare oak shimmered like a fairy-tale tree, the kind that would reach out and grab the hapless hero on his way by. Perhaps he'd stumbled into a parallel universe. No flying monkeys, though. He chuckled and pushed on toward the dead oak.

Jerry reached the lifeless oak. He was making a wide turn to go back the way he'd come, running out of the path, tripping over sticks and sliding on leaves, when he thought he heard a noise. He stopped. The noise stopped.

Probably only one of those splatballers.

But why did he feel as he always did before he had to give a speech to the assembly in the school gymnasium? His knees were rubbery, and he suddenly felt as though he were in the cross hairs of a rifle scope. And a little voice was telling him to run. Run while you still can.

Maybe singing would help. "Shall we gather at the river," he warbled, then stopped and listened. Was it the wind? He started moving again. "Yes, we'll gather at the river. The beautiful, the beautiful river." He stopped again, listening so hard he could hear his heart beat. "Gather...with the saints...at the river...that flows by the throne of God."

There was more, but that's all he knew. It seemed that if he could remember another verse he could ward off evil.

This time he was sure someone was running toward him. It sounded like a wild boar crashing through the underbrush.

He fled, sore feet and aching side forgotten. But he kept slipping and sliding on the wet leaves and patchy snow, as if he were in one of those dreams where a monster was chasing him and his feet were encased in cement. Behind him, somebody was wheezing and puffing. And closing. Jerry hit a dry patch and picked up speed, his legs stretching, pounding. He was pulling ahead; he had to be.

Suddenly, something hit him from behind. He tumbled head-long and rolled, got a glimpse of a bear of a man with thick, curly, black hair brandishing a baseball bat above his head. "What do you think you're doing, you son of a bi—"

And then someone was knocking, and there was pain, excruciating pain, and it was raining—sticky, saplike rain—and someone was hammering, like one of those jackhammers you hear early in the morning when you've had trouble sleeping and it's the middle of August with the dew point in the 70s, and there was a sound, like the grunting in a pornographic film, and he saw colors—red, blue, green, yellow, swirling in a vortex, and the hammering sound changed to a buzzing.

The hammering, grunting, and buzzing stopped. All was peaceful. The only sound was the chirping of the birds.

Jerry rose up above his body, looking down on a man spraying something on his back and legs with a can of paint.

Then the man kicked him in the face, and his body flopped over onto its back.

*   *   *

Martha Macintosh adjusted the focus on her field glasses. A white-breasted nuthatch was nosing its way down the trunk of a birch tree, a distinguishing characteristic, she knew. Such a pretty bird with its white breast, throat and face, bluish-black coloring and cute, little upturned bill.

As she followed the bird down the tree trunk, she noticed blood. Deerhunting season? No, that was long gone. A poacher?

Adjusting her field glasses, she honed in on a form at the foot of the tree. Then she dropped the glasses. She knelt to pick them up, her hands shaking—there was no mistaking it, the form was a human body, and the body had been wearing a Minnesota Gopher baseball cap. It was there, lying next to his hand. She only knew one person who wore a cap like that, her principal, Jerry Egge. The fool wore the cap to school, trying to be one of the kids. They poked fun at the fact that he didn't curve the bill.

Martha edged closer, and as she did, the smell hit her. She breathed through her mouth—knew that from one of the mystery novels she read during down times in the special education department where she worked afternoons with EBD students.

Maybe Egge had been out here playing splatball. She wouldn't put it past him. The kids had probably given him the slip, and he'd gotten lost and knocked himself out on an overhanging tree limb. No, too much blood.

As she got closer, she noticed his tongue, which looked like a piece of dried beef, then saw the detached eyeball, and she vomited on the body.

She screamed and screamed until her voice gave out, then ran to the nearest farm, home to an agoraphobic couple with no phone and whose car, an old Chrysler with a very sluggish battery, moaned and whimpered when the husband tried to start it. Finally the frustration of listening to the balky car got to her and she ran off on foot. She had to get help, couldn't take the chance on another farm.

Martha tried to flag down two cars on the road, but they ignored her frantic waving. Halfway back to town, clouds burst overhead, sending rivulets of water and mascara streaming into her eyes. Abruptly the rain quit, and a cloud of gnats took its place, hectoring her all the way to town.

Dear God, was she being punished? Her grandmother, who went to mass every weekday and twice on Sundays, had tapped a chicken-like talon on the Bible when she'd heard Martha had begun doing astrological charts.

"Martha, you hear me now. The Lord says, 'There shall not be found among you any one that useth divination, or an observer of times, or an enchanter, or a witch. Or a charmer, or a consulter with familiar spirits, or a wizard, or a necromancer. For all these things are an abomination unto the Lord.' You'll be in hell with your grandfather if you don't pay me no mind."

*   *   *

As she passed through town, eyes peeked out from behind curtains in every other household, wondering at the hysterical woman waving her arms at passing cars mouthing a soundless scream. Not much happened in Soldier, and the eyes weren't going to miss it when something did.

Chapter 2

Another Dog Gone

"Was it a vision, or a waking dream?
Fled is that music:—Do I wake or sleep?"
— John Keats

In order to reach the corpse, Dave Jenkins, deputy sheriff of Polk County, had to drive his Jeep down a deeply rutted track the farmer used to get in and out of his field. Twice he almost got stuck before reaching the clearing about a quarter mile in where Mrs. Macintosh said he'd find the body. He put the Jeep in neutral, letting it idle.

Miles Krueger's property. That odd little pecker, Les, was his son. Could he have had something to do with this?

Off to the left he could see what looked like a pile of dirty clothes, or maybe, a windblown scarecrow a farmer had staked in the middle of his cornfield to frighten away noxious birds. Only *this* scarecrow had been clubbed to death. Mrs. Macintosh said the body was in pretty tough shape. She'd been really freaked out, refused to come along. "I've been negligent," she'd said. "All I want to do is get to church and pray."

This was Dave's first murder. He didn't really want to go too close to the corpse just yet, thank you, so he pulled the bill of his USS Lake Champlain cap over his eyes and slouched, stroking the ends of the Old West mustache he'd grown to hide his baby face. Sheriff Kline and Larry Henderson of the Bureau of Criminal Apprehension should be here any time now.

Time passed. The body just lay there. Nobody came. He shut off the engine, got out and leaned against the hood. An Alberta wind was whistling through the trees giving him a chill. He snapped the top button on his Navy SEAL windbreaker and tried to stretch the cuffs of the sleeves over his hands.

Wasn't in the best shape to be investigating a murder after a night out with the boys. His head hurt a little and stomach was queasy. He'd been worrying about the recall petition his former

7

third grade teacher Hildegard Weiss—county clerk and power behind the scenes—had started on Sheriff Kline, and a few beers always quieted his braying conscience. Normally, he could sip coffee and recover at his desk. Who knew some crazy'd bump off the high school principal?

The sun chose this moment to peep through the clouds, the glare blinding him. He took off his cap, wiped the sweat away from his forehead with a bandana. He opened the buttons on his windbreaker, snuck another look at the corpse. Blood all over the place.

This wasn't going to be fun. He hadn't seen a corpse since Desert Storm—a couple of Saddam's boys—and he hadn't been too thrilled then. And this was somebody he knew. Egge had played right field and sometimes pitched for Dave's softball team, the Soldier Dogfaces. Just last night he'd called Egge asking if he'd like to join the baseball rotisserie league he was starting.

Had to suck it up. He was going on thirty after all, and this was the big one he'd been waiting for ever since he'd had the tin star pounded into his chest.

He wandered down the path away from the body, careful to stay on the verge. There were footprints moving toward Egge's corpse, lots of them, and they looked fresh. Size fourteen at least, if he were any judge. No time to follow the tracks now. Sheriff Kline would wonder where the hell he was when he showed up. Next to the path, some slob had discarded a twelve pack of empties. Rolling Rock barley pop. Green bottles, green cartoon. Never tried it.

High school kids and young adults in a state of arrested development used this place as a make-out spot. He'd been here himself not too long ago.

He looked around the clearing. Birches mixed with the occasional red-tinged pine, downed trees, unidentifiable weeds just beginning to sprout. There was a pond off to the right of Egge's body where the birches reflected off the water. Like mummy fingers. A ticklish shiver crept up his spine.

Guess he couldn't put it off much longer.

He strode toward the body. Egge's bowels had let loose when he'd expired, and the stench was worse than an open cesspool. He put his bandana over his face, bit his lower lip to control the gagging sensation.

When he looked down at the body, he had the sickening feeling he was going to fall, kind of like he'd felt that time in the Twin Cities when he'd looked down from the top floor of the IDS building. The corpse was totally unrecognizable from the neck up. The killer must have been in a frenzy. The bones of the face were virtually pulverized. It was Egge all right. Dave often saw him jogging before school in this same outfit: a Minnesota Gophers sweatshirt, gray sweatpants, and black socks with high-tops.

Dave stroked the corners of the mustache. Squatting on his haunches, he picked up the maroon baseball cap with the big Minnesota "M" lying near Egge's left hand, and looked at the inside. Sure had a big head, the one-size-fits-all snap was in the last hole. He ran his finger around the inside band, still wet from Egge's sweat.

And then a movie began to scroll through his mind. He was in an operating room. A baby was being born.

"Mary, you've been in labor for forty-eight hours," the doctor said. "I know you want a natural birth, but I assure you we do this all the time."

"It's for the best," the husband said.

"Clark is right," the doctor murmured. "If we wait any longer, the baby could be born dead."

The movie fast-forwarded to a kitchen scene where Clark, Mary and a little boy sat around what looked like a kitchen table. "He's three-years-old, Clark. He should be talking by now. I think we ought to take him to a specialist."

"Ach, Mary, my ma says nobody in our family was ever too talkative until they started school. Maybe he doesn't have anything to say."

"I'm worried the doctor futzed something up during that Caesarian."

"Mama," the little boy said. Mary and Clark looked at each other and smiled.

The movie scrolled ahead to a schoolroom—an old fashioned one with the desks bolted to the floor in rows. A boy with a homemade haircut and a big head was slumped in the front row looking embarrassed. The teacher was yelling at the class to 'fess up and admit who took Kitty Hoefer's pencil case or she was going to keep them after school and they'd miss their buses. The little boy's face got really red. The teacher said, her finger in his face, "You took it, didn't you?" Then a little girl raised her hand. "Found it, Miss Dalrimple, it got tangled up in my extra underwear."

The movie was gone. Dave stood, stumbled, nearly fell, then shook his head. He'd heard about this sort of thing before—a movie flashing through your mind as you're about to die. Thing is, it was supposed to be the dead guy reviewing his life just before he kicked off, not the first cop on the scene. Dave didn't know any Kitty Hoefer and his parents' names weren't Clark and Mary. God, he must be in shock. After all, it isn't every day you find your right fielder dead, looking like afterbirth. And Mom had said he'd always had a wild imagination. She'd said when he was three or four, he'd been in her and Pa's bedroom in the middle of the night complaining about seeing ghosts in the attic upstairs where he slept. The movie must be his imagination working overtime.

Then the corpse groaned, and Dave's hair stood on end. No! There was no way this guy could still be alive. He remembered something from his law enforcement courses about bodies passing gas and making other odd noises during autopsies. His mouth was as dry as cotton, and he couldn't swallow, but he got the mirror he kept in the glove compartment of the Jeep, held it under what was left of Egge's mouth and nose. Nothing. No pulse either. The man was as dead as disco, groan or no groan.

Enough of this nonsense. He had to try to do some police work. He stepped away from the body, grabbed a stick, and nudged the baseball bat lying in the weeds about ten feet from Egge's body. Different. A Wayne Terwilliger model. Twig had been first base coach for the Twins during the Series wins. Usually coaches didn't get any credit. Managers sometimes, never coaches.

Something tugged at his sleeve. Dave forgot to breathe.

"Holy crap, Dude. I ain't seen nothing like that since a fourteen car pile-up on the four-lane outside Mescalero."

Damn. Dave got his breathing started again and turned around. Mingo Jones, the night deputy, his fingers held over his nose, walked over and inspected the body. He looked out of place in a Polk County deputy's uniform, what with the long Apache hair, the turquoise belt with the number four etched into it, and the moccasins that increased the stealth factor.

"Jeez, you aged me ten years."

"Sorry, Dude, thought you heard me. D'ya know there's some cuss words painted on the water tower?"

"Must've missed it in all the excitement. What's it say?"

"Says 'Fuck You, Egg Man'."

"Those kids are getting downright verbose. Did you block off the road?"

"The sawhorses are in place and I tacked up the 'No Trespassing' signs on some trees, the orange ones that say, 'Keep Out! By order of Polk County Sheriff's Office. Violators will be drawn and quartered, entrails nailed to a tree.'"

Mingo stared down at the body dispassionately, as if he were looking at a department store window on Friday night when all the stores were open late. Then he made the sign of the cross, bowed his head, laced his fingers together over his groin, and began moving his lips.

When Mingo finished praying, he came back to stand by Dave. "You know the Egg Man very well?" he said.

"Not really. He was on my softball team. No hit, no field."

"The Egg Man and me got to know each other at the school. He had me rap with some of the classes. Multi-cultural education is a big thing there these days. Egge was a good shit, I don't want him stuck out there in limbo."

"Limbo like in babies who aren't baptized?"

"Kind of. Some people say that if a dude gets himself murdered, he could get hung up between this world and the afterlife. We Mescalero call them the Shadow World and the Land of Ever Summer. I think a formal ghost medicine ceremony may be in order."

Dave swallowed. He felt like he was the one stuck in limbo. Should he tell Mingo about the vision he'd had? Nah, he didn't know Mingo well enough yet to tell him something like that. This was the first time Dave had had anything to do with the Indian, since Mingo worked the night shift for the most part. Sheriff Kline had brought him on a few weeks ago to deal with the hordes of teenagers breaking curfew. He'd always wondered what would possess an Apache to take a job in Minnesota.

Rather than tell him about the vision, Dave said, "You believe that stuff, huh?"

"Sure do, Dude. Never did until I read up on it in college. The old Apaches used to burn down their tepees to make sure the deceased didn't try to take them with him."

"We aren't too keen on ghost medicine ceremonies around here," Dave said. "That was the sign of the cross, wasn't it? I didn't know you were a Catholic. "

"Born and bred. You know what they say—once a mackerel snapper, always a mackerel snapper. Most all Mescalero are R.C.'s to some degree. The Spanish padres, you know."

"Yeah, well, let's just keep this ghost medicine stuff between you and me, huh? It doesn't look like Sheriff Kline and the BCA are gonna get here anytime soon. I'm gonna backtrack. There're some prints over there. Looks like the perp ran Egge down. Waiting for him farther up the trail, most likely. I'd say the killer got away through the slough, probably had a vehicle parked back near the old quarry. I didn't see any other tracks coming in. Why don't you take a look?"

Mingo frowned, though it was pretty tough to tell since he always appeared to be frowning. "You don't happen to have a pair of waders I could use? These are very expensive handcrafted moccasins."

"You better get started before Sheriff Kline and the BCA get here. Who knows how bad they'll screw things up?"

Mingo saluted, took off his moccasins, put them in a coat pocket, and was off, bearing toward the swamp. Dave hadn't seen such an insolent salute since the last time *he'd* saluted Harry Kline.

Dave set off down the trail, careful to keep on the wilted grassy hummocks off to the side. As he proceeded, he noticed some of the trees had paint splotches on them. Those splatball fools had been playing war games around here. About a hundred yards in he found a clearing facing Miles Krueger's field, which ran parallel to the woods. That's when he spotted the tractor, a John Deere stuck so badly you could just barely see the smokestack, a little green, and the driver's seat. Miles's son, Les, had played for the Dogs for a while, but the kid was so hopeless Dave had to tell him to take a walk.

The tracks stopped in the clearing. It looked as though the perp had crouched there watching the trail. Dave knelt to retrieve a crumpled package of Old Golds by one corner, so as to save any possible fingerprints. Several butts were ground into the mud. He whipped out his evidence bags, scooped up the butts, and deposited them and the crumpled cigarette pack in separate bags, securing the zip lock on the top of each bag.

Dave knew somebody who smoked Old Golds. He sat down on a fallen log, and dialed Annie Kline, the sheriff's daughter, on his cellular.

"Hello?" Annie said at last.

"Hey, it's me." She and Dave had a kind of thing going on. But he didn't know what to do about her. He had feelings for her, but she was like one of the guys. That and Harry being her father put a damper on things. "Business, I'm afraid," he said. "You heard about Egge?"

"The whole town's heard about Egge. What can I do?"

"Little League started last week, right? I heard there was a fracas with one of the umps. I figured you'd know cause you're the coordinator, one of the bennies for being Sheriff Kline's daughter. I was thinking that umpire might've been Egge. I know he did some umping."

"You're such a smartass, I don't even get paid. That ump was Conrad White, a social studies teacher. Kind of looks like Jerry Egge, though he's about twenty years younger. Harley Barnhouser's son Butch was pitching. The score was five to five with the bases loaded in the bottom of the last inning with the count three and two. Butch threw a fastball, a foot outside easy, and White called ball four. Harley went after Conrad with a bat."

"Jesus."

"Never did catch him, just broke the headlights on his car."

"You really should have filed a complaint, Annie."

"Conrad wouldn't go for it. You know how many Barnhousers there are around here, and they're all just as mean as Harley."

He looked back down the trail kind of expecting Mingo to be sneaking up on him again. "Ain't this the shits," he said. "Another pitcher. Must be some kind of conspiracy."

Annie played short on Dave's softball team, the Soldier Dogfaces, who'd just lost their starting pitcher. The pussy'd moved to Arizona because he couldn't stand Minnesota winters. Jerry Egge had been the relief pitcher. Pretty good control, for a high school principal.

"You and your softball," Annie said. "I can't believe this has happened in Soldier. I guess there's no place to hide. Is Dad there yet?"

"Not yet. Mingo and I have matters in hand."

"You take care of him when he gets there. Don't let him do anything foolish."

"I won't. Thanks, Annie." He punched the disconnect button on the cellular.

Shit! He'd been hoping that bastard Barnhouser had done it. Barnhouser and he had been enemies ever since high school when Barnhouser'd hung him out the third floor window during freshman initiation for refusing to shine his boots.

He put the cellular back in his belt and thought about walking over to the Krueger farm to ask Miles if he'd seen anything. Instead, he hiked back to the murder scene, where he got out the yellow, crime-scene tape, picked out a likely number of trees, and began to mark off the area.

Still no Harry and the BCA. He was sorely tempted to examine the corpse himself, but Larry Henderson, the BCA guy, would eat him a new asshole if he did. Dave felt like the proverbial little boy confronted with the cookie jar. He knew he'd get a whipping if he took one, but he just couldn't resist.

Dave looked over at the body, half expecting Egge to sit up and ask what the hell had hit him, then walked over and took another look at him, trying to remember what he used to look like. Nothing came to mind, except a rather high forehead. He could imagine Egge slathering mynoxidol on his bald pate like a kid spreads jelly on peanut butter. Forty bucks a month. The smell wasn't quite as bad now.

What would it feel like to have your brains beat out with a baseball bat? He'd been knocked out during a smoker match in Navy boot camp once. Never saw the punch coming, hit him right between the eyes.

"I'll find the guy for you, pardner," he said. "And when we catch him, we're gonna forget about reading the guy his Miranda rights."

This time he heard Mingo running through the woods. "Found some tracks," the Indian said, "widespaced wheel span, lots of footprints like those around the body. Big man, regular Sasquatch. And some smaller footprints."

"Remind me to have the techs get casts of those tracks before the rain washes them away."

Dave tiptoed around the body, careful not to step on any footprints, then held his foot above one of the prints. The perp had a good six inches on him. "You're right about the fellow being a Bigfoot. I figured size fourteen. Looks more like sixteen."

Mingo wiped his feet on the dead grass, put back on his moccasins.

Dave had a thought: like it or not, the inspecting officer had to eliminate the person who discovered the body. "Mingo, you live at Mrs. Mac's boarding house don't you?"

"Sure do. Cheapest place in town."

"She sure gets around. Kind of a coincidence—"

"White squaw attracted to clearing like vampire drawn to Red Cross mobile unit."

"A Shirley MacLaine type, huh?"

"With all the bells and whistles. Tells me she's the reincarnation of Catherine the Great."

"Hmmpf. I don't suppose you know how well she got along with Egge?"

"Not very well, according to lounge gossip. Mingo partake of P&J sandwiches at the school after classes, learn all about the foibles of every student, faculty member, and janitor. I don't suppose you knew about the shenanigans going on between the Superchief and Mrs. Egge?"

"Sort of. I got a call to break up an altercation between two men in the Super Valu parking lot. By the time I arrived, Bronson and Egge were shaking hands, having apparently patched things up, but I hung around for a while and talked to the carryout boys. One of them said they'd been duking it out like Punch and Judy. Thought it was pretty funny."

"Cherchez le femme they always say," Mingo said.

"Yeah, the superintendent could have done it, that's for sure, if he was obsessed with Mrs. Egge."

"Not bad-looking, for an older broad. Kind of looks like the actress in *The Birds*."

Dave kicked a dirt clod. "It's a stretch to think that a man as well-respected as Charlie Bronson would bump somebody off over a woman, especially out here in the woods."

"That's true. He could get a hit man down in the Twin Cities for five K or so."

"Life is cheap," Dave said. He studied the body a little longer. The perp had hit Egge so hard that some of his teeth were lying on the ground next to the body. A couple of gold crowns. "When I was out there in the woods, I noticed some paint splotches on some of the trees. Let's say Egge is jogging through the woods. He runs into these crazies with the paint guns, some of them former students. They mistake him for the enemy, shoot him with paint pellets, mess up his little jogging outfit. Egge has a conniption fit and gets his brains beat out. Principals aren't exactly the most popular people in the world. If we take a branch and wedge it under the body, we can get a look at Egge's back."

"Henderson'll hate that. You know the Bureau thinks us little farts can't count to twenty without taking off our shoes."

"If Henderson doesn't want us to mess with the corpse, he should show up in a reasonable amount of time. What's it been, two hours since Mrs. Mac found the body?"

Dave looked around in the woods for a branch to lever Egge over a little bit but couldn't spot one sturdy enough. You'd think an ex-Navy SEAL would be able to find just the right tool for any job. He'd been trained to live on grass shoots and build a hut out of mud, leaves, and spit. He picked up a branch and rapped it against a tree trunk. Sounded solid. Dave rebuttoned the snaps on his windbreaker and put on his latex gloves so as not to leave any tell-tale deputy on the corpse, then wedged the branch under Egge, trying to ignore the dangling eyeball. The branch snapped, and the body flopped back to rest.

"Looks like he don't want you messing with him."

"Yah think?" Dave shook his head. "Help me get him turned over. I figure if there's paint on his body, we call for a roadblock, catch this guy easy, and you and I will have our pictures plastered all over the metro papers. We'll be heroes."

"We Indians don't like people taking our pictures."

"Heard that. You're afraid you'll lose your soul."

"That and all those old boarding school pictures with the bad haircuts."

There were no paint splotches on Egge's back. Something else, though, some kind of writing. Dave couldn't quite make it out. Better leave it alone until Henderson arrives.

Dave threw the branch as far as he could, then poked at the baseball bat with his toe. Why had the murderer left what was surely the murder weapon? Had he been interrupted? Or was this some kind of plant? And the cigarettes? A good lawyer would laugh at those—if they ever made a connection between someone who smoked Old Golds and the murder scene.

Egge's wallet was sticking out of his back pocket, almost as if the murderer had looked at it and put it back before running off into the woods. Could this have been a robbery?

"Yah see that?" Dave pointed at the wallet. "If this was a robbery, the perp'll have Egge's money and other personal effects on him. Another reason to set up a roadblock."

"I'd say the dude's long gone," Mingo said. "Like you said, it's been over two hours since Mrs. Mac found the body."

"This guy's arrogant as hell. Probably stopped off at Andy's Diner for a cup of joe. What can it hurt to check?"

"Okay with me, but if you keep toying with that corpse, the Egg Man is gonna latch onto you like Anna Nicole Smith onto an octogenarian millionaire."

"Knock it off, will you? You're giving me the willies. I'm going to go ahead and look. This is our case until Sheriff Kline says different. So what if Henderson goes postal when he finds out we touched the corpse." He yanked the wallet out of Egge's pocket.

Egge had forty-seven dollars in his billfold.

"I'm telling unless you give me half," Mingo said. Dave ignored him. The wallet also contained a birth certificate, credit cards, and pictures of Egge's towheaded kids when they were little. And one of Mrs. Egge and Bronson with Bronson's arm around her. Egge had drawn a mustache on Bronson and his wife and given them both horns. If the rumors were true, Egge would be the one with the horns.

"Bad vibes, Dude," Mingo said. "Salmon day for the Egg Man. A ghost medicine ceremony is definitely needed to sooth the evil spirits. Let the Egg Man rest. For now I need to prairie dog it, find the snotnoses who painted those cuss words on the tower. I know the ones who did it."

"You better, before Hildegard sees them." Dave swallowed. "Before you go, Mingo..." He stroked his mustache, looked down at Egge's body again. He felt as he always did when he walked under a ladder.

"Something you want to ask me?" Mingo said, smiling his coyote smile.

"Yeah, since we're to be working so closely on this case, I figure we should get to know each other better."

"You want to know what possessed a Mescalero Apache to move to Minnesota?"

Dave just couldn't bring himself to tell Mingo about the vision he'd had of Egge's life passing before his eyes. "Something like that," he said.

"After graduating college, I was planning on ridding the Rez of felons in New Mexico, but the council approved a nuclear test dump site. Mingo no fathom glow in the dark. Anyway, about that time, I scoped a Northern States Power Company license plate, 10,000 lakes. When you live in the desert, 10,000 lakes sounds like Paradise. That and the fact that my dad is from International Falls."

"The Icebox, huh? Well, get some sleep before you tackle Olive and Freddie." Olive Randall was Mingo's number one nemesis, an alcoholic nympho who slept through school and caroused all night. Freddie Cochran was her sidekick.

"How'd you know I meant the blond maniac and her sociopath boyfriend?"

"Educated guess, Dude."

"I'll check Andy's before I hit the hay," Mingo said. "Just in case the fellow's as cocky about this thing as you think he is."

When Mingo was gone, Dave put the billfold back in Egge's pocket. He ducked under the yellow crime-scene tape, and strode toward the fence separating Miles Krueger's field from the woods, mulling over what he had so far. A vehicle with a wide wheelspan, a baseball bat with an unusual endorsement, a man with awfully big feet, and a bunch of supernatural bullshit that he couldn't tell anybody about if he wanted to keep this case. Chances were he'd have a hell of a time keeping the case anyway, what with Mr. Larry Henderson of Baloney, Crappo, and Associates on the way.

Chapter 3

What a Joke

"The world has joked incessantly
for over fifty centuries.
And every joke that's possible has
long ago been made."
— Sir William Schwenck Gilbert

Dave was standing on the second strand of Miles Krueger's barbed wire fence, one hand braced on the post, getting ready to risk the family jewels by vaulting over the top, when Sheriff Kline and Larry Henderson, the BCA agent, drove up in the sheriff's cruiser. Dave had been so absorbed by what he planned to ask Miles he hadn't even heard the cruiser coming down the trail.

He got down off the fence. The doors slammed on the cruiser and Harry and Henderson, a regular Mutt and Jeff combination, walked toward the body. Or rather, walked and waddled. Harry was getting visibly heavier day by day. They were both smoking. Not a bad idea, considering the stench.

Henderson was a gray-haired, dignified man with a little David Niven mustache. He wore gray, pressed slacks with pleats and the ever-present BCA windbreaker. No hat—might muss the hair. He was carrying a black satchel that looked like a doctor's bag, which he placed next to Egge's shoe, on the edge of one of the footprints.

Harry leaned in, peering over Henderson's shoulder. "Holy Christ! He looks like he's been mauled by a Kodiak."

"I've seen worse," Henderson said. "Sorry we're late, Jenkins. My pilot had to set down in Alexandria, engine trouble. Did you touch anything?"

Dave, who was now standing next to Harry, shifted his feet, never could lie worth a damn. "I found some evidence out in the woods that some splatballers have been in the vicinity. Figured I'd better check his back so's we could set up a roadblock if it turned out...so I propped him up and took a look."

19

"You ought to know better by now—"

"So, did you find paint?" Harry said.

"Not that kind of paint, but there's something written on his back and legs." Dave smiled at Henderson. "I figured I'd better wait for you."

"Anything else?" Henderson said.

"I backtracked the perp to where he'd been lying in wait, found an empty cigarette package and some butts. And I remembered an old road back there by the abandoned quarry, so I had Mingo follow the perp through the swamp. He spotted some tire tracks that look like they may have come from the guy's vehicle." Dave handed over the evidence bags and Henderson put them in his valise.

"We'll take a look at Egge's back once we do the preliminary work," Henderson said. "Looks like lots of footprints. Awful big man, I'd say." Henderson removed a bag of what looked like powdered sugar from the satchel.

"Get me some water, will you, Jenkins? There's some in the trunk of Harry's car."

Harry handed the keys to Dave, and Dave went to fetch. Galley slave, that's what he was. And when he wasn't fetching, what was he supposed to do, stand there with his finger up his ass? There were just too many chiefs and not enough Indians, as far as he was concerned. He set the jug of water next to Henderson's valise, then looked over at the John Deere tractor stuck in a field a hundred yards or so away. Something had been added to the scene, possible witnesses—Les Krueger and his dad swearing at the tractor, kicking it, as if it were the tractor's fault that it got stuck.

"Say Larry, why don't Harry and me go talk to those two farmers over there? Could be we got ourselves an eye witness. That's where I was going when you got here."

"How am I supposed to cross that fence with my bad back?" Harry said.

Henderson was mixing plaster of paris for the footprints. "Do you know them?"

"Yeah, that's Miles and Les Krueger," Dave said. "They own this land."

"I don't see any harm in it. You want my tape recorder? It's in the cruiser there."

Dave waved his dictaphone at him. "All set."

Harry waddled toward a gate he'd noticed down the track a piece, Dave bringing up the rear. Actually, Dave had an ulterior motive for wanting to talk to Harry alone. He had to tell him about Hildegard's recall petition. For one thing, if he were Harry, he wouldn't want anyone running around plotting behind his back. For another, he was Hildegard's candidate for sheriff, and he wasn't sure he wanted the job. Then there was the Annie complication.

But somehow, he couldn't bring the subject up. Hated confrontations he guessed. Instead, he pointed out the blotches on the trees. "That's the paint I was talking about, Harry. Could be Egge ran into some of his old students out here, got into a fight, and they brained him."

"I don't think so," Harry said. "Those marks have probably been here forever. Splatballers are out here all the time. I'm surprised Miles hasn't complained."

"So who do you think did it?"

"Damned if I know." Harry went over to look at one of the paint splotches as if he were reconsidering what Dave had said— probably claim the theory later if it turned out to be true—then the two of them went through the gate and made their way along the edge of the plowed area where there was enough withered grass to keep their feet from getting muddy.

"You know what?" Harry said. "I'll bet any money that little bastard Les Krueger had something to do with this. That boy was born to be hung."

"Yeah, he's a real charmer all right."

They came to the end of the grass and Harry looked down at his feet, then at the soupy mud that had claimed the tractor. Dave knew from the times he'd been over for Sunday dinner that if Harry got mud all over his uniform, Brenda, his wife, would lecture him nonstop for at least a week. Harry looked at Dave beseechingly and he did what he always did when confronted with a quandary. He told a joke.

"Did you hear about the leper who made his living as a gigolo?"

"Yeah, Harry, he was doing great until business fell off. You told me that one last week."

Harry fanned himself with his hat. "You know what your trouble is, Jenkins. You don't have any tact. Sometimes you want to kiss up to the boss, don't you know?" They slogged off through the mud toward the tractor, both of them sinking down to their shoetops, feet making sucking noises when they pulled them back up. "Besides," Harry said, "if you think my jokes are bad, you ought to hear how blue it gets at deer camp. Why don't you come along some time? We could use some new fish."

"About the only way I'd be able to shoot a deer is with a camera," Dave said.

Miles Krueger was a very short man with a two-day growth of beard. One of his eyes was permanently droopy. His son Les, not much taller, was knocking the mud off his shovel against the tractor wheel.

"Hey, Miles," Harry said. "Got your tractor stuck, huh?"

Krueger eyed them and said nothing.

"Do you mind, Miles?" Dave said, waving the recorder at Krueger. Krueger nodded hesitantly, as if he'd never seen a tape recorder. Dave pressed the "on" button.

"I suppose you heard about what happened over there in the clearing." Harry tried to scrape some of the mud off of his shoes on the tractor hitch. "You two boys didn't happen to see anything did you?"

"I coulda seen the fellah," Miles said. "I did see somethin' unusual. How was he killed?"

"We can't really say, Miles," Harry said. "What did you see?"

"Fellah squatting at the edge of the clearing watching the trail. I was about to go over there and tell him to get off my land. I've had a hell of a time with city slickers playing war games over there spooking my cows. Then he ran into the woods."

Dave noticed that Les Krueger wouldn't look at either him or Harry. He kept shoveling mud away from the wheel. Occasionally he'd drop the shovel. His hands were shaking some.

"What did he look like?" Dave said.

Miles took one of those big blue hankies with the snowflake design out of his back pocket and blew his nose. "Seemed kind of big, dressed all in black."

Any normal human being would have been somewhat curious about the man in black, considering there'd been a murder. There'd been rumors, though, that the Kruegers still made Minnesota 13—high octane, homemade hooch—which would definitely fry your brain cells beyond hope.

"How big was he, Miles? About Harry's size? Bigger?"

"Jeez, I don't know. That's a ways away and I didn't have my glasses. I'd say he was big as Harry, thinner though." Miles repressed a snort.

"Why didn't you call me, Miles?" Harry said.

"I was tied up with this stuck tractor. I figured you'd get to me sooner or later."

"We're going to need to have you come in and make a statement," Harry said. "Did your son see anything?"

"He was at the house."

"That true, son?" Harry said.

"No, sir. I was in the barn spreading lime, as I recall."

The kid was lying. Dave would want to talk to him as soon as possible.

By the time Harry and Dave got back to the clearing, the medical examiner and the crime team had arrived. One of them was photographing the corpse and the blood spatters on the ground and on the trees. The body was now lying face down and the writing on Egge's back and legs was visible.

"Take a look at this," Henderson said.

Dave looked over Harry's shoulder at the writing.

The letters on Egge's back read, "D-Y-S-T-H," and "S-Y-Z" was scrawled on his right leg.

"What's that," Harry said, "some kind of vodoo, devil worship shit?"

"Beats me," Henderson said. "We'll let the shrinks figure it out." He began to put his equipment back in his satchel. "The blood, hair and fiber guys are just wrapping up. We got all the pictures, and the M.E. will do the autopsy tomorrow morning."

Henderson closed the snaps on the satchel, and stood, stuffing his hands deep in his pockets. "We should have the results tomorrow or the next day. The boys followed the tracks into the swamp and found this." Henderson held up a muddy boot. "It doesn't look good if there are no prints on the baseball bat or the boot. Did your farmer have anything interesting to say?"

"Says he saw a big fellow dressed in black run into the woods."

"I'd say that's pretty close to an eye witness. Do you know if the deceased had any enemies?"

"Are you kidding?" Harry said. "The man was the principal of a high school. Everybody hated him. I remember my principal, old cross-eyed Benboom, called him Baboon. The bastard actually had a paddle in his office he called 'the board of education.' Thought he was being original. Graduation night we broke into his office and poured pig's blood all over the place. They never caught us."

"Well, I'd suggest you interview Mrs. Macintosh," Henderson said. "I met her briefly before we came out here. She's the talkative type. She probably knows all of his enemies."

"Can't argue with that, Larry."

Maybe Hildegard was right about Harry. Who cared about Baboon and his board of education. Dave wanted to get in his Jeep and track the Bronson lead. He couldn't let the creep get away with killing a fellow Dog. He began pacing up and down along the border of yellow crime scene tape.

"I wish you wouldn't do that," Harry said. "It makes me nervous."

Good. Dave kept on pacing.

Harry lit up another nonfiltered cigarette, offering one to Henderson. Henderson shook his head. He smoked some kind of British-looking cigarettes he had in a silver case.

"I just can't get over this," Henderson said. "Homicides are up fifty percent from 1990, most of them juvies. You don't suppose this was a juvie homicide, do you? When's the last time you had a murder in Polk County?"

"Not so long ago," Harry said. "You remember that farmer we repossessed who shot my deputy in '84? And the school teacher who strangled that kid in '87? 'Course I guess that's getting to be a while now."

"The world's changing, Harry. How're your kids doing?"

"Driving me nuts. You know the one got a minor league contract—Mel? He bummed up his knee, and they dropped him. I tried to tell him baseball was no profession for a man, but would he listen to me? Not a chance."

"I know what you mean," Henderson said. "My girl Jesse's only seventeen, just out of high school, and she wants to marry this kid who, get this, sells encyclopedias for a living."

"Jesus."

"I want to send her to a girls' school like St. Ben's so she can get a good education and be able to support herself if her romantic life doesn't work out. And she thinks I'm a beast because I won't sanction this marriage."

"Such is life, Larry," Harry said.

Dave was getting tired of pacing; he wanted to boot Harry and Larry, the rhyming rumdumbs, in the ass. Then, out of the blue, Henderson said what Dave had been dreading, "You want me to take this one, Harry? You boys have your hands full the way it is."

"I don't think so, Larry." Harry tried to stretch out his back some. "If I let you do that, my constituents will begin to wonder why they've got me."

Dave stopped pacing. By God, Harry'd finally stood up for something.

The crime team stored the body in the back of the medical examiner's van, and Henderson reached down for his satchel and moved toward one of the criminalist's cars. "If you say so. I'll give you a call about the forensic results tomorrow morning. You'll be in your office?"

"That's where I'm usually at with this back of mine. See you later, Larry. Hope you work things out with your daughter. Well, Jenkins, I'm going to head out unless you can think of anything else. You'll head up the case. We'll bring Mingo in off the night shift if we have to."

"Thanks, Harry. I won't let you down."

Harry clapped him on the back and smiled. Dave wanted to throw his arms around the fat man and hug him. But he didn't.

Dave got in his Jeep, and followed Sheriff Kline down the cow-path that led to County Road 185 and the outskirts of Soldier. Now that he was without distraction, the images began to creep back in. The vision of the kid with the homemade haircut. The groan the body'd made. Mingo's ceremony request.

He'd see Father Mischke first chance he got. That would set his mind at ease. The old priest was a close personal friend of the Holy Ghost. And everything Dave said in the confessional was classified top secret.

First things first, though. He still needed to stop at Hildegard's. Had to try and talk her out of that recall petition before Harry found out about it.

Kind of proud of the stumblebum for standing up to Henderson that way.

* * *

"Rock of ages, cleft for *m-e-e-e*..." Sounded like the church choir yowling right outside Mingo's bedroom.

"Let me *h-i-i-i-de* myself in *Th-e-e-e*; Let the *w-a-a-a-ter* and the *bl-o-o-o-d*..."

He clamped the pillow over his face and ears but he could still hear them. Must have left the stairway door open again.

"Be of sin the double *c-u-u-u-re*; save from wrath and make me *p-u-u-u-re*."

He pulled off the pillow, looked over at his bedside clock. Ten o'clock. Since it was as bright as the day of the resurrection, that must mean he'd only had two hours of sleep. He rolled over, snagged his foot on the bedsheet, and fell out of bed on his bad hip, the one Cousin Cecil had nicked with a steel-tipped arrow when Mingo was four and wandered into Cecil's line of fire. Mingo got up, limped down the two flights of steps, and turned the corner into the living room.

And there they were, gathered around Mrs. Mac's tiny Wurlitzer, at least ten women, most of them with huge bouffants and fifty to sixty extra pounds. Then one of them noticed him and dove behind the couch. "It's a naked man!" And suddenly all of them were diving for cover, screaming high enough to make his teeth hurt. He clamped them shut and glanced down. Ah, shit. He'd been wearing a breechclout to reservation powwows for so long he'd forgotten the effect a pair of men's boxers might have on a bunch of middle-aged white women.

Mrs. Mac threw him a braided lavender shawl she'd had drapped over one of the chairs. He grabbed it and wrapped it around his waist.

"Sorry about the excitement," he said.

"Don't fret about it," she said. "Biggest thrill they've had in years. You had better put something on, though. We're doing penance. I expect to be wearing ashes for the next week at least, and I've cancelled all my readings."

She must mean the astrological charts she did. She got a hundred a throw for those.

"I'll be getting out of your hair pretty soon," he said. "I need to find Olive and get her to paint over the cuss words on the water tower."

"That girl is quite a handful, isn't she? She reminds me of me when I was that age. Had to get married when I was sixteen."

The other women began to crawl out from their hiding places.

Mingo tipped his Mountie hat, which he'd again forgotten to take off when he went to bed. "Hello, ladies. Sorry I scared you."

"Hello, Deputy," they ululated in chorus.

Back in his room, he got into his uniform, and went out the rear door where he'd parked his GMC 4X4 pickup. The shocks were shot and he only got about ten miles per gallon, but he'd paid just $2000 for it, so he couldn't complain. Had to borrow the money from the bank, get Harry Kline to co-sign for him. Thinking about painting her green with a camouflage design. Show Jenkins who had style.

He knew what he'd see even before he got to the tower, and there they were. A crowd lined up underneath pointing up, discussing what the world had come to. Hell, the graffiti was all they had, since they'd never get to see Egge's body.

Mingo parked his truck next to a fire hydrant and got out. The bakery lady, henna-colored hair styled like early Lucille Ball, was saying, "I'll bet it was that Green River killer I've been reading about in the Enquirer."

"Yeah, they say he's a long-haul trucker," the flower shop lady said.

The Soldier vagrant was leaning up against one of the tower supports, hunched over, clutching a brown paper bag. Mingo sidled over to the man. "I thought I told you to move on, Billy."

"Yes, officer," Billy said. Bloodshot eyes, tangled ZZ Top beard, gray fedora too small for his grizzled head. The man stunk almost as bad as the corpse at the murder scene. Mingo felt kind of sorry for the vagrant. Back on the Rez, his uncle Seymour stayed drunk on panther piss for weeks on end. Just last week, Mingo'd taken Billy to Crookston to the shelter, got him some walking shoes at the Good Will. They were gone.

"What happened to the shoes I got you?" Mingo said.

"Traded 'em for food." Billy shuffled off, heading toward the south side of town, still hunched, his overcoat so outsized he couldn't avoid tripping.

Mingo looked up at the tower. Quite a feat of derring do, climbing twenty feet along one of the tower supports to where the ladder started, carrying a bucket of paint and a roller. He was getting dizzy just looking up there. Had to be two of them at least and most likely a lookout—that friend of Olive's, Stormy, would be a good bet. He should go see her first. She'd spill her guts faster than spit freezes in February.

Gradually, people noticed him standing there and began crowding in on him.

"Hey, Deputy. Any word on who killed Principal Egge?" Mayor McCready said. He was the mayor in name only. Hildegard Weiss pulled his strings so readily some people called him "Howdy".

"Nothing yet, George," he said. "I'm sure Sheriff Kline will have a press release before the day is out."

McCready nodded and went back to looking up at the tower.

Mingo started his truck, turned onto Peach, drove past the Polaris snowmobile factory—the day shift was just coming in to work—took a left on Meade, rumbled across the bridge over Plum Creek, hooked a left into the Shady Brook Trailer Park, and pulled up next to the Randall trailer. He could find the place blindfolded he'd been there so often. Hated to hassle the mother, she worked at the Legion till past one o'clock, but there was no way to get around it if he wanted to see Olive.

A little girl, cute as a wolf pup, opened the door, Nancy or Patty. Must be Nancy, she was the older one, around eleven. Superintendent Bronson must have called off classes for the day. "Is your sister home, Nancy?" he said.

"She's up at the school," she said. "She had to make up time again for skipping. She'll never let us skip. It's not fair."

"Mind if I look around?" he said. Olive had used that ruse before.

The little girl shrugged, went back to the kitchen, and began drying the breakfast dishes for her younger sister who was doing the washing.

Mingo peeked into the mother's bedroom; she was curled up in a fetal position, dead to the world. He looked under the bed—nothing but dust bunnies—searched through the closet, stuck his nose out the window to check the roof. Nothing. As he left, he nodded to the girls. They giggled.

On the way to the school, he met Olive walking down the street headed back to Shady Brook. Long-strided, shoulders slightly hunched, blond tresses flowing in her wake, a light windbreaker doing little to veil the goodies underneath. The most beautiful white woman he'd ever seen, except for the perpetual sneer that marred her otherwise angelic face. And the girl was a Luddite, always trying to throw a wrench into the works.

He pulled up alongside, rolled down the window. "Got a minute, Olive?"

"Hey, Chief," she said. "You hear about Scrambled? They closed the school."

"Kind of a dastardly thing to do to get out of school, Olive."

She smiled a smile that would knock the birds out of the sky. "That's your opinion. Every second I spend there is like a month of Sunday school."

He rubbed his eyes, repositioned his Mountie cap at a tilt, trying to look nonchalant. "Sooo, you know anything about this, Olive?"

"Not hardly. I tried to...get along with him. The man was always hassling me about his stupid dress code, but I didn't hate him enough to kill him."

She worried her thumbnail with her teeth.

Mingo got out of the truck. "I didn't ask you if you did it, Olive. Was Freddie in town last night?"

"He's in Crookston. Got sent to Level Five for bringing a gun to school. You knew about that, didn't you? He was trying to scare these guys who were spreading stories about me."

"Crookston's only twenty miles away, Olive." She swept the hair away from her face and he caught a smell like freshly mown alfalfa. God, he had to get himself a woman. Maybe that red-haired schoolteacher he saw jogging every morning before the end of his shift. Debbie Meyer he thought her name was. "I'll give you the benefit of the doubt about the murder, for now, Olive, but I know you painted those cuss words on the water tower."

"The hell you say. Want me to take a lie detector test?"

A convertible drove by with a load of boys in it. Wolf whistles. "Hey Olive! How much for a quickie?" one of them yelled.

Mingo didn't know the car. He flipped open his notebook, wrote down the license number.

"Motherfuckers!"

"I wouldn't doubt it," Mingo said. "If Freddie didn't help you paint those cuss words on the water tower, who did?"

"I didn't do nothing."

"Olive, you've got red paint all over your fingers."

She took his arm, nuzzling up against him. "Chiefy, why don't you and me go someplace and talk about this." Damn girl would have been worth five or six ponies back in the old days. In the end the brave would wind up slitting her nose.

"The only place you and I are going is to pick up some paint and a cherry picker." Mingo opened the passenger side door, she got in, and they headed off toward Transportation. "Why'd you want to do the man that way, Olive?"

She shrugged, smiled a down-turned smile, her chin dimpling. "Nothing better to do." Then she gave a quick, convulsive laugh that caused her breasts to swing left, then right. "You should have seen his face. We were laying over there in the park next to the war monger statue watching Egge's house with field glasses. When he saw what was on the water tower, I swear he had a heart attack, knocked him right on his ass."

Mingo turned toward the girl. "You sound proud of yourself."

"I wasn't *trying* to give him a heart attack."

"You got yourself in some real trouble this time, Olive, whatever your intentions. I'm sure Deputy Jenkins is going to want to talk to you."

She folded her arms. "Fine with me. Like I said, I didn't do nothing."

* * *

After he'd returned from the murder scene, Dave had driven by the rectory at least a dozen times trying to make himself go in and talk to Father Mischke about the vision. But he just couldn't do it. The whole thing sounded too much like a bad acid trip. And besides, Father would ask why he hadn't been to mass since he returned from Desert Storm. Then he'd tried to talk to Hildegard, but her neighbor said she was in a school board meeting with Superintendent Bronson, where they were discussing the impact of Egge's murder. The meeting would probably run all day.

On the way back to the office, as he drove by Farmers & Merchants, he noticed a very pregnant blond woman coming out of the bank. He could've sworn the woman was Mary Lou Forman, the banker's daughter, but that couldn't be right, he'd heard she'd married some stock broker while he'd been in the SEALs and moved to Chicago. All through high school he'd watched Mary Lou, with the long blond hair that reached all the way to her ankles, captain the cheerleaders at the Friday night football games, lead the most popular clique in the cafeteria, and give the valedictory speech on graduation night. Once or twice he'd even mustered up the courage to ask her out. She'd turned him down like the knob on a radio dial.

Couldn't be her. He'd contented himself with filling out reports and checking with the BCA and FBI computer on a murderer with an MO that fit their man—the kinky lettering on the victim's back, the baseball bat. Nothing.

It was nearly six when he drove out Pickett's Road to Hildegard's house, an A-frame that looked like an old-fashioned Norwegian church he'd seen once in *National Geographic*. Hrothgar and Hagar, Hildegard's dobermans, galloped toward him until their leashes snapped them back, then stood barking and growling, the sound a cross between a lawn mower and a mountain lion.

"Tough talk for a couple of eunuchs," he said.

Hildegard came out, rapped them on their noses with a rolled up magazine. They whined, "We didn't do nothin'," and skulked off into a dog house almost as big as the main house.

Once inside, she led him to an armchair opposite her rocker, the old-fashioned wooden kind. Both chairs were positioned in front of a patio window overlooking the ancient pines bordering her property. Dave sat down but couldn't get comfortable. Must have been the antimacassars protecting the fabric of the armchair.

"Would you like some tea, dear?" she said.

"No thanks. Tastes like water to me."

"You'll like this. It's Earl Grey, you've never tasted it before." Before he could protest, she moved toward the kitchen and her two burner stove.

He looked around. He'd never been here before, usually saw her at town hall or the sheriff's office. There was a circular staircase that led to a loft where she probably slept. Immediately behind the rocker were two oval portraits of a man and a woman. The man had snow-white hair, a string tie, and a drinker's nose. The woman could have been Hildegard in an old-fashioned dress. Same schoolmarm countenance, same wispy hair. He'd always been amazed by her hair, done up in a kind of British-eccentric look, just right for her. She hadn't changed it in all the time he'd known her. He doubted she'd ever been to a beauty salon.

Hildegard returned, handed him a cup, and sat down in her rocker, cradling another cup and saucer in her lap. Her hands and her head were shaking just a bit, the hands chapped from all those years writing at the blackboard.

"There, I think you'll find that a bit more robust than usual."

There was a candy dish next to the rocker filled to the brim with bonbons. Hildegard was famous for them. Spelldown winners got bonbons when he had been in third grade. Everyone was a good speller.

She noticed where he was looking. "Would you like a bonbon, dear?"

"Thank you." He took the candy, then sipped his tea. It tasted like water with pepper in it.

Hildegard sipped her own tea, then set it aside.

"I can't believe this horrible outrage has happened in my town," she said. "I swear sometimes I think we're living through Armageddon. All that rape and murder. It wasn't this way when I was a young girl. Everybody went to church. 'Thou shalt not kill' was still one of the commandments, and if anyone ever touched a child, he'd be run out of town, or worse. Not that I'm advocating vigilantism, of course."

"No way."

"I'll be calling a town meeting for the end of the week to put the townspeople's minds at ease. By then you'll have something for me."

"Sure thing."

"Are you doing anything about the graffiti on the water tower? We can't have visitors being subjected to something like that. I can't imagine what that deputy was doing that those children were able to effect such boorishness right under his nose."

"Mingo's already taken care of it. And you can't really blame him. Those kids revel in trying to make him look foolish, and they work with military precision."

"Perhaps. Any likely suspects in the murder?"

"I had to break up a fight between Egge and Charlie Bronson once, but that's really stretching it...Miss Weiss, I came by to talk..."

"What makes you say that?" she said in a voice he remembered from third grade, the aristocratic one that would scare any third grade boy out of any "notions" as she called them. Bronson had run his own school board candidate against her once, and she never forgot. Evidently, the idea that Bronson might be innocent was a notion.

"If he and Egge's wife were having an affair," Dave said, "why would he want to kill Egge? He'd already captured Mrs. Egge's heart. Besides, Bronson isn't the type to get all dirty that way."

She sighed. "Any clues?"

"The murderer sprayed Egge's back with the letters, 'DYSTH' and 'SYZ' on his legs."

"Any tie-in with the graffiti on the tower? Seems like quite a coincidence to me."

"I don't think so. The perp was a big man—Sasquatch, Mingo calls him. He could have had help, though. There were other tracks near where Mingo thinks his vehicle was parked. Miles Krueger's boy, Les, is acting awfully guilty. Harry thinks the message on Egge's back is devil worship. Miss Weiss, I wanted to—"

"That man. You should have heard the joke he told at the Commissioner's meeting the other night, some awful jibe against lepers. I have already amassed a thousand signatures on my recall petition."

"Harry's not such a bad shit—"

He winced, anticipating a sharp rap on the knuckles. But she simply smiled.

"You're a grown man, David. If you can't control your tongue by now, I can't help you."

"Sorry. When you do what I do, the language gets a little rough. Jokes are a defense mechanism for Harry, Miss Weiss. He was brought up telling jokes in order to avoid genuine conversation. Lots of guys Harry's age know a million jokes."

She slowed the momentum of the rocker, and grasped a folder she had handy on a lamp stand next to it. "I have here a copy of the physical requirements a sheriff must maintain in order to do his job. Your Harry is a good fifty pounds overweight. The county commission notified him in writing over a year ago. I think the man has actually gained weight since then. And I understand he has a bad back as well. He won't be much help to you in the field."

"True, but—"

"Then there are the rumors about Harry and Shirley Pleasiac— not that I pay any attention to gossip, and Shirley's much too sensible to be involved in anything so tawdry. I'm afraid the recall is a foregone conclusion. I realize you're concerned about Harry's family, but I assure you he has a very lucrative retirement package. We need young blood. I think what we have here is a man who has overstayed his welcome."

"I don't think you're being—"

"Let's get back to the murder now, shall we? I think the spray paint is a ploy. Bronson could have told his hired killer to make it look like a psychotic episode. You have heard of Dr. Jeffrey MacDonald, haven't you?"

"No, who—?"

"The Green Beret doctor who killed his wife and children and tried to make it look like the Manson slayings. His daughters were five and two. I remember their names as if this happened yesterday. Kristen and Kimberly. That villainous man went so far as to stab himself with a paring knife."

"I don't know about this Jeffrey MacDonald person, but you won't be the only one to think that Bronson had something to do with Egge's murder." He hesitated for a moment, searching for words. He'd never disagreed with her before. "Miss Weiss, I want you to drop the petition. I definitely do *not* want to be sheriff."

"Oh, but this will be such an ideal opportunity to gather material, dear."

He sighed. Hildegard had always had literary ambitions for him, had read all of his papers in class, and she'd kept with him up all the way through high school. She'd been damn pissed when he'd opted for the Special Forces instead of college.

For a second he was tempted to tell her about the vision he'd had. She was such a no-nonsense person, though. Somehow he didn't think he could tell her, respect for his 'thick-coming fancies' or no.

Thick-coming fancies?

"How do you plan to proceed, dear?" she said.

"Ah...I guess I better talk to Mrs. Egge first and look around Egge's den at home, if he's got one." He cleared his throat, felt around in his pockets for a handkerchief.

Thick-coming fancies? He didn't even know what that meant. What had he been saying? Oh, yeah, Egge's den. "Maybe *he'll* tell us who killed him. If I don't turn anything up there, I'll sweat that Krueger kid some and beat the bushes around the trailer park."

"Get some sleep, dear. You'll be needing it." She handed him a little bag. "Take some bonbons with you. Candy is very energizing."

He slipped the bag into his windbreaker pocket and got up to go.

"I can't be adamant enough about how important it is for you to find this person before the town meeting," she said. "Mr. Henderson has been sounding me out about the feasibility of the BCA managing the investigation. He has so much more experience and I'm inclined to...if..."

Dave could feel the blood rushing to his face. The old woman knew everyone's Achilles heal. His had always been pride. "I'll handle it," he said.

The dogs didn't need to be told twice, but that didn't mean they liked it much. Low rumblings emanated from the dog house while he walked back to the Jeep.

Dave waved, watched her close the door, then kicked the front wheel of the Jeep. Five days. She expected him to find Egge's murderer in five days! Stupid old woman must think he was Houdini.

Chapter 4

No Casual Mistress

"It is easier to be a lover than a husband
for the simple reason that it is more difficult
to be witty every day than to say pretty
things from time to time."
— Honore de Balzac

Dave slid a TV dinner, one that had been in the fridge so long it had freezer burn, in the oven, skipping the preheat directions, then swept the crumbs from his morning toast off the kitchen table, sat down with a yellow legal pad, and tried to do what an FBI profiler might do, put himself inside the mind of the killer as he waited for Egge in the woods.

He needed a word that meant angrier than angry. Fuming, raging? Given the state of the body, the killer would have such a hard-on for Egge he'd want to do more than just kill him. Why was he angry? What had Egge done to him? Embarrassed him somehow, made sport of him in front of a woman? Dave tried to think back to the last time he'd experienced that sort of anger. The only incident he could come up with was when Harley Barnhouser pantsed him just as he'd been about to ask Mary Lou Forman to go to the Prom.

Ahh, nuts! He could never actually kill anybody, not even Harley. Dave threw down the pencil, got up and dug through his collection of Joseph Wambaugh novels and Ed McBain police procedurals stacked on the shelf under the TV, and came up with his beat-up Webster's Ninth New Collegiate Dictionary, coverless, missing some pages. He opened the dictionary to the word "die." The scribbling on Egge's back could mean: *Die you stinking, two-bit humbug*. But SYZ? He flipped to the S's and began to browse.

As he was working, the door opened and Howard "Moe" Pleasiac, his brown eyes sparkling, came in, his wiener dog Chopin trotting along behind. Moe was wearing a New York Yankees uniform top, probably to annoy Dave, a lifelong Yankee hater.

"Don't you ever knock?" Dave said.

"Since when are you so touchy?" Moe's toothpaste commercial smile was marred by a chipped tooth he'd acquired playing touch football with Dave. Really caught hell for that, from Shirley, his mother. Chopin stuck his nose in Dave's garbage can and came out with a piece of green salami.

"Hey, mutt," Dave said, "I was saving that for breakfast."

Moe went to the fridge, got himself a can of Lumberjack, then sat opposite Dave at the table. "What's that you're doing, J.W.?"

The kid always called him J.W., after Joe Wambaugh, the ex-Los Angelese detective turned author. Unfortunately, he'd told the boy about Hildegard's ambitions for him.

"Oh, the murderer wrote something on Egge's back with a spray can. I'm trying to figure what it means. Don't you dare tell anybody I told you."

Moe took a sip of Lumberjack, his face pruning up like a Dick Tracy cartoon. "God that's awful."

"Doesn't stop you from drinking it. Here, what do you make of this?" Dave showed him the legal pad with the killer's message scribbled on it.

Moe swept the hair out of his eyes; he had almost as much as his namesake, the slaphappy leader of the Three Stooges. "D-Y-S-T-H, S-Y-Z. Well, I'd say, considering the context, the 'D' means 'damn'. The fact that the three letters 'SYZ' are off by themselves has some import, perhaps a signature. I'll take it home with me. Have it for you by tomorrow night."

"Very impressive, Watson. I hope you're better at this than you are at housetraining that fricking mutt of yours."

"You're Watson, I'm Holmes on my chat line. Who's the smart one around here?"

"I'll have you know I skipped two grades in school. I'm Holmes!"

"It must have been the A's and the B's you skipped, but have your way, I'll be Sherlock's smarter brother Mycroft."

"Whatever." Dave took a drink of Moe's beer. "This is an awfully strange case. Out there at the murder scene..."

He paused. Didn't know how to say it. Maybe Harry's nauseating habit of telling jokes to cover his feelings wasn't such a bad trait after all, but he couldn't think of a joke about a ghost.

"Out at the scene," he said again. "Ah, Mingo said something awfully peculiar. He said Egge's spirit could still be lurking about. What do you think of that? Crazy, huh?"

"Makes perfect sense to me, J.W. If I'd been murdered, I don't think my spirit would rest either."

"You're really religious, though. I'm not so sure I even believe in an afterlife."

"Such a cynic."

"I guess." Dave took another pull on the beer. "Biggest case I've ever had and it has to be somebody I know, a guy from my softball team to boot. Hildegard practically threatened to let Henderson have the case if I don't get her something by Friday. She's calling a town meeting to reassure everybody that there's not a crazed killer in their midst. Or at least if there is, he'll be under lock and key soon. I'm not sure we can do much by Friday."

Moe downed the rest of the beer, making a sucking noise when he reached the bottom of the can.

"You can put your mind at ease. There are people on my chat line almost as smart as I am. We've been working on the Jon Benet Ramsey case, but I'm sure this one will take precedence. We call ourselves JESSICA, did I tell you?"

"Yeah, you named yourselves after Jessica from *Murder She Wrote*. Cute, really cute. We gotta get this guy, Moe. Egge was one of the Dogs."

Moe went over and grabbed Chopin by the collar, dragging him across the kitchen toward the door. "I liked him, too. We used to discuss the shortcomings of secondary education when I got sick of practicing my music. I'll get on the translation right now."

"Careful of that carpel tunnel thing."

On his way out, Moe let the screen door slam shut, not hard to do as the spring was shot and Dave hadn't had time to fix it. The spring, the hole in the screen, the leaky faucet, the broken recliner that wouldn't recline. And now a murder to solve by Friday or else—

What was that smell? The TV dinner!

Tossing Moe's beer can towards the trash, he hurried over, shut off the stove, and peeked inside. The turkey wasn't too badly burned. Didn't matter much, it tasted like cardboard either way.

He used his shirt tail to lift the aluminum tray over to the table, then flipped on the TV. A *Star Trek* episode was on, the new one with the bald-headed captain, where one of the crew was an empath, which is someone who can really, really feel someone else's pain. Maybe that's what all that crying, groaning, and hallucinating at the murder scene was all about. He'd always been a sensitive guy, why shouldn't he be an empath?

Well, card-carrying cowards who refuse to give blood because they're afraid they'll faint are not empaths. Armchair critics who laugh at Billy Graham are not empaths.

Had to tell somebody about the vision, should have told Moe when he had the chance.

He finished the least burnt parts of the meal, then shoved the rest in his garbage can for Chopin to find later.

Had to give Miss Weiss credit. Most murders are solved within the first few days, if they're solved at all. A little kick in the pants might be just the boost he needed.

He switched out the lights and went to bed.

* * *

Dave was up at six the next morning, feeling strangely elated. He finally had a big-time case he could really sink his teeth into.

As he was getting into the Jeep, Mrs. McKinney from across the street came running out of the house, clad only in her bathrobe and bunny slippers. For a moment he thought her house must be on fire or Matt, her husband, had had a heart attack. Before he could react, she came puffing up alongside his door.

"Deputy Jenkins," she said, between pants. "Matt is talking...about getting a gun. I need you...to talk him out of it."

He patted her shoulder. "You tell him I said not to worry. After all, I'm right across the street, and I've got mine, right?"

She nodded, still breathing hard, and he started the Jeep and headed downtown. It was awfully slow going. It took him a good half hour to get to work he was flagged so often. Warner's Hardware had had a run on deadbolt locks and the boys at the Legion wanted to form a neighborhood watch. The people in Soldier had been watching way too many serial-killer movies.

Shirley, Harry's office manager and Moe's mom, had beat him to work again. She handed Dave a cup of coffee as he strolled by. Fortyish, nice dark hair and eyes, must have been quite a looker in her younger days. What would she want with Harry?

"You look like you had a rough night," she said. "Have you and Howard got the murder solved yet?"

"Not quite. Have to hurry, though. Hildegard's given me until Friday."

Shirley raised her eyes to the ceiling. She'd had Hildegard for third grade as well.

"She's not the only one who wants this murder solved ten minutes ago," Shirley said. "Harry had to hire someone to help with all of the possible leads. He said to go right in as soon as you got here."

"Thanks."

Dave headed for the office. He'd tell Harry first thing about the recall petition, just come right out with it like he was talking about the weather. Yeah, that's what he'd do.

He stopped with his hand on the doorjamb, surveying the office. Wood-paneled, hunting decor, with a gun rack off to the right, a cane chair in front of Harry's battleship-gray desk, a cracked, leather couch up against the wall on Harry's right, a pile of outdoor magazines on a glass coffee table, an abandoned computer shoved off away from the desk, disconnected—occasionally, Dave would catch Harry staring at it vacantly. Yeah, if he were Harry, he wouldn't want some snot-nosed kid...

"Uh-huh. Uh-huh. Is that so?" Harry was on the phone, most likely talking to the Bureau of Criminal Apprehension. Harry lit one of his nonfiltered coffin nails and exhaled toward the ceiling, creating a haze of smoke in the room.

Somebody was breathing on Dave's neck. He spun around to find Mingo standing behind him. Damn Indian. Wouldn't be able to tell Harry about the recall petition in front of him.

Mingo took one of the folding chairs stacked in the corner and set it next to the cane chair. Dave took the cue, settled in the cane chair, and crossed his leg over his knee, holding his foot. Harry blathered on and on about the latest forensic bullshit, and Dave locked eyes with the head of the twelve-point buck Harry had mounted behind and above his desk. That deer had to be haunted. Its eyes followed your every movement.

Dave's eyes shifted to the desk. Harry had pictures of his wife and children lined up in front, facing outward as if he were showing them off. Five boys and five girls. Mace, Max, Mel, Mort and Marv and Alice, Annie, Alexia, Anastasia and Aimee. Alice and Annie were always over at Dave's place, trying to out cook each other. He didn't mind. TV dinners got pretty old after a while.

Harry handed the phone to Dave. "Wants to talk to you. It's Henderson."

"Yeah, Larry, what's up?"

"We matched the footprints at the murder scene with those at the quarry. The vehicle was some kind of van or truck. Interesting writing on Egge's back. The shrinks have no idea what it means."

"We think the first letter means 'damn'."

"Could be. Need anything? I can help out with the interrogation if you want."

"We'll muddle through, Larry. We'll try not to botch things too badly. I'll let you know if anything significant turns up. See you later." He hung up the phone.

Harry dragged on his cigarette. "Henderson says there were no prints on the baseball bat or cigarette package, the blood was Egge's, and it's a negative on fiber or any foreign hair. No results on the boot yet."

Mingo was fiddling with a piece of paper. He was just as antsy as Dave was to get going with the investigation. Dave stole a glance at the paper—just a bunch of names.

"Any chance this was a family affair," Dave said, "insurance or something? I hear he wasn't getting along with the old lady."

"Mrs. MacIntosh should be able to fill us in on all the dirt," Harry said. "I want you to interview her. Also, Bronson, and as many of the other teachers as you can this afternoon. Bronson says he can see you at three."

Dave looked down at Harry's hands, nicotine stained fingers with cracked nails. He was a heart attack waiting to happen.

"I thought I'd go to the autopsy this morning," Dave said, "then see Mrs. Egge."

"I don't know about that. People will think that's awfully bad form. Can't she wait?"

"I don't think so. I want to search Jerry's office if he's got one and get a look at Mrs. Egge's general demeanor. If the rumors I'm hearing are true, she and Bronson could have been in it together."

Harry smoothed back his few remaining hairs. "Fine. Just try to be tactful for once. What's that you've got there, Mingo?"

"Those splatballers, the ones defiling the woods, I have a list—you know, the treehuggers are always ratting them out. Thought maybe one of them might have seen something." The coyote smile was back. "And if not, maybe I can work them over just on g.p."

Harry smiled. He was getting used to Mingo's offbeat sense of humor.

"Great idea," he said. "You go ahead on that. And you want to coordinate the tips we've been getting. Shirley will introduce you to the new person, Lucille something I think her name is. She's a senior at North Dakota State Larry Henderson found for me. Me and Dave got to map out where we go from here. Let me know later today if you find anything new."

As soon as Mingo was gone, Harry said, "I needed to talk to you alone, Jenkins. There's talk that old bat Hildegard is going around collecting signatures against me. Do you know anything about that?"

Oh fuck. "I was about to tell you about that, Harry. I don't want to be the one in the middle."

"Well, you are in the middle as long as you go running to her with every little case."

"Shit, Harry, you know as well as I do that Hildegard has the final say around here. You can't even get a building permit without her okay. You won't see my name on that petition."

Harry mashed out his cigarette in the overflowing, yellow ashtray that had to weigh at least five pounds. "Are you denying you're her candidate for sheriff?"

"I suppose she might have some such addled notion, but I don't want your job. You know I can't stand paperwork. If you're so suspicious of me, why don't you give the case to Henderson?" Something he'd learned during all those pot limit poker games in the SEALs: always do the opposite of what they expect.

"Let this cup pass from me, huh? I don't think so, Jenkins. I'd rather chauffeur my mother-in-law than give up this case to Henderson. All I'm saying is I wish you'd do your level best to put a muzzle on that old pit bull."

"You know Hildegard, Harry. I have as much influence with her as you do."

"I understand you were over there last night."

This town. "I went over there to try to talk her out of the recall. For the last time, I don't want your job."

"The only way you're going to get my job is to beat me fair and square at the next election, kid."

"You'll be sheriff until you die, Harry."

"As long as you understand what's what. Oh, by the way, the wife and the girls want you over for Sunday dinner once this Egge thing settles down. You'll get an ulcer if you don't take time out to eat a nice solid meal. I remember what it was like to be a bachelor, always eating out of a can."

"I'll try to make it."

"Speaking of Hildegard," Harry said, "I heard she was so in love with her priest that she chased him around the church and grabbed him by the organ."

Harry erupted in a raucous "haw, haw, haw."

The deer looked down on Harry disapprovingly, Harry's laugh turned to a hack. Dave coughed in sympathy, then stood and tilted his USS Lake Champlain baseball cap low over his eyes.

"Gotta get going," he said. "Egge's ghost will be out to even the score if I don't get off my duff."

Harry's jaw dropped and his brows furrowed. "What did you say?"

"Just kidding, Harry. You always take me seriously."

*   *   *

On his way out of the office, his gaff about Egge's ghost still nagging at him, Dave ran smack dab into Annie Kline. Chicken, mashed potatoes, cole slaw, and hot buns flew out of the box she'd been carrying, the mashed potatoes and cole slaw landing face down on the linoleum.

He knelt to help her pick up the chicken, and Shirley swung into action with a broom, a dust pan, and some paper towels. "Jeez," he said, "I'm sorry, Annie. I wasn't watching where I was going."

"It's all right," she said. "You've got a lot on your mind."

"No, let me run down to Andy's and get some new."

Annie looked up at him with eyes, like chocolate quicksand, too dangerous for him to risk a swim.

"Look," she said, "it won't hurt Dad to miss a meal. He's been eating too much fatty food as is. You've got a murder case on your hands."

They took what was left of the chicken to the sink in the bathroom. Annie set the box down on the edge of the sink, checked herself out in the mirror, readjusted her Chicago Cubs baseball cap, her raven ponytail exiting out the opening in the one-size-fits-all snaps, and tucked her brother's flannel shirt into her culottes.

He watched her run cold water over the chicken pieces. Brown as a berry, she had to have been patronizing the tanning saloon at Hildegard's new strip mall. Her skin was offset by white tennis shoes that never seemed to get dirty playing shortstop for the Dogs, snaring grounders to her left or right with equal ease.

"He'll never know the difference once I warm them up in the microwave," she said. "Besides, Shirley keeps that floor so clean you could eat off it. Anything new about Egge?"

"Nothing I can tell you about," he said. "I'm on my way to the coroner's office to watch the autopsy. Want to come along?"

She made a face. "I think I'd rather have my appendix out."

He laughed, handed her a wing and two breasts, she ran water over them, and they took the salvaged chicken to the microwave in the outer office where Dave dabbed at the pieces with a napkin and Annie put them on the microwave plate. Over Annie's shoulder he could see Shirley typing away, a pleased smile playing across her lips.

* * *

When the Medical Examiner used his circular saw to open Egge's cranium, the headache Dave had at the murder scene returned with a vengeance. Egge's brain had an ugly greenish-gray tinge. No wonder he'd only been hitting .215 for the Dogs.

Cause of death: cerebral hemorrhage. No surprise clues. The ME said he'd send his full report as soon as possible.

Dave got to the Egge place at ten or so.

Carpenters' horses scattered about, plastic sheeting cordoning off one side of the house, men crawling around on the roof, sawing, hammering, measuring. Despite the nippy weather, most of them wore sleeveless T-shirts, showing off their muscles.

Dave rang the bell, and a Pekinese began yapping at him through the screen. He'd always disliked Pekinese. Dogs were descended from wolves and should have the same stature and arrogance. Had to apologize to Hrothgar and Hagar next time he saw them.

Finally, after a five minute wait, the girl Winona let him in and led him into the living room. The decor was more like sculpture than furniture and didn't seem to match the Victorian exterior. The walls were decorated with Renoir prints, mostly ballet motifs. The floor was bare and polished to such a high gloss that Dave could see his elongated body in the sheen. Egge must have really hated this place.

He took his hat off and set it on a glass structure attached to a claw-footed pedestal that he guessed was supposed to be a coffee table. He sat in one of the sculptures and immediately got a sore back.

Mrs. Egge looked nothing like the lady from *The Birds*. Her straight blond hair—so blond it was almost white—came to a point at the edge of her cheekbones, giving her a flapper look. Willie and Winona could have been anorexic models from one of those underwear ads. The boy was dressed in a red tank top and jeans. The girl wore a gray, baggy sweatshirt and hip-huggers. She certainly was beautiful, but he would never want to sleep with her. She'd feel bony and would never kiss him back. The three of them, very blond and pale, almost invisible, sat speaking in whispers. No crying, no red eyes.

He cleared his throat, "Um...you folks have my most sincere sympathies. I'm so sorry for your loss. I just need to ask a few preliminary questions and then I'd like to see Jerry's office if I might. Mrs. Egge, can you tell me if your husband had any enemies?"

"You mean besides Charlie?" she said in a voice that seemed to fade before it reached him. "Everybody knows Jerry and Charlie didn't get along. You can put me on that list, too. We were talking about divorce."

Dave looked over at Willie and Winona. They didn't seem too bothered by what their mother was saying.

"Any threatening phone calls?" he said.

"Our home phone is unlisted. Nothing in the mail that I know of. If he got any at school, he didn't tell me about them. We didn't talk much, he spent most of his time at school."

The dog was now chewing on a slipper. Nobody took it away. Dave thought about driving by here periodically on the off chance that he could catch the dog out in the road.

"I need to ask you some questions about your marriage, Mrs. Egge, and about this rumor...We could talk in private—"

"My children know the facts of life," she said. "Jerry and I didn't sleep together anymore, and, yes, Charlie and I have been seeing each other."

"Daddy didn't love us," Winona said. She picked up a magazine from the coffee table and began paging through it.

Dave felt more alone than at any time he could remember. Poor Egge. "Er, Mrs. Egge, I have to ask about life insurance."

Mrs. Egge gazed over at him—she had hooded, aristocratic eyes, the kind that let you know you weren't worth much. For a moment, he didn't think she was going to answer, but then she must have thought better of it. "Two hundred fifty thousand dollars," she said, "double indemnity. I think he had himself killed, Deputy Jenkins, hired someone to do it. He was very unhappy in his job, but I wouldn't let him quit. He never came home until late at night."

He could see an almost imperceptible upward turn of the mouth. Too damn smart for her own good.

Willie tore his eyes away from the TV. "My father would never kill himself. Anybody that self-possessed isn't about to commit suicide."

Little snot. Reminded Dave of the dog. "Mrs. Egge," he said, "did your husband have a study? I need to check out his bedroom, too, if I could."

"He kept everything in his den up in the attic. I have a key to his file cabinet." She rummaged through a little, black clutch, came out with a ring of keys, removed one of them, and handed it to him. "He has a computer, about which I know nothing. You'll have to figure it out for yourself."

Winona offered to show him to Egge's den. As soon as they were out of the room, she got very friendly, her arm crooked in his, her breast nudging up against his bicep.

"Here we are," she said at the door to the den.

"Thanks."

"Anything you need, you just whistle." She raised her brows at him. "Cops really stir my ashes. You want to go out?"

"I'm engaged," he said and closed the door on her. Not exactly a lie. He was engaged in investigating a murder.

The musty-smelling room was sparsely furnished, with a lived-in maroon recliner under a sky light, a Macintosh computer—elaborate cords everywhere—centered on a small desk, an oak file cabinet, and, up under the eaves, an overstuffed bookcase behind which he could just barely see a battered fold-a-bed. A pile of old newspapers and *National Geographics* barricaded a closet door and blocked the only window. Egge's leather slippers were positioned next to the recliner and a briar pipe straddled an ashtray on the desk. Dave picked up the pipe—teeth marks along the stem, didn't look as if it had ever been smoked.

And suddenly he could see Egge in his car, hands gripping the wheel so hard his knuckles were turning white, his wife sitting up against the passenger side door, as far away from him as possible.

"You certainly made a spectacle of yourself tonight," Egge said. "Flirting with Bronson like a teenager in front of God and everybody. If it weren't for the children, I swear I'd move out now."

"Don't worry about the children," she said. "They're not yours."

"What the fuck do you mean, the children aren't mine? That's the most hateful thing you've ever said to me. You'd say anything to get back at me."

"I can't help it. They're not yours."

The vision disappeared.

Dave set the pipe down and collapsed into the recliner, breathing hard. Then he picked the pipe back up. He wanted to know who the father was.

Nothing.

His hands shaking, he sat down again and put his head between his knees. Damn, he had to tell somebody about these hallucinations or he'd go out of his rabbit-assed mind. The priest didn't seem to be an option and Mingo, with his highfalutin degree in criminal justice, might try to use it on him to take a step up in rank. That left Moe.

He picked up the phone and dialed Shirley's home number, chancing it that Moe'd be skipping school again today. He needed some help here anyway, and the only person who didn't make him feel as if he should be under investigation rather than doing the investigating was Moe Pleasiac. Besides, Moe could spot dandruff in a snowbank.

Moe got there in fifteen minutes and was shown to the den. The boy was wearing bib overalls with a bowler hat with Looney Tunes tattoos on his arms, the stick-on kind.

"They really, and I mean really, didn't want to let me in," Moe said, appropriating the recliner. "When the dog licked my hand, they relented."

"Sorry about that. I didn't think they cared about anything. How'd you make friends with the dog? I don't think he trusted me."

Moe tossed his hat on the pile of *National Geographics* and swept back his hair. "It's the dog fraternity. Chopin and he probably know each other. I'm a master and you're not. I'm surprised he's not in here trying to get me to pet him."

Dave surveyed the room, looking for a place to start. The room was so stuffy he could barely breathe. Such a big house, and Egge had been stuck up in the attic. Felt sorry for the guy, probably why he'd conjured up the vision about the wife.

"Well, let's see what we can find," he said. "You check the desk while I hit the file cabinet."

Moe got out of the recliner and skipped over to the desk, where he turned on the computer. Dave jiggled the key to the file cabinet. It was fighting him. Keys never wanted to open for him. Finally, he kicked the bottom drawer and the top drawer opened. He reached into the file cabinet and came out with a heater.

"Whoops!" he said. "Got a gun, .38 special, piece of junk. Must have been expecting some trouble. Wonder if he had a permit for this."

The gun and the most recent vision certainly went together. If Dave had a couple of grown kids, and his wife told him they weren't his, what would he do? Wouldn't feel too good about himself, that's for sure.

After a cursory inspection of the file cabinet, Dave moved to the bookshelf and began sifting through the books looking for bookmarks, entries in the margins, secret compartments. Egge had a lot of books about Shakespeare.

Over at the desk, Moe was wearing a frown instead of a smile. "Egge's got a privacy program on this thing," he said. "It'll take me all day to find the password."

"Try 'relief pitcher,'" Dave said.

Moe's fingers clattered over the keys, then waited. "Nope. Any other suggestions?"

"Look in the drawers. I'll bet passwords are like house keys. People put them above the door or under the welcome mat."

Moe typed in some more letters and the screen came to life. "He had it scratched on the housing. Would you believe, John Dewey?"

"See if there's some kind of file about a private detective. I have a feeling Egge knew about his wife and Bronson and he wasn't happy about it."

"There's one labeled 'documentation.'"

Dave pulled up a chair next to Moe. "That could be anything. Principals document everything when there's trouble with a student or a teacher. It's about the only way to expel a kid these days."

Fingers zigzagging down the screen, Moe skimmed the document. Dave shifted a gooseneck lamp to see better, watched him read. The boy had the kind of face that would never get old, but the eyes were those of a hypnotist.

After a few minutes of scanning, Moe said, "Bunch of dates with a few comments. The first one is about a New Year's Eve party where Bronson made a pass at Egge's wife. Then on the way home, she told Egge the Bobbsey Twins downstairs weren't his."

Suddenly the room seemed gray, and Dave was feeling nauseous. The fucking visions were real.

"What's the matter with you?" Moe said. "You look like you did when the North Stars moved to Dallas."

"Nothing, just feeling a little queasy lately."

"Don't breath on me, okay? I always get what everybody's got."

"I'll try not to."

Moe turned back to the screen. "Ooh, here's a real goody. He says, 'This morning I found irrefutable evidence that Bronson has been intimate with a student. I plan to confront him and the student with this information before I go to the authorities.'"

"Does he mention any names?"

"Not that I can find. I suppose he was worried the information might fall into the wrong hands, despite the privacy program."

"I guess we've found our real motive, haven't we? Can you make me a copy of his desktop files?"

"Sure. It'll take a while, though."

Moe ran floppy copies of the desktop while Dave had thick-coming fancies about what ECT treatments must be like. Then they spent another hour or so alternately digging through Egge's desk, file cabinet, and the bookshelf before Dave had a flash of inspiration. "I'll bet he's got a safety deposit box," he said.

On the way out, Dave and Moe found Mrs. Egge in the kitchen eating breakfast, Wheaties with strawberries.

"Once again I want to offer my condolences," Dave said. "I don't know if you knew, but Jerry was on my softball team, and I take his murder personally."

Her eyes squinted as if he'd just told her Jerry'd been a closet bigamist. "Oh yes, he was fanatical about that team. Too bad he never got involved in...Forget that, I'll be seeing you tomorrow at the funeral, won't I? Jerry was an organ donor and he'd wanted to be cremated, but that BCA person—Mr. Henderson I think he said his name was—wouldn't allow it."

Might need that body again later. Typical Buttinsky Henderson behavior. If he did the job right in the first place, he wouldn't be needing to exhume.

"I'll try to make it, Mrs. Egge," Dave said, then Moe tipped his bowler and they left.

On his way to the Jeep, Dave noticed something in his pocket. He reached in and found he had unconsciously misappropriated Egge's pipe. Didn't want to bother her. He'd keep it until he saw her again.

Back at the office, Mingo was sitting in Dave's closet of an office in *his* chair, flipping playing cards into his Mountie hat.

"Finished with the splatballers," Mingo said. "As a whole they look as if they'll soon grow bored with paint and move on to bigger highs. None of them saw anything and there's no evidence that they were involved. I told them not to leave town. Not that they would have—some of them have never been *out* of town—but I always wanted to say that. I'm waiting for a roster from the Crookston team, one of the local boys gave me the name of their fearless leader."

Dave chased Mingo out of his chair and sat down. "How about tips, anything good?"

Mingo overturned the wastebasket and sat down. "Nothing much so far." He gave his coyote smile. "Some of them are pretty funny, though. Old Man Hoover reported a suspicious stranger. Turns out it was the Watkins man who's been selling him household products for over thirty years."

"Egge's funeral's tomorrow," Dave said. "I better check it out. Sometimes these creeps like to push the envelope and show up at the funeral. He should stick out like a sore thumb if those footprints mean anything."

"I don't know, Dude. My Cousin Cecil has size thirteen shoes, and he's only five foot six."

"You're the one called him Sasquatch," Dave said, handing Mingo a copy of Egge's documentation. "It's looking bad for Bronson."

Mingo read over the indictment.

"Listen to this: 'January 15, followed Bronson to the Bluebird Inn in Crookston. The bitch showed up fifteen minutes later. They spent two hours together.'"

"Nice they could keep each other entertained so long." Dave stood up. "Let's go, I've got an appointment with Bronson at three. See if you can get a warrant for Egge's bank records and safety deposit box. I have a feeling Banker Forman will be somewhat reluctant to let us see what's in that box without a court order. I could've asked Egge's wife for the key I suppose, but she's a suspect you know."

"No problem. I'll get the warrant."

"I appreciate your taking the extra added responsibility. How much is Harry payin' you, if you don't mind my askin'?"

"The money's not the best, only $25,000, but the perks make up for it. I get to fish all I want, you know. The Chippewa and the Sioux, my relatives, they got fishing rights, and a game warden can't tell a Sioux from a Kickapoo."

"Yah we got the good fishing all right. Didja know Minnesota means land of sky blue waters?"

"Yeah, I seen the beer commercial."

"I've already talked to Harry about gettin' you on days."

"Nah, don't need much sleep. When I saw the listing in the placement office at Johns Hopkins, the night hours were part of the allure. Most Apaches, you know, would rather ride sidesaddle than work during the evil night hours, but I'm not your usual Apache."

"You went to Johns Hopkins?"

"Sure did. On an athletic scholarship."

"Football?"

"Lacrosse. Johns Hopkins is the best Lacrosse school in the country. Indians invented the game, you know. We call it baggataway, little brother of war."

"Never seen the game played. You'll have to explain the rules sometime. I don't suppose you've ever played any softball?"

"You want me to play for the Dogs, right? I'll think on it, let you know next time we blink each other. I'm pretty sure I want to, but we Mescaleros don't do things on the spur of the moment." Mingo stood and moved toward the door. "I'll go get that warrant."

"And when you're through there, you might want to ferret out Lester 'the Molester' Krueger. He was acting awfully hinky at the murder scene."

"Right, Dude." Mingo put on his hat, which Dave noticed now sported an eagle feather. "Mingo look under nearest rock."

Chapter 5

Cock of the Walk

"And I will punish the world for their evil,
and the wicked for their iniquity;
and I will cause the arrogancy
of the proud to cease..."
— Isaiah 13:11

Dave arrived at the school at three o'clock sharp. Bronson's secretary—gray perm, half-glasses balanced on the end of her nose—told him to take a seat without looking up from her machine gun fast typing. When the phone rang, she picked it up, said, "Soldier High School," tucked the phone under her chin, and continued typing. Dave knew if he tried that his brain would start to smoke.

There were no magazines to read, so he took out his notebook and went over what he had so far: Bronson and Mrs. Egge were definitely having an affair; Egge knew about it and he'd most likely confronted Bronson at least once at the Super Valu. Egge had a lucrative life insurance policy, double indemnity yet. Egge's children didn't seem too upset about their father's murder. Egge's children didn't look anything like their father and he'd been told they weren't his. Bronson was looking awfully guilty all right.

Dave dropped his notebook in his lap. No way, not the superintendent of schools. Egge was just unlucky. He'd run into some weirdo out in the woods as was evidenced by the demonic markings on his back. No matter how smart Bronson was, he wouldn't think of such a nutty scheme, despite Hildegard's Jeffrey MacDonald scenario.

"You can go in now," Bronson's secretary said.

He glanced at his watch as he moved down the plushly carpeted corridor leading to the Big Chief's office. Fifteen minutes he'd been woolgathering.

Bronson's office was a spacious room with a huge walnut desk, polished to a high sheen, virtually clear, except for a telephone and an IBM computer. Bronson was on the phone, his big mitts, with black, kinky hairs on their backs, dwarfing the receiver. There was a ring—the size of a robin's egg—with a ruby stone on his right hand, and he wore a slate-gray suit with a blue tie knotted in a very precise windsor, the suit binding at the shoulders, as if he were still a growing boy. As he gabbed, Bronson ran his hand over his curls and they popped right back into place.

"Have a seat, Deputy, I'll be right with you." Bronson pointed to a chair.

Dave scrutinized the room. Philodendrons were hanging from all four corners and on either side of the big picture window overlooking the football field. Other than the plants, the room took on a sporting motif. Two of Bronson's sons had been basketball and football stars for the Soldier Commandos. Bronson had newspaper action shots of both boys, enlarged and framed, throughout his office.

The superintendent plopped one very large foot up on his desk.

"We'll need two men," he said, "and we can't pay you over fifty a day. It'll max out my substitute budget as is."

Dave hadn't had much to do with Bronson other than his work with DARE. Just enough contact to develop a dislike for his perm and the wing tips. The clodhoppers in those shoes could have made the tracks out at the murder scene.

The superintendent had dark lines under his eyes. Dave knew that Bronson was under pressure concerning an upcoming referendum. The high school had been built in 1934, and the building inspectors kept threatening to condemn the place. Bronson had tried twice previously for a new building and got voted down. The buzz at Bud's Tavern said it could mean his job if it didn't pass this time.

Bronson glanced over at Dave. "Got to get back to you, there's a guy here from the sheriff's office. Right. I'll call you in about an hour or so. Take it easy." He put the phone down, rubbed his chin, and squinted at Dave. "I never quite placed you before, Deputy Jenkins. You played football with my son Tom, didn't you? Was it safety or middle linebacker?"

"I played both ways, Mr. Bronson," he said, "defensive end and offensive center."

"Kind of small for a defensive end, aren't you?" Bronson said, smirking just a bit.

"Well, you know, in high school, the coach has got to take what he can get. Coach Schmeck thought I was pretty quick off the ball."

Bronson's face brightened. "Yeah, I remember those UCLA teams in the Rose Bowl who were awfully small on the line but always beat Woody Hayes's Ohio State teams off the snap."

The man picked up his phone, set it back down, then started tapping his pencil. The phone buzzed. He grabbed it like a lifeline.

"Sylvia, hold all my calls...I don't care whose parent it is, god-damn it! Have him call me back in an hour."

Bronson put the receiver down without saying good-bye, then leaned back in his chair. Hmm, no empathy for his subordinates? Could be a sociopath.

"Now how can I help you, Deputy?" Bronson said. "This thing has been one big black eye for the school district, let me tell you. Had to call in outside grief counselors for the kids and hire securi-ty to put their minds at ease. That was them on the phone. And we lost a day. Lose another half day tomorrow for the funeral. Every day we lose, we have to make up in the summer when the humid-ity is high, and we don't have any air conditioning. The kids are impossible."

Dave thought of Egge's documentation about Bronson's having sex with a student. Cock of the walk, in more ways than one. Dave wanted to pop this guy up alongside the head. "Yeah, it gets pret-ty hot," he said. "Look, Mr. Bronson, I need to know—"

"You want to know if our little altercation in the parking lot of the Super Valu went any further. Look, I'm not the only one who didn't get along with Egge. He was a very abrasive man. And prin-cipals—especially principals who handle their own discipline as Egge had to because the district was too cheap to hire a vice-prin-cipal—are hated by practically everyone."

Dave shifted in his chair. "Er, Mr. Bronson—"

"It's Chuck. Mr. Bronson is my father."

"Yes...Chuck, could you tell me a little bit about your disagree-ment. I'm sure it was nothing."

Bronson got up and poured himself a cup of coffee. "Would you like some?" he said.

Dave said, "I believe I will. Just black, thank you."

"I'm sorry," Bronson said. "I'm just a little edgy. I suppose you think I'm insensitive. Terrible thing about Egge, terrible thing. Nobody deserves to die like that."

"But...you and he did have some difficulties?"

Bronson handed Dave a roundish cup with a University of Michigan emblem on it. "I...tried to fire Egge."

"Over anything in particular?" *Fear he'd report the child abuse, for instance?*

"I felt he was insubordinate over some curriculum differences we had. The ah...Board disagreed. Excuse me, I need some sugar. Got this infernal sweet tooth." Bronson moved over toward the coffee bar, his back toward Dave. And when he did, a pencil lying on Bronson's desk seemed to take off on its own and roll off the edge. Dave was sure Bronson hadn't touched it. The pencil bounced and rolled under Bronson's desk.

What next? What was that guy's name? Uri Geller, that was it, the psychokinesis guy who could bend spoons with his mind. Dave had thought that was a bunch of bullshit. Until now.

Bronson strode back to his desk, sat down in his luxurious swivel chair, and put the big pontoons back on the desk, took a sip of his coffee. "That's better. What were we saying? Oh yes, the Board wouldn't fire Egge."

"Um...yes," Dave said, still bothered by the rolling pencil. "Ah...lots of people have personality conflicts, I'm sure. I'll tell you what, you give me the names of people who had gripes with Mr. Egge, if you will, if it doesn't violate any confidentiality legislation, and then, if it's okay, I'd like to operate from here for a few days. I'll try to be as inconspicuous as possible."

Bronson frowned. "I don't think we can do that, Dave. I do everything in my power to protect the educational environment at Soldier High. If I allow you to do your interrogations here, you'll be a distraction."

Dave shook his head. He hadn't planned on asking to set up office in the school when he'd come in here. Hmmm, actually, it wasn't such a bad idea.

He took a sip of coffee and said, "Let me try to explain where I'm coming from. I need access to Egge's file and everyone who worked with him. I can't be constantly running back and forth from the sheriff's office to the school. If you don't cooperate, your teachers will lose more time at the sheriff's office than they will if they talk to me here."

Bronson considered this for a moment, then reached over and pressed the intercom button. "Sylvia, would you send Fran Ellis in here."

A few minutes later a small, round, balding man dressed in brown came into the office and sat in the chair next to Dave. Bronson introduced them, and they shook hands.

Bronson looked over at Ellis. "Fran, I'd like to get your feelings on an unusual request the deputy has just made. He wants to set up shop at the school. What do you think?"

Ellis's face brightened. "I can't think of a better idea. You know we're always calling over there anyway; we can't handle assault or drug incidents on our own, and I can't get my scheduling done what with all the interruptions. This way we'll get an immediate response. He can have Jerry's office, I never use it, and I'd be willing to supervise the deputy if that's what you want me to say."

"I don't think that was the deputy's intention," Bronson said. "He won't want to be bothered with our needs if he's interrogating people."

Ellis shrugged. "Whatever you'd like."

Bronson turned his swivel chair toward the wall, steepling his hands under his chin. Deep in thought, like Harry Truman before his decision to drop the bomb. Dave's head was spinning. It would be awfully creepy working in a dead man's office. He kind of hoped Bronson wouldn't go for it.

Turning back toward them, Bronson said, "If Fran's willing to be responsible for you, we'll give it a try. It should be okay as long as you don't need more than the few weeks we have left of school."

"I appreciate this—"

"I have another consideration besides the investigation." Bronson stood and moved to the window. "I've been mulling this over for a number of weeks. We'd like to institute a police liaison with the school. You'd be here every day for an hour or so, talk to a few classes occasionally, familiarize yourself with our malefactors. Of course, I wouldn't expect you to bother with any of this until after the Egge case has been closed. We can't afford a lot of salary, but we can pay you something."

He should have anticipated Bronson's cost-saving maneuver. He'd have to check with the Crookston police to see what a liaison officer should get.

"I don't see that as a problem," Dave said. "I'm here all the time as is."

Bronson moved back toward his desk, sat down, and put his feet back up. He was Dave's boss now and back in command.

"Could I start tomorrow?" Dave said. "And, oh yeah, I'll file a report on our interview, but the sheriff may want to talk to you himself, okay? Don't be too surprised if he covers a lot of the same ground."

Bronson, who had very heavy beetle brows, frowned and said, "Tomorrow's fine." He really did resemble the movie actor.

On their way out of Bronson's office, Ellis slapped Dave on the back. "Forget what Bronson said," he said sotto voce out of the side of his mouth. "Just do whatever you think is kosher."

Dave intended to. He didn't like that cat's attitude one bit. The next time they talked, the wing tip would be on the other foot.

And the old black ram never did admit he'd been tupping Egge's ewe.

He stopped, watched Ellis escort one of the kids who'd been waiting to see him into his office. The old black ram tupping Egge's ewe? Othello?

Egge's den was packed with books on Shakespeare.

He shook his head. No, he could have remembered it from high school. That was the kind of line all the boys would snicker over when the teacher read Shakespeare to the class. He looked at his watch. Only three forty-five. He'd try to squeeze in a preliminary interview with Mrs. Macintosh if she was still here.

Dave moved through the library toward one of the conference rooms at the back. There he found Moe playing chess with Dan Cardwell, the librarian. Cardwell was an old high-school classmate of Dave's with early-Beatle hair shot with premature gray, little pig eyes, a broken nose, and a beard. Both of them were so engrossed they didn't notice him walk up, so he stood next to the table and watched the game for a while.

Moe eventually looked up. "Hi, J.W. Are you here about Principal Egge?"

Dave laughed. "What was your first clue?"

Moe swept the hair out of his eyes. "Actually, I thought you'd call all the people you wanted to talk to down to the cop shop and interview 'em on your own turf."

"You need a haircut. I thought I'd stop and talk to Mrs. Macintosh while I was here. I was just in with Mr. Bronson. He offered me the principal's job."

Moe grinned. He'd always been Dave's best audience. "Sure he did. And he's doubling the principal's salary so's some other school doesn't grab you first."

"You'd doubt my word? I can't imagine why. Any progress on that puzzle we were discussing?"

"JESSICA and I are still noodling it over. We don't want to be hasty."

"I wish you two would clue me in," Cardwell said.

Dave gave Cardwell the upraised eyebrow look which meant, you know better than to ask something like that. "Do you think it would cause any trouble if I interrupted Mrs. Mac's class for a few minutes?"

"Nah, they never do anything in there anyway," Cardwell said, "except maybe watch movies and play loud music. I had to ask

Jerry to tell Gigglebox to keep it down. That's her room over there, 305."

"Gigglebox?"

"That's what we call her around here," Cardwell said. "You'll understand why when you talk to her. Say, did you know Mary Lou Forman's back in town? Seems like I remember you had the hots for her once."

So it was her. "Why would I care?" Dave said. "I don't have the bucks to satisfy that woman."

Cardwell grinned and Moe's derisive smile became audible. "Huh huh huh." More fodder for the mill.

Dave mussed Moe's hair, turned, and headed for Mrs. Macintosh's door. "I can't stand here gabbing with you clowns all day. Don't beat him too bad, Dan."

"That'll be the day," Cardwell said. "It hasn't happened yet. I don't know why I bother trying."

Mrs. Mac's door was open, but Dave knocked on the doorframe anyway. She was huddled over a table with two girls. She glanced up, noticing him, maintaining eye contact. Big woman, comfortable-looking with a round expressive face and an indelible smile.

"I'll be right with you, Deputy, I was expecting you. Allie, Gina, this is Deputy Jenkins."

"Hello," they said in unison. He nodded.

"I just need to finish here," Mrs. Mac said. "There's coffee if you want some."

She pointed to a coffee maker in the corner. He went over and helped himself, wondering about the purple hair, rather unusual for a woman her age.

Dave glanced around the room. Mrs. Macintosh had decorated the place with all sorts of posters: R.E.M, Nirvana, Nine Inch Nails. A magazine rack held *Popular Mechanics*, *Hot Rod*, and *People* magazine. A little radio in the corner was tuned to a rock station.

He looked back at Mrs. Mac and her students. They were both overweight. *Which is symptomatic in the rare discipline problem with the fair sex.*

Damn. He hadn't heard *that* in high school.

Dave unconsciously fingered the pipe in his windbreaker pocket and a phone rang, once, twice, three times. A very busy Egge, who was trying to schedule classes for the coming year, snatched the receiver. "Yes?"

"This is Mrs. Larue, Mr. Egge. I'd like to file a harassment complaint. Those boys in my daughter's P.E. Class have been calling her The Walrus."

"Do you have any names, Mrs. Larue?"

"All of them. The whole class, Mr. Egge. I want them punished and punished severely."

The woman was eating something.

Egge reached inside his desk and came out with an economy-size bottle of aspirin, swallowed a handful, and washed them down with a tumbler of water he had on his desk.

Raucous laughter brought Dave back from wherever he'd been. Mrs. Macintosh was laughing so hard tears had come to her eyes. The infectious merriment had wreathed Allie and Gina's faces in smiles, mutating them into cover girls. Thank God for the chuckles, they hadn't noticed he'd been spacing. Lord, what was happening to him?

Mrs. Mac stopped laughing, held Allie's palm, tracing the lines with her finger.

"You have what is called the Earth hand, Allie," she said. "Square palm, short fingers, deeply lined. You are a serious person who would be happiest working as a carpenter or a farmer."

"I do like to work in the garden," Allie said.

"Let me see your hand, Deputy Jenkins," she said. Dave walked over and proffered his hand, a little reluctantly since he wasn't sure he wanted anyone poking through his psyche at the moment. Mrs. Mac took it gently. "Now this is an Air hand, Allie. Long fingers, square palm, etched with fine lines. Expressive, high intellect, very curious. Certainly fits, don't you think? Oh, wow, conic fingertips. That means you rely more on intuition than reason."

Allie wrote something in her notebook.

Mrs. Mac stroked his fingertips, which, now that he noticed it, did come to a point. "Eventually you'll be drawn to the arts, poetry, music. Do you play?"

"Just the occasional chopsticks. Moe taught me."

"You really should pursue it. I suppose you're wondering what we're doing here, Deputy?"

"Some kind of...activity I suppose."

"Hands on. Hands on, Deputy. That's my educational philosophy. The girls are trying to prove the metaphysical realm has a rational basis. It's so hard to put your finger on it, though, isn't it, Gina?"

"Most people think we're crazy." This from the blond, curly-headed one with protruding eyes.

The bell rang and one of the girls left, after enduring a smothering hug from Mrs. Macintosh. The one called Allie hung back.

Mrs. Macintosh got up and took Dave by the arm, moving him out into the library area where Moe and Dan Cardwell were playing chess.

"You wanted to speak to me?"

"Only on a preliminary basis. I need to arrange a good time for you to talk to me in detail about the Egge murder, but I don't want to disrupt your class. It could take quite a while, I'm wondering if tomorrow is too soon."

"I'm so ashamed of myself." Her hands fluttered about like hummingbirds. "Me a professional, acting like such a ninny at the murder scene. All day yesterday for that matter. The neighbor girls and I wore out our rosaries and harried the neighbors with atonal hymns from dawn to dusk. I hope I got that out of my system. This morning I got up, looked in the mirror and said, 'That church lady you ain't, Martha. All that Hail Mary stuff is for Mother Teresa.' I hope the Lord doesn't strike me dead for sayin' this, but I gotta be me. I'm perfectly fine now, and back to dabbling in the black arts. The girls and I should make contact with Jerry any time now."

"Ah...contact?"

She took a card out of her dress pocket and handed it to Dave. It read: Martha Macintosh, Soothsayer and Matrimonial Agent. Dave slipped it into his breast pocket.

"You'll have to talk to the superintendent about the interview," she said. "If he'll release me, I'd be happy to come anytime. I don't want to be docked any pay, you see."

"As long as I'm here, Mrs. Macintosh, if you don't mind that is, do you know if any of the students harbored a special grudge against Jerry Egge?"

"Oh, my word, I wouldn't want to get any of them in trouble without proof."

"That's fine then. I'm sorry for taking up your time."

"Don't mention it, Deputy. You go see the superintendent. I'm sure he can help you."

"Thanks again, Mrs. Macintosh," he said, tipping his cap and moving toward the red exit sign.

"Isn't he the cutest thing, Allie," she said, when she thought he was out of earshot. "He looks like a movie star, I swear. If I were only twenty years younger."

Some kind of big mouth she was. He'd thought she'd fall all over herself trying to tell him who killed Egge, and not a word.

He took the card out of his shirt pocket. Professional soothsayer? Getting in contact with Jerry? He thought back to the pencil moving on its own in Bronson's office and this most recent vision where Egge had apparently been showing him what a tough job he had. What would Mrs. Mac think about the visions?

She seemed like kind of a nut, though. One day she's singing hymns and saying the rosary, the next she's reading palms and passing herself off as Jeanne Dixon.

Dave stopped, his hand on the door handle, looking back over his shoulder at Moe and Cardwell deep in concentration. No, that game wouldn't do it for him. He yearned for his old football days when he could bump helmets with a big old defensive tackle when things got too complicated.

Fuck it. No way was he going to talk to Mrs. Macintosh about anything other than what she knew about the Egge killing. Just the facts, ma'am. No psycho bullshit.

What next? Oh, yes, the manager of Shady Brook. Most of the residents were either career felons or apprentice felons. The manager practically lived at Bud's Tavern. He should be easy enough to find.

*   *   *

Harry and the new girl, Lucille Robinson, went out the back door of his office where he'd parked his cruiser. Harry kicked the front right tire, which was a little low. He'd stop at the Amoco and have Pigeon pump her up. He'd look pretty foolish if it went flat and he had to call a garage for help.

They got settled in the front seat—for once the back wasn't acting up.

"I'll just show you the hot spots around town," Harry said. "I usually do my rounds in the morning, but you know with the murder and all—"

"Don't I know it," Lucille said. "I've been on the phone nonstop. Most of my tips are from people who just want reassurance. Would you like a doughnut?"

They were the nutty kind he liked. He took one. Lucille had to be a good fifty pounds overweight, which might present a problem. Otherwise she was very personable and laughed at all of his jokes. He'd promised her if she handled the tipline for a minimal salary, she'd get first crack at a full-time deputy's job if one opened up.

"So, where you from, Lucille?" he said. Should have remembered that from the interview. Seems like it was one of the Dakotas. Never could keep them straight.

"Lead, South Dakota, sir. That's near Rapid City."

Harry finished his doughnut, sucked the crumbs off his fingers, then started the cruiser. "Just call me Harry. My daughter find you a place to hang your hat?"

"She didn't tell you she's letting me stay with her? Just temporary. Mr. Jenkins says he'll have the case solved by Friday."

"The boy has a different sense of humor. Pay him no mind. Hildegard, she's the county clerk, is calling a town meeting for Friday. She wants to reassure the townspeople. Anybody report any overgrown oddballs?"

"There was a tip from the trailer park about this fellow who lived there four, five years ago who was always threatening the neighbors. They haven't seen him since. I put that one on my maybe pile."

"I doubt that's anything. You maybe want to sit in on the Lester Krueger interrogation with Mingo. I hope you've met Mingo."

"Oh, yes. What's a Mescalero Apache doing in Minnesota?"

"Says he likes the four seasons. Didn't have the heart to tell him we usually only have three."

She giggled. "We're lucky we get two in the Dakotas."

The girl had an easy way about her. Maybe he should offer her a job now before somebody else snapped her up.

Harry backed the cruiser into the alley. Some kids were playing kickball in the park near the convent. Usually they were out there by themselves, but today several older kids and a few mothers were watching them. He turned onto Peach, heading toward Meade Street, the main drag.

Turning north onto Meade, they drove past the volunteer firemen practicing with the hose. It fought them like a giant boa constrictor. His daughter Annie was the first woman in Soldier to qualify as a fireman, and she didn't like him interfering, as she put it, so he didn't stop to talk.

"There's Annie," Lucille rolled her window down, stuck her head out and waved, but Annie didn't look up. Lucille rolled the window back up. "I guess she didn't see me." She looked sad, as if people ignored her quite a bit. He hoped she wasn't the kind to pout.

"She's always been a very focused girl," he said. "The only one of my kids who likes to hunt. You meet any of the boys yet?"

"Just Mel. What a handsome man. I can see where he got his looks."

Harry blushed.

"Of course," she said, "he'd never have anything to do with a person like me."

"Oh, don't sell yourself short," Harry said.

He never should have let Jenkins get away this morning without asking him about the press conference Hildegard had planned before the town meeting. Reporters would be there from the Twin Cities and Duluth, and what was Harry supposed to tell them? Their readers wanted to know about what the body looked like, and the murder weapon, and the devil worship stuff on Egge's back. Damn right they'd want to know about the spray paint, he'd want to if he were them. But all he could say was, "The sheriff's office has no comment at this time, as any details we could give you would most likely hamper the ongoing investigation." Unless he let something slip.

The Amoco station was only a block from the fire station. Pigeon Hackett was just finishing with a customer when Harry and Lucille drove up to the pumps. "Fill 'er up, Pigeon," he said, "and check the right front. She looks a little low to me."

Harry got out and went into the station for a candy bar. When he came back out, Pigeon, a short man with ears that almost flapped in the wind, was just replacing the nozzle on the pump. Lucille was standing next to him with her hands in her back pockets.

"Me and the boys at the Legion been talking, Harry," Pigeon said. "What do you think about us starting up a crime watch?"

"No, I don't think that's such a good idea, Pigeon. The night deputy might get offended." Harry took a bite out of his Baby Ruth. "And you know Mingo when he gets the idea people are questioning his ability. Dave and I can handle it otherwise."

Actually, Pigeon and his friends would only get in the way, probably shoot themselves in the process, if Harry let them form a crime watch. Besides, Pigeon liked to drink.

Pigeon wiped his hands on his greasy coveralls.

"I think a crime watch is a good idea," Lucille said. "If you want, I could coordinate matters."

Another damn know-it-all. He was cursed. "We're pretty sure this is an isolated incident, Lucille."

"I'm sure the sheriff is right, Miss—"

"Lucille Robinson," she said.

"Terrible thing. Terrible thing. Jerry was such a nice person."

"Me and Brenda is having a mass said for him," Harry said. "Didja ever think of something like that?"

"Can't remember ever seeing Jerry in church, Harry. Are you sure he was Catholic?"

"Couldn't hurt, could it?"

Harry put the cruiser in gear and drove off before Pigeon could raise another protest.

He rolled down his window and hung one arm out. All along Meade people were grouped in little clusters talking, some of them pointed at Harry and Lucille as they drove by. One or two tried to flag him down, but he ignored them as he was intent on doing his rounds. He couldn't remember the last time anything had actually happened during his rounds, but it was a good idea to let the constituents know their sheriff was on the job. He turned off Meade onto Peach, heading west toward the Polaris Snowmobile factory.

Silver and black demonstration machines, glistening in the sun, were lined up in front of the retail part of the Polaris building. It was break time and the workers were clustered around the big red and white Coke machine, the kind that took dollar bills and charged a buck and a half for a plastic bottle of pop. Harley Barnhouser and his cousins Delbert and Alquin, who'd been working at Polaris ever since they'd quit high school, were lounging in lawn chairs smoking and taking their ease. They watched the cruiser go by as if it were a parade float. Harley was drinking on the job again, and he didn't care who knew it. In his rearview mirror, Harry could see Harley lift the Budweiser can in a mock toast. Harry didn't have the energy to call him on that. No sense stirring up a hornet's nest.

"Those things cost mor'n a used car," Harry said. "The boys're after me to get them a new one. Burned out the motor on the last one."

"They're fun though," she said.

Harry passed the three huge elevators, the bins bulging with accumulated wheat. The farmers were storing their crops waiting for higher prices.

He turned left onto The Angle, moving toward the hydroelectric plant, which was bordered by a hurricane fence with triple barbed wire at the top. High voltage signs were conspicuously displayed on large placards in bold type. A kid had been electrocuted here only last year. All three gates were open on the damn, the water gushing down into the river with such force the rocks below seemed to teeter on the verge of toppling.

"Beautiful, isn't it?" Lucille said. "I could watch that all day."

"Yeah, I guess so. When you've lived here as long as I have you don't seem to notice."

Harry nosed the cruiser south, past the big glass house where Blaze Forman lived, and turned onto Seminary heading toward the high school where Mel had a temporary job as a bouncer and part-time coach.

"We'll just stop and say hello to my son. He's helping out at the school. Mr. Ellis, the athletic director and temporary principal, is relying on him quite a bit to pick up the slack since Egge's murder. Not what you'd call a real job, though."

Harry stopped the cruiser in front of the athletic field where Mel and Marshall Preston, the physical education teacher, were working with the baseball team. Mel was pitching. The batter belted one over the center fielder's head, slid into second, and scored on the overthrow for an inside-the-park home run.

"He really got a hold of that one," Harry said. "Reminds me of when I was a boy growing up in Eveleth—that's on the Iron Range. We played ball every day. Just about everybody in Eveleth had a large family. We never had any trouble finding a game."

They got out of the cruiser and stood behind the backstop. He waved to Mel and Mel waved back. The batter was joking with Mel about the advisability of wearing a cup.

Harry missed that friendly banter boys seemed so good at. "We played everyday until it got too dark to see the ball," he said. "Until I hit Judge Hasting's house, broke the big picture window in front. Boy did I get a whippin'."

Whipping? Nowadays they'd probably call it a beating. Never played baseball again, and he quit high school in his sophomore year to join his father in the iron mines. Always trying to please his old man.

"Mel's limping," Lucille said. "What happened, he sprain his ankle?"

"Tore his anterior cruciate ligament playing minor league ball. Needs an operation, but the team won't pay."

Maybe he was too hard on Mel.

They got back in Harry's cruiser and headed toward Andy's Diner, the hub of Soldier, Minnesota. Jenkins's Jeep was parked diagonally out front, in the midst of the thirty-some-odd trucks parked up and down the street.

"That's Dave's Jeep there. Most likely in there hoping to pick up some helpful kernels of gossip regarding the Egge case."

Harry and Lucille went in and Harry purchased a handful of beef jerkies and a hard-boiled egg. Lucille bought a bag of Cheetos. Jenkins was deep in conversation with Ben Voigt, the manager of the Shady Brook Trailer Park.

"We better not intrude," Harry said. "Let's head on back to the office.

Once inside, Lucille went back to work on the tipline and Harry tuned the radio to an easy-listening station. After sitting at his desk a few minutes, he reached inside a drawer and pulled out a picture of old Sheriff McCloskey. Mac had big, bulging eyes that could see inside your heart. Sometimes if he stared at the picture long enough, Harry could swear he heard Mac's voice.

If you want to fire the boy, I go with him, Mac had said that time Banker Forman was trying to get Harry's badge. *The kid is the best damn deputy I've ever had. He's worth ten of you and your kid put together.* Harry'd stopped the banker's son for driving over the center line. The kid had called him an awful name and Harry'd hit him with a flashlight. Brenda had been pregnant with their first at the time. If he'd lost his job, he didn't know what he would have done.

"Who's that?" Lucille said.

Harry started. He'd been so lost in thought he hadn't heard her come in.

"That's my father-in-law, the old sheriff," he said. "Sometimes I talk to him when I have a stressful situation like the Egge case. That doesn't mark me crazy, does it?"

"I wouldn't think so. Are these your children?" She fingered Annie's graduation picture.

"All ten of them and none of them married." Lucille's eyes lit up. "Oh, I wanted to tell you, this farmer named Ray Miller called. He says somebody's been stealing his gas."

"I don't see what that would have to do with the Egge killing. Still, I'll have Dave check it out. You get back to work."

Harry buzzed Shirley. She came in, waiting with her hands crossed in front of her. She still wore her wedding ring, although it had been years since Dan had killed himself. Such an attractive woman—a healthy head of brown hair, really knew how to dress. Today she had on a little, sleeveless blue jumper with red buttons on it, and she wore blue, button-like earrings to match. There was an endearing smallpox vaccination on her upper arm. Harry wanted to touch her. So far he'd managed to resist.

He asked Shirley to sit down. She perched on the edge of the cane chair.

Harry lit a cigarette. "Shirley, do you remember Alvin Franklin?"

She gazed up toward the ceiling as if trying to remember. "Any relation to the Franklins that live on that section southwest of Fertile?"

"Damned if I know. You know I'm from Eveleth originally. Anyway, Blaze Forman needed us to go out and help repossess this farm. I had a bad back, already eating Doan's pills like they were candy. I couldn't go, and Alvin got killed in my place. Farmer shot him getting out of the cruiser."

"Oh dear."

"The farmer's wife made him go see Father Mischke, and they brought him in."

"Must have been terrible," Shirley said, "but I wouldn't be so hard on myself if I were you."

"Then there was the teacher."

Shirley looked at him with those raised eyebrows, which made him feel that she was really trying to understand. Unlike his wife Brenda.

"A few years after Alvin Franklin, Milt Kapass strangled one of his students who'd been harassing him. The poor guy had been on tranquilizers, kept the kid after school, blacked out, and strangled him with his necktie. Fr. Mischke brought Milt in, too. I was thinking of deputizing Fr. Mischke there for a while."

Shirley smiled. She had a little dimple in her chin, and she had a way of pursing her lips that made her look like a little girl.

She scratched the side of her nose. "And now we've got this Egge thing. Makes you wonder if teaching is a safe profession."

The outer door opened, and Shirley went to see who it was. He moved over to the couch trying to stretch out his back, unsuccessfully.

He'd been building toward telling her about the boy he'd killed in Vietnam. All of the Cong were so young, the boy couldn't have been more than fifteen. And then he'd almost killed the Forman boy as well.

Well, he couldn't wallow in the past all day. He went back to his desk, dialed Andy's Diner, and asked for Jenkins. Harry wanted to know if he had a lead on the case. It had certainly appeared so, what with Jenkins being so engrossed with the manager at Shady Brook, and Jenkins would never tell him without being asked.

Sometimes he'd like to take the razor strap to that boy as he had with his kids when they wouldn't toe the line. Of course, he couldn't do that anymore. It wasn't politically correct. And besides, the boys all weighed over 200 pounds.

Harry moved the phone to his other ear. He could hear the clock, clock of the foosball table in the background, never could play that game worth a shit. What would he do if Hildegard's recall petition were successful? Harry sighed. Sounded like a whimper.

Jenkins took the phone. "Yeah, Harry?"

"I was just wondering if you had a lead," Harry said. "You seemed pretty busy when I was in there earlier."

"Nah, just talking to Ben Voigt, the Shady Brook manager, about suspicious characters and unruly clients. He said there were plenty of those. We've just been dishing the dirt really. And then some other people overheard, and they had to put in their two cents."

"Did you find out anything from Mrs. Egge or Bronson?"

"Bronson's trying to pretend he never had an affair with Egge's wife. I didn't buy it. And we found a journal on Egge's computer. Some interesting info on it."

"Who's we, Jenkins? Tell me you didn't have Shirley's kid with you again."

"Without him I never would have been able to get into Egge's computer. Egge was tailing Bronson and his wife and keeping a record. Moe's practically got the code on Egge's back cracked already. Says the writing on the leg may be a name."

"Funny kind of name if you ask me. If that kid gets hurt—"

"Speaking of kids, Lester Krueger looks like he may have had something to do with this. I've got Mingo on his case. When I see Hildegard again, I'll tell her you noticed he was acting guilty."

Harry cleared his throat. "Well, you know we do have other cases. Ray Miller just called. Says somebody's been stealing his gas. You got time to check it out?"

"I'll run out there as soon as I get a chance. I'm going to the funeral tomorrow. Maybe the guy'll be dumb enough to show up. Then I'll do Mrs. Macintosh. And Bronson again, formally, on our turf. It's all coming together, Harry. We might even make Hildegard's deadline. Well, gotta go."

Jenkins hung up the phone before Harry could bring up the press conference. Harry dropped a pencil on the floor, and when he bent over to pick it up, his back seized up on him.

"Shirley!" he yelled.

Chapter 6

JESSICA

"Abash'd the Devil stood,
And felt how awful goodness is..."
— John Milton

Moe moved the cursor over the apple, dragged it down to PPG Config, and released the mouse. Next, he pressed "open", and the modem began communicating with the server in Crookston. When the four yellow lights blinked on, he went back to the menu, selected Netscape Browser, depressed the icon, and was on the World Wide Web.

Soon Moe was talking to a kid from Philadelphia named Newton who claimed a perfect score on his PSAT. Moe thought Newton had an awful lot of gall naming himself after the famous physicist and suspected he was really a forty-five-year old bachelor living with his mother.

Newton had been arguing that the message on Egge's back was a tag sign from a gang. "Could be Dylan, Stan, and Hank, something like that."

"All we got around here are wannabes, Fig," Moe typed. "I'm thinking the 'SYZ' part is the killer's name. You know, like a painter signs his work."

"SOS" in Buffalo, New York, thought that was a great possibility. He was combing through the Manhattan phone book looking for names that fit.

Funny how things work. Only the day before yesterday, Moe and the others in the JESSICA chat group had been working on the missing TV anchor in Mason City, Iowa, and now they had their very own case.

Marjorie Rawlings in Tampa Bay made another contribution. "FWIW, could it be the killer is trying to tell us where to find him? Some of them want to be stopped, you know. Something like 'Drive your Scooter to Hooters'?"

"LOL, Marj," Moe typed.

"No, no, methinks it's an exclamatory sentence," SOS said. "The killer is cursing the high school principal."

"I think U right, SOS," Moe typed. "Nice try, though, Marj. Got anything yet on the name?"

"Syzaro, Syzstma, Syzstelian, Syzcks, Szyplinski."

"I think it's a long name," Marj said. "Could be one of those splatballers U were telling us about interrupted the murderer before he could write the whole thing."

"I noticed U inverted the letters on that last name, SOS," Moe said. "That's a definite possibility."

"I've got it," Newton typed. "Damn your soul to hell! And as Holmes says, the 'SYZ' is the killer's name."

"I'll pass it on, Fig," Moe said. "Thanks, U-all."

Moe shut off the machine and went in to brush his teeth. JES-SICA had been fun before, but these days it was up there with pulsating universe theory.

Gargling for the required thirty seconds, Moe thought about the rough day he'd just experienced. After he'd seen Dave, he'd gone with his mother to a therapy session in Crookston. Dr. Maine, who reminded Moe a great deal of Walter Cronkite, was one of those therapists who make the patient do all the work.

At the end of last week's session, he'd told Moe to find all he could on Durkheim's theories of suicide and decide which one he thought fit his father best.

Today, twirling in Dr. Maine's swivel chair, he had made his report. "I think I've got my father pegged," he said. "Durkheim talks about anomic suicide, the inability to adjust to change, and my father was just about to retire from the Navy after twenty-three years."

"What do you remember about your father, Howard?" Dr. Maine said.

"I was only eight at the time, and I adored my father, but even to me, he seemed awfully nervous, and I remember he had to be early for everything. Church, weddings, sporting events. He always needed lag time. And, oh yeah, he insisted on a planned menu for each day of the week."

"You seem to remember a lot. Anything else?"

"He had a hair-trigger temper. He hit my mom once."

"Do you remember the circumstances?"

"She couldn't get the checkbook to balance or something. I don't know, I think it was about money. We didn't have any."

Moe was bored with the suicide talk. He stopped the twirling, stood, and went to sit on the arm of the couch where the doctor lay with his eyes closed. "I've been helping my friend work on the Egge murder," Moe said.

The doctor opened his eyes. "Oh, I don't think that's a very good idea. Your father's death was so traumatic."

"But it's been eight years, Dr. Maine. It doesn't bother me all that much anymore."

"How do you account for the nightmares your mother's been telling me about? Let's talk about something more pleasant. Tell me about your music. Have you written anything new?"

Moe wiped the dribble off the mouthwash bottle, put it back in the medicine cabinet, then went to do his laps on his exercise bike. He usually did twenty miles, full tilt as if he were chasing a purse snatcher. Tonight, he was after the man with the spray paint, and he planned to use a little hoodoo on him. He'd been reading about programmed dreams, or lucid dreaming as it was called in the trade, and he'd been making some progress learning the technique. All you needed to do was concentrate on a mantra like, "Tonight I'll dream about the murderer, tonight I'll dream about the murderer."

The drag wheel made a whirring sound as he picked up speed. Supposedly the dream would delve into his subconscious and reveal something he hadn't realized he'd known. Of course, it would help if he could get his pal Dave to do the dreaming, since he was the official investigator. But Dave would think that lucid dreaming was akin to channeling or Rolfing, *another candy-assed, egghead fad*. He was such a lout.

Moe got off the bike and went to the window. Chopin was howling at the moon. The dachshund wanted to sleep at the foot of Moe's bed, as he had when he'd been a puppy, but the dog just smelled too bad, no matter how much baking soda Moe used in his bath.

He went down the backstairs to say good night to Chopin.

"Say, boy," he said, "did you have a good time riding in the Honda today?"

His mom had let him drive to Crookston for the doctor's appointment and Chopin had sat in his lap and hung his head out the window.

He ruffled the dog's ears, and Chopin licked his hand. "I don't think I'll ever pass that drivers' test, Chopin."

The dog looked up at him with mournful eyes.

"I don't suppose you know there's a killer loose, Chopin. Are you afraid? Don't worry, though, Dave's on the case."

Chopin chuffed, a cross between a bark and a sneeze.

"That's why you're afraid? I'll have to tell him you said that."

He knelt down and adjusted Chopin's collar, checking it to make sure it wasn't torn. The dog wasn't neutered and was always looking for romance. Once he'd been gone for a week.

Music drifted from down the street. Moe thought it was the Smashing Pumpkins. "Got a piano recital coming up," he said. "I hate piano recitals, I keep trying to convince Mom to let me quit. I feel like such a geek!"

Someone was standing behind him, he could barely see her out of the corner of his eye. He spun around.

"Talkin' to the dog again?"

Olive Randall, the scariest girl he knew, had snuck up on him again, and Chopin hadn't warned him. She'd been doing something to her hair—one side was much shorter than the other. But then she was one of the only girls he knew who could look beautiful with a safety pin in her nose.

"Oh, hi, Olive," he said. "I was just checking Chopin's collar. He always manages to break out of it and disappear."

"Regular lover boy, ain't he?" she said. "Not like some people we could mention. Jenkins tell you any more about the Egge thing? My mom's been thinking about sending me and the girls to live with my uncle in Duluth. He works on the boats. You know, iron ore."

That was a laugh about sending her away. Her mother was rarely ever home and had no idea where Olive was most of the time.

"Dave is pretty sure it was just an isolated case," he said. "Looks like whoever did it got the wrong guy. There was a message..."

Chopin growled at Olive. He didn't like to share his personal time with Moe.

"What kind of message?...Never mind, I know you don't want your deputy friend losing faith in you. Telling a nobody like me'll do that."

"You're *not* a nobody. It was some spray paint. On his back. We think the killer signed his work."

"No fucking shit? Wanna hear something freaky? I was out there around the same time it happened. Before school, right? Me and Rita and Freddie were playing war games. It's really fun, you oughta try it sometime."

"Did you see anything?"

"Nah, they had us pinned down pretty good. I'm interested in one of the guys on the other team who goes to school in Crookston.

Ma says it's a whole lot easier to fall in love with a rich man, and the guy's old man is a stock broker."

Moe found her whiskey voice riveting. Standing there in the darkness, he could have mistaken her for a much older woman.

"Tell me this much," she said. "Everybody at school says it was this huge mother who left tracks you could wade in during the spring floods. If that's true, sure does sound like Brontosaurus, doesn't it? I ever tell you he got fresh with me once?"

"Really?" he said.

"Yeah, he's a real asshole. The kind of guy who thinks a woman ought to be thankful he's letting her suck his dick."

Moe could feel the blood rush to his face. Thank God she couldn't see him in the darkness.

"He'd've been the one I'd'a picked to see all mangled out there in the woods," she said. "Don't get me wrong, I never exactly liked Egge, always ragging on me about what I was wearing, but he sure didn't deserve to die like that." She paused, scratched an insect bite on her leg. "Look, I won't lie to you, the real reason I'm over here is cause His Highness Mr. Conrad White insists I take a makeup test or I'm gonna have to go to summer school, else take American History over again next year with the freshmen. God forbid. I was wondering if you could help me study."

"Any time, Olive. Just say when."

"I'll make it worth your while." She winked. "I miss so much school. Ma needs me at home...Say, you know that name you say was sprayed on Egge's back? Did you ever think that maybe 'Egge' wasn't really Egge's name? Maybe he's one of those whatchamacallits. You know, one of those guys who testifies against the Mafia."

"You mean Witness Protection?"

"Yeah that's it. I always thought there was something weird about him."

"That's...a thought."

She stood so close he could smell the tacos she'd had for dinner, then she sidled up alongside and nudged him with her hip. He hadn't felt anything that good since Chopin was a pup.

"You know, Howard, I can get out of class just about anytime I want. Want to meet me in the hall and—"

"I don't get to school much," he said.

"Too bad, you don't know what you're missin'. Gotta go." She knelt down and patted Chopin on the head, then got up and ran off into the dark.

Now why hadn't he thought about the possibility of Egge going under an alias?

The water in Chopin's dish was frozen. He knelt and broke the ice with a rock he found next to the sidewalk. Had to remember to tell Dave about what JESSICA had come up with today.

There were no lights on at Dave's place. Either he'd called it an early night or he was still out working on the Egge case.

Moe gave Chopin a doggy biscuit, then knelt, reflecting on why anyone would want to kill a nice man like Mr. Egge. Moe never called Mr. Egge "Scrambled" as the other kids had, and Mr. Egge always treated Moe like another adult. Mr. Egge reminded him of Dave, kind of a kook, but with hidden depths. Egge'd been on Dave's softball team, although he didn't think they'd been what you'd call friends.

Sure would like to get a load of that murder scene.

Chopin caught sight of the shadow of his tail in the moonlight and began a frenzied whirl, until he wore himself out, flopped on his rump, and looked up at Moe. Moe laughed, ruffled Chopin's ears, and trotted up the creaky backstairs of the remodeled schoolhouse.

It was only ten o'clock, awfully early for him, but he decided to hit the sack. He took a shower and said his prayers, a special one for his poor father and one for his mom to help her find a husband.

As he climbed beneath the covers—he slept in the upper level of the cluttered bunk bed—he began to repeat the mantra: "I will dream of Principal Egge's murder. I will dream of Principal Egge's murder." He'd set the alarm for three o'clock, just as the REM researchers had done in the book he'd read.

At first the mantra didn't work. He dreamt that Olive had him cornered in a stairwell at the school and he was only able to save himself by flying around squawking like a magpie. He had another nightmare about Sheriff Kline handing him a subpoena to appear in court—the neighbors were suing over Chopin's amorous forays.

The alarm went off and he wrote down the two dreams. He was surprised at how vivid they were and how much detail he could remember.

He had no trouble getting back to sleep, and he began to dream again. Everything was yellow, his least favorite color, and there was a nauseating smell rather like a cross between his grandfather's socks and a dead body. A jowlish fat man, his remaining strands of hair combed down over his forehead and shaped in the form of horns, sat on an oversized toilet, probably meant to be some kind of sadistic throne. Fat boy was mumbling commands in some foreign language, or maybe it was the kind of English they speak in the deep South. By concentrating hard, Moe was able to make sense of the utterances.

"Ernie, you little muthafuck," the man was saying, "don yahl know it a sin to off yoself, especially in the manna yah done by crashin' yo mamma's car into that there bridge abutment? What yo think yo punishment gonna be, bowah?"

Moe couldn't stand up. He was sliding all over this icelike stuff—rather like a Minnesota country road in early April, one of those days it wasn't safe for the school buses—and he had to go to the bathroom really bad. His stomach began to distend like those starving children in Africa and a whiff of urine pinched his nostrils.

"You have me confused with Ernest Hemingway," he squeaked.

"Murdah is murdah," the fat man said.

Suddenly Moe was running along a path in the woods, and he saw this big man with curly black hair, wearing duck hunting waders, chasing Mr. Egge with a baseball bat. Just at the last minute, Mr. Egge turned and saw the man, but the brute smashed him right across the crown of the head, which must have fractured his skull immediately, but the big goon wouldn't stop hitting Mr. Egge. He kept swinging down at Mr. Egge's head as if he were chopping wood with the baseball bat, and eventually the connection made more of a mushy sound, as if the bat were making contact with rotting vegetables instead of bone.

Stop the dream and focus, he told himself and the action stopped, the man with the bat raised over his shoulder, a spray of blood frozen in midair. Moe zoomed in for a closer look. Under the goon's rain slicker, he could see the beginning of a word on a T-shirt. *B-E-R-K.* He was about to turn his attention to other details when, off to the left over the behemoth's shoulder, Moe could see his father and an older man with bug eyes wearing a fisherman's hat, the kind with all the lures. They sat on the lower limb of a tree, taking it all in. His father smiled at him, something he had rarely done in life.

"Your boy interested in girls yet?" the older man said.

And then Lardbutt, dressed in a long duster, high-top boots and a plantation hat, was back, pacing up and down in front of this platform upon which Olive was standing, naked except for a sheet covering her private parts. The room was smoky and very humid, and the men, all of whom looked like Superintendent Bronson, were fanning themselves, smoking cigars and sipping on mint juleps.

One of the Bronsons said with booming voice, "Let me see her naked and have her turn around. I want to see her ass."

Lardbutt ripped the sheet out of Olive's hands. "Yah! twirl some for us, girlie."

Olive turned, her arms held flat against her sides, her breasts jutting. Her nipples glistened, as if they'd just been sucked. Her pubic patch was tufted, like corn silk. As she turned, her butt cheeks jiggled, like Jell-O on a rickety card table.

A kind of groan—OOOOAAAH—ascended from the audience.

"I bid $1,500," one of the Bronsons said. "She looks like good breeding stock."

Olive wriggled her toes—somehow the chains binding her ankles made her even more alluring—put her fist on a hip, and transferred her weight to one leg. She could have been standing in line at the Bijou she looked so nonchalant.

"I'll give $2,000," another Bronson said.

"She's mine," Lardbutt said. "Ah'll boost it to $4,000."

Moe leaped up on the platform, grabbed Olive's hand, and they jumped in tandem to the ground, Moe swinging a suddenly-materialized sword left and right at the Bronsons closing in. The lights went out. He could feel the impact of bone as he lashed about with the sword, and the shadowy figures screamed and swore.

He stopped the dream again. Then he added music, Chopin's Polonaise, his favorite classical piece. The shadows disappeared and he was lying in a meadow of clover and Olive, still naked, was kissing him on the neck.

Moe awoke, stuck to the sheets. The best damn dream he'd ever had. He had to tell Dave about it. J.W. would cream his jeans.

He rushed outside without putting on his shoes and covered the fifty feet of near-frozen ground between the converted schoolhouse and Dave's crooked, little, white frame house in a hop, skip, and a jump.

Dave's door was open. Not too shocking considering this was Soldier, Minnesota, but rather puzzling since Dave was a deputy sheriff after all, and the cynic didn't trust anybody.

"J.W! J.W! Are you up yet? I've seen the murderer! Come, Watson, come. The game is afoot!"

The house was as quiet as a Shaker rocking chair. He could hear the ticking of a clock and the suction and release of his bare feet as he crossed the kitchen linoleum. He barged into Dave's bedroom, ignoring the possibility that Dave might shoot first and ask questions later.

Dave and Annie Kline were coupled in spoon fashion, the bed covers thrown aside, his arms around her waist, their legs entwined. Not a blemish on their bodies. They resembled an erotic Greek statue he'd seen in an art book. So beautiful—he wanted to touch them. His eyes locked onto Annie's breasts. If he could run back to the house and get his camera in time...

His breathing must have been audible because Dave turned, looked right at him, and yelled, "Get the hell out of here! Don't you ever knock?"

That broke the moment. Moe turned away and Annie dove under the covers.

"Sorry," Moe said, "but it's important. There may be a break in the case, I think I've seen Egge's murderer."

"Hold on there," Dave said. "Let me get some clothes on; wait for me in the kitchen. Didn't your mother teach you any manners?"

Moe went into the kitchen and sat on the edge of a stool, his toes clasping the rungs. He looked around the kitchen. The month on the DNR calendar above Dave's stove hadn't been changed. Most likely because of the picture of the Alpha male wolf snapping at a pesky pup. Dave loved wolves.

A few minutes later, Dave materialized in the kitchen, wearing jeans and no shirt.

"You and Annie Kline?" Moe said softly. "I thought you must be a misogynist or something. You never even sit on the same side of the table as my mother when you come over to our house to eat."

"For the last time, your mother isn't my type. What's this about your seeing the murderer?"

"It was in a dream," Moe said. "Ordinarily I wouldn't bother you with psychobabble, but you said the casts they made were from waders like they wear fishing, and I saw the waders in a dream. The murderer had curly black hair, with broad shoulders, like a football player wearing pads. And my father—"

"Your father?" Dave said. "Have you been in the communion wine again?" He was spooning coffee into a filter. He had bags under his eyes this early in the morning. A dead ringer for Mr. Magoo. "Dreams don't mean diddly. You were thinking about the evidence when you went to bed, and that wild imagination of yours went berserk."

"Dreams don't mean diddly? Did I hear you right?"

"Spare me the lecture on Jung's theory of the collective unconscious. I'm just not in the mood."

"Just let me explain the dream symbols and how they impact the case."

Dave poured water into the top of his coffee maker and flipped the switch. "Tell it to your JESSICA friends."

"You devil. You just want to get back in there and make a little deputy. You are using a condom, aren't you? The world is way overpopulated."

"Okay, okay. Anything else in the dream besides a big guy with curly hair who looked like a linebacker? We already knew that much."

"Get a load of this smooth move," Moe said. "I stopped that dream like a video on pause, zoomed in on the murderer and scoped some lettering on his T-shirt. B-E-R-K. And I was going to tell you about my fath—"

"Speaking of letters, JESSICA get a reading on the spray paint yet?"

"Damn your soul to hell."

"There's no need to get nasty."

"No, I meant that's what we think the lettering stands for, the 'SYZ' is the killer's signature. Some long Polish name most likely."

"Coffee's done, help yourself."

Moe turned up his nose at the messy kitchen. Didn't the slob ever wash the dishes? He went over to the cabinet and got his Cincinnati Redlegs mug, which he always washed before he left.

"And another thing, for what it's worth," Moe said. "Olive says Bronson got fresh with her once. She doesn't have all that much credibility, but there was that entry on Egge's computer, so I thought I'd tell you about it. I'm helping her study for a make-up test. I'll pump her for all she's worth."

Dave smirked, stroked his mustache. "I would if I were you," he said.

Chapter 7

Sign of the Fish

"Give me your arm, old toad;
Help me down Cemetery Road.
— Philip Larkin

A fter Moe left, Dave went into the bathroom, found the little scissors he used to groom his mustache, and began to snip away. His whiskers had a reddish tint to them he couldn't ordinarily see unless he trimmed it, and the little hairs, like sawdust, drifted down on the sink, where they'd stay until the buildup got too crusty and he was forced to swamp the place out. Once he had the soup-strainer down to manageable proportions, he lathered up and shaved the remaining bristles with his safety razor. Today, he *wanted* to look young.

He splashed water on his face, wiped the remaining lather on a towel, and dabbed aftershave on his raw upper lip. Stung like salt on a cut. Now where in the hell had he put those field glasses? He moved into the bedroom, rummaged through his dresser drawers. Found them buried beneath the dozens of black socks he no longer wore from Navy SEAL days. Sleepyhead Annie had dozed off, and when he kissed her on the nose, her eyelids fluttered, and she opened her eyes.

"Is he still here?" she said. "I've never been so embarrassed in all my—"

"Forget about it. Moe'll never tell anybody."

"I won't know how to act when I see him again."

"Just do what everybody does, pretend it never happened."

"I hope you don't think that I—"

Dave sat down next to her and put his arm around her neck. "Annie, you and I have been chums ever since I returned from Desert Storm and just because we fell into bed together is no reason why I'd think any less of you. I gotta go."

"But how will I—?"

He kissed her on the lips, gave her another hug, and said, "You were great, I'm proud to have been your first." She sunk back down on the bed and put the pillow over her head.

On the way out of the house, he grabbed his tinted aviator glasses and a cowboy hat out of the hall closet.

He'd parked the Jeep on the south side of the house in the shade of the big ash tree, which functioned as camouflage, discouraging thieves who might want to hotwire a valuable WWII classic. What he saw when he turned the corner caused him to take off his sun glasses and drop them on the ground. All four of his tires were slashed and the words "Die, Cop" were sprayed on the windshield.

He walked on the grass off to the side of the Jeep so as not to disturb any possible footprints, then grabbed his cellular and dialed the Amoco station.

"Yallow."

"Pigeon, this is Dave Jenkins. Somebody's gone and slashed my tires. You got any retreads?"

"If I don't I can always scare some up. You want me to put 'em on for yah?"

"Why don't you wait a bit, Pigeon. I want to take some pictures first."

"You think this is the same guy who killed Egge?"

Dave switched the cellular to his other ear, put one foot up on the bumper of the Jeep, careful not to step in the dirt. "Nah, probably some kid I nailed speeding."

"Jeez, if I was you, I'd sleep in a jail cell."

"Keep this under your hat, huh? People will jump to conclusions."

"Won't tell a soul."

Shit, if he knew Pigeon, the news would be all over town before he got to work. Dave pushed the disconnect button on the cellular and redialed.

"Sheriff's office," Shirley said.

"Dave here, Shirl. Is that new person there yet?"

"Lucille? She was waiting at the front door when I got here. Why?"

"Send her over to my house, will you? Tell her to bring a crime scene kit with her. I need to use your car, too, okay?"

"Help yourself, the keys are in it. Aren't you going to tell me what happened?"

He took his foot off the fender as it was beginning to fall asleep, then crouched down on his haunches, little pin needles stabbing at his leg. "Sorry, I'm a little preoccupied. Some kid slashed the tires on my Jeep."

"Oh, Dave. Are you sure it wasn't...?"

"If it was, he's just given me more of a reason to hunt him down. And when I do..."

"Please be careful. If Howard loses another—"

"I hear you, Shirl. Bye."

Ten minutes later, Lucille, her hair done up in a French twist, her new uniform pressed neatly enough to shame a marine, pulled up in Harry's cruiser. She shut off the ignition and got out of the car.

"My God," she said. "Who could have...? Oh."

"You know the drill, Lucille. Fingerprints, casts of any footprints you find, Polaroids of the windshield. When you're done, I want you to get some turpentine out of the shed over there and wipe that stuff off the windshield. Keep the rag so's we can try to trace the paint. Then call Pigeon at the Amoco and tell him to change the tires. And don't tell him anything else, okay?"

"Yes, sir."

"The name's Dave. And, oh yeah, when he's finished, bring the tires back to the sheriff's office."

She nodded, then turned to look at the Jeep, shaking her head as if the Jeep were Egge's mangled body.

Dave drove Shirley's Honda down Meade over the bridge. The water was rising from the spring runoff, and the wind had whipped up whitecaps that looked like laundry detergent. He had to wait for another car to cross as the bridge was too narrow for two cars at once, and he was tempted to just pull over to the side of the road and stare down into the water and brood about what he'd do to the bastard who'd massacred his Jeep. Truss the scrote up like his great grandmother's corset, then cinch him to the trailer hitch, leaving only his legs free. Then drive away, slowly at first, the scrote walking along behind. Pick up speed so the scrote would have to trot, and then run when Dave nudged the accelerator another notch. Finally, he'd floor it and the scrote would fall on his ass, getting hauled over rocks and stones and broken glass, until what was left resembled a Jackson Pollack drip painting.

Nobody touched his Jeep!

After the other car had passed, he drove on, past the Legion, the flag at half-mast in honor of Egge, past Immaculate Conception, the bell announcing Egge's funeral mass. Past Finkle's barbershop, standing cheek to jowl with Emerson's beauty salon, both places fairly buzzing with the latest dirt concerning the murder. Past Bud's, Andy's Diner and the Merry Widow Motel—one of the few places in Soldier not named after something at Gettysburg—and the Value Stop, after which he turned down the dirt road leading to the rear entrance to Evergreen Cemetery.

He parked the Honda in the entrance and walked the rest of the way, passing the little white crosses that reminded him of those at Arlington Cemetery. Babies and small children who'd died in a diphtheria epidemic around the turn of the century. The crosses always made him sad.

Dave climbed the footpath, which rose to a little knoll where a copse of maples offered some cover. He wanted to get a good look at the crowd before they saw him, despite the disguise. When he got to the top, he realized this was the same knoll where his grandmother, from whom he'd inherited his house, was buried. He'd only been there once, the day she'd been buried. Hated graveyards. Since he was a little early, he poked through the ankle-length grass looking for Gram's grave. Niemann, Alexander, Swanson. All of them born around the turn of the century.

Pleasiac. Dan Pleasiac, Moe's dad. He shuddered, glanced at the grave next to it.

Sheriff McCloskey.

Hmph. Harry's father-in-law. Harry'd said McCloskey had been a virtual dictator of Polk County, so well-respected that he'd been able to move the jail from the county seat in Crookston to Soldier, where he lived because he didn't like to drive the twenty miles.

The old sheriff's headstone read *Ben McCloskey, 1901—1962. Law is Order, and Good Law is Good Order*. A vandal had tried to chip away the first "r" in the word "order".

Dropping to one knee, Dave traced the inscription on McCloskey's headstone. And when he did, he could see McCloskey out in the woods dressed in camouflage, aiming a scoped rifle at a man walking through a clearing below. The man bent to pick a flower, sniffed it and looked up at the sky just as McCloskey pulled the trigger. The man's head exploded like a watermelon thrown up against the side of a building. McCloskey jacked the shell out of the chamber, then went down and dragged the body over to a prepared grave, kicked the dirt into the hole, and covered it with leaves.

Dave took a deep, gasping breath, like he'd been underwater a little too long. Then he leaned up against the tombstone, scratching the hair on the back of his head so hard he drew blood. The headstone teetered—a touch more pressure and it would topple.

Too many more of these hallucinations and he'd have to commit himself. Hallucinations happened to crazy people, like that looney David Berkowitz he'd read about for his criminal psych class at vo. tech. He'd read how the wingnut's neighbor's black Lab, supposedly a six-thousand-year-old demon named Son of Sam, had told him to target women with long, flowing hair.

A thunder clap caused Dave to jump, and droplets of rain began to slap at his face and the backs of his hands. Beneath him, he heard car doors slam, and he could see a white hearse traveling toward the awning protecting Egge's open grave. Two altar boys helped the old priest out of the hearse, the wind whipping at his vestments.

What else did he know about psychosis? Some people had delusions of grandeur, thought they were Napoleon or even Jesus Christ. Those people that had those hallucinations—schizophrenics he thought they were called—were introverted, loner types who thought the Russians were bugging their phones. They were paranoid. *Nothing* like what was happening to him.

No, he certainly wasn't paranoid, and his visions had such a ring of truth about them! Egge's life passing before his eyes, the parent complaining to Egge about her daughter being called a walrus, Egge swearing at his wife. And now this one. There'd been a rumor circulating for years that McCloskey had killed his wife's lover. But what did McCloskey have to do with Egge?

Or maybe somebody at Andy's had slipped something in his beer just for kicks. Just to watch him go slowly bonkers. Hell, it'd happened before. What was that stuff some jerks slipped in women's drinks? Some hallucinations were drug inspired. LSD flashbacks, like that.

He took another deep breath, adjusted the focus on his binoculars, and studied the mourners. Egge was being buried in a new part of the cemetery, nothing but grass and look-alike headstones. Egge would have been pleased with the turnout. Kiwanis and Rotary Club members, the school board, the rest of the softball team. Thirty or forty Shriners. A large contingent from the old folks home with their leader Hildegard Weiss. Multicolored umbrellas gave the scene a carnival aspect. Not too much black, lots of reds and blues and greens, an occasional plaid.

Father Mischke, who had to be at least eighty and had been the parish priest in Soldier for twenty years, was leading the prayers over Egge's coffin. He was a bald man with a few stray wisps of hair standing straight up on his head and more wrinkles in his face than a hound dog. He wore a muffler around his neck and leather gloves. One of the servers held an umbrella over the priest's head while the other turned the pages in the prayer book when the priest gave him the cue.

Too bad he couldn't bring himself to talk to the old priest about the visions. Pretty much knew what he'd say anyway. *Psychic phenomena is the devil's work. You need to pray more, my son.*

Mrs. Egge sat in the open door of the hearse, crying this time, for public benefit most likely. Willie and Winona consoled her.

He surveyed the crowd once more, checking for anybody suspicous-looking. Would the murderer show up, and would he be able to pick him out if he did?

Ah, there was Mrs. Macintosh. Kind of liked her. What she'd said about him resembling a movie star. He checked his shirt pocket for her card. Soothsayer, huh?

Mr. Charlie Bronson, his new boss, stood next to Mrs. Mac, wearing a bulldog expression. The superintendent was scanning the crowd as well, probably looking for his lover Sue Egge, whom he couldn't see from where he stood behind all the umbrellas.

Dave shifted the glasses. Paydirt. Slouched over, leaning up against a tree. Billy, the Soldier vagabond. Hadn't thought of him. Big enough to fit the description of the murderer despite the slouch, but gray, really gray. Couldn't be him, though. Harry said Billy and he fought together in 'Nam. According to Harry, Billy had a silver star. When Dave'd first taken the job, Harry'd told him to cut Billy some slack.

On the off chance that this could be something, he took out his cellular, dialed Mingo's number.

"Yo, Mingo Jones here. It's your quarter."

"Jenkins. You perchance see Billy Bum the day of Egge's murder?"

"Sure did. When I went looking for Olive, he was hanging out under the water tower getting smacked on Old Grandad. Why, you don't think he's a suspect, do yah?"

"I'm looking right at him out here at Evergreen. Never noticed what a big boy he was before. I'd say he could fit those tracks out at the murder scene."

"Wears size thirteen. I got him some shoes at the Good Will the other day. I hear you had a little problem with the Jeep."

"Word gets around, don't it? Probably just some kids."

"You hope. Anything besides slashed tires?"

"Yeah, I'll tell you when I see you. Look, if I can't head off Billy, why don't you swing around and stop him at the front gate."

"Sheriff Kline isn't going to like us harassing Billy."

"He'll like it less if it turns out Billy's the one."

"Guess you're right, Dude. I'll be right there. Caio."

Dave punched the disconnect button and turned to another part of the crowd. There were few, if any, high school kids at the funeral and no teachers, other than Mrs. Mac. Dissension in the ranks, or had Bronson warned them off? Dave needed to talk to them all. Bring Mingo along to look for suspicious behavior.

When he swung his glasses back to where Billy had been leaning up against the tree, he was gone. Shit. Dave edged around behind the crowd, hoping to bump into Billy on the way. No such luck. He came up behind Bronson and his wife Emily. No mustache, the cowboy hat, the shades—they wouldn't recognize him. He listened in on their conversation.

The big bruiser dwarfed his petite wife. "Calm down, Charlie," she said. "Robbie's grades will improve. He's got football practice and a girlfriend. C's aren't that bad. You take everything so seriously."

Most people in Soldier thought Emily was a saint for putting up with Charlie. Eventually Dave'd have to talk to her about the affair. He wrote her name in his notebook.

Giving up on the Bronson conversation, he glanced over at Willie and Winona. The towheads looked really put-upon, as if they hadn't wanted to come and been ordered to by their mother. Moving away from the Bronsons, he rubbernecked the two Calvin Klein types. "I get the Rolex," Willie whispered.

"The hell you do." Winona turned and stared at Dave as if she'd smelled something bad, then smiled when she recognized him. So much for the disguise. He wiggled his fingers at her. Fratricide? Was that what you called it when children killed their father? Or was it patricide?

Sue Egge, who'd found Bronson behind the umbrellas, whispered something in Bronson's ear. The dour man actually smiled.

Dave thought back to the picture he'd found in Egge's billfold and the vision he'd had in Egge's den. Sue had gone straight for Egge's gonads when they'd argued in the car. Telling a guy his kids weren't his would probably be worse, in some ways, than being hit with a Louisville Slugger.

As the mourners started to disperse, Dave seemed rooted to the ground, watching the caretakers shovel dirt onto the coffin, the sand pellets seeming to sting his eyes. The mound of black earth began to accumulate and he couldn't help but cough and choke. His eyes watered and he turned away, toward the string of cars jockeying for position as they left the parking lot. Some of them were honking their horns, not the usual thing with Minnesotans, who were usually good at waiting their turn.

Dave recognized Bronson's Lincoln Continental and Mrs. Mac sitting beside him in the front seat. He trotted over to Shirley's Honda, got in, pumped the accelerator twice, the car turning over like a pampered kitten, and followed them down Hancock Lane, which ran east, a shortcut back to the school. As he drove, he drummed his fingers on the wheel in accompaniment to the thwack thwack of the windshield wipers. Maybe he'd talk to a few kids before he got settled in his new office.

Bronson parked the big Lincoln in the reserved parking at the front of the school, walked over and opened Mrs. Mac's door. Hmmph, never would have expected it. Feeling naked without his mustache, Dave doffed the cowboy hat in favor of his trusty USS Lake Champlain cap. Hot on their heels, he followed them right through the throng of kids parting like the Red Sea when they saw the superintendent. The kids, who were standing umbrellaless in the rain and looked like a pack of wet rats, were just coming to school due to the late start because of the funeral.

The big clock above the office doors said 11:10. Lots of kids were milling in the hall. Lockers were banging and clanging, kids were yelling at each other. He hadn't heard such language since Navy bootcamp when he'd first been exposed to guys from New York and Chicago.

Bronson didn't stop to talk to any of the students as he moved toward the main office, losing Mrs. Mac almost immediately as she became engrossed in several giggling contests with some of the girls.

Two girls who lived near his house, came up to him. Tina and Mandy he thought their names were, or was it Sandy and Trina?

"You shaved off your mustache!" the blond one said.

"We wanted to tell you about Freddie Cochran," the little one with jet-black hair and matching fingernails, said. "He brought a gun to school."

The one he thought was Mandy, rail thin with granny glasses and freckled complexion, said, "Yeah, he's always in dutch for telling teachers to fuck off."

He shivered. It wasn't his job to wash her mouth out with soap. He touched the brim of his cap. "Thank you, beautiful ladies. I'll keep that in mind." Their faces lit up and they ran to tell their friends.

Freddie Cochran's gun fetish wasn't exactly new information. Dave'd been called in on the gun charge, and for other problems.

Freddie could have been a movie star or a model, he was so good-looking. Pretty actually. Maybe that was his problem. He wrote Freddie Cochran's name in his notebook under Emily Bronson's, then looked over at the office. He could see Fran Ellis, the athletic director and acting principal, through the glass partition, sorting a bunch of little slips at the counter.

Dave turned back toward the locker banks, searching for a credible informant. A boy in a football jersey was necking with a little redhead in a very short mini-skirt. Dave fingered Egge's pipe, and Egge popped into the hall, elbowed his way between the two, and the boy said, "What the fuck..."

"How many times do I have to tell you people? No public display of affection." Egge was wearing an awful, plaid sports coat, cobalt blue and emerald green. He must have got it at a rummage sale the thing was so grotesque. What a job, almost as bad as Shore Patrol in the navy. The swabbies called them sex protectors. When Dave's eyes refocused, the affectionate couple was giving him a *get-a-life* look.

Dave took Mrs. Macintosh's card out of his shirt pocket, ran his finger over the raised lettering, the ink smearing from the sweat and the pressure, then moved toward the office where he'd prepare for his interrogation with the woman with the purple hair.

* * *

When he answered Mingo's summons later on in the day, Lester Krueger was wearing dirty coveralls and work shoes caked with dirt. Mingo had thought Shirley was going to run him out of the office when he tracked in all that mud, but she'd stoically swept it up, just as she always did.

Mingo had been paging through a stack of old annuals he'd gotten from Dan Cardwell at the high school. He'd unearthed one interesting bit of information: Lester Krueger had been on Jerry Egge's junior high baseball team.

Lucille had provided some additional info regarding Lester Krueger. She'd gotten a tip from a lady at U.S. West. Egge had once complained about some threatening phone calls, and he'd thought he recognized Krueger's voice. Wanted to know if he could put a trace on the calls.

The boy took a chair and slumped down into his clothes. Creepy-looking kid. Duck-hunter's hat, two day's growth of beard fighting for recognition among the acne scars. Green teeth. "This place sure is a fuckin' dump," Les said. "You'd think a hotshot deputy would rate a better office." He laughed nasally.

Jenkins's office was a converted storeroom with cement walls and a definite mildew smell. The desk took up most of the space, the wastebasket was overflowing, and Jenkins had a dog-eared Raquel Welch poster, the one from the stoneage movie, taped up on one of the walls, so Mingo couldn't argue with that assessment.

"Suits us fine, Lester," Mingo said, putting the emphasis on the first syllable, as in Les is less. He paged through a folder, xeroxed forms from different cases he always kept on his desk for times like this. He'd found that just about everybody, especially uneducated greaseballs like Krueger, thought the government was keeping a file on them.

"How'd an Indian get to be a deputy sheriff?" Les said.

One Mississippi, two Mississippi...Instead of going for his hunting knife, Mingo said, "I went to school on an athletic scholarship."

"Kind of like that guy Jim Thorpe."

"You know about Jim Thorpe?"

"Sure. He got his Olympic medals taken away and he drank himself to death."

Mingo debated whether it was worth it to tell the kid Thorpe's family got the medals back. "Yes, he did have a problem with alcohol. Now, Lester, we'll be needing your fingerprints, but I have a few preliminary questions. Why don't I get right to the point. Deputy Jenkins says you looked awfully nervous out there the other day when he and Harry talked to your dad. Do you know anything we should know?"

Les put his hands on his knees and rubbed. Dirt was caked under his fingernails. "Ain't you supposed to read me my rights?"

"We're not accusing you of anything, Les. Why would we want to read you your rights?"

"I don't know nothin' about any murder. Why dyah need to take my fingerprints?"

"It's our understanding that you made some threats when Egge cut you from the baseball team. Our source says that you made several calls to Mr. Egge's residence and that he recognized your voice."

"They were never able to prove that."

"You didn't like him much, did you? "

"So? I don't like you much either. Doesn't mean I'm gonna try to fuckin' kill you."

"Sorry to hear that, I'm awfully fond of *you*. You didn't answer my question, Lester. Did you make those calls?"

"I refuse to answer on the grounds it may tend to incriminate me."

"This isn't a courtroom, Les, and I don't have a tape recorder back here. You can level with me. Your teammates say you were bragging about making those calls."

"Those creeps never liked me."

Mingo reached under the desk and came up with the Louisville Slugger found at the scene of the murder. "I want you to take a look at this baseball bat, Lester. It has an unusual inscription on it."

Krueger's eyes got so wide he could have been a stand-in for Stepin Fetchit, if he'd been a darker shade of brown. "Is that the murder weapon?"

Egge's blood was still caked on the baseball bat. "No, Lester, we always keep Wayne Terwilliger bats on hand. So, have you seen it before? Remember now, if you don't tell the truth, it'll go harder for you later."

Krueger bit his lower lip. "I'd never use a piece of crap like that. Terwilliger is just a coach."

"That so? Must be hell to have to live up to such high standards." Mingo paused, stood, inspected the poster of Raquel, then looked down at Krueger. "That big man your father saw standing on the edge of the woods, do you know anybody like that?"

Les just stared, as if he thought Mingo might have some sort of special vision. "Ah, I might. There are lots of big guys. Ever watch football? Some of those guys weigh three hundred pounds. Maybe one of them killed Egge."

Mingo moved over to Krueger's side of the desk, still staring down at him. "Yeah, but you don't know any Viking football players. Maybe you know somebody like that from someplace else? How about Billy, do you know Billy?"

Large blotches of sweat were expanding beneath Krueger's underarms, and the wetness seemed to increase when Mingo mentioned Billy Bum's name. Krueger was leaking so much he could've spent the last hour in a sweat lodge.

"Nope, don't know nobody like that," Krueger said.

"You don't know Billy Bum?"

"Whyn't you say so? Everybody knows Billy Bum. He gives me a swig out of Old Grandad every once in a while."

"You ain't seen him lately, have you?"

Krueger took off his cap, scratched his head, as if to check his computer-like memory. "Not since before the murder."

Mingo thought he'd try a different tack. "We'd like you to take a polygraph test. Do you know what that is?"

"Sure, that's a lie detector test, seen it on television. I ain't taking one of those."

Mingo tapped Krueger on the chest. "I don't know why not, Lester. You say you don't know anything about any big man. You say you didn't have anything to do with Egge's murder. If you take a polygraph and pass, you'll be off the hook. Come on, I dare you."

"I ain't takin' no polygraph test. You can't make me incriminate myself."

"You're just too sharp for me, Lester." *Maybe a little good cop, bad cop.* "I'm forgetting my manners. Would you like a coffee or a soda pop? It'll only take a minute. Your mouth must be awfully dry."

"I wouldn't mind a Coke."

Mingo hit the intercom. "Shirley, would you bring my man Lester a Coke, please?" Mingo moved his chair to the other side of his desk, close to Krueger's. "You know, Les, I've felt kind of bad about Jenkins kicking you off the Dogs. Me and him we don't get along so well, professional jealousy, you know. I think I should be the chief deputy around here. Did you know I went to Johns Hopkins on a LaCrosse scholarship? We won the Wingate trophy my senior year."

"What's John Hopkins?"

"That's Johns Hopkins, a very prestigious school out east where I majored in criminal justice. Jenkins has this laughable degree from a vocational school. He thinks you did this, and he says he's going to send you to the electric chair."

"You must think I'm some kinda idiot. Minnesota doesn't even have the death penalty."

Mingo got up and stood behind Krueger. The boy turned to look up at him.

"We have these footprint casts we found out at the scene where we think the assailant's vehicle was parked. Your feet look like they just might fit those casts. You go with Mrs. Pleasiac now and get fingerprinted. I'll be with you in a minute to take foot casts."

"I don't have to give you my fingerprints."

"Au contraire, my man. The law says you must. Kind of like when you get arrested for driving drunk. You gotta submit to a breathalizer or give up your license."

Surprisingly Lester didn't argue, nor did he ask for a lawyer. Shirley, on the other hand, gave Mingo the evil eye through the open door as she pressed Lester's finger against the ink pad. Mingo got up to get his Mountie hat off the stand, realizing at the last moment he still had it on. Next stop, Farmers and Merchants State Bank.

The phone rang. "Yo, bro," Mingo said.

"It's me. I'm at the school. Did you snare Billy?"

"When I got there, you were just leaving in Shirley's Honda."

"Funny, I didn't see you."

"You weren't supposed to. I'll run Billy down the next time I visit the shelter in Crookston. Stay there some nights. Harry don't pay me much, you know."

"My heart pumps purple peanut butter. Got a little job for you, you doing anything?"

"Gotta cast Lester's tootsies for the Walk of Fame, then I'm on my way to the bank."

"When you're through there, I want you to sweat Freddie Cochran about the gun thing. How'd the Krueger interrogation go?"

"He damn near shit when he saw that bat. I don't think he did it, but I think he's seen that bat before."

"I gotta do Mrs. Mac. Let me know if there's anything interesting in the safety deposit box."

"10-4, Dude."

*   *   *

Egge's in-box was piled at least a yard high with rubbish, the floor was cracked linoleum and there were no windows. The room's sole redeeming grace, in Dave's mind, was a bulletin board decorated with senior snapshots and articles about kids taken from the Crookston Transcript that took up an entire wall.

Before he'd talk to Mrs. Mac, he'd need to try to track the baseball bat. The only detail that had any particular relevance was the unusual endorsement. Wayne "Twig" Terwilliger, the Twin's first base coach for both World Series victories in 1987 and 1991, had hit about .200 for his entire career, so there couldn't be a whole lot of those bats in existence.

He dialed Johnny Logan's sports shop, and Johnny gave him a phone number for the Louisville Slugger sales rep, who, in turn, gave him an 800 number for the home office. The public relations person, a Miss Montrose, who had a very sexy voice, didn't know how many bats had been made with the Wayne Terwilliger endorsement, but she would try to find out. Miss Montrose said that it sounded like a custom-made job since she'd never heard of Wayne Terwilliger. He assured her the Twig was a great hitter. Dave gave her his office number and the school phone number.

After hanging up, he flipped through Egge's file he'd gotten from Bronson. A picture of a young Egge with all of his hair and horn-rimmed glasses was paper-clipped to the inside cover. Moe had this crazy idea that Egge had been born with a name other than Egge, hence the invective damning his soul to hell. Not according to Egge's file he wasn't. He'd been born in Silver Bay, Wisconsin, although he'd gone to school in Soldier. Should be easy enough to check. Dave called the operator and transferred the charges to the sheriff's office. She then gave him the number for the county courthouse.

"Here it is," the clerk said, "Gerald Egge, born September 8, 1944. Parents Mary and Clark."

Dave fell off the chair, hurting his tailbone on the hard linoleum. He'd dropped Egge's file and the papers were strewn all over the office; he set about picking them up, on his hands and knees.

"Hello, Deputy Jenkins? Are you OK?" The phone was dangling over the edge of the desk, the cord snagged on a pencil holder. He reached up and put the phone back in its cradle.

That did it. He'd talk to Mrs. Macintosh about the visions, swear her to secrecy, and if she blabbed, he'd deny everything. Would people believe, a whacky, purple-haired special ed. teacher?

When he finished picking up Egge's file, he buzzed Mindy, the principal's secretary. "Mindy, can you page Moe Pleasiac for me? I think he's down in the band room practicing his music."

Back to the file. Egge'd gone to St. Cloud State. He had a degree in English. He'd taught three years in Mankato, Minnesota.

Rat-a-tat-tat. Moe's clever knock. The door was ajar, and Moe stuck his head in through the opening. Behind him, Dave could see the alcove was crowded with kids waiting to see Fran Ellis in the adjoining office.

"Get in here, will you?" Dave said. "Park it over there."

Moe sprawled in the chair across from Dave's desk. The baggy sweatshirt with the hood could have been a monk's cowl. He was finally putting on a little weight, and the rounded cheeks gave him the appearance of a mother squirrel, with hazel nuts stored there for its babies. Still the ever-present smile, despite the refrigerator on his back.

"Hey, J.W., what can I do you out of? You know, of course, that you just interrupted a brilliant virtuoso performance. I had the whole band and choir at my mercy. The bravos were ringing throughout the halls like the bells at Chartres."

"Enough already. I need you to check something for me on the Internet. I was going through Egge's things and I found this magazine from the National Association of Secondary School

Principals. I want you to see if you can find a membership list. See how many names start with 'SYZ'."

Moe pulled the strings tighter on the hood, bringing to mind another image, Little Red Riding Hood. "So you think the murderer got the wrong principal?" Moe dropped the hood, took out a rattail comb, and raked it across his moptop. It flopped back down over his eyes.

"Can't hurt to check. There are no names starting with 'SYZ' in the Soldier, Fertile, Climax, or Crookston phone books."

Moe sniffed, rubbed his nose on his sleeve.

"Take a Kleenex, will you? How soon can you get me that information?" Dave put his shoes up on the desk.

"Card won't mind me using the machine in the library. I might have to hack my way into their records. If not, it shouldn't take more than a few minutes."

"About that dream you had—"

"Don't tell me you had one too!"

"Not exactly. Not what you'd call a dream dream..."

Before he could explain, the fire alarm went off, and all four hundred students marched to their assigned shelters in very orderly fashion. Mindy apologized for not telling Dave about the scheduled tornado drill. He was assigned to the safe where the public address system directed everyone to assume the fetal position. Everybody did, including some very attractive senior girls, giggling all the way, and Dave. Mr. Bronson was above it all, standing there with his arms crossed, glaring at the giggling girls.

When he got back to Egge's office, the lady from Louisville Slugger called back. She said, "We got a call for Wayne Terwilliger bats right after the Twins' World Series victory in 1987 and again in 1991. The order came from a store in Minneapolis called Pitch and Slide on Nicollet Ave. There were about two hundred of those bats in existence."

"Thank you, Miss Montrose. You ever get to Minnesota?"

"That's Ms. Montrose, Deputy," she said. "And I'm not even sure where Minnesota is."

Dave shrugged, hung up the phone. As good a put down as any he supposed. She couldn't be serious about not knowing where Minnesota was. What, was she born under a rock?

Mrs. Mac was right on time. Upon closer inspection, he noticed that her eyebrows were drawn on, her cheeks were a bit too red, and she'd missed the lines with her lipstick. Her red and white print dress with a maple leaf design clashed with the purple hair.

He was dying to find out about the purple hair. That and the sooth-sayer thing.

She placed her saddlebag of a purse on top of Egge's desk, coming dangerously close to knocking over Dave's cup of coffee.

"Sorry about that," she said. "I'm like a bull in a china shop, always been that way, ever since I was a little girl." She looked at her watch. "I'm not late am I? The clocks around this place are always off. The power goes off and it takes them weeks to get them back on sync. Sometimes I think they do it on purpose— There I go again rambling on. You want to know about Jerry Egge. Such a terrible thing. He and I didn't exactly hit it off but...some men are like that, they don't like loud, brassy broads. I can see by looking at you you're not like that."

"Mrs. Macintosh, could you tell me—"

"Could I tell you if Jerry had any enemies? Charlie Bronson would be the big one." She was giving the gum she was chewing quite a workout. "Bronson and Mrs. Egge were having an affair, and Jerry found out."

"I hadn't heard that," he lied, hoping she'd expound on the matter.

"Oh, yes, there was a big fight and everything. It was all over school the next day."

"Yes, I knew about the fight. The boys at the supermarket said they'd been arguing over sports. How about otherwise, how did they get along professionally? Did they have any curriculum differences?"

"Only that Jerry didn't like to sit in the rooms for an hour evaluating teachers when he could tell in a few minutes if they were good teachers or not. Bronson said he was insubordinate."

"So then, how did Jerry handle it—I mean the affair?"

"Classical avoidance for the most part," Mrs. Mac said. "He spent all of his time over here."

Dave kept thinking about what had just happened when he'd called Silver Bay. Instead of asking her what she knew about extrasensory perception, he said, "Were there any other people Jerry didn't get along with?"

"I hate to badmouth one of my kids...Freddie Cochran. You were involved in that little episode with the gun, weren't you? I thought Jerry handled that whole incident very well. Some principals would have wanted Freddie expelled permanently. I don't really see where Freddie would have had a grudge against Jerry. But you never know with kids."

"That's true."

Mrs. Mac removed some hand lotion from her purse, squirted some into her palms, rubbed them together lavishly. Suddenly she remembered something else she needed from her purse. She opened the purse again and removed what looked like a grocery list.

"What's that you've got there?" he asked.

"Just a grocery list for my EBD—that's emotional and behavior disorders if you didn't know," she said, removing a rubber band from her purse and winding it around one of her fingers. I keep forgetting the treats, and believe me, they let me know about it."

"Can you think of anybody else who might be a suspect?" he asked.

"I assume you'll get around to me sooner or later. Jerry didn't think much of special ed., especially EBD. Thought Attention Deficit Disorder was a crock. Jerry felt EBD should be there to help the teachers with discipline, kind of a holding pen. We went round and round, almost came to blows."

He said, "But you got him help after the attack." He remembered where he'd seen her. She played left field for the Jackrabbits. Her hair had been covered by a baseball hat, which was why he hadn't recognized her.

"It could have been a clever ruse," Mrs. Mac said. "I used to wrestle with my five brothers who were on the wrestling team. I could have taken him out easily. If I were you, I'd really sweat me."

She flexed her muscles. He hadn't had any teachers with a sense of humor when he'd gone to school.

The phone rang. He picked it up and set it down on the desk, punching the disconnect button. "You seem to be enjoying this. Let's just say you're not at the top of my list of suspects. One more thing before I let you go. Mrs. Macintosh—"

"You want to know about my card, what I mean by soothsaying. I thought it sounded less formal than parapsychology—you know, psychokinesis, clairvoyance, telepathy, that sort of thing. Once we—we's the girls and I, the ones I was saying the rosary with—contacted my old great-grandmother who came over from Bavaria. My maiden name was Schueller. Very religious woman let me tell you. She bawled me out for not doing my Easter duty."

"Ah, you mentioned telepathy. I get those confused. Telepathy is when you can read somebody's mind, is that right?"

"More common than you think, Deputy. Animals do it all the time. Did you know we only use ten percent of our brains?"

"And what am I thinking, Mrs. Macintosh?"

"You're thinking what a crazy old bat I am, right? And you're wondering if I'm color blind."

Dave smiled, noncommittally, he hoped. "I think you're one of the most singular people I've ever met."

"We call that a euphemism around here." She clasped her fingers on her stomach. Her card was lying on top of Egge's personnel file in clear sight. "I've been expecting a call from you, Deputy," she said. "I see you've still got my card."

"Well, Mrs. Macintosh, considering what I do, it's very hard for me..."

"Let me tell you where I'm coming from, Deputy Jenkins. You know about identical twins, right? I'm not a twin myself but I had twin sisters, Bridgette and Gina. They had their own language, strangest thing you ever heard. Bridgie and Gina were very seldom separated, but all of us children had to work outside the home to help support the family, and often they had to work for different people. 'Gina broke a dish and cut her finger,' Bridgie would suddenly say, and sure enough, when Gina got home that night her finger would be bandanged and Bridgie would say, 'I told you so.' They'd finish each other's sentences, sometimes they'd even finish mine. Being around them so much, I got where I could do it, too."

"I guess I'm just a doubting Thomas..."

"You want some sort of sign. They all do. My forte is really astrology, Deputy Jenkins. I'm originally from Baton Rouge, you know. Learned it from an old black woman whose housekeeping I used to do—she won the lottery and she wanted a white servant. 'Wants to know how I won all this money?' Miss Mattie Harper would say, waving the greenbacks like a fan on a muggy day. 'You gots to know the signs,' she'd say. Isn't that a kick in the head?" The laugh got louder. "Why don't I do a little demonstration for you, Deputy Jenkins? When were you born?"

"March 15. I don't know the time."

"March 15! The ides of March. That's when Brutus and those senators skewered Julius Caesar. Little matter about the time you were born, we'll just do a cursory reading. The Pisces sign is two fish swimming in opposite directions. Part of you wants to fly, the other half wants to walk, if you get my meaning. Part of you wants to have sex, the other part wants to be a monk. Ideally, you want to link up the two parts, kind of like Albert Einstein. He was a very mystical man as well as being a great scientist, wasn't afraid to get a wild hair up his ass upon occasion. What you got to do if you are a Pisces is get your kinky self to talk to your buttoned-down self."

Dave rubbed his eyes and scratched his head. Had to admit that sure sounded like him all right. The visions had been right about Egge's marital problems, and they'd been right about Egge's parents' first names. Mrs. Macintosh, she'd know about this sort of thing. And she wouldn't think he was crazy. She wouldn't even think anything was wrong with him.

"Mrs. Macintosh, if this gets out—"

She took a pair of glasses out of her purse and looked at him intensely. "Did you know that you have two—"

"If this gets out, I'll be a laughing stock."

"I can assure you, Deputy Jenkins, that we'll keep it under our hats, so to speak. Lots of police departments use clairvoyants these days."

"We'll need to visit the scene of the murder."

"Oh, no, I never want to see that place again. I acted so disgracefully. You'd think I would have been able to veer off before losing my lunch on the poor man's body."

"But Mrs. Macintosh—"

"I suppose you're right. They've cleaned it up some I hope. I never saw so much blood. Reminded me of the time I worked at a slaughterhouse. It's going to cost you, though. I get forty dollars an hour."

"This is a police investigation, Mrs. Macintosh. We don't ordinarily pay—"

She smiled revealing teeth that belonged on a piano. "Come now, Deputy, we both know I'm your only refuge. What're you gonna do, go to the priest?"

"Ah, I have a call to make in the country this afternoon. Could we make it first thing tomorrow, say seven thirty?"

Mrs. Mac stood, straightening her dress which had snagged on her panty hose. "I'll take a personal day," she said. "Will you be picking me up?"

"I'll be there with bells on. I hope you don't mind riding in my Jeep."

Dave smoothed out the crumpled list of names the superintendent had given him. The people on it and their supposed difficulties with Egge all seemed so innocuous. Nothing that couldn't wait till tomorrow. He checked his watch. Where had all the time gone? It was three o'clock, and he still wanted to get a sense of what the classroom behavior was like. Maybe the place was out of control. "I think I've just got time to visit a class or two."

She said, "You're welcome in EBD anytime."

"See you tomorrow, Mrs. Macintosh," Dave said, opening the door for her.

She curtsied. "You can call me Gigglebox," she said as she snapped shut her purse. "Everybody does, even the kids."

They left the office together with Mrs. Mac stopping to collect her messages, dropping several on the way out. Mindy picked them up and put them back in her box. She winked at him.

He was drawn to the nearest classroom, which happened to be Miss Meyer's English Nine class where she was teaching *Romeo and Juliet*. The students were all dressed in period costumes, and Miss Meyer had blocked the play. Miss Meyer made him wear one of the berets with the feather and take the part of Mercutio since Mercutio was absent. He had less trouble with the Queen Mab speech than he thought he would.

Every so often they'd stop and discuss what was going on. He found himself discussing up a storm. One of Debbie Meyer's students, Gene Gant, an effeminate little twerp with blond strawlike-hair and tortured skin said, "This play sounds an awful lot like a soap opera if you discount the poetic language. Can Shakespeare really expect us to believe the messenger who's supposed to tell Romeo that Juliet is faking her death is delayed by a plague and is quarantined? Nobody's that unlucky."

It was as if Dave were wearing an earpiece and a producer was cuing him. "If I recollect correctly, Gene, that's because of the theme of the fickle finger of fate which is prominent in the play. Rather like the soldier who goes through the Invasion of Normandy without a scratch and is hit by a car when he goes home after the war."

Suddenly Dave found himself confronted by a sword-wielding Gene Gant who was portraying Tybalt. Dave got to do his dying act, when Tybalt stabbed him under Romeo's arm, and put a curse on everyone's houses.

After school Dave went back to the office where he'd meet Moe. He still had to check out Ray Miller's gas theft and Moe wanted to go along. Dave also needed the results on his computer search of the National Association of Secondary School Principals.

Dave sat in his office with his feet up on the desk and his fingers laced behind his head, staring at his Raquel poster and processing what he'd found out. That Shakespeare class had been his strangest experience yet. More hoodoo. He hadn't realized he knew anything about Shakespeare. Thirty-six plays, dramas, comedies, histories, and farces. And Shakespeare didn't write those plays. It was a man called the Earl of Oxford. Once he'd tried to watch a Shakespeare play on PBS—Julius Caesar he thought it was—he'd fallen asleep inside of five minutes. Maybe he should see Mrs. Macintosh again *before* tomorrow morning.

Dave dialed a number on his cellular. "Lucille? This is Dave Jenkins. Any prints on the Jeep?"

"Just yours, Deputy Jenkins. And the sand was too fine for any decent footprints. The slashes in the tires look like they were done with a switchblade. I sent them to the BCA lab along with the paint samples. That okay?"

"Perfect. I have a little job for you. You ever do an interrogation?"

"Sure, lots of them in school, but never a real one."

"I want you to arrange to see Mrs. Bronson, the superintendent's wife. I need to know how she felt about her husband's affair with Mrs. Egge. You're a woman, so it should be easier for you."

"Gee, I don't know if I can do that."

"Just get her talking. Ask her if she liked Jerry Egge. She should take it from there. Watch her body language."

"I'll do my best."

"That's all I ask." He punched the disconnect button, went back to communing with Raquel.

Chapter 8

String Theory

"A lively understandable spirit
Once entertained you.
It will come again.
Be still.
Wait."
— Theodore Roethke

Mingo stopped in front of a squat, yellow brick and granite building on the corner of Meade and Zouave Road, next to Logan's Sport Shop. According to the cornerstone, Farmers and Merchants Bank, one of the oldest buildings in town, had been built in 1895.

When he entered the bank, the three teller windows were busy, so he sat on the bench next to the door. The place had the atmosphere of one of the banks in the pictures of Jesse James holdups—strong smell of varnish, no spittoons though. He'd heard the James boys and the Youngers had held up a bank in a place called Northfield, Minnesota. Got shot up pretty bad, and the Youngers did time in Stillwater, the state prison. Dillinger had a hideout in St. Paul, too, if he wasn't mistaken.

Mingo crossed his legs and thought about what he'd need for the ceremony he was going to do out at the crime scene. Tobacco, pollen, some jet or cataline. He'd want to load up with powers. And some gifts from the Egg Man's family. That might present a problem. He'd most likely have to trick them into giving him something that belonged to the Egg Man.

He sighed, reached in his back pocket, got out the letter he'd received from his mother. She wanted to know if he'd seen his father yet, and if he was going to Sunday mass. His mother had always been a strict Catholic, and had disparaged Apache religion as had some of the other mothers. As a result, he and the other young people laughed at the old men who'd danced in the ceremonies. Superstitious nonsense. He and his homies had been much more interested in heavy metal and partying. But then he'd gone away to college, and he'd needed a minor to go with his Criminal Justice major. Native American studies seemed like a good sluff choice. But during his first class he'd read a poem called "Passages" by Aldo Ramirez.

Mingo put the letter from his mother back and took out his wallet, where he kept the poem in with the paper money. He unfolded the wrinkled poem and began to read it again, although he could probably recite it from memory by now. Mingo felt happier whenever he read the poem.

Buffalo cows and calves graze on a grassy hillside.
Mountain God dancers in buckskin and beaded moccasins
twirl and prance.
Eagle feather headdresses reach four feet high.
Jingling tin cones contend with the pulse and
throb of drums.

A dancing clown enters the scene, a paper sack for a
headdress, ratty tennis shoes instead of moccasins,
his chest painted with the words "Injin' Funk" and
"Whitey's Toys" scribbled on his back.

"Singing wires work better than smoke," the people
murmur. "Lariat 4X4's run faster than Indian ponies.
We will borrow some of the white man's ways. We will
sell our fancy blankets to the storekeepers, trade
our coup feathers for casino cash.

But we will never surrender our beauty or desert
the gods who roam the woods, swim the rivers, and
soar across the sky.

Funny how that poem had grabbed him. It had the effect of his first taste of alcohol. Couldn't get enough Apache culture. After weeks of nonstop reading, eyes swelling like hemorrhoids, he'd learned that the Apaches were fairly recent arrivals in the Southwest, around the fourteenth century, along with the Navajos. The Pueblo Indians had called them both Apachu, which meant stranger. The Apache were strong minded, individualist people who refused to mimic the rituals of the Pueblo tribes as the Navajo had and who revered the second born, Water Boy, rather than

Monster Slayer of the Navajo. And, as he'd told Jenkins, they feared the dead.

While Mingo was rereading the poem, the door opened and an old man shuffled in and sat down next to him. The old man turned and looked up at him. He had blue watery eyes and the lower half of his face protruded like a monkey's. He was wearing a black slouch hat, buckskins, and boots that reached his knees.

"You're an Indian," the old man said. "Ain't cha?"

"Yes, sir. Mingo Jones. And you are?"

"Albert Gahan. Glad to meet you."

Mingo didn't know whether to shake hands or run. Gahan was the Apache term for Mountain Spirit, and this one looked like the Grey One, the clown in the poem, who made fun of the other dancers during ceremonials.

They shook hands. The name could be a coincidence.

"Ain't seen you around before. You're Harry Kline's new deputy?"

"Yes, sir. I'm mostly on night duty, but since the Egge murder..."

"Waiting to see Skinflint Forman, I suppose?"

"As a matter of fact I am. It's pretty much standard procedure to check the victim's financial records."

"That so? I come to deposit my social security check. Used to be a harness maker in town here, until the tractor put the kibosh to that. Didn't trust banks much until somebody robbed my cache. Must have seen me dig it up."

"That's too bad. Did the sheriff catch the culprit?"

"Are you kidding? That man couldn't catch cold."

"Sir, excuse me for changing the subject, but I was curious, you know, because of the Dillinger gang in St. Paul, if this place has ever been robbed?"

"Sure was. Gang drove up in a brand new Packard. Shot up the place with one of those Tommy guns you see in the movies, and got away with ten thousand dollars. Skinflint Forman's been trying to get it back ever since, though it was his old man's money."

"Anybody killed?"

"The teller. Name of Isador Golsch. He hung on for a few days, then died of pneumonia."

Could be Izzy Golsch was stuck between the Shadow World and the Land of Ever Summer, too.

Finally one of the windows cleared. He tipped his hat to the Mountain Spirit and went to the window.

"Could I see Mr. Blaze Forman?" he asked the fortyish woman behind the glass. She gave him a look as if she didn't recognize the deputy sheriff's uniform. Perhaps it was the eagle feather. If Jenkins could wear a baseball cap, he could have a power symbol.

"May I say who wants him?" she said.

"Just tell him it's a criminal matter. That'll spark his interest."

Mingo had never been one for tact. Of course, he'd never been on the day watch before, so there hadn't been much need for it.

A little man with snow white hair that could have been a wig came out from behind the partition separating the banking elite from the hoi poloi.

"I'm Blaze Forman," the little man, who couldn't have weighed more than a hundred twenty pounds, said. "What can I do for you, Deputy Jones?"

Hmm, he didn't remember telling the suspicious teller his name. Perhaps this man was a worthy adversary. The little man held out his hand and Mingo shook it. Surprisingly firm grip.

"It's about a criminal investigation, Mr. Forman."

"Won't you come back to my office?"

They went through a side door, back through a narrow hall to a room that looked as if it had once been a vault. Narrow, very high, stamped tin ceiling, one window, floor to ceiling. A view of the parking lot.

Forman gestured toward a chair and Mingo took it. Forman sat in his Scrooge-style leather chair that must have cost half a grand, if not more. Then again, maybe he'd foreclosed on a furniture store.

"I hope I didn't keep you waiting, Deputy. I've been very busy. Everyday seems to be doomsday around here lately. Sugar beet payments just came in from Crystal Sugar. More Bad news for the farmers I'm afraid, they're eleven dollars a ton below what they got last year."

"I heard about the flood."

"Yup, the flood and wheat scab. We've had weather and disease problems six years running, and commodity prices are just unbelievable."

"I'm sorry to hear that."

"With commodity prices the way they are because of the crisis in the Far East, farmers can't turn a profit. Wheat is down eighty cents from last year, corn a dollar, soybeans over two, and barley seventy cents. The FSA's declared a commodity disaster in ten of the last eleven years. Over forty percent of our farmers have exhausted their credit."

"FSA?"

"Farm Service Agency. Forgive me, Deputy. I shouldn't burden you with my problems."

"No, I'd like to hear."

"It's not just the farmers. Fertilizer dealers and other businesses aren't selling anything because there's no money out there."

"I can empathize, Mr. Forman but—"

"It's just that when those payments come due, I'm going to look like the villain...I'm taking up your time, what can I do for you, Deputy?"

Too bad about those farmers, but Mingo couldn't help but think about Little Crow and his tribe, who, after begging for federal beef allotments that never came, went on the warpath against the people of New Ulm, Minnesota, only to be beaten down by General Sibley and his troops. Thirty-eight warriors had been hanged, the largest execution in American history, and there would have been more had it not been for Lincoln's pardon which spared some lives. Little Crow himself had been shot down in a farmer's field like a rabid dog.

"Deputy?"

"Sorry, I was just thinking about those farmers. Ah, I'll try to make it quick, sir. We're investigating the Egge murder, and we have reason to believe that Jerry Egge had a safety deposit box in your bank."

Forman rested his elbows on the desk, clasped his fingers. "It made me sick when I heard what happened to Mr. Egge. I'd like to help in any way that I can, but I can't tell you anything about Mr. Egge's personal business, Deputy. You ought to know that."

"A file on Egge's computer implies that there may be something in his safety deposit box which may point toward the murderer."

"I can't help you, Deputy Jones. If you want to see what's in Mr. Egge's box, you're going to have to get Mrs. Egge to show you."

"That or a court order," Mingo said, dealing the warrant across Forman's desk like a trump card.

Forman's face caved like a snowbank during the spring thaw. The little man took on the look of Custer before the massacre on the Washita: *You many have outsmarted me this time, Indian, but I'm going to butcher your tribe's wives, children, and old people.*

Forman took him down a winding staircase to the bowels of the bank where he personally opened the steel grating guarding the safety deposit boxes.

"We'll need to drill and punch the lock," Forman said. "I'll get the maintenance man down here for you. Just ring this button when you're finished," he said, touching the said gizmo near the door.

As the maintenance man drilled, Mingo struck up a conversation about how well the local Indians got along with the Caucasians. In the process, he discovered that the maintenance man was one-quarter Ojibwa.

"Ever hear of Russell Means?" the man said. "Wounded Knee ain't too far from here."

Enough said.

There was an envelope in the box labeled "indictment". Mingo removed the clasp and perused what Egge had written.

"Holy shit," he muttered.

*   *   *

At four-thirty Moe finally showed up. Dave and the moptop said goodbye to Shirley and, with Chopin in tow, went out the back door on their way to check out the complaint about stolen gasoline at the Miller farm. Dave knew that gasoline used for farming was not taxed. As a result, most farmers had massive, two-hundred gallon tanks in their yards. Some brazen thieves could not resist the temptation, despite vicious farm dogs who would serrate your gluteus maximus if you got within a half mile of the farm.

As Dave cranked up the engine of the refurbished Jeep, he noticed Moe pointing at the statue in Veteran's Park. "Will you look at that?" Moe said. Dave looked where Moe was pointing. Colonel Colvill, the leader of the First Minnesota Regiment at Gettysburg, had become an amputee.

Dave shut down the engine and they walked over, scanning the ground looking for the missing appendage. It wasn't there. They sorted through the bushes and searched under the park benches and the children's merry-go-round and swing sets. The arm was nowhere to be found.

"I suppose Hildegard will be after me to find the damn thing," Dave said.

"You'll probably find it in your bed," Moe said. "Remember that scene from *The Godfather* with the horse's head?"

"Not funny. I'll be right back."

Dave couldn't find his gun, so he grabbed one of Harry's carbines and they were finally on the road.

As they drove down Meade, despite the late hour, people were still out in their yards, raking leaves or preparing their gardens for planting. It was the first day of the year the temperature had risen into the seventies. Soon the dew point would soar into the seventies and Dave's clothes would stick to his back, and the Minnesota state bird, the mosquito, would be out in force, like Japanese zeroes honing in on a pokey destroyer tender.

"What's with the rifle?" Moe said.

"Any coward who'd stoop to slashing the tires on a man's Jeep wouldn't hesitate to call in a false police report trying to lure me out into the country."

"I hadn't thought of that. I think I hear my Mom calling."

Dave was exceeding the speed limit by a good twenty miles an hour.

"Don't you think you ought to slow down," Moe said. "You're setting a bad example."

"What's that Charles Barkley says about role models?...Oh yeah, up yours."

As they passed the strip mall construction, Moe said, "Considering this most recent development, the fact that they chose the statue of Colonel Colvill, I'm wondering if...JESSICA thinks that what we have here is a symbolic murder. A high school principal is an authority figure. Can you think of a more demanding authority figure than a military colonel?"

"A military general."

"Wiscnheimer."

"Vandalism of a statue doesn't necessarily have anything to do with Egge's murder."

"I suppose you're right. Can I drive? I'm taking the test again next week."

"Are you sure you want to? There's no power steering."

"I need the practice. After driving this thing, driving my mom's Honda ought to handle like a Rolls-Royce."

Dave stopped at intersection of Meade and Climax Road, where Soldier's one and only light was stuck on red, and they shifted positions. The Jeep chugged ahead, gasping and snorting, black smoke rolling out of the exhaust, the stink of gasoline outdueling the Christmas tree air freshener Dave had strung around the rearview mirror.

"Don't you think it's time to put this thing out of its misery," Moe said.

"I'll have you know a collector would pay at least a hundred thou for this little beauty."

"Dream on, J.W."

As they approached Evergreen Cemetery and the scent of pine wafted over their heads, Dave began to have another vision. Olive,

Freddie, Stormy and Lester Krueger were sprawled on a bench in Veteran's Park drinking wine and smoking pot.

"See that statue," Olive said. "I'll bet I can knock his head off."

She got up and threw a rock at the Colonel. Freddie and the others joined in. One of the larger stones thudded up against Colvill's arm and it fell against the base, splitting into two pieces.

They stopped throwing stones and it got quiet, as if they realized they'd done something heinous.

"The old war monger looks more realistic this way," Freddie said, slurring his words. "I read where if you were grazed by a bullet from a Sharps rifle, your arm was automatically bound for Armour meat packing."

"I'm taking that arm home with me," Olive said, cackling like Janis Joplin on Everclear. "It's just the thing I need to keep the bathroom door from swinging shut all the time."

"Better pick up those rocks," Freddie said. "Too easy for Deputy Dog to finger out what happened. It'll be a little diversion for him."

When Dave came out of it, they were out in the countryside and Moe was still talking about the Jeep. "I suppose if you fixed it up some you could get something for it. Most collectors want their antiques in pristine condition."

"What's that?"

"The Jeep, we were talking about antique collectors."

"Forget the collectors. You and Olive have your study session yet?"

"Not yet. I've been meaning to ask about you and Annie Kline. How you go about—"

"Keep that to yourself, huh?" Dave said. "I feel like shit about it. This could ruin a great friendship, or worse, I could lose a great leadoff hitter. I had a little too much to drink at Bud's, and she had her way with me. I think it was the cleavage that did it. I'd never seen her cleavage. Usually she dresses like a boy."

"You two are such buds, I'd marry her if I were you."

"Bite your tongue," Dave said, as he reached over to turn up the radio. "Just play your music and become a big star so I can say I knew you when, and don't worry about what this kid does."

"Kid is right!...I don't want to play my music. I want to be a sleuth like you, only not so bumbling and uncoordinated. What's Sheriff Kline gonna do when he finds out? You're not much, but you're all he's got. He can barely get out of his chair with that bad back of his."

"I think it must have been subconscious behavior," Dave said. "I've been rather bored with the job until this Egge case came along."

"You do have a low threshold for boredom," Moe said. "Seriously, did you learn anything new from Bronson?" He rubbed Chopin's ears, and Chopin tried to reciprocate by licking his face.

"Only that he's got awfully big feet, just like Mr. Bigfoot at the crime scene, and he's got a hell of a temper. That reminds me. What about the computer check? Give you one little job—"

Moe dug around in his back pocket with one hand, fought the wheel with the other, then handed Dave his hand-tooled wallet with the saddle on its face. "I wrote out the name on a piece of paper. Look in the money fold. His name is Del Szymanski, he lives in Steubenville, Ohio. What do you think?"

"How good are you at statistical analysis? What are the odds you'd find a person with that name on a membership list of the National Association of Secondary School Principals?"

"I'll need to find out how many Szymanskis there are in the country and how many people belong to the group. Is tomorrow soon enough? I guess Brontosaurus does resemble the maniac in my dream, seems the guy was younger, though."

They came to what passes for a hill in Minnesota. Moe downshifted rather smoothly.

"Something's bothering me about that baseball bat," Dave said. "Would you believe I had a dream about it last night. I was playing in the World Series, I could tell because I could see the monuments in center field at Yankee Stadium and there were too many cameras around for it to be just a regular game. And Sandy Koufax was pitching. I almost wet myself. Anyway, all I had was the Wayne Terwilliger bat. I got a couple of loud fouls before he struck me out with that big jugeared curve."

"Must be hell to be a failure, even in your dreams."

"I was proud of my loud fouls."

Dave's hat almost blew off. He took it off, tightened the one-size-fits-all snaps. "Mingo talked to the splatballers we knew from Soldier," he said. "What about the opposing army? Egge could have been mistaken for another stooge wearing a Minnesota Gophers outfit...I wonder if I put any gas in this thing lately."

"Jeez I'm an idiot," Moe said. "Olive told me she was out there playing splatball during the time of the murder and I forgot to tell you. She says she has the hots for a member of the opposing army. If I were you, I'd talk to her."

"I don't understand that girl. What's with the slutty attitude?"

"You got me, she scares me silly. I'd always thought my feelings had something to do with a possible religious vocation. On my part, of course."

*   *   *

The Millers had a very long driveway. Dave felt it must be hell to get in and out of the place during the winter. A small black and white dog tried to tear the mud guards off the Jeep as they approached the farmhouse.

Moe and Dave spent about an hour at the Miller farm, trying to find tracks and other evidence. It was hopeless. So many vehicles had been around the gas tank that it would be easier to find a gray hair in one of Cher's wigs than to find the thief's tracks.

The little dog kept trying to nip at Dave's heels.

Miller, who had been manuring out the barn when they drove up, yelled at the dog, "Get down, Lady." The dog looked shameful, and three minutes later, she was sneaking up on Dave, trying for another nip.

Ray Miller was chewing snuff, expectorating freely. He said, "When you fellas gonna set up the stake-out?"

Dave, who was trying to keep his distance, said, "Ray, you know the county couldn't afford to set up a surveillance."

Miller added a wad to the already bulging cheek. "Gonna take some fingerprint samples then, ain't 'cha?"

Dave sighed. "I doubt that there'd even be a record of this scofflaw's fingerprints. I hate to say this, Ray, but the crook is most likely one of your neighbors. Maybe even a member of your family. Did you ever think of that? You got a girl old enough to drive, don't yah?"

Miller had about a million chickens. Occasionally one of them would get the notion to fly a few feet, spooking Dave no end. Chickens had always given him the creeps.

"I ain't lettin' Rita take the test till she's eighteen. She can get her own car then."

"I don't know what to tell you, Ray, other than that you might put a lock on the nozzle."

Miller cogitated on that some. "The horse is out of the barn, Jenkins. Why'm I payin' taxes? I should be able to get some police protection. You ken go, I'm'na talk to the sheriff."

"Suit yourself. Sorry, we couldn't help."

He went to wait for Moe in the Jeep where Lady and Chopin were sniffing each other. His phone rang. Mingo with a report on the safety deposit box.

*   *   *

Rita, Ray's daughter, was feeding the chickens and Moe had gone to talk to her. She was wearing a white t-shirt with holes in it—no bra—and jeans with turned up cuffs; her feet were bare. Curly black hair and cross-eyed, she reminded him of one of those girls he'd seen in that movie about Charles Manson, only she had more hair.

"How's it going, Rita?" he said. "Don't see you in school much, not that I'm there that often myself."

Rita spat on the ground. "Since when do you talk to me, you little weasel? You ain't never said more than two words to me."

"Come on, Rita, you never looked like you *wanted* to talk to me." He looked around the yard, reveling in all the animals. "You know what, I'd trade places with you in a minute. Can you show me how your dad delivers calves, how the steers are castrated? And what kind of feed you give the chickens and the diseases they get? What your dad's profit margin is?"

"You're a funny little guy, ain't you?" she said. "You'd last out here for exactly one day, if that long, before you called your mama to come get you. This place is backbreaking hard work. How'd you like to help me shovel out the chicken coop? Got that job coming up pretty quick."

"You just tell me when you want me here, Rita."

*   *   *

"Sooo, got yourself a new girlfriend, huh?" Dave said on the way back to town. He was sitting on the passenger side, trying not to lean up against the door.

"She's the biggest nutcase in school. If it weren't for Miles Krueger's statement, I'd say she had something to do with Egge's murder. I'm going out there this Saturday to help her clean the chicken coop and learn everything I can about farming. I'm going back to nature and I plan to stay there."

"While you're at it, quiz her some about Olive, will you? They're always together. You know, I wish you'd get over on your side of the road. This isn't England after all and we're coming to a hill."

Dave's hands were cold because the top was down, and when he put his hands in his pocket, he touched the pipe again and flinched, afraid he'd see Egge lying on the ground, the brute murderer above, hammering away at his face with the sledgelike ball bat, blood spattering every which way.

Moe was now weaving from one side of the road to the other. Dave was trying his darnedest not to grab the wheel.

"Mopester, you've taken a lot of psychology courses, haven't you?"

Moe looked over at Dave anticipating a joke. "No, mostly I read about psychology, trying to understand the human condition, you ought to try it sometime. Why?"

"I know I'm going to regret telling you this. You have to promise you won't laugh."

"I can't promise that. Tell you what, I'll try not to laugh." Moe pulled the hood of his sweatshirt up over his head.

"Are you cold? I can put the top up."

"See what I mean? That top has more holes than a pasta strainer."

"I think I may be going insane. I had this hallucination out at the murder scene."

They were nearing the outskirts of Soldier just coming up on the cemetery. Dave wiped his forehead with his sleeve. He was very tired. Driving with Moe always drained him. Chopin chuffed.

Moe turned his way, a concerned look on his face. Dave reached over and pushed his face forward since he was closing in on a parked car.

"What kind of hallucination?" Moe said.

"I think I saw Egge's life pass before my eyes."

Moe slammed on the brakes and Dave got his hands up just in time to prevent smacking into the windshield. Moe pulled off to the side of the road. "What did you say?"

"I saw Egge's life pass before my eyes at the murder scene."

Moe picked Chopin up off the floor and scratched his ears. "You didn't fall down and hit your head?"

"I should've known better than to—"

"Hold on, hold on, don't get your water hot. It's just that that's supposed to happen to the person being killed."

"I'm thinking I was in shock or something."

"That's possible I suppose. Anything else spooky happen?"

"Just before you got to Egge's house the other day, I saw him arguing with his wife and she told him his kids weren't his."

"That was on the computer."

"And when I called Silver Bay to find out if Egge was his real name, I found out his parents' names were Clark and Mary."

"So?"

"That's what their names were in the vision I had at the murder scene."

"How many more of these have you had?"

"I'd say seven or eight. I had one on the way out of town about the severed arm on the statue. Olive and Freddie Cochran did it, according to the vision. Of course I can't use that..."

"I wonder what the Amazing Randi would say about this. He's that guy who goes around debunking spiritualists and such."

"Who knows? Who cares? Do you think I need to see a head shrinker?"

"Yes, I do, but not because of the visions." He tapped his lower lip, then smiled. "You're so *damn* lucky. Why don't I ever get to have a supernatural experience?" He snapped his fingers. "Mrs. Macintosh, people say she's a psychic. I've been thinking of going to see her myself just to check her out, see if there's anything to it. I was thinking that maybe she could help me delude myself into thinking my father is all right, wherever he is."

"I'm sure he is, Moe."

"Then there's that dream I had, you know, the one about Egge's murder. I've never had such a vivid dream before. I wonder what those letters on that guy's shirt meant? Couldn't be Berkeley, could it? You know, the college where they had all the protests? If it was, JESSICA's idea about the symbolism—"

"You're not patronizing me, are you? I'm kind of surprised a kid like you who's so heavily into quasars and quarks would advocate parapsychology."

"I hate naysayers. Anything's possible in my book."

"I thought all scientists were atheists. Can you give me a scientific handle on this, something I can live with? Lay some cosmological bullshit on me, it'll make me feel better."

"Have you ever heard of string theory?"

Dave shook his head no.

"I don't suppose you know anything about quantum theory or the theory of relativity?"

"I know a little about that. Einstein—everything is relative. Depends on your perspective."

"Groovy. Anyway, science has had a hard time resolving the discrepancies between the macrocosm and microcosm, or Einstein's grand scheme of things and electrons, neutrons and protons. Mathematically, the only way to do it is a formula which allows for ten dimensions. See where I'm going?"

"Kind of."

A semi went by, exceeding the legally prescribed speed limit. The Jeep rocked.

"Let's look at a hypothetical," Moe said. "If we lived in a two-dimensional world, a three-dimensional person from another world could reach down and pluck us out of our two-dimensional world, and we would seem to disappear to all the other two-dimensional people who wouldn't have any depth, only length and width. If you extrapolate to ten dimensions, who knows what we can get scientifically."

"I feel *much* better," Dave said.

"I can't wait to tell JESSICA about this."

It was eight o'clock, still light out, though, because of Daylight Savings. Moe and Chopin got off at the new McDonalds. As Dave drove away, Olive Randall, a beautiful girl about Moe's age, with long alabaster legs and a figure that would tempt Liberace, if he were alive, accosted Moe and tried to pull him over to the takeout window. Probably begging again. She'd even asked Dave for money once or twice. Einstein and Jezebel. He felt like a shit not trusting Moe enough to tell him he'd already made arrangements for Mrs. Macintosh to revisit the murder scene.

As he was kicking himself, a black sports car approached the stop sign on Seminary, did a rolling stop, and turned in his direction. The driver, her long blond hair blowing in the wind, honked. Mary Lou Forman, she'd been bugging him of late almost as much as Egge. He'd been thinking of asking her out again, now that they were both grown up and she was apparently separated. So what if she was pregnant. She might be impressed by a pistol packing cop with a murder case on his hands.

The Jeep sputtered as he neared Little Round Top and it died as he parked in the shade of the humongous ash tree. His luck was improving. Usually, he ran out of gas in the middle of nowhere, miles from civilization. Had to think about where he'd park Nellybelle tonight so as to avoid a reoccurrence of the slashing incident. He slammed the door of the Jeep, and it popped back open. To hell with it, he needed to call Superintendent Bronson and tell him the sheriff wanted to talk to him. Not exactly true. Needed to talk to him about what was in the safety deposit box.

Dave knelt to pick up his copy of the Star-Tribune, scanned the headlines, tossed it on the kitchen table, then went to the phone.

Bronson's wife answered. She said he was in the den watching CNN.

"Sorry to bother you at home, Chuck," Dave said when Bronson took the phone, "but the Sheriff wants to talk to you again about the murder."

"I don't know when I'll find the time," Bronson said, "I'm buried right now."

Dave had to hold the phone away from his ear as Bronson was being his usual blaring self. Sounded as if he was coming down with a cold, though. Dave moved to the frig, took out was left of a moldy loaf of bread—what the hell, penicillin—slathered some mustard on two pieces of crust, slapped a piece of bologna, also green around the edges, between the slices. He took a bite, and said, "Jeez, I'm really sorry, Chuck. Something has come up that we didn't know about before our first session."

"But I already gave you a statement. Egge and I didn't like each other much, but we were able to put that aside and work together regardless." His voice was taking on a higher pitch. "I'm so damn busy," Bronson said, sniffling, then honking into what must have been a tissue. "What's wrong with before school?"

"No can do. I have a previous appointment first thing in the morning." Dave swallowed the last piece of sandwich and washed it down with a slug of Lumberjack.

Bronson reluctantly agreed to be at the sheriff's office at 9:30. Dave had been expecting some flack about making a special case scenario for the superintendent since he had an office in the school he could use for the teachers and staff. Why not interview the superintendent there? That would have been a tough grounder to field. He needed to talk to the superintendent in his own bailiwick, to put the man on the defensive.

Dave decided to make one last phone call, hoping that Johnny Logan was still up.

"Johnny, glad you're still awake. Say, remember those baseball bats I called about? I forgot to ask, did you ever do any business with Pitch and Slide on Nicollet in Minneapolis?"

"Sure, lots of times," Logan said. "I stop there and trade war stories with the owner. He gives me stuff on consignment."

"Did you ever have any Louisville Sluggers with a Wayne Terwilliger endorsement?" Dave asked. He twirled the phone cord around his finger.

"Sure did. Got a special request from Sheriff Kline. Twig had one pretty good year. He hit .242 with 10 home runs for the Chicago Cubs in 1950." Logan, the second baseman for the Dogs, liked to tell everyone he was related to the shortstop who had played for the Milwaukee Braves before they moved to Atlanta. Dave was pretty sure he was full of shit.

"Got the *Baseball Encyclopedia* handy, eh?" Dave said. "Pretty quick fingers. Thanks for the info, John, you've been a big help."

"Does this have anything to do with the Egge murder?"

"If you tell anybody I asked, you'll have to leave town, John, because of all the police harassment."

"I'm scared."

Dave hung up the phone. In a few hours everybody at Bud's and Andy's would know about the baseball bat.

So Harry had purchased a Wayne Terwilliger bat. Not only was the man obese, he also had amnesia.

He dialed another number.

"Amoco Station."

"Pigeon. Glad you're still there. Got any room in the shop? I need to park my Jeep there tonight."

Chapter 9

Telltale Lingerie

"You spotted snakes with double tongue,
Thorny hedge-hogs, be not seen;
Newts, and blind-worms, do no wrong;
Come not near our fairy queen."
— Shakespeare, *A Midsummer-Night's Dream*

Dave unlocked the door to the evidence room, a closet-like chamber, slighter smaller than his office, and flipped the light switch. He found the baseball bat and took it back into his office.

It was seven o'clock in the morning and here he was already at work, going over the bat with a magnifying glass. Nothing. He'd like to get that blood off, but if he steamed it off or whatever, Henderson would be sure to want to know what happened to it. He stood the baseball bat in his wastebasket and reached for the BCA report on the crime scene. The results were in on the boot and the footprints found at the murder scene. No fingerprints, but the report said the boot showed extensive wear, probably worn by an avid sportsman. There was enough left of the lot number on the boot to show that it had been made in 1972. The report also revealed that the smaller shoe prints were the same size as Lester's.

Dave tapped his pencil on the desktop, considering whether he should have Mingo and Lucille search the Krueger farm for shoes to match those at the quarry. Would Lester be dumb enough to keep the shoes?

He tossed the pencil into a mug on his desk, reached into a drawer, and took up a pair of panties. The laundry tag read *O. Randall*. They had come with the indictment Mingo had found in Egge's safety deposit box that said Egge had fished them out of Charlie Bronson's wastebasket. You'd think the Super Chief, as Mingo called him, would have been a little more careful. What would Bronson do when he whipped these babies out in the middle of the interrogation?

Before he met with Mrs. Mac, he had to take care of one more little piece of business. He put the panties away, reached into his shirt pocket, and stared down at the name Moe had given him. Del Szymanski, Steubenville, Ohio. Kind of a longshot, but what the hell, in a few minutes he was going out to the murder scene with a self-styled soothsayer with purple hair.

According to the NASSP bio, Szymanski was seventy-eight. Long retired, but still a member of the principal's association. Should be eight o'clock in Ohio. He dialed information and got a phone number for a Del Szymanski in Steubenville. The operator dialed the number for him.

A woman answered.

"Is this Mrs. Szymanski, Mrs. Del Szymanski?"

"This is she," she said.

"Mrs. Szymanski, this is Deputy Sheriff Jenkins in Soldier, Minnesota. May I speak to your husband, please?"

"He's not here right now, Deputy Jenkins. He has breakfast with his Lions Club chums every morning. May I ask what this is about?"

"Oh, we have this lead on a case we're investigating. Could you have him call me back at 612-555-3099, please..."

"Is my husband in any trouble, Deputy?"

"No, we're just doing some checking; your husband isn't in any trouble."

"He'll be back around ten, Deputy Jenkins. I'll have him call you."

"Thank you, Mrs. Szymanski." He replaced the receiver on the cradle.

His watch read seven-fifteen. He'd walk over to Mrs. Macintosh's house. Hopefully, Annie, who'd recently moved out of her parents' house and taken a room at Mrs. Mac's, would still be in bed.

Not looking where he was going, Dave bunged up his chins on Harry's cruiser, which Harry'd parked right up against the back door practically. God that hurt! Harry's eyesight was probably going, too.

Dave cut through the church parking lot, veering toward Mrs. Mac's house across the street from the rectory. He was nervous. *Mrs.Macintosh is the best person for the job*, he told himself again. *Besides reading palms, she does tea leaves, holds séances, the whole nine yards. She's probably seen lots of ghosts.*

Mrs. Mac lived in an old three-story house that must have at one time been some kind of official building—the windows oversized—a cumbersome-looking fire escape winding down one side of the house. About two acres of lawn, with a garden the size of Eden. She must have really liked birds—she had bird baths, bird feeders, even multi-level, hotel-sized bird houses. Everything a little birdy could possibly want. When he leaned on the doorbell, he could hear what sounded like birdsong echoing through the interior.

Annie Kline answered the door. "Oh, it's you," she said. She was still wearing her bathrobe, her hair was wet and her feet were bare, the paint chipping on the nail polish. He wanted to jump her.

"How'd the game go last night," he said. "I was hoping to get in a couple of at bats."

"I don't suppose that would look too good," she said. "We lost 14-4."

"Damn," he said, "Our first loss. I came to see Mrs. Mac. Is she up?"

"I think she's in the dining room," she said. She rubbed her wet hair with a towel, then turned, heading back toward the bathroom.

He wandered into the ground-floor dining room where the boarders were having breakfast. Two bachelors from the snowmobile factory, three of the ever changing foster children Mrs. Mac usually accommodated, and George McCready, the ersatz mayor, occupied some of the fifteen, sixteen straight-back chairs gathered around a huge mahogany table which dominated the room. Flowers everywhere—on the fireplace mantel, functioning as centerpieces for the table, geraniums hanging from the ceiling. The room smelled like a fricking funeral home.

Mrs. Mac was dishing up the oatmeal. "Good morning, Deputy," she said, so enthusiastically he could have been her prodigal son. She was still in her dressing gown, her hair in curlers. Apparently she'd forgotten their appointment.

She set the pot down next to George McCready and said, "You boys help yourself; I need to talk to the deputy." She grabbed him by the arm and pulled him toward the rear of the house. "Come into the kitchen where we can be more private. I've got some coffee on and some fritters. You like fritters, don't you? I've been doing charts on everyone involved in the case, and I've come up with some fascinating information. I can't wait to get out to the murder scene."

He removed his cap. "Frankly, Mrs. Macintosh, I feel like a complete idiot—"

"Did you know that you have two auras, Deputy Jenkins? I've never seen anything like this before. Come right in here, and we'll do an examination."

"I've been having some unusual experiences, Mrs. Macintosh," he said.

"I'll bet," she said, chuckling, "You're not a multiple personality are you? Either that or you're possessed. Can you turn your neck 360 degrees? Just kidding. I loved that movie."

As they entered the kitchen, he was met by the most wonderful aroma he'd ever smelled. Must be the fritters.

"Let's take a look at those auras, shall we?"

She sat him down in a window seat. He could see out into the backyard: huge maple trees, the biggest tree house he'd ever seen in one of them. She took his cap off, and massaged his forehead. He almost jumped, as her hands were icy cold.

"Talk to me, Deputy," she said. "Don't be bashful. You've been having some unorthodox experiences. Tell mama all about them."

The hands had the effect of an emotional laxative. "I've seen Jerry's life pass before my eyes, among other things," he said, feeling as if he'd just told her about his bashful kidney.

"What sort of other things?"

He told her about the spat Egge had with his wife and about the fat girl's mother and the public display of affection scene at the school. And about how he knew who Jerry's parents were before he called Silver Bay.

Dave tried to get up, but she pushed him back down. "I was thinking of talking to Father Mischke," he said.

A momentary spasm of pain crossed her face when he mentioned the priest's name. She sat down next to him, crossed her legs, and said, "The awful way Jerry died jarred the train off the tracks if you'll pardon the metaphor. And believe me, he's not the only departed undulating in the ether. Obviously he feels some sort of connection with you."

"We played softball together. That's the only tie I know of."

She looked at him like a homicide detective who knew he was hiding something. He hadn't told her about Sheriff McCloskey. "Let's get going then," she said, "time is a'wasting."

"Don't you want to change clothes?" he said.

"We don't have time, Deputy," she said. "I'll just get some shoes."

* * *

They walked back to the sheriff's office where he'd left the Jeep, Mrs. Mac clinging to his arm. Warning her about the door on the passenger side, he dusted off the upholstery and laid an old flannel shirt he got from the back on the seat for her to sit on.

On the way out of town, she went into a discourse about how Ronald Reagan had planned public policy based on astrological readings. When he braked for the stop sign on Meade, he could see Blaze Forman out in front of his bank poking his finger into a farmer's chest. Dave thought it was Ray Miller, but he wasn't sure.

They drove by the Legion on the right. Mrs. Randall, Olive's mother, was unlocking the outer door. Besides bartending, she also cleaned the place. He waved; she didn't see him. Mrs. Mac was still blathering on about how Mrs. Reagan was the greatest first lady of them all and didn't seem to notice Mrs. Randall at all.

The sun had come out, causing Dave to don his shades to avoid squinting as they drove down County Road 185 and made the turn onto the cow path which led to the murder scene. As he arrived at the clearing and shut down the Jeep, he noticed the John Deere had finally made it out of the mud pit and was dueling exhausts with another one as they plowed the adjacent field.

Mrs. Mac put her hand over her mouth as if she were about to be sick.

"Are you all right?" he said. Stupid of him, he'd been so embarrassed about talking to a psychic that he'd forgotten she'd discovered the body.

"I'll be fine," she said. "Mind over matter. I'm a professional." She got out and began walking around, swinging her arms as if she were power walking. She looked up into the trees, and she knelt down, fingering the wet grass and weeds.

Suddenly she stopped and stared right up into the sun. Didn't she know she could hurt her eyes? He moved closer. No wonder, her eyes were rolled back into her head.

She began chanting, "I smell sweat, dirty socks, talcum powder and rosin. Boys are yelling, 'Belt that tater,' 'We got ducks on the pond,' 'that one's a big can of corn,' 'watch fer the suicide squeeze,' and 'whatta rubber arm.' I see a curly-headed, broad-shouldered young man wearing a baseball uniform."

Her eyes returned to normal. "Do you know anyone who plays baseball professionally who might have curly hair? It's so curly it may be permed. He's wearing a skirt with that uniform! But it's a man, I know it's a man!" Her heels were sinking into the soil, so she took them off and tucked them under one arm.

"The only professional baseball player in these parts was Harry's son, Mel," he said, "but he got hurt and they dropped him."

"Do you have anything that belonged to Jerry?" she said.

He had to think for a minute, then remembered the pipe.

"This is rather embarrassing. I picked up the pipe when I was searching Egge's den, put in my pocket, and forgot about it."

He handed her the pipe, which she examined. "Just the thing. I need to keep this while we're out here. Let's follow the trail of the killer. Do you remember where it was?" She reached down and put her shoes on.

"Sure thing. We've got it marked off." He led her through the trees, trying to keep away from the wet areas.

"I come out here quite often, for the birds you know," she said. "You'd be surprised at the variety. Just the other day I saw a white-breasted nuthatch—" She put her hand to her lips as if she were about to throw up.

"What's wrong, do you feel ill?"

"I just remembered. I saw the nuthatch just before I discovered Jerry's body."

He patted her on the back and she leaned up against his shoulder, then her expression changed and she stood bolt upright. "I'm getting something, Deputy," she said.

"Something about the murder?"

She held the tips of her fingers against her temples. "It's a man...a very confused man. He does drugs, as the kids say."

"Is it the murderer?"

"I think so. He has a number of associates. Children, they're children. Good God, this is awful. He has sex with the children!"

"We have some evidence that—"

"He lures them in with a false sense of outrage. He was a veteran...No, that's not right. He wears fatigues, I was thrown for a moment. He was a protestor against the Vietnam War—our man was an agitator."

Mrs. Macintosh visibly shivered. "One of the children has a very unusual first name. Something about the weather. Rainy, no that's not it. Stormy. Could it be Stormy Guck?"

He stopped short. "You say Stormy has something to do with this killer? She's my paper girl!"

If this were true, Stormy could have been the one who slashed his tires.

"I'm positive. I'd bring her in and talk to her if I were you."

"Mrs. Macintosh, I need probable cause. Harry'd take away my badge if I did something like that."

Mrs. Macintosh sat on a tree stump.

He said, "You're going to get your wrapper wet. Here, let me put my coat over that."

"Oh, it's an old one. Don't bother with it. Couldn't you bring her in on a drug charge? She's intimate with this man, I'll bet he's giving her drugs."

"We've talked to Stormy before, mostly about breaking curfew. I suppose the next time Mingo brings her in I could bridge the topic, if only to watch her reaction. Are you sensing anything about Egge?" he said.

She closed her eyes, fingered the pipe and was quiet for a moment. "Do you believe in an afterlife, Deputy Jenkins?"

He leaned up against a dead tree. "I haven't been to church in a while. I guess I'm more of an agnostic these days after what I saw during Desert Storm."

"Do you see these dead leaves, Deputy? They're mulch. They help regenerate the forest. Everything is cyclical. A leaf is born, it dies, it's reborn in another guise. I think it's sad that you don't believe. You need your religion. But that's neither here nor there. Jerry has found some fellow travellers, one of them an older man; I'd say he was in his sixties when he died. The other man is younger, a suicide. They're searching for redemption." She got up and took him by the arm, leaning into him.

Then it dawned on him that she'd said "suicide."

He said, "Do you have a first name or anything for the suicide? I have a friend whose father killed himself."

"Oh yes, Howard. Could be, I can't be certain."

Although it was the middle of the morning and the sun was shining, he felt as if he were alone in a cemetery on Halloween.

"How about the other man, the older fellow?"

"He's wearing a fishing hat, and a vest. He has a small mustache and his eyes kind of pop out. I have it; it's the old sheriff, Sheriff McCloskey. Now we're getting someplace. There's a rumor that McCloskey killed his wife. He'd need to compensate for that."

Which would explain the vision at Evergreen Cemetery. If he believed this shit. "Could you talk to Jerry, Mrs. Macintosh?"

"I wish you'd call me Gigglebox, or Martie. All my older friends call me Martie. I could try to talk to Jerry, but I need my implements. I have to hold the séance under controlled circumstances, and we'll need three or four other participants. It's better if they're people Jerry knew. Also, it's very expensive. Four hundred dollars. Do you have four hundred dollars?"

He should have known this was coming. The Amazing Randi would be rolling around on the ground laughing his guts out.

They stopped on the edge of the slough. "I need to think on this some, Martie. Let's get back to town."

She seemed offended. "You expect to be paid for your work, don't you, Deputy? It's not so much the money. If you don't respect yourself, no one else will. And so I charge four hundred dollars for séances, with no exceptions, even for you."

As they headed back toward the Jeep, Mrs. Mac's face scrunched up, her eyes crossing just a bit.

"I'm getting something else," she said. "I see a very beautiful girl. She's a banker. Could that be right? She's not just beautiful, she's very intelligent, and her name is Mary Beth, no Mary Lou, that's it."

Mrs. Mac appeared to be even more pleased with herself than she had when she'd sensed the curly-headed man wearing the skirt.

"Mrs. Macintosh, I think you're getting crossed signals." He stared down at his shoes like a penitent schoolboy. "Mary Lou is a girl I knew in high school who wouldn't give me the time of day."

"You don't mean there's someone else besides Annie Kline? I've always felt that you and Annie Kline were an ideal couple. Men! You don't know what you've got until you lose it. That girl is so considerate; she even remembered my birthday. None of the other boarders ever remember my birthday. What happened with this Mary Lou person?" she asked, moving in closer.

"Her father is Blaze Forman."

"God forbid. You must be a glutton for punishment. Wouldn't have surprised me a bit to find his mangled body in the woods, excuse me for saying so."

They were back at the clearing where Egge had been killed. She was looking out into the field at the dueling tractors with her hand over her eyes in kind of a scouting pose.

Mrs. Mac crossed her arms and stepped back just a bit, assessing him. "Tell you what I'm going to do. If this Mary Lou person is so important to you, I'll sell you a potion. I'll feel like a traitor to Annie, but money's money. Fifty-five dollars for the potion. Your money back if it doesn't take."

Her feet must have hurt, for she'd taken off her shoes again. She was holding them by the straps, kind of swinging them like a lariat.

"I don't believe in potions, Martie. That man you were talking about... If you were going to speculate, who do you think the man was?"

She gave him back the pipe and he put it in his windbreaker pocket. She put her shoes back on and stomped back to the Jeep with a kind of hemorrhoidal gait. "Talk to that wife of Egge's and those awful children," she said. "I'll bet those sociopaths had him killed for his insurance. Find the boy in the baseball uniform."

Another suspect. But the only evidence he had against Mel Kline was a matchmaking psychic, and Harry would take a rifle off the rack in his office and pop him like a carnival balloon if he even suggested Harry's own son might be involved in the murder.

As he drove Mrs. Macintosh home, he put his hand in his pocket and touched the pipe. The movie was scrolling again and he had to pull over and stop the Jeep.

Egge, dressed in suit and tie, was sitting at his desk, looking at the clock. It was eight o'clock. *I hate my job,* he said to himself, *been here since six this morning.*

A man and a woman were seated across from Egge. The man looked like a rough customer, short-sleeved golf shirt, sunburned, tattoo of an eagle on his right forearm. "I can't believe these grades," the woman said. "A 'D' in geography. She's always loved geography."

"All kids go through a rebellious stage," Egge said.

"Never got over it myself," the rough customer said.

Egge laughed. "I know what you mean."

"Were you involved in the movement?" the rough customer said.

"What movement is that?" Egge said.

"The sixties. The fight against oppression and tyranny."

"I marched. Somebody took away a cop's revolver. Some other idiots burned a dog."

The man laughed derisively, shaking his head. Hairy chest, big, meaty, woodchopper's hands. "Man, you don't got any credibility."

"You don't *have* any credibility," Egge said.

The big man looked as if he were going to come over the desk after Egge.

"Was that an epileptic fit, or did you have another vision?" Mrs. Mac said.

He told her about what he'd seen. "Sounds like the man in the dress," she said. "I'll bet the girl with the poor grades was Stormy."

Dave felt a back headache coming on. "This is all so..."

"Frustrating?"

"Yeah, I guess that's the word. If Jerry is really trying to help me find his murderer, why doesn't he just tell me who did it?"

"Spirits rarely talk to mortals directly. Except in the Dickens stories and others of that ilk. It would scare them too badly. Visions are like dreams and we all have dreams. Sometimes we even see things in the daytime, mirages in the desert, hallucinations when we're overly tired."

"You didn't answer my question, Martha."

"I don't think he knows who killed him. If he were going to talk to a living person, it would be someone like me who knows the ups and downs. When he's ready, he'll talk through me."

When he got back to town, he dropped Mrs. Macintosh off at home, and he stopped off at the office to go over the Louisville Slugger again.

He checked the baseball bat out of the evidence room, got out a rag, and started rubbing some of the blood away from the sweet spot. As he rubbed, the initials "M.K." began to show. This didn't make any sense. If Mel Kline had killed Jerry Egge, why would he leave the baseball bat with his initials on it behind?

*   *   *

The pink room at the sheriff's office was ordinarily used for interrogation purposes because somewhere Harry Kline had heard that the color pink soothed potential violent behavior, which was kind of strange because Harry had also agreed to let Mrs. Travis's art class do a mural of Custer's last stand on one of the walls. It had started snowing, which, along with the pink, put Dave in a mellow mood.

A picture window faced the Immaculate Conception Catholic Church. He was staring out that window, remembering his first confession when he had taken the little blue book with all of the sins in it into the confessional. It was dark inside the confessional, but after his eyes adjusted to the light, little Dave was able to review the whole book with the Father, holding up the line for at least a half hour. If he ever went to confession again, he'd have to tell Father Mischke what he'd just done with Mrs. Macintosh. Probably a sacrilege. Father'd have to get a dispensation from the Pope to forgive him.

The buzzer on his phone went off and he picked it up. "It's me, got the results on that statistical analysis you asked me to do. There's one chance in ten million that there'd be initials beginning with 'SYZ' on Egge's back and a man named Szymanski belonging to the NASSP."

"You don't say? How did you figure that out, if you don't mind my asking?"

"According to the Mormons, there are only three hundred Szymanski families living in the United States, and the literature from the NAASP claims 20,000 members. I'd say it's quite a coincidence that one of them has a Polish name beginning with the letter 'SZY'. JESSICA concurs by the way."

"Really? Well, that clinches it."

"I knew you'd think so. Gotta go, going to school for a change. Have to prove to those ninnies once again that I'm in charge of my own destiny."

"Good luck on that."

Dave hung up the phone and it immediately buzzed again.

"Is this Deputy Jenkins?" the caller said.

"Yes, sir. What can I do for you?"

"This is Del Syzmanski in Steubenville, Ohio. I understand you've been trying to reach me."

The man had a gravelly voice, sounded like something out of *The Godfather*.

"Yes, sir. We're investigating the murder of a high school principal named Jerry Egge. Some evidence we found indicates that the murder may have been a case of mistaken identity."

"And what does this have to do with me?"

"Ah, we were given a name similar to yours and you were on the membership list of the NASSP. We'd like to know if any of your students have ever tried to—"

"No, I was a disciplinarian, Deputy Jenkins, but I think most of my students realized it was for their own good."

"You were never threatened, no one ever tried to assault you?"

"Oh, an occasional boy tried, but times were different then, if you get my drift."

"Gee, Mr. S., you sound like *my* high school principal."

"If that's all, Deputy, I'd like to get back to my friends."

"That's all. Thanks for your time, sir."

Dave hung up the phone. Kind of a stupid idea that one. What the hell, though, Son of Sam had been caught because of parking ticket. A guy had to check every possibility.

When Bronson arrived at 9:45, Dave could hear Shirley, simultaneously tapping away at her computer, greet him. Dave's hackles rose, sweat emerged on his upper lip, and his stomach turned suddenly sour.

Shirley showed Bronson to the pink room where Dave stood, still looking out the window. Bronson, who was dressed like a detective from film noir in his double-breasted, pinstriped suit with pleats, apologized for being late.

They shook hands, Bronson squeezing a little too hard, then took seats opposite each other at the conference table. Bronson said, "We had a walkout this morning over the dumbest thing you could imagine. I'd be kind of proud of my students if they stood up to me on matters of curriculum or scheduling differences, but wearing hats in the classroom? Common sense should tell them they can't wear hats in the classroom. About two hundred of them went out, and when I threatened to have them make up a day after school got out, a hundred or so went back in, but the others stayed out, even when it started snowing. We had to take attendance, pull their cards, with the help of some of the teachers who had their prep periods, and start calling their parents. Mindy and Sylvia were about half finished when I left."

Dave pulled his USS Lake Champlain baseball hat down over his eyes. "Well, Chuck, I know what you mean. We see a lot less respect in our line of business, too, these days, especially from teenagers. I appreciate your loaning me that office."

Bronson's upper lip was very red and he kept flicking at it with a wadded up tissue. "Surely, just let me know when you need it again."

The words *Adulterer!* and *Baby raper!* kept occluding Dave's mind, like specks of sand lodged in his eye. He shook it off. Had to appear dispassionate. "I kind of enjoyed myself," he said. "I got a chance to look in on Debbie Meyer's class. It was as if I'd had some experience at it. I've always felt I'd maybe make a good teacher."

Bronson wiped his forehead with his handkerchief. "Yes, Egge was a big Shakespeare fan as well. My first year on the job, we took the wives down to the Guthrie to see Hamlet."

"That's a long one, isn't it?"

"Five hours. Thought it would never get over and we had to fight rush hour traffic on the way back."

The superintendent looked as if he hadn't shaved at all that morning, kind of like Richard Nixon in his debate with J.F.K., the one that had lost the election, which Dave seemed to know about for some reason, almost as if he'd been alive then. The super was very nervous, clicking his pen in and out. He caught himself and put it back into his upper left pocket. A pocket protector would have helped—an ink smear seemed to be expanding as if his pen was leaking.

Did the ink smear go with the pencil that had moved by itself and with the visions? What would Mrs. Mac think of this kettle of lutefisk? He wrote it in his notebook.

Dave was starving to death. He was always hungry these days. Seems as if he was eating for two. "Excuse me for a minute, Chuck." Dave buzzed Shirley. "Shirley, can you run over to the Super Valu and pick me up a sub sandwich? Corned beef if they have it. Thanks."

The super loosened his tie. "Before we get started, Deputy Jenkins, I'd like to clear something up. I realize I may have put myself in an untenable position because I neglected to tell you about Jerry's wife."

Bronson was obviously a consummate politician, revealing only as much as he thought Dave already knew.

"Anything else you left out, *Chuck*? Now's the time to tell me, if there's something else you forgot."

"No, not that I can think of. What is this, Deputy—?"

"You're a suspect is what this is." Dave let the words drift down on Bronson like ashes on the people of Pompeii. "We have an eye witness who saw a tall, broad-shouldered man run into the woods, just before the murder. And there was that time you had that fight with Jerry."

"I've heard of this kind of thing before," Bronson said. "A successful man is resented by—" Bronson finally noticed the expanding stain, withdrew the ink pen from his pocket and threw it in the wastebasket.

"Yeah right, you're being framed."

"Let me explain my situation with Mrs. Egge," Bronson said, his voice getting higher again. "She worked as a library aide at the school, and one day we got to talking about our children. She was so easy to talk to, and it just came out how unhappy she was in her marriage."

"That so?"

"My wife, Emily, and I got married because we had to."

"There's another thing, *Chuck*," Dave said. "What about Jerry's going to the school board about your affair? We have reason to believe that he was about to do just that."

Shirley popped in and out, leaving the sub on a paper plate and a can of Pepsi.

"You should excuse me, Chuck. I didn't get any breakfast." He took a bite, keeping his eye on Bronson, who was gripping the heavy yellow ashtray on the conference table as if it were a life buoy. The sandwich tasted bland. Why the hell had he ordered corned beef? He hated corned beef!

"I—I wasn't aware that he was going to the school board. Jerry never would have jeopardized his family by getting our indiscretion in the newspapers."

Dave clenched his jaws. "Little indiscretion, eh? Let me get this straight. You just implied that you and Mrs. Egge had the greatest love affair since..."

Bronson pushed back his chair and crossed his arms over his chest. "I think I better call my lawyer, Deputy."

Dave took a swig of Pepsi, trying to wash the taste of corned beef out of his mouth. Unusual tastes these days. If he didn't know better he'd think he was pregnant.

"Why don't you just tell me where you were when Egge was killed?"

"I don't know. Probably at school. I make it a point to be the first one there."

Should he show him Olive's pants now, or let him dig himself a deeper hole?

"We checked, *Chuck*. Your secretary says you didn't arrive until ten thirty that day. Would you like to try again? It's only been four days."

"I don't like your tone, Deputy."

"Please don't report me to the sheriff, *Chuck*. I promise I'll be good."

Bronson tried to grin. The smile looked more like a twitch. "I may do that. I have an alibi, although I'd rather not let it get out. I was with Mrs. Egge at the time they say Jerry was killed."

"That would be rather like a wife testifying for her husband, *Chuck*."

"We were at the Bluebird Motel in Crookston. They know us; we've been there on a regular basis. I've already checked it out, and they'll testify, Deputy."

"Anything else you'd like to tell me about?" Dave said. "This is your last chance." He finished his sub and washed it down with another swallow of Pepsi.

"What do you mean?"

"Mrs. Egge thinks Jerry had himself killed. *Hired* it done. Now if you're the smart man I think you are, *you* could have made a discreet phone call or two—"

"That's stupid," Bronson said. "I don't have a lot of time, Deputy, and you're wasting what little I have. If there's nothing further, I'll be—"

"I'd really like to do that liaison thing," Dave said. "I don't know about the money, though. Hardly seems worth my while."

"I thought we had a deal. Is this a shakedown, Deputy?"

"Not hardly. Can you explain these, *Asswipe*?" Dave threw the panties at Bronson hitting him in the face. They bounced off and landed on the floor. Bronson stared down at them as if they might explode, then put his hand to his chest, breathing heavily.

"We found a document in Jerry Egge's safety deposit box that says you had sex with Olive Randall. That's her name on the band of those panties. Now, if that's not a motive, I've never seen one."

Bronson smiled through the sweat. "This isn't evidence. My attorney would laugh this out of court and—"

"You can go, *Chuck*. I'll be checking on that alibi, don't you think I won't. And if you're lying, you better get your toiletries together, cause you'll be spending some time in the hoosgow, if you're familiar with that word."

"You'll rue the day—" Bronson reached down and swept the heavy ashtray off the table and it crashed to the floor, scattering cigarette butts and ashes every which way, then he turned on his heel and stalked out the door, not looking back. Shirley said, "Good day, Mr. Bronson." Bronson ignored her.

Dave had been about to go over the table after Bronson. So damn sure nobody could touch him. He had a feeling he'd have done okay against the guy, despite his size. Kind of wanted to test himself.

After Bronson left, Dave reflected for a moment, then wrote two words in his notebook, next to what he'd written about the ink blotch on Bronson's shirt, "corned beef". Then he picked up the phone and called Mingo, who had been on duty last night and was most likely trying to sleep.

"Yeah! What the hell you want?"

"Sorry to wake you, Dude. I need you to check out an alibi for me. Bronson says he was doing an all nighter with Egge's old lady at the Bluebird Motel in Crookston at the time Egge was killed."

"What time is it?"

"It's early. I'll get Lucille to handle it."

"Nah, I'm awake. Anybody who needs more than three hours sleep is a wiener."

"If you're sure. When you're through there, I want you to get a search warrant for Miles Krueger's farm house, and pick up every shoe you can find."

"Including the ladies'?"

"Jeez. You talk to Freddie Cochran yet?"

"Negatory. Too much else on my plate. As a matter of fact, my plate runneth over."

"When you're through with the alibi and the shoes, I want you to give Freddie Cochran first priority. Grill him about his problems with Jerry Egge, I keep hearing that boy's name."

"Might take me a while to track him down."

"Want to take the Jeep?"

"No thanks, I'll take my 4X4. I'd like to get there."

Everybody was a comedian. As he was hanging up the phone, there was a knock on the door. Lucille.

"Come in, Lucille. How'd the interview with Bronson's wife go?"

She took one of the conference chairs opposite him. Her hair was mussed and her face was flushed. Her uniform looked as though she'd worn it in a sauna. "It was kind of embarrassing, Deputy Jenkins. I'm sure I was blushing every minute."

"Why, was she angry?"

"Hardly. She says she and Mr. Bronson have an open marriage, that she was well aware of all of his extramarital excursions, as she put it, and that she'd been involved in a few of them herself. Menage a trois, she called it."

"I'll be damned. Tell you what you do now. You call her back quick and see if she can substantiate the bastard's alibi. He just told me he was with Mrs. Egge at the Bluebird Motel in Crookston the morning Egge bought it. If their marriage is so open, there's a chance he told her where he was going."

"Do I have to?"

Chapter 10

The Sheriff's Boy

"Always suspect everybody."
— Charles Dickens

After the Bronson interview, Dave asked Harry to join him in his Jeep on the morning rounds. As they drove by the Wal-Mart construction site, monster Caterpillar graders drowned out the organ music coming from the fundamentalist church across the way. The yellow machines reminded Dave of enormous junkyard dogs, snarling and snapping at each other, as they fought over a bone.

"Dja hear Warner's hardware is closing down?" Harry said. "Don Warner says he's getting out while the getting's good."

Dave slapped his hand on the dashboard. "There goes the next generation." Warner had six daughters, ranging in age from fourteen to twenty-one.

The Wal-Mart store was another bone of contention between Dave and Hildegard. He'd been opposed, arguing that the store would kill the downtown area, but Hildegard had decreed the store would bring jobs to Soldier, which, along with all of the Red River Valley, had been suffering through flood, crop disease, and low prices for ten years now, so the town board had rubber-stamped her decision.

Harry was chain-smoking, having just lit a cigarette from the old butt, which reminded Dave he should check at the Super Valu to see if he could find anyone else besides that shit Harley Barnhouser who smoked Old Golds. A teenager squealed out in front of the Jeep, almost daring Dave to race, but he just ignored the kid, preoccupied by what he had to tell Harry about his son. Somewhere a car backfired, or else, somebody was shooting somebody, but Dave continued down Pickett, his left foot drumming the floor mat.

"Goddamned dandelions all over the place," Harry said. "Can't get rid of the motherfuckers. You'd think the frost would kill the bastards." He was quiet for a moment, then said, "How'd the Bronson interview go?"

Dave made a U-turn at the deserted railroad terminal and headed back toward Meade.

"He's guilty as hell of statutory rape, if nothing else. I don't expect him to cooperate much more, though. He mentioned a lawyer and it sounds like he's got a pretty good alibi. Says he was at the Bluebird Motel in Crookston with Mrs. Egge at the time Egge was killed. I've got Mingo checking on it."

He glanced over at Harry, who tried to open the window on his side, but gave up when he realized the handle was broken.

"Bronson could've hired it done," Harry said.

"That's what Hildegard thinks."

Dave took a left on Meade, cutting off a Winnebago just coming out of the Amoco Station, and headed south toward Evergreen cemetery.

Harry said, "If Superintendent Bronson has an airtight alibi, we're right back where we started. Hildegard wants this case solved."

"We're in this together, Harry," he said. "Did I tell you she gave me till tomorrow?"

Harry slapped his forehead. "That's right, tomorrow's that goddamn press conference. I'd rather have my fingernails plucked."

It was cold and overcast. Dave rolled down his sleeves and buttoned them. "Got something new, Harry. I found the initials 'M.K.' under some blood on the baseball bat."

"M.K.? Miles Krueger? Nah, he doesn't care anything about baseball. Maybe his son? Lester could be his middle name."

"Harry."

Harry's face took on a sudden awareness. "You've got to be kidding...You think my son was involved somehow?"

For once the light at the intersection of Meade and the road to Climax was working, and Dave cruised through on green. "Did Mel have a Wayne Terwilliger bat?"

"I'd forgotten he had that thing," Harry said. "We went down there to the Dome for a game once, and Twig was the only one who was nice to my kids. Mel's birthday was coming up, I thought it would make a nice present."

Harry had moved over with his back against the door. Dave wondered if he should warn him about that lock. When he got to the cemetery, he made another U-ball and headed back toward downtown.

Dave glanced over at Harry, then back at the road. "I'm going to have to talk to Mel. If only to find out what happened to the bat."

They were driving by a vacant store, across from the town hall and the firehouse. Another goddamned graffiti artist had painted "Michael Bolton sucks" on the windows since Dave had seen it last.

Harry lit another coffin nail and reached over, shutting off the ignition. Dave pulled over to the curb. "You're just doing your job. There's something else, though, Dave." He took another drag on his cigarette, the ash flaring up. "This is hard for a father...to even bring up. I was young once myself...I remember...I know about Annie. I need to know what your intentions are."

The windshield was beginning to fog, so Dave reached up and wiped a spot clear with his sleeve. "Annie and I are just buddies, Harry. I don't know what they told you but—"

"She was crying this morning. I can never stand to see her cry. She's so beautiful, I can't really believe I ever had anything to do with bringing her into the world. When I asked her what was wrong, she told me all about you two. I was kinda surpised, she's never told me anything about boys before."

Harry picked at the calluses on his hands, then turned to meet Dave's eyes. "Annie was always my favorite. You know, a father usually favors his boys, but she was the only one who would go fishing and hunting with me."

"I don't know what to say, Harry. I'm sorry."

"She wants you fired." He reached inside his coat, searching for another cigarette, came back empty. "I told her I couldn't do that, you're the only one who can solve this case. Other than Henderson that is. That man makes me feel inferior, and I don't like to feel inferior."

"I'll go see her tonight, Harry. I have to review the tipline with the new girl—they live together, you know."

"I feel kind of sheepish about this. Like I should at least take a swing at you or something."

"I know you're not afraid of me, Harry. If you want to, you can go ahead and hit me."

Harry sighed, then wound up and belted Dave on the arm about as hard as one of his Navy SEAL mates had done when they'd been jockeying to see who could take the hardest hit. His arm hurt like hell.

Dave restarted the Jeep. On the radio Linda Ronstadt was telling him he was "no good, no good, no good."

"You go ahead and talk to Mel," Harry said. "I'm sure there's a reasonable explanation."

Before Dave could put the Jeep in gear, Harry's door popped, and he almost fell out. Harry shut it and moved over cautiously.

"I'm really sorry, Harry. Annie's my best friend. I wouldn't hurt her for the world."

"Forget about it. Just think about the consequences next time, and watch your drinking."

Harry wouldn't be so understanding if he knew Dave was thinking of giving Mary Lou Forman a call. The woman was plaguing his mind so much he could smell her face powder and perfume when he woke up in the morning. He craved that woman. She could be expecting triplets and he'd still have the hots for her.

Dave dropped Harry at the office and headed over to the Kline residence on the corner of Peach and Wheat Field Lane, where he parked his Jeep.

Mel must have seen the Jeep through the window because he came hobbling down the porch steps, still limping from the baseball injury. Since it was kind of cold for April, Mel was wearing a flannel, black and red hunting shirt over a smiley-faced T-shirt. The limp gave Dave an idea. The crime team should be able to tell from the casts the BCA made at the scene whether the murderer had an injury to one leg.

"Want to go for a walk?" Dave said.

Mel nodded. He didn't seem to need a reason, any excuse to get out of the house. Spotty work up at the high school.

As they walked, neither said a word. One of Mel's more appealing attributes was that Dave never felt the need to talk around him. They walked down Peach, past Veteran's Park, where a young mother was painting iodine on the knee of a kid who must have fallen off a swing—several other little curtain climbers were watching, fascinated. They walked past the convent, where a nun was working in the garden.

"What's red and white and black all over?" Dave asked.

"A wounded nun," Mel said, laughing. "That one don't work. They don't wear the habit no more."

They walked past the firehouse. Some of the sopping-wet volunteers were washing the truck.

"Whyn't you volunteer for the fire department?" Dave asked.

"They don't take crips," Mel said. They both laughed.

They turned left, heading south on Meade. Dave's mind began to drift. Should he call Mary Lou, just to say "hi"? Would she even remember who he was?

"What's that you say?" Mel said.

"Nothing. Don't mind me. I've got a lot on my mind."

Before they got very far on Meade, it started raining hard, so they ducked under the awning at the Super Valu, which reminded Dave he needed to talk to the manager. Mel did some browsing while Dave asked Pete Funk if he knew of anybody who smoked Old Golds. Pete said he'd ask the checkout clerks and get back to him. By the time he'd finished talking to Pete, the rain had let up and he and Mel continued on toward the south side of town.

They got as far as Andy's Diner before the smell of ham and eggs sucked them in off the street. Doc Bailey, the vet, and George McCready were playing their daily game of cribbage at the counter. Two old guys in one corner were yelling at each other about the school referendum, not so much because they were angry but because they were hard of hearing.

Mel had a two or three day growth of beard. He was rubbing his hand back and forth over the stubble. No hat, his black hair wet and hanging in his eyes; he took after Brenda with her close-set eyes and high cheek bones. He was big enough to play defensive lineman for the Vikings, very little fat on him. Dave wouldn't want to tangle with him.

They ordered coffee.

"So, Bud, whatcha gonna do now that you got dumped from the team?"

Mel always spoke in a whisper, almost as if he were telling a ghost story before a fire on a Boy Scout outing. "I don't know, the school thing seems like a dead end since I ain't got a degree. I was thinking of doin' what you did. Maybe join the service or somethin', then fall into somethin' when I get out, maybe run against you fer sheriff. What was it like in the SEALs?"

Dave cleared his throat. "Turned me into a killer. Very rigorous, swimming through mud with your hands and feet tied, underwater demolition, swinging from vines in tsetse infested jungles." He took a sip of coffee.

"Whyn't you make a career of it?"

"Too childish for a level-headed sort like myself. Your skivvy checks—you know SEALs don't wear underwear. Your Duponting—that's their idea of fishing, with a grenade. Besides, I was never going to be any Meateater anyway."

"What's a Meateater?"

"That's the elite of the elite, the toughest nut in the bushel."

Mel stirred some sugar into his coffee and said, "I don't suppose they'd want me either with my bum leg."

"Have you ever thought about a civil suit?" Dave ran his finger down the menu, which he knew like his own social security number.

"Nah, I had to sign a waiver when they signed me. It's different in the minors. I don't want nothin' that I didn't earn anyway."

The waitress smiled at Mel as she walked by, and Mel smiled back. Stormy Guck. Dark, pencil thin, boyish haircut, thirteen or fourteen earrings in each ear, way too young. He'd forgotten about what Mrs. Mac had said about her. Might as well have, still didn't have any reason to interrogate her. He had a feeling he'd do better with Olive.

"Well, let me know if I can do anything for you, a recommendation maybe," Dave said, grasping Mel's arm.

Mel searched Dave's face. He must be thinking *it's not every day Deputy Sheriff David Jenkins invites me for a walk.*

"Mel, let me tell you what we got here," he said. "That baseball bat we found at the scene, it's got the initials 'M.K.' on the fat part, and your dad says you had a Terwilliger model just like it. Do yah know what happened to it?"

The two old guys got up and paid their tab. Stormy, who was bussing a table, dropped a cup on the floor, and it shattered into hundreds of little pieces. Momentarily everybody watched as she swept up the mess.

"Johnny Logan had lots of those, and plenty of guys have the initials 'M.K'."

The ceiling fan, which was on for some reason, whirred and hummed, making it awfully hard for Dave to hear Mel's whispered rebuttal.

Trying to assume a tone of friendly disbelief, Dave said, "You also match the description of a suspect a witness saw going into the woods just before the estimated time of the murder."

For the first time Mel spoke above a whisper and his voice cracked as if he were about to cry. "Look, the last time I saw that baseball bat was in jr. high when I played for Egge. It was my lucky bat. One day I got two homers with it, and afterwards, when I went to take it home, it was gone. I'd know it, though, if you'll show it to me. You see, I used to hone down the handle for better bat speed, even when I was in jr. high. I'd know my bat all right."

Probably the longest speech Mel had ever given, but the slouch was gone and Dave would bet, if he were a lawyer, that this man would make an awfully good witness.

"We'll show it to you," Dave said. "So how did you get along with Egge, Mel? We heard you had some hard feelings 'cause he

recommended you sign that contract instead of going to school."
He drained his cup, motioning at Stormy for more.

Mel played with the sugar, sifting it back and forth in his
hands. "So?" he said. "He never put a gun to my head. My dad
warned me to settle for a sure thing and go to school, but I would-
n't listen. Who told you I had hard feelings?"

Stormy filled Dave's cup, smiled her Chiclet smile, and wiggle-
walked back behind the counter.

"I really can't say," Dave said. "I want you to check out this picture we found it in one of the yearbooks. Can you tell me about
these other kids?" He handed him the photo.

Mel took the picture and held it close to his eyes. "Les Krueger,
there's somebody who really hated Egge. He was obsessed by
baseball, thought he was gonna be the next Roger Clemens or Jose
Canseco, and Egge wouldn't even let him play once he realized the
kid was going to hurt himself if he did. You know, he lives out
there where Egge bought it."

"Don't I know it," Dave said. "His father gave us the description I was telling you about. Their tractor was stuck in a field at the
time. I tell you what, Mel, the casts of the footprints we found
should clear you. You should go in and get those casts made and
take a peek at the bat to see you can identify it."

Dave left fifty cents for that Stormy girl. Her family probably
needed it.

The defeated look in Mel's eyes changed to a glimmer of mis-
chievousness. "One more thing, Dave," he said. He paused and
licked his lips. "Annie wants me to kick your ass. I can't believe
she's broadcasting this all over town."

Dave tried to remain calm. "I know, so your dad said. You
know how it is, Mel, the thing has a mind of its own."

"Actually I don't know how it is."

What the hell was this? Was the guy telling him he was a vir-
gin? All the guys he knew would make it up before they'd admit
something like that.

"You've got the right idea," Dave said. "Who needs women. If
I had my druthers I'd live out in the woods, only come to town
once or twice a year for salt and sugar."

Two blue-haired old ladies sat down in the booth next to
theirs—Dave had never seen them before. Stormy took their order.

"Kind of like the Unabomber, huh? So what are you gonna do
about Annie?"

"Like I told your dad, I'll see her tonight when Lucille and I go
over the tipline."

"You better, she's my favorite sister."

"Say, you were in the same homeroom as Mary Lou Bronson, right?" he asked, trying to change the subject. "What did you think of her?"

"Extremely fine, but I wouldn't turn my back on her. Everybody thought she was a narc."

Dave toyed with the money on the table, checking the date and the mint location. Nothing but newly minted junk. "I think I saw her coming out of the bank the other day. Thought she was married and living in Chicago."

Mel scoffed. "I'd stick with Annie if I were you. She worships you. Mary Lou Forman is never going to settle for Soldier, Minnesota."

"I guess you're right, but I can't agree with you on Annie. She's like a sister to me."

Mel gave him a dirty look, probably thinking about incest. They got the check and left, Dave heading back to pick up his Jeep, Mel limping toward the sheriff's office to get those casts done.

A call was waiting for him when he got back to the office. Hildegard. She was crying. He'd never heard her cry before, never even knew she had tears ducts. "Something terrible has happened," she said. "I need you to come over here right away. Someone has poisoned Hrothgar and Hagar."

When he got there, she was kneeling in her front yard with Hrothgar's head in her lap. She was wearing a man's fedora hat, a cardigan sweater, and baggy corduroys. Hrothgar didn't look dead. His eyes were closed and he had a look of contentment on his face, as if he'd gone to doggie heaven and was cavorting with the poodles who'd been off limits since his sex life had been nipped in the bud. Hagar was lying over by the dog house. He'd experienced a much more gruesome death if the torn up lawn was any indication. Strychnine poisoning affects the central nervous system, causing convulsions.

"I found them this way when I got up this morning," she said. "You know I've had them since they were just little fellows a day old. Couldn't even see yet—I fed them with a baby bottle. Do you think the children could have done this?"

"Anything's possible, but I doubt it. Maybe if you were still a teacher..."

"Someone could have put them up to it," she said.

"I'll need to take the bodies, Miss Weiss. I'll take them over to the vet. If they used strychnine, there'll be a record."

"I think Charlie Bronson had something to do with this," she said. "He found out that I'd pegged him as the principal suspect in the Egge murder and he was letting me know I'd better keep my mouth shut."

"Not likely, Miss Weiss. Something like that would only make you madder. Everybody in town knows how close you are to those dogs."

She stroked Hrothgar's ears, gently set his head down on the lawn. "I suppose you're right." She stood, dusted off her hands. "Anything new on the murder?"

"I think I know whose baseball bat it was, Lester Krueger is involved somehow, and Mr. Charles Bronson has more of a motive than we thought."

"Mr. Henderson has been calling me every day asking if I'd like him to take charge. I'm thinking he needs a big case to boost his credibility with the higher ups. I told him we'd stick with you a little longer. Are you ready for the press conference tomorrow?"

"As ready as I'll ever be, I guess," he said. "The paparazzi give me the hives."

She rubbed her eyes. "I don't know what I'll do without Hrothgar and Hagar."

He knew better than to suggest she get a puppy.

Chapter 11

Batter Up

"Every man hath a good and a bad angel attending on him in particular, all his life long."
— Robert Burton

Dave pitched Hrothgar and Hagar's stiff carcasses into the back of the Jeep, threw a tarp over the dogs so as not to attract attention, and started the Jeep. He drove down The Angle, past Blaze Forman's fancy glass house—the black sports car in the driveway—turned onto Seminary, then almost immediately took another left onto Reynolds, and finally made a right, pulling up in front of Doc Bailey's office, a one-story building next to the radio station on Zouave Road.

Doc, a bearded mountain man type, paced up and down pounding his fist into his palm. "The bastard that done this ought to have his balls ground up in a vice. This is the second such case in a week. I'd'a called you, but I figured it was just some dumbass trying to kill gophers."

"Looks like strychnine to me," Dave said. "I'll check over at Warner's and see if there's a record."

"You do that," Doc said, easing Hrothgar's remains gently down onto the operating table. Doc raised his brows. "You don't suppose..."

"That there's a connection between what happened with Egge and these poisonings?"

"You're a mind reader."

"Who else had a dog poisoned?"

"Blaze Forman's border collie. He's been known to let Buddie off her leash, and I thought she got into somebody's garden. I gave him what for about it, I guess I should apologize."

Dave shrugged. "I'd say it's too late, Doc. You better hope you never need a loan."

On his way out of the vet's, Dave had a thought. Blaze Forman had money and power, a definite turnoff for some of the local yokels. Hildegard was probably *the* most powerful person in Soldier, although she didn't have a whole lot of the green stuff. And Egge had been right up there, too, on the power register. Was some psycho sending the other two a message? Had the nut sent Egge one before he died, a little more graphic than the smut on the water tower?

When he got back to the office, just as he was about to leave for an appointment at the school, Dave got a call from Mrs. Szymanski in Steubenville.

"Deputy Jenkins, I had to phone you." She sounded upset. "My husband won't listen to reason. You see, several years ago he was involved in a hit and run incident. He insists it was an accident, but he was walking down a dirt road facing traffic and he was hit from behind. Both his legs were broken and he had a bad concussion. I think one of his former students was responsible."

Dave shifted the receiver to his other ear. "Any idea who would do such a thing, Mrs. Szymanski?"

"I'm afraid not, Deputy. Del never talks about his problems. You see, he was at Guadalcanal, and he swears anything after that has to be anticlimactic. He thinks he's indestructible, insists that no one could possibly want him dead, especially his former students."

Dave reached over across the litter on his desk, found his notebook, and wrote *WWII, Szymanski* on a clear page.

"Would it be possible to get a student list for the years your husband was principal?" He drew a circle around what he'd written.

Children were hollering and clunking around in the background. Grandma was babysitting. "I'll try to get that for you, Deputy. It should be quite extensive, though, Del was principal for over thirty years."

Dave drew a box around the circle. "Thank you, Mrs. Szymanski. Anything you can do will help. I'll be looking forward to hearing from you." He hung up the phone, got his baseball cap off the rack, and headed out the door. "Going to the school, Shirley. Don't know when I'll be back." She nodded, not missing a beat in her typing.

* * *

Dave stood in the hall at Soldier High, surveying the activity between classes. The halls were strewn with crumpled notebook paper, gum wrappers, and even pop cans. There were posters advertising an end of the year dance with a rock band called "Man

O' War" providing the entertainment. The word "admission" was spelled with one "s".

Three muted bells, similar to the kind you hear in an elevator, sounded, and a wall of students, all charging in the same direction bore down on him. He flattened himself up against the wall to avoid being trampled to death. Then, when the hall cleared, he headed for the social studies department, where he intended to talk to Conrad White who was on the list Superintendent Bronson had given him. White, the same guy who'd had his headlights bashed in by the estimable Harley Barnhouser, had been accused of assaulting a student.

White looked like every teacher Dave had ever seen—thirtyish, crewcut, horn-rimmed glasses with heavy black frames, the kind of guy you saw on campus during the summer wearing walking shorts with tube tops and brand new sneakers. When Dave entered his room, White was chiding various students to take the gum out of their mouths, remove their hats, and sit down. He finally won the class's full attention, directing them to read the next chapter and answer the questions at the end while he talked to the deputy. Mr. White stepped out into the hall with Dave.

Mrs. Mac had said that if White had killed Egge, she'd come to school naked for a week, wrapped in a large pink bow. Dave lectured her about not being able to ignore any tip. She had looked at him cross-eyed. What a goofy broad.

White turned to give Dave his full attention, his eyes magnified by the thick glasses. "Deputy Jenkins, I'll admit I was rather upset with Jerry Egge for calling in the police over such a minor matter. I'd told that particular student to keep his feet under his chair at least a hundred times, but I didn't actually kick him, I tripped."

Dave pretended to write something in his notebook since this was basically the same thing White had said when he'd confronted him with the original charge.

White glanced over his shoulder to check on his students, then continued. "I'm on the on-site management team. The negotiating committee also. Egge called you in about the supposed assault to embarrass me. He was fighting on-site, said he didn't want to be a glorified office manager. The man had been principal so long he didn't know how to form a consensus."

Over White's shoulder kids were throwing erasers, chalk and pencil stubs.

Unsure whether he should bring this pandemonium to White's attention, Dave said, "I appreciate your cooperation, Mr. White. Is there anything else you can tell me?"

"I have this visceral feeling," White said, "Maybe the murder was drug inspired."

"A visceral feeling, eh?"

"Yes, a gut reaction to use a more blunt expression."

"You and Egge ever have a physical confrontation? I understand the man had quite a temper."

"I suppose you heard about the fight in the parking lot of the Super Valu?"

"I got there just as it was ending."

"No, nothing like that, although he did try to goad me into it."

"Really? What did he say?"

"Said some people just weren't cut out to be teachers. Kind of tough to take coming from a man with only three years experience."

"That all it takes to qualify for principal?"

"Last I checked. I've just about got my specialist's degree. They won't be able to say that about me, though, I've been teaching going on ten years."

"So then, you didn't kill Egge?"

White laughed. He didn't turn red, he didn't flinch.

"Not hardly. The wife wanted me to kill a bat that got into the house the other night. I opened the door and let it out."

"I'll check into that drug thing, Mr. White. I'll let you get back to your students." As he walked away, Dave could hear Mr. White yelling at his students to pick up the debris, which hadn't been there before they'd come into his immaculate room. Mrs. Mac had been right about that one.

On his way past the library, Dave noticed Olive Randall leaning up against the water fountain, one foot overlapping the other, a sandal dangling by its strap. The girl wasn't wearing much: a very short miniskirt, a sleeveless, braless T-shirt. Her blond hair was moussed, combed straight back, and tied in a bun.

"Are you still looking for Principal Egge's killer at the school, David?" she said, shifting her weight. He hadn't seen such a smooth shift since he'd test-driven a brand-new Corvette. "I don't think you'll find him here, David."

"Now, how would you know that?" he said, trying to keep his eyes on hers.

"Intuitively," she said, smiling like a synchronized swimmer. "We women are known for that."

"Shouldn't you be in class, Olive?" The girl would make some of the super models look like knuckle-dragging primates, and she was definitely giving off pheromones. Perhaps he'd been a little rough on Bronson.

"Oh, I just came out here to rendezvous with my boyfriend," she said. "There's so much going on in Home Ec. that Mrs. Clooney can't keep track of everybody. Somethin' must have happened to him." She looked down the hall toward the stairs.

"I've been meaning to talk to you, Olive. Can you make it down to the sheriff's office sometime today? I have something that belongs to you that I want you to identify."

"Sure, I don't work tonight. I can be there around four if that's all right. Are you sure that's all you want, David? I've had my eye on you."

Dave could feel himself start to blush. "Maybe if I were a little younger."

"I like older men. Besides, what are you, twenty-five? That's not that much older."

"I'm a little older than that, Olive."

"Adults have so many hang ups." She touched the top of her head checking for stray curls. "Did you know your friend Howard is helping me study?"

"No, I hadn't heard that."

"He is *so* cute. He probably thinks I'm not good enough for him, though. Just trailer trash, you know." She paused, looking vulnerable. "I'm sorry, it's just that a girl gets typed as soon as she steps in the door around here. I wanted to do well, I really did, but I had to stay home and help my mom with my baby sisters, and I got behind, and the only way I could be accepted was...you know."

"You've got two more years to do better, Olive. Moe can help you."

She bowed her head and slouched her shoulders. "I can't believe he'd want anything to do with me."

Go figure. Here was a girl who could walk into any room, snap her fingers, and have the entire male populace fall at her feet slavering, and she didn't think she was good enough.

"I'll tell you one thing, Olive. If you keep dressing like that, you'll probably scare him away. He'll give you a chance, though. He's the most fair-minded kid I know."

She put a hand on his arm. "I'll try not to corrupt your friend." She moved toward the library, discarding a wooden lavatory pass in a wastebasket along the way.

Dave returned to Egge's office where some messages awaited him: According to Pete Funk at the Super Valu, none of the clerks could finger anyone in particular who smoked Old Golds—he wrote himself a reminder to try the Value Stop. The other message was from Doc Bailey, confirming that Hagar and Hrothgar had died from strychnine poisoning.

He checked his watch—almost time for the period to end—then moved past the library headed for a classroom on the other side of the building.

* * *

Mrs. Grant was one of those neckerchief ladies, at least fifty-five, still wearing those funny glasses attached with a chain—in case she made a sudden move and they jumped off her face, Dave thought. According to Bronson, she was a very strict disciplinarian with the bad habit of pulling the bangs of students who didn't come up with immediate responses to her questions.

Dave hadn't planned on interviewing Mrs. Grant, couldn't think why Bronson had put her on the list of people with a gripe against Egge in the first place. But he figured he could maybe check with her about what Conrad White had said about Egge's fighting on-site management. He had three minutes to interview her since she refused to meet with him in Egge's old office as he'd already blown two appointments.

"I can't believe Mr. Bronson put me on that list," she said. "Over something so foolish. It doesn't really hurt them when I pull their hair. If I'd grabbed a handful and yanked as hard as I could, I could see their point, but tugging at their forelocks is rather like spurring a horse when you want to make him go. I've been doing it for forty years."

"My principal kicked me in the butt once for horseplay in the lunch line."

"You should have reported him."

"He caught my attention. The next time I thought about skylarking I checked to make sure he wasn't around."

She laughed. "What can I do for you, Deputy?"

"Something Conrad White said about Egge having some problems with the faculty."

"Oh, you must mean on-site management. A really good idea, if they'd give us the time to do it. When you teach five sections, you're not exactly in the mood to grapple with the budget after school. I assure you the faculty is very ambivalent about the concept."

"I hear you. Did you kill Jerry Egge, Mrs. G.?"

"Not too blunt, are you, Mr. J.? Physical violence of the kind you're talking about makes me ill. You have my oath that I never touched the man."

"That's enough for me, ma'am. They make it rather difficult for you to do your job these days, don't they?"

"You have no idea, Mr. Jenkins. When I was younger, I swore they'd have to drag me out of here kicking and screaming. This will be my fortieth year, and my last. I'm afraid I'm giving away my age, Deputy."

"Don't let it worry you, ma'am. I never was any good at math." The bell rang and Dave was mugged by a herd of eighth graders arriving for the next class.

He tipped his hat, and she surprised him by winking.

After talking to Mrs. Grant, he went to a pay phone in the lobby and called Warner's Hardware about the strychnine. Don Warner said he had a recent name, but he didn't want to give it over the phone. He'd send it down to the sheriff's office.

Charlie Bronson I'll wager.

Dave dropped another quarter in the slot, punched in Henderson's number. Needed to know if the crime team could tell whether the murderer had a limp.

"And why would you want to know that, Deputy?" Henderson said.

"I found the initials 'M.K.' under some blood on the Louisville Slugger. I'm pretty sure the bat belongs to Mel Kline. It's unlikely that he's our man, though, since he blew out his anterior cruciate ligament while playing minor league ball. I'm trying to eliminate him."

"Sounds reasonable. I'm sure the sheriff is relieved. Does Mel have any idea what happened to the bat, that is, if he didn't use it?"

"He implied Lester Krueger, one of our leading suspects, could've taken it. I've got Mingo out at the farm trying to match Krueger's shoes with the footprints at the scene."

"He has a warrant?"

"I wasn't born yesterday, Larry."

"Don't be so touchy, I was only checking. Most of the time that's what I do, double check and triple check. We'll be expecting the shoes."

"Thanks."

Dave hung up the phone, turned in a circle, then honed in on Fran Ellis's office, a closet next to the principal's. When he arrived, Ellis was on the phone, but when he heard Dave's knock, he immediately made amends to the caller and hung up. They shook hands, and Dave took a seat.

"I suppose you're wondering why I'm not using Egge's office," Ellis said. "Let me tell you, if I tried to move my desk, I'd be even more lost than I am now. You wouldn't believe how complicated this job is. I take care of all the events for senior, junior high and elementary, and we have eleven sports, twelve pretty soon because of gender equity."

Dave took a closer look at the athletic director. He'd been pre-occupied that day in Bronson's office. The man could have been a monk, with the bald spot in the middle of his head, the obligatory paunch and a fondness for brown. He wore his watch on the wrong hand and backwards. Ellis was sucking on what smelled like a cherry cough drop, mixed with the aroma of too much after-shave. There was a picture of an overweight lady with a bad perm on his desk. When Mindy, the principal's secretary, came in with a message, Ellis reached over and turned the picture face down.

Ellis read the note. "Goddamn it," he said, "Level 5 has nixed one of our students. They say he's incorrigible." Ellis put the note in his *in* slot.

"Let me guess, Freddie Cochran, the gun fetisher."

"The one and the only. He goes with one of the nicest little pieces in the school," Ellis said, with a lewd grin. "It's the highlight of my day when they send her in here for not wearing her Maidenform."

Dave perked up at the mention of Olive. "Oh, yes, I ran into Olive just a few minutes ago." He fiddled with his cap. "Er, Mr. Ellis, I need to ask you about Freddie."

Ellis raised his eyebrows. "Excellent athlete when he works at it, I had him out for wrestling one year. His trouble was he wasn't mean enough, and he could never stay eligible. I think he just needs to get older like all of us."

"You think so?"

"I was watching this interview with George Foreman on ESPN last night, and he said that when he was young, he used to mug people. Didn't even know it was wrong. Sometimes I think it's just a matter of defiance of authority. We all do that, don't we, Deputy?" Ellis massaged a tattoo of an anchor on his upper right arm.

"Say, were you in the Canoe Club?" Dave asked, trying to fig-ure this guy out. He could see a single guy like himself talking about Olive that way, but this guy was married. Yet he seemed to really care about Freddie. "I was a Navy SEAL myself," Dave said. "What was your rate?"

"Those days there were no government loans. I went in just when the Cuban missile crisis broke out, thought I was dog meat for sure. Made it to Radioman 2nd class before I got out. Should have stayed in, though, you should see the pensions these days. That's why I'm a teacher, for the pension. But I just couldn't stand the ridiculous hierarchy. If you were second class or over, your index finger curved permanently from holding a coffee cup, and you got calluses on your butt from sitting around doing nothing. I just barely made second class before I got out." Ellis picked up the picture of his wife and put it back in its previous position.

"You forgot to mention the nincompoop ensigns," Dave said.

The telephone intruded on their reminiscences. You could hear a very loud woman on the other end of the phone just reaming Ellis's asshole. Ellis said, "Yes, Mrs. Hackbart," about twenty times, and then, after about five minutes, he finally squeezed in an "I'll look into it, Mrs. Hackbart," and hung up.

"That's the worst part of this job. Those women who think their kid could do no wrong. No wonder they're all on drugs."

"So you don't think Freddie killed Egge," Dave said. "Is there anyone else I should talk to?" He jotted a few notes in his notebook: the reaction to Mindy, the overturned picture, his reference to Olive.

Ellis looked uncomfortable. "I don't want to get anyone in trouble," he said. "I'll tell you what. If anybody should be a suspect, it would be me. Jerry was advocating dropping baseball instead of adding soccer for girls. I couldn't see high school sports without baseball, it's the national pastime, after all. We had some wild yelling matches, let me tell you. Called my wife a moth-eaten poodle." Ellis reached into a drawer and withdrew an autographed ball. It was from the 1956 World Series. He had everybody's signature on the ball: Mickey Mantle, Yogi Berra, Bill Skowron, Hank Bauer, even Casey Stengle. He let Dave touch it, then put it back in the drawer.

"Nice ball," Dave said. "Wish it was mine. You'd think Egge would have been more sympathetic since he used to coach. Too bad I didn't know sooner what a fan you were or I'd have asked you to join our rotisserie league. Funny though, you're the second person in this school who has offered himself as a suspect."

"Gigglebox I'll bet. We're pretty much in the open around here, Deputy. Somebody would have told you anyway." Ellis got up to check out the situation in the office foyer. It was getting crowded.

Dave rose and stood near the athletic director. "You've been most helpful, Mr. Ellis. I'll let you get back to work, looks like you've got quite a crowd out there." They shook hands again, and Ellis crooked his finger at one of the kids waiting in line.

After he left Ellis, Dave drove to the Value Stop to ask Sid Hoffman, a newlywed whom he routinely fleeced during Friday night poker games, if he had any regular Old Gold customers.

Sid was spraying the vegetables with one of those little spritzer bottles. He was blond with his hair combed in a part down the middle of his head, reminiscent of characters Dave sometimes saw in old black and white movies. A long white apron covered his entire torso down to his oxford shoes.

"There's one guy comes in very rarely," Hoffman said. "I remember him 'cause he looks so much like that actor on *Hill Street Blues*, Ed Marinaro, who played for the Vikings. He always pays cash. Why, is he wanted for something? I'll bet I know. This is about the Egge murder. Everybody says it was a big curly-headed guy."

"I didn't say that, Sid. You got my twenty bucks?"

"I can only let you have ten. You know how it is with the new wife and everything. Did I tell you she's pregnant?" Hoffman untied his apron, reached in his wallet and extracted a ten, handing it to Dave. "I'll let you know if he comes in again."

"Thanks, Sid, you can call me on my cellular. Here's the number. Call me as soon as you see him, right? And don't tell anybody about this."

Hoffman smiled. Another blabbermouth.

Dave walked across the street to Andy's Diner. So much was going on his head was spinning. He had to hash things out. Maybe he could get in a couple of at bats during the Dog game tonight— they were playing Barnhouser's team. Probably not, the townspeople would think he was jerking the gherkin.

He got settled in a booth near the can. For once the place was deserted, except for him and Stormy. He looked at his watch. Three-thirty. Stormy served him coffee, then sat down opposite him.

"Are you gettin' your paper all right?" she said.

"Some people complain they never get it. That's bullshit."

She had an undeveloped face: wide forehead, an almost non-existent chin, teeth like Chiclets imbedded in clay. It was a face you had to grow into. Ten years down the road, he was sure he wouldn't recognize her.

"No complaints, Stormy," he said. He thought back to what Mrs. Mac had said about the man who'd been preying on children.

"How's life, Stormy? You getting along better with the folks?"

"Gotta give them half my paycheck. That's the pits."

"You just can't win, Uncle Sam gets mine. How're you and Olive hitting it off?"

"She's not buying me booze if that's what you want to know."

"Just asking. You know it's not good for you. You're still a growing girl. That stuff can really mess up your kidneys."

She laughed. "You oughta know, I seen you drunk."

"I'm of age, not that that's an excuse. I've been meaning to ask, Stormy. You know anything about what happened to my Jeep?"

"I didn't know anything happened to your Jeep. It looks okay to me."

"Somebody slashed the tires, all four of them."

"Too bad."

"Another thing, Stormy. You know anything about any dogs being poisoned?"

Her eyes blinked as if in anticipation of a slap. "I didn't have nothing to do with Miss Weiss's dogs."

"I didn't say anything about Miss Weiss's dogs."

"It's all over town, I think I heard it from the vet. He comes in here all the time to play cribbage."

"Forget that for a moment. Did your teachers ever tell you anything about Vietnam?"

This time it was worse. Her eyes took on the look of a horse being broken to the saddle. She got up and stood next to the table, doing a little inadvertent tap dance. "I gotta get back to work or Andy's gonna fire me. I need this job."

"There's nobody in here, Stormy."

"He says for me to wash the dishes when it's not busy."

Without so much as a by your leave, she turned and practically ran through a door next to the counter. He could hear the sound of water running and dishes and forks clattering together. Have to put the squeeze on her when he found the time. First things first, though. Olive would be meeting him at four. Something unusual was going on with Soldier's teenagers—that was for sure. He wondered how Mingo was doing with Freddie Cochran.

* * *

Mingo and Sheriff Kline were leaning on the doorjamb in Dave's office, Harry munching on a bag of pork rinds, washing them down with an orange pop.

"So you think Billy Bum may have had something to do with this?"

"Not really, but we've got to check him out," Mingo said. "He fits the general description, if you exclude the gray hair."

"Nonsense. Billy is an educated man. We had a long discussion once; told me he went to UCLA before he got drafted into the army. Studied anthropology. He's just got a little case of post traumatic stress is all, they're generally harmless unless they aggravate the condition with dope."

"I'd say he's aggravating the condition plenty with the liquid drug. Can't find him anyway. Been calling down to the shelter two, three times a day, and they haven't seen him since before Egge's funeral."

"Anything on Krueger's shoes?"

"I found three pair that look like they might fit Lester. Sent the whole package to the BCA just a minute ago."

Harry finished the pork rinds, licked his fingers. "What you got going next?"

"Freddie Cochran is due anytime."

Harry tossed the empty bag at Jenkins's overflowing wastebasket. "I'll let you get to it then."

When Harry left, Mingo put his feet up on Jenkins's desk, and began tossing playing cards into his Mountie hat, ruminating on the message on the Egg Man's back. Indian women castrated the enemy after battle to prevent him from reproducing in the afterlife. Perhaps the lettering was similar in intent.

A curse would tend to aggravate the corpse's spirit. Mingo was having a hard time getting clearance from his Cousin Cecil, a bonified Mescalero shaman, to hold the ghost medicine ceremony for Egge. He also had a theological dilemma on his hands: whether it was kosher to allow a woman to watch if he ever got the okay from Cecil. Miss Debbie Meyer, at Soldier High School, had asked him to speak to her ninth grade class on Mescalero culture, and he'd just happened to bring up the ceremony when they'd talked on the phone. She'd wanted to know if she might observe. He really doubted it. Religion was a male prerogative in Mescalero culture.

Freddie Cochran stuck his head in the door of Jenkins's office. "What's crackelating, Chief?"

"Damn," Mingo said when the forty-sixth card caromed off the brim of his hat onto the dusty floor. He'd been close to a new record.

Freddie, a very good-looking boy with jet black hair and extremely white teeth, ignored the swear word, strolled into

Jenkins's office, sat on the edge of a chair, and looked Mingo right in the eye, something Mingo would ordinarily find offensive, if Freddie were another Apache. Freddie, barefoot, painted toenails, no less, was wearing a T-shirt with the message, "I'm a Fuck-up and proud of it," scrawled across the front and a gangsta-style baseball cap tugged way down over his eyes. Rumor had it the boy was gay. Not that that was a big thing with the Mescaleros.

"Thanks for coming, Freddie," Mingo said. "Would you like a soft drink?" Mingo had a grudging respect for Freddie, ever since he'd orchestrated the incident where his 4X4 had been hauled up to top of the Legion.

The boy shook his head no. "Got anything stronger?"

Freddie had a definite trickster mentality, something Indians usually appreciated more than the whites.

Mingo ignored him. "I think you know why I called you in here. Mr. Egge had to expel you for packing a gun at school. Some people seem to think you may not have taken that too kindly."

Folding his arms, Freddie said, "The piece didn't even have a firing pin. I got it from my Grandpa who took it off a dead Nazi. I just brought it to school to scare these creeps who were spreading stories about Olive. I told them once before, but it didn't do no good."

Mingo pushed his chair back and took his feet off the desk. "And Mr. Egge wouldn't listen to your explanation?"

"Scrambled just brought out my record and explained how he had no choice, there were no gray areas where weapons were concerned. He said he'd get me in another school which would really help me. Level 5 is for nut cases, though, so I gave him some shit."

Mingo tugged at his ear, cupped his chin in his hand. He kind of knew how Freddie felt about boarding school. His grandfather had told him horror stories about having to get his hair cut like a white man and go to school out East.

"What kind of shit, Fred?"

"The usual, a couple of crank calls."

"You too, huh?"

"Why, who else called him?"

"Nobody. You know anything about any dead dogs, Fred?"

"Miss Weiss, Banker Forman. You mean there are more of them? Why, you think I had something to do with that?"

"Can't blame me, can you?"

"Look here, Deputy. I might pull a truck up top the Legion, and violate the curfew once in a while, but I don't hurt animals. Sickos start with animals and move on to people. That ain't me, Babe."

"How 'bout your friend, Rita? Would she do something like that?"

"Got me, ask her. I doubt it, though, she lives on a farm."

"How well do you know Lester Krueger?"

"Lester Krueger is a jerk. I wouldn't walk across the street to piss on him if he were on fire."

"How is it I always see him hanging out with you people late at night if he's such a pariah?"

"Olive says it's not nice to treat people like everybody treats Lester."

"Maybe she's right. No one is discriminated against in Apache society. Not even homosexuals." Mingo searched Freddie's eyes. The boy didn't even flinch.

"So then, do you think Lester had anything to do with the Egge murder?"

"Nah, he's all talk. He'd shit his pants if he ever got in a scrap with anything bigger than a chihuahua."

"Our best information says you were in Crookston at the time of Principal Egge's death. Is that the case?"

Freddie crossed his legs, braced his elbows on his knees, and cupped his chin in his hands. "I'm not supposed to leave campus, but you know me, I'm a night owl. And, besides, I got my walking papers. I'm what you might call incorrigible."

"I appreciate your honesty," Mingo said. "Let's try another. You helped Olive spray-paint the water tower?"

"What do you think?"

"Well, I don't know if you've heard or not...The whole town seems to know more about this case than I do...But the murderer spray-painted some nasty shit on Egge's back. Quite a coincidence, don't you think?"

There was a scar through one of Freddie's eyebrows. Could have gotten that in a fight with a bunch of gay bashers.

Freddie smiled as if he were proud of himself. "We used a paint roller on the water tower, Chief."

Mingo glared at the boy. The eyes didn't seem to match, one was smaller than the other, and his eyelids were whispy and off-color. "Word has it that you and Olive were in the woods the morning Egge was killed."

"So? We're out there most every day, me, Rita and Olive play-ing army against some kids from Crookston. It's a gas, you oughta try it. Olive has this thing for one of the guys on the other army. I don't suppose an Indian would care for—"

"As a matter of fact, we do have a similar game. It's called bag-gataway, Little Brother of War, the precursor of lacrosse. Sometimes 1,000 players on each side with the goals miles apart. A game could last as long as three days. The object was to disable as many of your opponents as possible. But the Indians were careful not to get any war paint on the trees where there were any."

"Touché, Chief."

"And you're not jealous of the boy Olive has this thing for?"

Freddie took off his cap and began toying with the one-size-fits-all adjustments. He needed a haircut and he had a bad cowlick.

For once the boy was caught off guard. "No...we're just really good friends."

"You'd die for her and she'd die for you. That about right?"

"Exactly."

"We have some information that the superintendent slept with Olive. Were you aware of this?"

"No chance. She doesn't dig old dudes. She told me she flirted with him once, but that was all. Olive flirts with everybody."

Mingo pursed his lips, wound his finger around a strand of his hair, glanced over at Raquel to see what she thought. The boy seemed like a stand-up kid. If he'd killed Egge, Geronimo was as white as Marcel Marceau. "What's up with you, Freddie? What's with the chip on your shoulder? I've been going over your disciplinary record at the school and—"

Freddie made a moaning sound and slid down in his chair. "I hate school, it's so god-awful boring."

It was so quiet he could hear Freddie's belly rumble.

"When I was your age, I hated everything, too, especially those old Apache grandfathers. Thought they were a bunch of squares. Me and my homies started drinking and taking drugs. The grandfathers said that we should stay away from peyote, it was evil, so, of course, we ate those buttons too. Anyway, to make a long story short, I got it out of my system, realized that the old time religion was part of who I am, and studied up on Athapascan mythology. The white man would do well to take a page from the Indian initiation rites. I learned some of the ceremonies, got to give myself a new name. You know, you white people are stuck with the ones your parents gave you."

"Got any more of those peyote buttons?"

"The elders were right. It was a really bad trip. I have to ask you something, Freddie. Did you kill Principal Egge?"

"Hundreds of times with a needle right between his eyes."

"And besides voodoo? Did you McGwire Principal Egge to death with that baseball bat?"

"I didn't particularly have any use for the man. He was using up perfectly good, breathable air."

"But you didn't kill him?" Freddie shook his head no. "Do you know anything about who did kill Mr. Egge?"

This time the kid flinched ever so slightly. "No, I couldn't kill anyone, and I don't know anything about the murder," he said. "Sounds like some crazy person did it, lots of those running around these days."

"If you did kill Mr. Egge, or if one of your friends did, we can probably plea-bargain down to second degree. I mean if you can prove that he was harassing you. You got into an argument with the man, lost your temper, and brained him with the club, not really intending to kill him or anything. Is that how it went?"

"Everybody knows that Scrambled's face was—I didn't kill him, Chief. Second Degree, third degree or any kind of degree. Read my lips. I didn't do it."

Mingo had a hunch. "What does your dad do, Fred?"

Freddie yawned, reversed his cap. "What dad? Mom says he was a long-haul trucker. Must have met some babe on the road."

Fatherless boy. He'd be looking for a father substitute. Unfortunately, some of them found somebody like Charles Manson or Timothy Leary.

"I didn't know my father either. Would you believe he's a white man? He was in the army at Fort Hood, met my mother, married her, and left her within the year. Culture clash I guess it was. He lives in International Falls."

"You're a half breed?"

"We don't use that expression, Fred."

When Freddie left, Mingo went back to tossing the cards into his hat, thinking about when he might get a chance to go see his dad. About whether his dad would even *want* to see him.

* * *

Olive examined the panties, then dropped them on the conference room table. "I lost these at the Merry Widow Laundry. We don't have room in the trailer for a washer/dryer, so I always do the laundry there. Then there's this creep, Pigeon at the Amoco, who's always following me around. He could've taken them. Some guys get off on women's underwear."

The girl put the three middle fingers of her right hand in her mouth and bit, a definite tell if Dave were playing poker. But he wasn't playing poker. The brown eyes turned liquid and the fore-head above the blond eyebrows furrowed.

"Mr. Egge found it in Superintendent Bronson's wastebasket, Olive."

She didn't hesitate for a moment. "I have no idea how they got there, David. As a matter of fact, I don't think this is even my laundry mark."

"You're not lying for Mr. Bronson, are you Olive? Why would you tell Moe that he got fresh with you once?"

Her eyes were slightly down-tilted. Feline, he guessed you'd call them. "Oh, that. I was just joshing him. He's such a little puritan."

"This is a very serious matter, Olive. Even if Mr. Bronson had nothing to do with the Egge murder..."

"I'd never protect a perv. I have little sisters, you know."

"Let's drop that for a moment then. Do you know anything about the recent poisonings? Strychine poisonings. Miss Weiss lost her Dobermans. Mr. Forman's Border collie."

This time she shivered. "That son of a bitch turned down my ma's loan request. We need a car so's she can get a better job in Crookston. But I'd never take it out on his dog and I don't know nothing about any Dobermans getting poisoned. If that's all, I've got—"

"The splatballers, Olive. We need the name of the boy you were interested in."

"Oh shit. I was only tryin' to make you jealous. There wasn't any boy."

"We can check this out, Olive."

"Check all you want. I just like to hang out in the woods. No law against that, is there?"

"I guess not. Get up, we're going out to Shady Brook."

"What for?"

"I'm going to search your trailer. Want to see the warrant?"

Dave didn't have a warrant. He would have had a hard time getting one from a judge when he told him he was looking for Colonel Colvill's amputated arm.

When they got to Shady Brook, the door to the trailer was locked, and Olive claimed she didn't have the key. Dave reached above the door and felt around. Nothing there. Then he looked under the welcome mat and in a flower pot next to the stoop. The key was in the flower pot.

"Imagine that," Olive said. "My mother really ought to tell a girl—"

"Tell me another one, Olive."

Colonel Colvill's arm, in two pieces, was holding open the bathroom door just as Olive had said in Dave's waking dream.

Dave rubbed his eyes, shook his head. The arm was still there. "Could I have a glass of water, Olive? And some aspirin if you have any."

She went to the sink, got the water and the aspirin from a cupboard nearby. She opened the childproof cap, dumped the aspirin into his hand, handed him the glass. "I have no idea where that arm came from," she said. "Patty or Nancy must have picked it up in the park. They're like cats, always dragging in stray carcasses."

He took four of the aspirin, washed them down with the water. "I don't want to give your mom any more grief than I have to, Olive. I want you to come in tomorrow and talk to Harry and Hildegard about compensation and maybe some therapy."

"Come on now, David, are you serious?"

"You're damn right I am. We had to call in the original contractors to paint over the graffiti on the water tower. Hildegard said she could still see it. And you better hope we can get that arm back on the statue. You know how much grief that old women has been giving me about that?"

"I've heard about her, almost had her for third grade. I'm not going to talk to her about any stupid therapy. Tell you what, drop your pants and I'll give yah a hummer. A freebie. I get fifty bucks a throw from the boys at Polaris."

"Damn it, Olive, you just don't get it, do you?"

"How about a hand job then? I use vaseline or vegetable oil. You've never had a better one. Or we could fuck. Come on, you know you want it, I seen you looking down my dress."

Dave had a sudden realization. The long blond hair, the figure that would tempt a sailor on saltpeter, the bee-stung lips. This girl could be Mary Lou's younger sister, and he felt like slapping her because Mary Lou had never used the f-word in her life, would never even think of using profanity, and if she did, the words would cut her lips.

* * *

Dave parked Nellybelle in the McKinneys' garage across from his house on Little Round Top—they had an extra stall where they usually kept their boat—then walked across the street to his house and turned the door knob. It was closed tight as a drum. Hadn't locked the place in all the time he'd lived there. He let himself in, making a beeline for the phone, where he called Olive's mother at

the Legion. She'd seen the arm holding open the door, but she had-
n't noticed Colonel Colvill had been missing one. She'd assumed
the arm was some sort of art project from school. She said she'd
make sure Olive was at the sheriff's office around ten the next day.

After talking to Mrs. Randall, Dave dialed Mingo's cellular,
hoping he was awake, as it was five o'clock and the man had to
sleep sometime.

"Safe Haven Bingo Parlor, B-9 speaking."

"Hey, guy, what's the word on Bronson's alibi? Olive says she
never bonked Bronson and she has no idea how Egge got hold of
her underwear."

"Interesting. What would you say the odds are that's true? Has
she ever come on to you?"

"Stupid question."

"Yup, I'd say the girl doesn't have much taste if she hadn't come
on to me too."

"The girl has a definite hard-on for the world, that's for sure. I
found the Colonel's arm holding open the bathroom door at her
trailer."

"Somehow that don't surprise me, Dude, but I didn't know she
was a hermaphrodite."

"Jeez. The Bronson alibi?"

"I showed the motel clerk a picture of the Super Chief I got out
of the Crookston paper. He says Bronson was there with a blond
woman who looked like the lady from *The Birds* the night before
the Egge murder. Registered under the original name of Mr. and
Mrs. John Smith. The clerk says he saw her the next morning
around eight eating in the snack bar, but he didn't see him at all
that morning, so I guess it's possible he could have snuck out during the night sometime."

"I don't think she looks like the lady in *The Birds* at all. When
did she turn in the key?"

"Shortly after she ate. He didn't see her drive away."

Dave had dinner, watched the evening news, and a rerun of
M.A.S.H. on cable. Hawkeye doing some nurse, which brought to
mind Olive's offer and, by association, Colonel Colvill's arm and
the clairvoyant vision. He shut the TV off, turned out the lights and
went for a walk.

As usual he was drawn towards the river and Mary Lou's
house on The Angle. He must have walked by that glass house a
thousand times, and he still got a thrill to his solar plexis. This
time, after crossing the bridge, he veered left toward music coming
from the holy roller church. *Rock my soul in the bosom of Abraham.*

Deep, dulcet tones, a heavy reliance on the bass section. *Oh, rock my soul*, they sang. *Too high, can't get over it, Too high, can't get over it.*

Because of storm clouds, the street lights were lit. There was a light drizzle, the light reflecting off the accumulating puddles. As he walked by the church, the choir returned to the refrain. *Rock my soul in the bosom of Abraham, Oh, rock my soul. Too wide, can't get round it, too wide can't get round it, Gotta go through the door.*

The music had hooked him, soaked through his tough, agnostic hide, and he was tempted to go in, just to watch, tap his foot, and maybe clap in accompaniment. No, couldn't do that. Not the chief deputy of Polk County.

At one of the Andy's Diner gossip sessions, he'd heard the holy rollers had stormed several school board meetings, demanding some form of prayer in the schools and the teaching of Creationism in the mandatory biology class. Egge had hit the ceiling, the walls had quaked with accusation and recrimination. Religious types had committed some mighty heinous acts in the name of God. Would the fundamentalists be as fanatical as the abortion clinic bombers?

He continued on past the church, splashing through the puddles, his hands jammed deep in his windbreaker pockets, going no place in particular. *Too deep, can't get under it, Gotta go through the door* reverberated through the air.

Funny thing about Olive's proposition. He'd acted like your basic Young Republican—shocked beyond patience by the depravity of the underclass. She did look a lot like Mary Lou; albeit Mary Lou always had all of her snaps snapped and buttons buttoned. When would he get over her? It was almost as bad as that obsession thing John Hinckley had for Jody Foster. Used to write her letters and everything. Thank God he never mailed them.

A couple of blocks down he could see lights on in the school, Ellis's office he thought. The man was putting in some mighty long hours.

Rather than continue on down Wheat, he found himself turning on Peach, angling toward Veteran's Park and the statue. Nothing out of order there, the Colonel still had his other arm. Hildegard should be thrilled he'd found the lost appendage, and maybe, just maybe, she'd transfer some of the grief she gave him to Olive when they had their little tete-a-tete. Have to be a quick one, the press conference was at eleven thirty. He strolled past the sheriff's office, Mingo's 4X4 parked out front, on toward the firehouse, then turned onto Meade, and found himself standing in front of

Mrs. Mac's house, which was when he remembered his promise to Harry and Mel that he'd go see Annie that night.

He walked up the path and knocked. Mrs. Mac answered the door. "I was expecting you," she said.

"You were? I didn't know I was coming."

"Come in here. We'll go in the kitchen and have some of those fritters. And a nice glass of warm milk. It's too late for coffee."

They took seats around the kitchen table. The checkered curtains, the waxed hardwood floor, the nice linen tablecloth reminded him of home.

"Something tells me you've had a revelatory experience," she said.

"That's an understatement," he said. He told her about the corned beef, the ink stain, his unreasonable anger during the Bronson interrogation, and finally about Colonel Colvill's arm.

"You poor boy," she said. "This whole thing has been awfully . stressful for you, hasn't it? I'll waive my fee." She handed him a big glass of milk and the biggest sweet roll he'd ever seen. "We'll mark it down to building amicable relations between the police and the spiritualist profession."

"That's awfully big of you, Mrs. Mac."

"I hope that wasn't a pun," she said. The explosive laugh almost blew his head off. "We'll do the séance as soon as I can clear my schedule."

"Annie's not here then?"

"No, she went with Lucille to Crookston to see a movie. I have something for you, though. I promise I didn't peek." She handed him three files bound by rubber bands. "Lucille gave me these for you."

The files were labeled in grease pencil: "priority", "maybes" and "losers".

"She especially wanted you to look at this one," Mrs. Mac said, handing him a slip of paper. The note said that the caretaker at Evergreen Cemetery had found an overcoat (size 50), motheaten tennis shoes, and a pair of twill pants in a garbage can shortly after Egge's funeral. "Mean anything to you?" she said.

"Quite a lot actually."

"You're not going to tell me are you?" she said.

He laughed, shook his head no.

Back at home, Dave felt a little better. Confiding in Mrs. Mac was like putting himself in the hands of his mother, and his mother would never do anything to make him look foolish. He still wasn't sure about that séance, though. If he went through with it, he'd have to make sure security was awfully tight.

Later on, Moe brought over some Chinese takeout, they played gin rummy for a while. Dave told Moe about Lucille's note and about finding Colonel Colvill's arm (but not about Mrs. Mac agreeing to the séance or Olive's sexual advances). They discussed JESSICA's newest theories, then Dave flipped on the TV, which drove Moe away as he'd sworn off TV unless the program had some educational merit. Dave passed out watching a Bonanza rerun.

He woke up just in time for the ten o'clock news, too depressing by half, so he shut the TV off and went to bed. Tomorrow would be the big town meeting/press conference, probably his last day on the case if Hildegard wasn't just blowing smoke, and he'd never even seen her light up.

Chapter 12

Designated Hitter

*"The haft of the arrow had been feathered
with one of the eagle's own plumes."*
— Aesop

The phone rang, wrenching Dave out of his recurring dream about hitting against Sandy Koufax's yakker in the World Series. Rubbing his eyes, he looked over at the red digital numbers on his Sears alarm clock, which read five A.M. He snatched up the phone and mumbled, "Jenkins here."

"Larry Henderson, Jenkins, over at the school. We've had another murder I'm afraid. Fran Ellis, the temporary principal. How soon can you be down here?"

When Dave arrived, Harry, Henderson and Bronson were standing just outside Ellis's office, while the fingerprint specialists stepped over Ellis's body dusting the room. The body, resembling a department store mannequin resting on its back waiting to be put in the display window, was in much better condition than Egge's had been. The athletic director's little office looked as if it had been through a quake, with paper strewn about, drawers in the file cabinets half-open, pictures on the walls askew, and a big crack in the plate-glass wall separating the office from the lobby.

It was very quiet, so quiet that at times Dave thought he must have lost his hearing, but it was just that the others were whispering. Maybe it was because the monklike Ellis's body had not been removed.

Bronson glared at Dave as if he was an ex-wife who was suing him for the family fortune. Dave scowled back at him. Next time he'd throw a fist.

"Okay if I go in there?" Dave asked Henderson.

"Sure, if you don't mind wearing these booties. Just don't touch anything."

Dave slipped on the elastic coverings, moved into the office, sidestepped the fingerprint techs, and knelt to close the dead man's

165

eyes. Ellis had been wearing a tie with a fish design, something Dave hadn't noticed the day before. Same brown suit, though, same tan shirt, same Hushpuppy shoes. The glass in the picture of Ellis's wife was broken, and her picture had been removed and torn in half. Dave checked under Ellis's fingernails. Nothing he could spot. "Bag these, will you?" he said to one of the criminalists, then moved back outside the office and stood next to the BCA investigator.

"There's no blood," Henderson said. "Looks like somebody clipped him upside the head with that Big Bertha there, he's got a lump behind his ear. The killer left this."

Henderson handed Dave a note written on memo paper in black ink encased in a transparent envelope that read:

Dear Officer Jenkins,

Please excuse my formality, but I wanted you to know that I'm aware you're on the case. If I were you, I'd start locking my door. Does it scare you that I know you sometimes leave your front door open? Well, you see, I've been there, early in the morning and late at night.

You'll need more help than Kline or that BCA clown to catch me. Let me save you some trouble. Bronson didn't kill the coach, nor that kid with the gun, nor the Sheriff's boy, nor that Lester kid. Let me give you just a little hint. You'll need it. I have no need for a gun or a knife.

The Designated Hitter

Dave handed the note back to Henderson.

"I think we've got something here," Henderson said. "The killer knew you sometimes leave your door open. That must mean you know the guy. Somebody in the neighborhood would have noticed a stranger snooping around."

"Nobody saw the scrote slit the tires on my Jeep," Dave said. "I suppose it's too early to know for sure who was the last one to see Ellis alive?"

Henderson toyed with his David Niven mustache, looking as if he were preparing a statement for the press. "You're not going to believe this, but Mrs. Macintosh was involved again. She saw him at six last night. She'd been working with one of her students, and as she was leaving, she stuck her head in his office to say good night. She said he seemed to be expecting somebody. She was the last one here, as the janitor goes home as soon as he's finished cleaning, and the athletic coaches have a key to the building.

Marshall Preston, the baseball coach, was the only one on the road last night, and he says he didn't notice anything funny. I called him as soon as Mr. Bronson showed me the schedule."

"We had to eliminate the night janitor due to cutbacks," Bronson said.

"Ellis's wife says he never came home for dinner," Henderson said. "She called the office at six thirty, and again at seven. She thought to call Mrs. Macintosh since she was aware she liked to work late. That's how we knew he was still alive around six. Mrs. Ellis didn't really get worried, though, because he sometimes goes along on an away game without telling her."

Intruding on the quiet, the double doors at the entrance to the school worked like subway turnstiles as the criminalists came and went.

"I can't believe this has happened again," Bronson said, running his hands through his hair.

Henderson clapped his hand on Bronson's shoulder in commiseration, then turned back to Dave. "She didn't realize the buses would have been long gone by six. When he didn't show up by midnight, she called the superintendent, and they found him at around one this morning. Looks like a woman's handwriting," he said, holding the note up against the light.

Dave flashed to the previous night, the lights on in Ellis's office, his meeting with Mrs. Mac. She'd seen Ellis alive no more than a half hour before Dave had talked to her.

"Did anyone check his appointment book?" Dave asked. "Mrs. Macintosh said he was expecting someone."

Henderson fished in his pocket, passed a transparent envelope to Dave. "There's a page missing," he said.

The crime team, groaning with the effort, grasped Ellis's body by the arms and legs, heaved it onto a cot, and rolled it out into the hall, waiting for the meatwagon.

"It's all right to go in there now and take a load off, guys," Henderson said. "We've got whatever's to be gotten. The boys did a grid, combed every inch of the place. Just don't step on any glass. We might be able to get some partials off that."

The four men moved single file into the office.

Harry gargled, a smoker's attempt to clear his throat. "We've got a principal and his replacement dead," he said. "I think that's too much of a link to ignore. If this is a serial killer..."

Bronson wedged between the wall and Ellis's desk and took a chair. The superintendent had taken the time to put on a suit and tie before showing up at the school in the middle of the night. His blaring voice broke the stillness. "To me this guy really sounds childish. I hate to say it, but I'll bet it's one of the kids."

Dave's hackles rose once more, sweat re-emerged on his upper lip. The acid sensation was back. The son of a bitch had a lot of gall calling *anybody* childish.

Bronson's lips were moving but Dave perceived what he said in a different context: *Mr. Egge receives low marks in conflict resolution among faculty members. Nor does he handle constructive criticism well, or delegate authority when called for. As an illustration, I cite his constant interference in matters properly the province of the athletic director and the special education department. He has shown questionable decorum during faculty meetings, has used language unbecoming a professional.*

Dave removed his cap, mopped his forehead with his handkerchief. "Ah...What's that you said, Mr. Bronson?"

"Just thinking out loud, Deputy. I'm sure you people know more about this sort of thing than I." He grinned. "I would hope."

Harry yawned cavernously and said, "Well, we can't take the murderer's word that it's not the Cochran kid, that's for sure. Looks like whoever did it, lost his temper and bopped him one, and the Cochran kid's got a mean disposition."

"Mingo seems to think Freddie's basically harmless," Dave said. "Freddie was at that special school in Crookston when Egge got killed. I checked it out."

"Didn't you say the boy got kicked out of Level 5 and was coming back to Soldier High?" Harry said.

"Yeah, Ellis got the message yesterday while I was talking to him."

"What can we do about the other coaches, Henderson?" Harry said. "Both of those guys were coaches at one time, the others could be in danger." Harry was still whispering. "I don't see what we can do other than close the school."

Bronson, fiddling with his twenty-dollar silk tie as if he hardly ever wore one, shook his head. "No way! We don't close the school for longer than two days. We can't allow terrorism to disrupt...Sheriff, we're going to expect some help with security, until this murderer is apprehended." He finally gave it up and removed his tie, putting it in his pocket.

Dave felt a spasm run up and down his backbone. Every time Bronson opened his mouth, Dave's knuckles itched. He wanted to rip that tie out of his hands, and garrote the pompous bastard. The same way he felt when he spied a heckling Harley Barnhouser at second base when the Dogs played Barnhouser's collection of dere-licts, perverts, and misfits.

"I guess we can call in some of the police reserve," Harry said.

"May I have a word with you in private, Mr. Bronson?" Henderson said. Bronson nodded, and the two left the office and crossed over next to the trophy case away from the body.

Dave was thinking: *that son of a bitch Henderson is still trying to find an advocate to sponsor his takeover bid and he'll never find a more likely candidate.* He could just hear him blowing his own horn: *Mr. Bronson, we have proven expertise in capital cases, our forensic resources are so much more superior to anything Polk County can bring to the table...*And why had Dave been the last one called this morning?

Harry and Dave studied Ellis's bulletin board. Harry spied a lunch menu and went into a long discourse about how bad school food was.

A while later, Mindy, who hadn't heard the school-closing announcement on WCCO, arrived for work with a bag of dough-nuts, rosy cheeked, smiling cheerfully, until she saw the body. Then her complexion turned pea-soup green, her eyes went to half-mast, and she fainted. Bronson, who'd finished his consultation with Henderson, scooped her up, splashed water on her face to revive her, and sent her home.

Dave and Bronson stood watching one of the criminalists sweep up the broken glass. Harry and Henderson had stepped outside for a smoke break. Neither Bronson nor Dave spoke for what seemed like a week, then Dave said, "We should let the teach-ers know that they're all at risk. And that they should avoid being alone with anyone." His eyes became riveted on a plaque on the wall which read *Whosoever looketh on a woman to lust after her hath committed adultery with her already in his heart.* Matthew-5:28.

That Ellis would have this saying on his wall seemed especial-ly ironic after his behavior around Mindy and after what he'd said about Olive. If Ellis's wife knew about his philandering, she'd be a suspect. She could have torn up her own picture.

Bronson noticed where Dave was looking. "Ellis was born-again. I've told him to take it down over and over again."

Dave managed to swallow the loathing he felt toward the man. "Really? Did he belong to the fundamentalist church?"

"Hell if I know. I try not to involve myself in my people's per-sonal lives."

"What sort of stand did he take on the prayer in the schools issue? I understand there were some hard feelings during some of your school board meetings."

"Oh, I made it plain that he better stay out of that. The Constitution is pretty clear on separation of church and state."

Dave felt like mimicking the man's imperious tone.

"Mind if I take this with me?" he said, unfastening the plaque from its hook.

"Help yourself," Bronson said.

Dave doubted the holy rollers had anything to do with Ellis's demise. The church fanatics might have had enough reason to smite their enemy Egge, but why would they want to eliminate one of their own? Rather, he thought these murders were some kind of sick joke: both of the principals clubbed to death, one with a Wayne Terwilliger bat, of all things, the other with a Big Bertha. And the goofy Jack the Ripper note.

The meatwagon came to get Ellis at 7:30, and the voices returned to normal.

* * *

The press conference was being held in the high school gym, where there was room for anyone from the town and surrounding area. Annie and Lucille found a seat next to Superintendent Bronson in the third row behind all of the reporters. Annie had heard the press conference announced on WCCO. As a result, there were about twenty reporters in all, including those from Minneapolis-St. Paul, Duluth, and Fargo, or so Annie'd been told.

Annie noticed Hildegard Weiss sitting near the outside entrance, probably making sure no young people slipped through the perimeter. The elderly woman's brows were knitted, her lower lip protruding, and she was tapping her foot. When she assumed that Madamn Defarge expression, it could only mean that someone's head was going to roll.

The place was packed to the rafters, with more people outside trying to squeeze their way in. The noise was deafening, rivaling a close basketball game, something Soldier wasn't used to since the team was a notorious loser. The press conference had been scheduled for eleven-thirty and was already fifteen minutes late.

Dave, Hendersen, and Harry were huddled together on the stage, surrounded by the set for "Camelot", which the amateur theater group would be performing that evening if the play hadn't been cancelled. Dave was still wearing his usual Navy SEAL attire, the USS Lake Champlain baseball cap, the special forces windbreaker with the white lettering on the back.

How stubborn could he get? Annie wondered. One would think for such a somber occasion he'd change to his uniform. But what did she care? She didn't even know what she was doing here in the first place. She'd finally gotten him into bed, thought that'd hook him since they were all consumed by sex, but no! he was pretending it never happened. The man was a hopeless case. And so was she. Just this morning one of the teachers at the high school, Marshall Preston, the physical education teacher, had asked her to go out on a date again. She'd turned him down flat.

Lucille grasped Annie's hands. "Isn't this awful?" she said. "Two principals. I don't think I'd want to be the next one."

Annie pried herself loose. "This town is going to shut down," she said. "You'll be able to shoot a bazooka down Meade and not hit anything."

"I don't know, Mr. Jenkins seems to think this one was an accident. Don't tell anybody I said this, but Mr. Ellis only has this one little bump behind his ear."

"That so?"

"I suppose this means there won't be any game tonight. Mr. Jenkins asked me to join up with the softball team."

"I kind of figured, I play shortstop."

"Don't I know it, Mr. Jenkins says you're awfully good. He says once this is all over I can get on the rotisserie league, too. You know, that's where they gamble on the outcome of major league games."

Annie adjusted the collar on her dress. "Are you sure you want to do that, Lucille?"

Lucille shifted forward in her chair, the folding chair threatening to collapse in on itself. "Sounds like fun. What they do is they bid on all the players and each person forms their own team. Everybody gets 260 units to bid, 23 players each. Mr. Jenkins has this computer software that accumulates stats all year on eight categories: batting average, home runs, pitching etc. The team with the highest total in each category gets ten points at the end of the year. Second place gets nine and so forth. The team with the highest overall total wins $450 for its owner."

"I'd check the stats myself if I were you," Annie said.

"Oh, I don't really care about the money. I want to join because of your brother Mel. I thought that was pretty fair-minded of Mr. Jenkins to let me join. Male law enforcement officers are usually chauvinistic."

Annie had tuned Lucille out, until she heard the word "chauvinistic."

"Oh, don't let that fool you, he's chauvinistic enough. When's this clambake gonna start? It's ten to twelve already."

"Look at all those reporters. I wonder if I'll get to be on TV. Speaking of rotisserie, he ever ask you?"

"I was at the first meeting. He needed somebody to pop popcorn, and put out the pretzels and potato chips."

"And you let me tell you all about the rules. I'll bet that was just an excuse about the snacks. Are you scared, about the Ellis matter, I mean?"

"Not me personally. I'm kind of anxious for my father, though. Maybe if he didn't weigh so much."

Lucille's face turned crimson and she lowered her head. Annie was thinking *me and my big mouth*. The girl had such a sweet face and such an amiable personality. Put her on four light meals a day, get her to exercise more, can the junk food, and she'd be a doll. Any man would be lucky to have her. Annie touched her hand. "I'm sorry, I wasn't thinking. Tell you what we'll do, we'll get you in the volunteer firemen. So far I'm the only woman, we need to let these men know we can handle anything they throw at us."

Lucille brightened. "I'd like that, do I need to pass any tests or anything?"

"Nothing you haven't come up against studying for your degree in Criminal Justice."

"They expect me to lose fifty pounds before I graduate, they gave me a special diet—rabbit food, mostly. I don't know how I'll stick to it."

"I'll help you. I go to the gym three times a week, and you'll go with me."

They both looked back up at the stage. "Thanks," Lucille said. "Aren't you afraid for Dave? He got his tires slashed, you know. And someone's been going around poisoning animals."

"He can handle himself; I don't know why I bother with him. The man obviously thinks he can do better."

"He adores you, I can tell."

Annie looked over at Bronson sitting next to her. He smiled back at her. Now there was a man who knew how to dress. Blue pinstripe, three-piece suit, silk tie, tasseled loafers shined to a high gloss. And he must get his hair cut once a week at least. Her girlfriends said the man was on the make, that he'd been doing it with Egge's wife. Would he be passionate enough about a woman to commit murder? If only she could get Dave to be that feverish about her.

Lucille whispered in her ear. "I wonder what it would be like to go to bed with him?" She giggled.

"Who, Dave?"

"No, him," Lucille said, motioning her head at Bronson.

Annie whispered in Lucille's ear. "He'd probably crush you. And I thought Paul Bunyun was a myth."

Lucille put both of her hands over her mouth, but the giggling broke through, spraying the people sitting directly in front of her, who traded seats with another couple.

Annie bit her lower lip. Why had she assumed Lucille's sexual reference referred to Dave? Dave. Dave. Dave. She'd never believed that hogwash about love at first sight, but it was almost like Pavlov and his dog. You ring the bell, and the girl goes weak in the knees. She couldn't believe she'd sicced her old man on him. Maybe guys are right when they say women are too emotional and impulsive.

"I'm starving to death," Lucille said.

"Lucille, remember what you said about losing weight."

"But it's past dinner time. If I don't get something, my stomach starts to growl. I wonder if I got time to run over to Andy's."

"This time. I'll want to see you on that diet after the press conference. Go ahead, I'll fill you in if anything important happens."

Lucille smiled, scooched across the knees of the other people in their row, and trotted toward the exit.

Bronson leaned over and said, "What are you doing now that you've graduated, Anne?"

She managed a shy smile. "Did you say something, Mr. Bronson?"

"I was just wondering what you've been doing with yourself?"

"I've been spending a lot of time with the volunteer fire department," she said. "I think I might want to do that professionally."

He scowled down at her. "Isn't that rather dangerous? I've heard that women have a hard time qualifying."

"I've got five brothers, Mr. Bronson. Believe me, they have trouble keeping up with me."

"I'll bet they do, I understand you're also the Little League coordinator. You must get the phone calls."

"Not too many. When the boys first apply, some of them say, 'I *want* to be pitcher', or 'I *want* to be the shortstop.' Those are the boys who can usually play, probably because they have the confidence to get it done. Other boys say, '*Can* I play third or *can* I play the outfield?' My answer always is, 'I don't know, *can* you?'"

Annie looked back up at the stage. Dave was holding a piece of paper and Henderson was pointing to something on it. They seemed to be arguing.

"That's an unusual insight for someone so young. I was a catcher myself. Catchers aren't afraid of the bat, we have to make the long throw to second, we call the pitches, and we don't cry when we take a foul ball in the crotch."

"That's my hardest position to fill."

"I thought it was the easiest way to the majors. It didn't work out quite the way I thought."

"You didn't do so badly," she said.

"Thank you. You're a sweet girl."

Still nothing going on the stage. A maintenance man was futzing with the sound system. Harry—she'd called her father Harry for as long as she could remember—was sitting on the end of the stage, his feet dangling over the side, probably telling jokes with the mayor, George McCready, and Doc Bailey. There was no such thing as an inappropriate time for a joke in Harry's scheme of things. Several of the reporters were listening. She hoped it wasn't the one about the lesbian Eskimo he'd told her this morning when she'd seen him at Andy's. He'd had to explain to her why Klondike was a punch line. She hoped those reporters wouldn't make Harry out to be a fool.

Sylvia, Bronson's secretary, tapped him on the shoulder and whispered in his ear. He stood up, put on his coat and said, "I've got to go back to the office and meet with the police reserves. It's been so enjoyable talking to you, Anne. Stop in and see me sometime."

When they shook hands, her hand, engulfed by his, felt as it had when she'd held hands with her dad as a little girl.

"I'll do that," she said. He smiled, buttoned the middle button on this coat, and left.

Marshall Preston took Bronson's vacated seat. "There you are, I've been looking all over for you."

"I was just talking to the superintendent."

"You sure you want to be seen with him? He's the principal suspect in the Egge murder, you know."

During that first rotisserie meeting, Marshall, a friend of her bother Mel, had helped her pop popcorn, had stuck to her like Velcro the rest of the evening, and had finally asked her out.

When she'd finished popping corn, Annie had gone over and sat on Dave's knee. She'd put her hand on his leg, massaging his thigh. He took her hand away. "What were you talking to Marshall about?" he whispered.

"Jealous, huh?"

She bent down and bit Dave on the ear. "Cut that out, will you? Everybody's watching," he said.

"You know you love it," she said.

At the time she'd glanced over at Moe Pleasiac, who'd been watching them with a little grin on his face. Horny little devil. Her little sister Aimee worshipped him. Maybe if she set them up, he'd stay out of the way. She was rather worried about that relationship. The kid was competition, worse than another woman almost.

"Annie, are you in there?" Marshall said.

"I was just thinking how sad this all is," she said.

"Yes, Ellis was a good man. You think any more about going out with me?"

"Why not?" she said. "Where we going?"

"How about a nice restaurant in Fargo? You can pick it."

Lucille sat down on her left side, handed her a sub sandwich and a can of Dr. Pepper. "Made it just in time," she said.

Annie looked up at the stage where Dave was moving toward the microphone.

Dave flipped the microphone 'on' switch, and the gym immediately quieted, as if he'd muted the volume on the TV. He cleared his throat. "At approximately one o'clock this morning, Fran Ellis's body was found in his office by Superintendent Bronson and Fran's wife. Mr. Ellis had been hit on the head with a blunt instrument. We have the murder weapon and a message left by the assailant."

Annie spied Mary Lou Forman sitting in the first row behind the reporters, smiling encouragingly. Annie'd heard she'd divorced her husband. The bitch was looking at Dave as if he were a Popsicle on a sweltering August afternoon.

Dave took a drink of water. "At this time we will take questions. We have a microphone available for your use. Please use it rather than yell out questions. Mrs. Johnson."

Mrs. Alva Johnson was the reporter and editor for the *Soldier Clarion*, a weekly paper that had been in existence for over a hundred years. Mrs. Johnson was the granddaughter of the founder, Ben Eich.

"Deputy Jenkins, can you tell us if this murder has any similarities to the Egge murder?"

Dave leaned down to confer with Henderson. He whispered in Henderson's ear, and Henderson whispered in his.

"Ah, we think it's a separate incident."

"Would you explain why you feel this way, Deputy Jenkins?" Mrs. Johnson said.

"Mr. Egge's murderer was frenzied, whereas, Mr. Ellis was hit only once. I'd say he was rather unlucky that the blow killed him. Also, the murderer took the time to sit down and write a taunting message. Ah, let me clarify that. The taunting message was directed toward me personally."

Henderson tugged at his sleeve. Dave nodded.

Mrs. Johnson said, "A taunting message? You mean like Jack the Ripper? What was in the message?"

"Disclosure of said information would seriously impede our investigation," Dave said.

The bald man who grabbed the microphone next was wearing horn-rimmed glasses that had been out of style since before Buddy Holly and his plaid jacket and polyester trousers had been banished to most people's garage sales almost as long. "Bill Hanover of Reuters, Deputy Jenkins. Our sources tell us that the Egge murder had satanic elements? Some kind of spray paint on the victim's back. Can you acknowledge this for us?"

Pencils were moving furiously and notebook pages were flapping. A flashbulb went off, and Dave looked blinded.

"We can't acknowledge that. No. We can only say that Mr. Egge's death most likely resulted from blunt force injury."

"Fine then," the Reuters man said. "No suspects have been announced as of yet in the Egge murder. Can you tell us if you have anyone under investigation? I have a follow-up."

"Yes, we have several suspects under consideration."

"Could you elaborate. Just generally."

"There's a possibility, just a possibility you understand, that the Egge murder was a case of mistaken identity. We have a name we're pursuing who could have been the intended victim."

Obviously Henderson, Harry, and Dave had decided to throw them a bone, Annie thought. She hadn't heard anything about mistaken identity.

The Reuters man moved to the end of the line, and a much more imposing person took the microphone. Annie would say she was in her late forties with iron-gray hair, wearing a muted-plaid business suit and high heels which made her at least six feet tall. "Erdra Reardon of the St. Paul Pioneer Press, Deputy Jenkins. Our sources tell us that Mr. Egge's back was spray-painted with the letters 'DYSTH' and 'SYZ' was scrawled on one of his legs. Can you confirm this for us?"

Dave turned off the microphone, met Henderson's eyes, and knelt down in front of his chair. He stood, started to talk into the microphone, realizing at the last moment he'd turned it off. He flipped the switch and it screeched like a banshee on crank. He moved back away from the microphone.

"Ms. Reardon, your question is out of line. We'd like to see you after the press conference."

The tall woman, who seemed unperturbed, reeled in the slack of the microphone cord.

"You've heard of confidentiality of sources, Deputy?" She hesitated a moment, brushing back her hair, revealing long, red talons. "So then you can't confirm that such a message was left at the scene."

Dave shrugged. "No, I can't."

A photographer chose this moment to blind Dave again. "Would you please refrain from taking pictures until after the conference," he said. "I'm going to have to leave. I have an interrogation in a few moments. Mr. Henderson of the BCA will answer any further questions you might have." Henderson was caught off guard. He whispered in Harry's ear. Harry shook his head.

* * *

When Dave threw the curtain to the right of the stage, his gut clenched. Mary Lou Forman was waiting for him.

Her hair was piled on top of her head, she wasn't wearing lipstick or any jewelry, and she was very pregnant; yet, she still looked like Lady Godiva, Cinderella, and Jean Harlow all rolled into one.

"I hope you don't mind my being so forward, David," she said. "I thought you might like to get together before I have to go back to Chicago. We haven't talked in ages."

Never. They'd never had a conversation longer than it takes to say, "Will you go out with me?" on his part and "I have to study for a test" on hers.

"I'd like that, Mary Lou, but I don't have a lot of time these days."

"Surely you have time for a cup of coffee. I'll buy."

Chapter 13

In Nomine Patris

"There is no refuge from confession but
suicide; and suicide is confession."
— Daniel Webster

Earlier that same morning, Father Mischke had been hearing confessions just before the eight o'clock mass. His tour in "the box" was an everyday obligation, as the parishioners at Immaculate Conception had not embraced face-to-face confession. Nor had they approved of examination of conscience during mass, without the intercession of a priest, which would also absolve their sins. If they had a firm purpose of amendment.

Mrs. Adelmeyer was one of those diehards who insisted on a partition between the priest and the confessant, although Father Mischke knew very well who she was and could recite her sins by rote. It didn't help that she'd grown childish. "I had impure thoughts five times," she'd say in that scratchy voice of hers. Father was nigh on certain she hadn't had any sex in thirty years.

The confessional was becoming increasingly claustrophobic for Father Mischke, one of the reasons for his impending retirement. It was difficult for him to sit in the dark in the coffin-like room, and he had such a hard time listening. It was as though he'd regressed seventy years and was at Sunday mass woolgathering during ancient Father Rauschendorfer's sermon.

Mrs. Adelmeyer hesitated for a moment, and he began to give her absolution. "God the Father of mercies, through the death and resurrection of his Son, has reconciled the world to himself and sent the Holy Spirit among us for the forgiveness of sins—"

"Just a minute, Father," she said. "I'm not finished."

He wanted to tell her it wasn't necessary for her to come to confession anymore, that she was too old to commit a sin, but he couldn't very well do that since the old woman had been taught to confess for the grace the sacrament afforded. Telling her not to come to confession would be like telling her not to come to church.

179

There she'd be, each and every morning, in the very first row, even during weddings and funerals when the first pews were reserved for family. Arthritic, one hand resting on a cane, rosary entwined in her fingers—a real-life caricature of an Ellis Island photo. He got so depressed when he saw her out there every morning—she reminded him so much of himself.

Finally she was finished and he was able to give her absolution without rushing the words too much. Something else he'd had in common with the boy he'd been—hell-bent-for-leather prayers. Those interminable rosaries his mother had made him say.

Someone entered the confessional. Father opened the partition. "Forgive me, Father, for I have sinned," the man, whose voice was basso profundo, said. "My last confession was thirty years ago."

Thank God for a little dissonance, Father thought.

"I've missed mass, let's see, what's fifty-two times thirty, plus all the holy days? Something like sixteen hundred, right? Math was my worst subject."

Levity in the confessional? That hadn't happened very often— usually some smartass college kid who'd discovered philosophy—and when it did, Father would tear out of the confessional, fling open the confessant's door, and pin the little twerp's ears back.

"What was that sin I used to confess?" the man said. "Something about disobeying my parents. My father was a goddamned drunk, and I haven't seen the old lady in over twenty years. She was, or I guess I was, just a biological accident. But the ten commandments say I should honor her anyway, right? Are you still there, Father?"

Father heard what he thought was a match being struck. Was the man smoking? A spark could ignite the entrance curtain and this box would go up like a rotten log.

"Please don't use profanity, you're in God's house. You're not smoking in there, are you?"

"Did I swear? I'll try not to do it again. Can't guarantee it, though. You folks haven't been too effective lately censoring the mass media. You could say I've been corrupted."

"If not television, a profane parent, dissolute friends," Father said, trying to match the man's sarcastic tone.

"I suppose you're wondering what I'm doing in the confessional after all these years."

"Not especially. I get one like you every few months or so, usually they're older, though. Go ahead, get it off your chest, whatever it is."

"You asked for it. I've been copulating with a young girl."

"Did the Bishop send you here to test me?"

"Trouble in paradise, Father?"

"Never mind that, how young is she?"

"Old enough to bleed...she's only sixteen, but she's mature for her age. We do it all."

Father Mischke coughed, tried to clear the congestion from his voice. His eyes were watering from the strain. "If this...is a practical joke, I'm not...too old to come out there...and box your ears for you, young fellah."

"No practical joke, Father. And she's not the only one."

"You don't sound at all repentant. I don't think I can give you absolution, and you're taking up valuable—"

"Oh, who wants your old absolution. The church absolved the Nazis...Nothing to say? Aren't you going to defend yourself? Still mulling over what I said about Ol—"

Father dug his nails into armrest. "If you don't leave—"

"Don't throw me out yet, Father. There's more." The man's breathing was clearly audible as if he'd been running all out. "I killed this guy, see?...I clubbed him to death with a baseball bat, what do you say to that? Hey, I'm a poet. I clubbed him to death with a baseball bat, what do you say to that."

"I think you should turn yourself in. You must know that anything you say in the confessional is confidential, but I don't believe you'd be here if you weren't sorry. Even if you think you're 'pulling my leg' as the young people say, I feel subconsciously you're ashamed."

"Damn these kneelers are hard. Why don't you put a chair in here?" The man paused again, his breathing less audible. "What if, just what if...I don't have a conscience? You must know about sociopaths, Father."

"I don't personally believe there is such a thing. I know you're going to mention people like Gacy, Bundy and Ed Gein, but those aren't real people. They're manifestations of the Devil."

"The Devil, eh? Well, why can't I be a manifestation of the devil, then?"

"Lucifer was prideful, and pride is a deadly sin." Father coughed again, wiped his mouth with a tissue. "I don't think you'd be too happy if you lived where he is. You sound like an educated man and you should know better. Logically you should be able to figure it out, even if you don't believe in Christ, that murder and sex abuse are wrong. We can't have chaos. You need to turn yourself in. When I was your age...You young people make me sick. It's always somebody else's fault."

"You can't possibly believe that free will crap. What kind of free will does an eighteen-year-old sent to die in a rich man's war—"

"I can't explain why God allows war. We can't hope to understand God's ways."

The silhouette disappeared—the man must be standing—but then the shape leaned over, and spoke into the screen. "There is no God. I believe in...I believe in a force, a disinterested force. God or Jehovah or Allah or whatever you want to call him created the world, then left or died. Those who have faith are fools."

Father Mischke coughed again. "Ah, yes, deism. Franklin and some of the other founding fathers believed in that. Maybe you really are the devil. The silver-tongued devil who talked Eve into eating the apple."

"That's probably politically incorrect these days, Father. You'll have to change that myth before long, or you'll wind up losing all your female parishioners. Look, it's been real, but I've got to go. Remember your oath now."

"Before you go, son. Can you tell me why you killed Principal Egge? He was a good man from what I understand."

"You don't understand much. He was a very arrogant man, and as you say, pride is a deadly sin."

The silhouette disappeared from the partition and Father could hear the whisk of the confessional curtain and heavy footfalls retreating down the aisle.

Father Mischke was in a quandary. Surely confidentiality didn't apply to something like murder. Somebody had to stop this man. He opened the door an infinitesimal crack. A big man, well over two hundred pounds with black, curly hair, was just leaving the church. As the man opened the inner door, he turned and caught Father Mischke's eye.

* * *

Three bikes made the turn connecting Shady Brook Trailer Park and Meade Street. Olive Randall (who was pondering how she'd spend the money she expected to earn panhandling), Stormy Guck, and Rita Miller were on their way downtown to beg from the crowd who'd come to town because of the press conference. Rainclouds loomed overhead, but the three had disdained umbrellas.

As they crossed Plum Creek bridge, Stormy hung back as she was having trouble with her brother's bike with the bar down the middle, and her oversized carpenter pants and extra-large Green Bay Packer jersey kept snagging on the wheel sprockets.

"I feel sick about what happened last night," Olive said.

"Watch what you say in front of the kid," Rita said.

As they cruised by the Amoco station approaching a residential area, Rita let go of the handlebars and rolled up the sleeves on her flannel shirt. Olive thought the sweat band holding back her curly black hair made her look like Jimi Hendrix.

"You thought any more about the burglary?" Rita said.

"I don't know about that, it might be a little soon," Olive said.

Rita was watching the houses which lined Meade Street closely. "How about the spinster lady's house?" she said, standing on the brake.

"Not her," Olive said, pulling up alongside Rita. I won't rob Miss Brown. She spends weeks baking cookies and other treats for the kids in the neighborhood. The kids eat the cookies, but none of them hang around for long."

"And how long have you ever hung out with Miss Brown?" Rita said.

Stormy stopped her bike next to theirs and said, "What's going on?"

"Nothing you got to concern yourself with," Rita said. She turned to Olive. "I see Miss Brown in church quite a bit. She's got this sapphire broach that has to be real. If we can find it and get out, she won't know it's gone until she wants to wear it to church. By then, we should be able to hock the rock."

"Let's get going," Olive said. "I got a feeling there's gonna be a lot of generous people downtown."

The three got on their bikes and steered toward the downtown area.

"Awfully bossy today, ain't we?" Rita said. "And what the hell are you dressed for? On parade, riding through town in a miniskirt, no underwear, your hair done up like Madonna. What're you doin', counting the number of guys who give you the eye?"

Olive did her Janis Joplin laugh. She thought Rita was a stitch. Most of the time. "You're just jealous," she said.

Rita let go of the handlebars, took out a cigarette, lit it and blew the smoke in Olive's direction. "Did I tell you your lover Howard is coming out to the farm tomorrow to help clean the chicken · coop?"

"No shit."

"Yeah he wants to learn all about agriculture. I got a feeling it's a guilt trip, though."

"How so?"

"You know, hobnobbing with the underclass. That sort of thing."

"But his mom lives in that old school house. They don't have any money."

"There's more to it than money. He's a teacher's pet, ain't he?"

"I suppose. What I don't understand is why he'd come to you if he wanted to learn about agriculture."

Rita took another puff and scowled, unable to think of a comeback for once.

Suddenly the pedals on Olive's bike were turning, but she was slowing down. She jumped off and put the bike down on Mrs. Macintosh's lawn. The other two slammed on their brakes, kicking up gravel and small pebbles, and walked their bikes back to where Olive was standing, looking down at her bike. "Damn, slipped the fucking chain. You two ever fix one of these?"

"Don't look at me," Rita said. Stormy just shook her head.

As Olive was trying to decide if she should appropriate Stormy's bike, the banker's daughter drove by in her brand-new black sports car.

"It's just not fair that girl gets everything she wants," Olive said, "and Mom, Nancy, Patty and me have to live in a trailer."

"Wish I had that girl's hair!" Stormy said, tugging at the strands of her bob cut.

"Mary Lou Forman-Guild," Olive said. "Word has it she has her cap set for that hunka burnin' love Dave Jenkins."

"I would have given a newborn heifer calf to see his face when he saw those slashed tires," Rita said.

"Wish you hadn't made me do that," Stormy said. "He gives me a tip on collection day and he never tries to get out of paying."

"You were the only one who wouldn't look conspicuous foolin' round the man's house," Rita said. "And don't give me any more lip or I'll beat your ass."

Mrs. Macintosh had just raked her lawn. Olive took off her sandals, wriggled her toes in the velvety sod. "Like to have Mary Lou's nose, too, instead of this bulbous thing I got," Olive said.

"Your English teacher would have a conniption if she knew you used the word 'bulbous'," Rita said.

"Someday learning a new word every day'll pay off," Olive said. "I could be a great author like that Mary Higgens Clark."

Rita choked on her cigarette smoke. "Yeah and I'll be the next big super model."

Olive watched the black sports car make a left turn onto Pickett. She wondered what it would be like to be friends with Mary Lou Forman, such a sophisticated person. She needed to get new friends. Rita was too fucking strange.

"How'd your little meeting with Old Lady Weiss go?" Rita asked.

"Oh God, you don't want to know. You're probably next, you know. I'll be cleaning those ditches for the next year, and she wants to see me every week. She's going to teach me deportment, whatever the hell that is."

"I think that's where you learn how to balance a book on your head," Stormy said, imitating a woman with her arms flat against her side walking a straight line.

"I think I'd almost rather go to therapy," Olive said.

"Where's Freddie?" Stormy asked.

"When he found out I was going to have to take the rap for the Colonel's missing arm, he confessed to the Indian. He's in the park helping the Chief solder the sucker back on."

Freddie was always doing things like that, like the time he took the gun to school to stick up for her. Olive loved him more than anyone, but he just couldn't learn to deal with his sexuality. Instead of finding gay friends, Freddie acted out by causing trouble. He was the first boy she'd done it with, although he basically only liked oral sex, which bothered Olive some because she was so obsessed by cleanliness.

The girls stood and moved on down the street, Rita and Stormy walking their bikes, Olive on foot, careful not to step on any cracks.

"I wish you wouldn't do that," Rita said.

Olive knew she'd lose the vision in her right eye if she stepped on a crack; once she'd told herself if she didn't count all the telephone poles on the way to her Aunt Tilley's in Thief River Falls, her little sister would fall and break her arm. Sure enough, she got bored and quit counting. Then, only two months later, Nancy had fallen out of an apple tree.

"Mind your own business," Olive said.

"I think it's nuts, you need a head shrinker."

"You're going around poisoning dogs and you think I need a psychiatrist?"

"I gotta get going," Stormy said, "I gotta be to work in a few minutes."

"Whyn't you say something?" Olive said. "That only leaves two of us to do the panhandling."

The girl shrugged, looked guilty. "I thought we'd be done by now."

Rita gave her a withering look. "Get out of here, then, nobody wants you around anyway."

The girl ducked her head, most likely anticipating a punch, then pedaled away down the street, looking back at them, as if to check whether they were chasing her.

"She makes my nipples hard," Rita said.

"She's only thirteen, Rita. Why don't you leave her alone?"

"Sure, like you've never done it with a girl. Madonna does it with girls, so why not?"

"Because it's gross, that's why. Don't you know about Sodom and Gomorrah?"

"Fuck Sodom and Gomorrah. Lester Krueger's fucking Stormy now anyway."

"Lester the Molester. You ever do it with him?"

"Let's just say for a little guy, he's got the biggest dick I've ever seen."

Olive got up behind Rita's bike and they zigzagged down the sidewalk. A little boy and his father were pulling a red wagon along the sidewalk across the street. The wagon was heaped full of black dirt. The little boy looked very purposeful. Olive Randall's father had left when she was three years old. She could not get her mother to talk about him at all, but she found pictures of him in the bottom drawer of the old dresser in her mother's bedroom, those and the sex manual she learned so much from.

The boy and his father came to a bare spot on the lawn; the little fellow couldn't be more than three or four, Olive thought. He was wearing a sailor's hat turned down over his ears, and he had a small scoop shovel. The man was very patient, although the boy was getting most of the dirt on the sidewalk. Occasionally, the man tipped a bunch of dirt out of the wagon onto the bare spot, and the boy would get down and smooth it out with his hands.

The man noticed Olive watching them and smiled. *What kind of smile is that, I wonder?* Olive thought.

Ordinarily she'd flash him, but not around the rug rat.

Not too bad looking, black, thinning hair, smile like an evangelical preacher. "Looks like he works out," Olive said. "I'm pretty sure he's a teller at the bank." Maybe he'd like to get together later.

"You'd have sex with your own father," Rita said.

"No, I wouldn't. Why don't you just shut up."

They were coming up on a vacant store with the faded words *Gail and Ax Chewing and Smoking Tobacco* painted on one side. Five cents. Had cigarettes ever cost five cents? The store's windows were boarded up.

Rita stopped her bike and looked back at Olive. "That episode in the park going on your record?"

"Not as far as I know. I didn't see a judge or anything."

"Not like the shoplifting thing, huh?"

"That was a total misunderstanding. I put that compact in my pocket, just until I could take it to the counter to pay, I had my birthday money from Grandma. Didn't know about the goddamn security camera until the store detective stopped me outside." The experience had been humiliating, but also kind of exhilarating.

"Tell that to somebody who ain't seen you pull the five-fingered discount hundreds of times."

"Jeez, I was only nine years old. They acted like I was a hardened criminal."

"You ever been in jail?"

"Yeah the time Freddie and me got caught vandalizing the school. We snuck out at three in the morning and Freddie had a can of spray paint, and he dared me to write 'fuck you' on the double doors in front of the school. Harry Kline caught us, kept us in jail overnight, then made us clean up the ditches around town for two weeks."

"They have a thing about those ditches, don't they? Wish I had an old man like that guy back there. He looks like he takes the time to be with his kid. My pa begrudges us the food we eat."

"At least you've got one. I tell you I had a dream about you last night?"

"I knew you wanted me."

"Not that kind of dream, you were just in it. It was kind of weird—I think it was about my father."

Rita laid her bike down on the grass in front of the bank, and they sat down Indian style. "Tell it then," Rita said. "You have such cool dreams."

"Okay, but don't interrupt like you always do. Let me see, how'd it go? You and me were at one of those Renaissance festivals where everybody pretends they're characters from the middle ages and you and me we were charging at each other on these big old draft horses that the farmers have. I had a white one, yours was black, of course, since you're evil."

"Fuck you, Goldilocks!"

"Shut up, will you? You're makin' me forget. The horses were armor-plated, and we had these big pig stickers, lances I think they're called. We came charging at each other and I rammed that thing right down your fuckin' throat. The blood came gushing out the back of your head. It was orgasmic, let me tell you."

"Hey!" Rita crossed her arms over her chest and gave Olive the evil eye.

If she got too testy, Olive would put her in a hammerlock and make her say, Who's your mama? "You wanna hear this or not?" Olive said.

"Go ahead, knock yourself out."

"I think that was a very sexual dream, you know, with the penis implications."

"What?"

"The lance symbolizes a penis. Howard told me."

"Oh, in that case."

"That's not the important part. It's who was in the crowd watching us. After I got down off my charger to administer the coup de grace with my sword—"

"The coup de what?"

"I was gonna make sure you were good and dead. Anyway, I noticed Scrambled and these two other guys out in the audience, only their faces weren't smeared like most of the other grunges. They didn't take a lot of baths in those days. Scrambled had on his usual dippy looking running outfit and this other guy was a short fat joker wearing one of those fishing hats with all the lures. He had kinda bug eyes, too. Then there was this big tall dufus who looked a little like Howard Pleasiac. They had the same hair, you know. Scrambled said, 'Hello, Olive. You need to turn him in, you know that, don't you?'"

"No shit?"

"I'm thinkin' since he hated Bronson so much that's who he meant. They had a fight over me, you know. Scrambled doesn't know—"

Rita uprooted a dandelion and set about plucking the petals, staining her fingers with yellow. "Anything else?" she said.

"Yeah. That's when my dad showed up. My real one, you know. He was with the maintenance crew that came to pick up the bodies and clean up the broken lances and that. Kind of looked like Deputy Sheriff Dave Jenkins, only taller and more muscular."

"You really got the hots for that guy, don'tcha?"

"Not really. He likes that Forman bitch. Anyway, I was telling him that not only was I good at jousting but I also got good grades in school, and wasn't he proud of me? And you know what he said?"

"No, what did he say?"

"He said, 'You're a fuckin' liar. I know you don't go to school very much.' Then he hopped on his Harley and rode away into the sunset and the background music was playing 'Eye of the Tiger'."

"Where'd the Harley come from? I thought this was about the middle ages."

"Dreams are like that."

"Whew, you're a bigger head case than I thought. You better not be plannin' on stickin' any pole down my throat." Rita looked up at the clock on the Farmers and Merchants bank, which read twelve o'clock. "Jeez, I hadn't realized it was so late. Here, take the bike, I gotta get going. My pa's got a meeting at the bank, and he's picking me up afterwards. If I'm late, he's not going to be in a good mood."

"You too? I was planning on panhandling at least twenty-five bucks among the three of us."

"Can't be helped. See you later." Rita trotted up the steps of the bank, opened the door, and was waving back at her before Olive got a chance to ask why her father was meeting with Banker Forman.

Every so often, Rita would show up at school with black and blue marks on her arms and face and the teachers would ask if she was having trouble at home. That's when Rita would raise holy hell and wind up in the principal's office for making threats.

Olive turned and walked the bike toward the church. Would she cover for her old man if he hit her? The closest to a father she'd ever had was her mom's live-in, Bob. Bob was the one got her started on her word for the day, said he was an instructor at U of M, Crookston. A young lady ought to learn how to articulate, he said.

Bob could have been Nancy and Patricia's father, he'd been around long enough, before her mom had told him to hit the bricks. The girls were with Grandma today, out at the farm, learning how to quilt. Olive made her little sisters flapjacks every morning. Her mom was usually too tired to cook after working until two at the Legion. Olive made sure the girls did their homework every night, and she made them say their prayers, too, although Uncle Bob said religion was just superstition.

Olive stretched, yawned, and looked up at the church steeple with the giant numerals, which read eighteen eighty-eight. She'd been counting on the money she got panhandling to buy some lottery tickets. Olive invested every spare dollar on the lottery. She couldn't buy the tickets herself, so she had Pigeon Hackett at the Amoco station, who'd do anything for her, get them for her. Pigeon was an old bachelor who lived with his mother. She could imagine him fantasizing about her.

She parked Rita's Schwinn in the bike rack, and looking all about her to make sure no one was watching, crossed the lawn separating the church from the rectory. Maybe she'd go see the old priest, who seemed to be a nice old man, tell *him* about her fucked-up life.

Mrs. Spahn, Father Mischke's cook and housekeeper, let Olive in. Rumor had it that there was a romantic relationship between the two. Olive couldn't fathom anyone having sex with such an old man.

Father Mischke was sitting at his circular kitchen table under a blue dome light, drinking coffee and reading the *Minneapolis Star Tribune* turned to the sports page.

A tomcat was sleeping next to Father's leg, and "My Boy Bill" was blaring from an old-fashioned, console radio. Father Mischke put down the paper and smiled when he saw Olive.

"What a nice present on a drizzly, Friday morning. I haven't seen you in church for some time, Olive. What can I do for you, sweetheart?" Father Mischke was getting really old; his clothes were too big for him, and his face was so shriveled it looked as if the bones had dissolved. His little eyes peeked out of the folds, rheumy and yellow.

Olive sat on a hard chair with an embroidered cushion on the seat. "I needed to talk to you, Father. You see, I wouldn't feel right going to confession in church since the tongues would start to wag."

"Have you met my cat, St. Peter?" Father Mischke said. "I call him St. Peter 'cause he's always denying me when the cock crows. I really ought to have him fixed." St. Peter gave him a dismissive look. Nobody was going to neuter old Pete. "If you're expecting absolution, Olive, I'll need my clerical garb." He closed the paper, smoothing it down on the table.

Olive touched her hair. "No, no, I just need to get something off my chest. I don't really believe in absolution, Father. I'm sorry."

The old priest pushed out his bottom lip at her. "It's all a matter of semantics, don't you think? Go ahead then, my dear. I'm all ears."

He certainly was. His face seemed to have shrunk since Olive had seen him last. St. Peter had gone back to sleep, purring in accompaniment to the show tunes on the radio.

Olive reached over to stroke the cat. "I'm sure you've heard the rumors, Father," she said. "I've done it all. I don't want to be crude, but I don't know how else to say it. I've even done it with older guys. One of them was a lot older, at least fifty. He's a real big shot. I just wanted to see if I could seduce him, you know what I mean? I was kind of surprised that I could. We did it right there in his office, right in the middle of the day with four hundred kids milling around outside the door. I suppose old guys have their needs, too, but this guy has the kind of job that should be above it all, if you know what I mean, kind of like a priest. He should have been able to resist the temptation, even if it was kind of my fault."

The telephone jangled, causing Olive to start. Father Mischke picked it up, listened for a few minutes, his face registering no emotion, then said, "You don't mean that, Mr. Barnhouser. It's my job to counsel my parishioners." He listened for a few minutes more, then said, "I'm not trying to make trouble for you; your wife asked me to find a shelter for her. Frankly, Mr. Barnhouser, I could have, and probably should have, called the police." He listened for a few more minutes, then set the phone down. "He doesn't mean it. I can't get him to come in here with his wife for counseling."

Olive rubbed the tops of her hands, which had turned blue from the cold, and they hadn't warmed yet to Father's log fire. "Did he threaten you, Father?" she asked. "With all that's been going on around here, I wouldn't take any chances. I saw Mr. Egge's body. We were out in the woods playing army with those paint-pellet guns—It's really fun, you oughta try it—Anyway, I tripped right over the body. His face looked like what comes out of a meat grinder, a real mess. I heard somebody coming, so I ran away. I get blamed for everything, you know, so I didn't tell any-body." Olive crossed her bare legs. She had already kicked off her sandals. Her micro-mini rode up some on her legs.

Father Mischke's face turned red, and he practically shouted at her. "Knees together, young lady! Put on your shoes and sit up straight in the chair."

Olive obeyed, smiling to herself as if relieved.

"Yes, Father," she said. "I really think you ought to report that call to Sheriff Kline. It would be different if Mr. Egge and the A.D. hadn't been killed, but I wouldn't chance it. So you think I should tell on Charlie Bronson then?"

"I would if I were you, Olive," he said, feeding St. Peter a sardine from a can he had on the table. The telephone had roused the cat who looked irritated, although he accepted the fish. "But it's really up to you, since what you tell me is strictly confidential, despite the fact that it's not a formal confession."

"That boy is in so much trouble," she said. "This is just one more reason he's the most likely suspect with Egge, but I'm wondering why he killed Ellis." Olive knew Bronson hadn't had anything to do with Ellis's murder, but she wanted to punish the superintendent for ignoring her when he saw her in the halls.

Father Mischke took one of the sardines and nibbled on it. "Who knows, Olive," he said, taking St. Peter off of his lap and putting him on the floor. "It's all so sad. The only consolation we can have is that it's over for them, and they're with God now."

"I wish I could believe that," Olive said, showing her dimples. "One more thing, Father. I need to know if you believe in ghosts. Some mighty strange things have been happening around here since Egge's murder. I keep having these strange dreams, and sometimes it's as if I've got somebody talking to me over my shoulder, and when I turn around to look who it is, there's nobody there."

He was looking at her as if he felt sorry for her.

Father Mischke glanced down at the front page of the paper. "I only believe in the Holy Ghost, Olive, although we call him the Holy Spirit these days. I'd take my own advice if I were you and talk to the sheriff about Charlie Bronson."

Olive scuffed across the polished entrance to the rectory, stooping to scratch the big cat's ears.

Chapter 14

Get Me to the Church on Time

"Every one fault seeming monstrous till
his fellow fault came to match it."
— Shakespeare, *As you Like It*

Dave eased the Jeep onto Meade and cruised past the firehouse, doing a sensible twenty miles an hour as he didn't want to upset Nellybelle's delicate dispositon. He'd noticed the oil gauge had dipped below the Mendoza line again. The thirsty girl drank more than a skid row dipso. He was on his way to the Krueger farm to confront Lester about the baseball bat Mel Kline said Lester'd snitched.

He pulled up to the pumps at the Amoco station, shut down the engine, and sat there thinking. His mind was not on his job. After the press conference, over coffee, Mary Lou had told him she was separated from her stockbroker husband, and she'd angled for somebody to hold her hand in the delivery room when she had her baby, which was due any day.

"I can't see my father having much of a bedside manner," she'd said. *Why me?* he wondered. She knew he adored her. Perhaps that was the reason. No one else around to fight off fire-breathing dragons and child-pilfering dwarves. Dave said he'd be honored, but he had a bad cold and didn't think the doctors would let him. She said that's why they wore those masks. He said if she could clear it with the doctors, he'd be happy to. Damn right he would. She'd be indebted to him for the rest of her life.

Pigeon rapped on the windshield. "Fill her up?"

"That and two quarts of oil."

He got out and stretched his legs. A block down he could see Olive Randall on the sidewalk adjacent to Immaculate Conception, doing jumping jacks, either that or she was waving at him. If she didn't cease and desist, he'd have no choice but to arrest her for indecent exposure.

When Pigeon had finished gassing and oiling Nellybelle, Dave steered the Jeep in Olive's direction, did a U-ball, and pulled up next to the curb in front of the church. Olive jumped into the front seat, damn near impaling herself on an exposed spring.

Olive was breathing rather heavily, either from all those jumping jacks, or she really was upset about something. She'd been in the sun. Freckles were beginning to sprout on her nose, and when the sunlight hit her face just right, he could see the downy fuzz on her cheeks and upper lips. She looked about fourteen.

"I thought I should tell you about what I just heard, considering what happened to Mr. Egge and Mr. Ellis." *The low-down and bluesy voice didn't match the freckles and the downy cheeks.* "I overheard this man—Father said it was Harley Barnhouser—threaten Father Mischke. I didn't think he'd tell you himself so I thought I better—"

"Harley Barnhouser is mostly hot air, Olive."

"But Father looked so afraid," she said.

"I'll watch the rectory, Olive. If only to set your mind at ease. Mind me asking what you were doing in there?"

"Not that it's any of your business, but I was telling Father about Charlie Bronson. That underwear you showed me was mine. I hope you don't hate me."

"I'm not exactly a footwashing Baptist myself, Olive," he said. "But you're only sixteen, and the law says Mr. Bronson is totally at fault."

She chewed on a thumbnail. "Doesn't seem fair. I knew what I was doing."

"Help me put the baby-raper in Stillwater where the cons'll show him what it's like to force himself on defenseless young..."

She crossed her legs, the mini skirt riding up on her thighs. Little nicks and cuts marred the otherwise statuesque legs. "Come on now, David. We both know that age is relative. Charlie's a sixteen-year-old football player, and he'll be one when he's ninety-four if he lives that long."

Amazing, she even sounded like Mary Lou.

"You know what he told me when we had sex?" she said. "He said he made all-state his senior year. Does that sound like your basic well-adjusted adult? And, besides, Charlie didn't really have a chance once I set my cap for him. Just like you wouldn't stand a chance if I decided I wanted you, David."

Every time she said his name, Dave felt an electric tingle surge through his loins. She winked, then hopped out of the Jeep and headed toward the bike rack, looking back at him over her shoulder. That smile made him feel like Paris must have felt the first time he saw Helen of Troy and decided to steal her from Melaneus. Melaneus? Who the hell was Melaneus? Who was Helen of Troy and Paris, for that matter?

More of that Shakespeare stuff most likely. Next thing he knew he'd be going to one of those operas, the kind where nobody understood a word. He sighed, put the Jeep in low gear, and swung out onto Meade on his way to the Kruegers. Didn't figure anything could happen to the old priest in broad daylight.

* * *

Dave parked the Jeep next to the Krueger's three-story, rambling farmhouse. The Krueger yard measured about the size of a supermarket parking lot. The barn and outbuildings were grouped in a circle and protected on the west side by a windbreak of evergreens. What looked like a new machine shed, all metal, the front door big enough to admit an F-14, commanded most of the yard. At first Dave couldn't see Miles anywhere. Then he noticed Miles's feet sticking out from under his combine.

Splashing through the mud puddles to where Miles was working, Dave knocked on the metal housing protecting the machine's vital parts. "Hey, Miles. Dave Jenkins here. Can I talk to you for a minute?"

"Hand me that wrench, will you?" Miles said. "I almost got this. Just a few more minutes should do it."

A half hour later, Miles crawled out from under the machine, chicken shit spotting the seat of his overalls. "What can I do for you, Deputy?" he said.

"Like to talk to your boy Lester."

"He ain't here. Right after the Indian talked to the boy, he left for the Cities looking for a job. Said he wouldn't be back till Monday. The boy's been trouble ever since he was born, he just ain't got no sense."

"Do you ever remember seeing him with a baseball bat with a narrow handle?"

Miles knelt and began to collect his tools. "He played for the junior high school team for a while is all I know. Spent hours throwin' the ball up against the silo. Got so's it was interfering with his chores, and I had to threaten to make him quit. I never was much for athletics myself."

"But you didn't see any bat?"

"Well, I can't say that. Seems like he had one, but I thought that Egge give it to him, so I didn't think nothing of it. If that boy stole,

I'll tan his hide." A look of enlightenment crossed Krueger's face. "You don't mean to imply that my boy...? The neighbor lady says Egge was killed with a baseball bat."

"No, we have no conclusive proof of anything, Miles."

"About those shoes the Indian took?"

"We'll get those back to you. They don't match the tracks we found at the murder scene."

* * *

"Shit!" Dave said, when he finally got the Jeep started after grinding the battery down to a minimal groan. He left the Jeep in idle and sat there drumming his fingers on the wheel, so deep in thought he didn't notice he'd turned off the radio. Why the hell hadn't he nailed Lester when he had the chance? Would an all points bulletin do any good? More ammunition for Larry Henderson. This afternoon when they met to plan strategy, Dave was going to have egg all over his face. Henderson would call Hildegard the minute the meeting ended.

What next? He had to see Mrs. Ellis, although he didn't really believe the jealousy angle was worth a fiddler's fuck.

There was a smudge on the windshield, and when he reached into his pocket for a rag to wipe it off, he touched Egge's pipe again. This time a group of teens were sitting around a fire listening to a man read. The book jacket read *Soul on Ice.* He recognized several of the kids: Olive, Freddie, Lester Krueger, Stormy Guck. Freddie and Lester were passing a doobie back and forth. The man put the book down and said, "This morning I read a story about a rich man who built his dog an elaborate house, with its own bathroom, gold-plated fixtures on the plumbing."

The teenagers chanted, "Kill the rich bastards!"

Dave tried to focus on the scene as Moe had on his dream about Egge's murder. A small creek was running just behind the fire. Some of the kids were wandering in and out of what looked like a lean-to with a barbed-wire fence in the background. Somebody's pasture?

There was a knock on the windshield. Dave jumped, let go of the pipe, then rolled down his window. "Anything else I can do for you, Deputy?" Krueger said.

"Nah, I was just thinking. Let me know if Lester shows up." He put the Jeep in gear and drove off.

That afternoon, as he was talking to Mrs. Ellis, who claimed she didn't even know about Ellis's flirting, he got a call from Mingo.

"This is going to break your heart, Dude," Mingo said, "but one of those splatballers has fallen and he can't get up. Fell down a gulley out there in the woods near the Egge scene and broke his fibula in three places."

"Was he pushed?"

"Yes, I think so. But we can't prosecute the mountain spirits. You want me to handle this?"

"Yeah, you talk to the guy. Sound him out good, make damn sure there's no connection with the E&E murders. You know about the meeting at Bud's?"

"That's affirmative. There's another little development, though. I got a letter in the mail today; Forman is repoing on my pick-up. Can he do that?"

"If you missed a payment. Jeez, I just thought of something, I owe the bastard for the roof job I did on my gram's house. I better check my mail."

After leaving Mrs. Ellis's place on Wheat Field Lane, Dave drove down Meade. Every other house had a wrap-around porch. Usually housewives were out on their porches shooting the breeze, even at midday. One thing about Soldier—you never went begging for company late at night when there was nothing on television, providing you didn't want to talk religion or politics. Today, the porches were deserted.

He stopped at a little white split-level on Hancock near the cemetery. Wilbur Small had been out of work ever since the sugar beet processing plant had closed. Didn't stop him from having kids. The youngest was only two he thought. Mindy was the oldest.

Dave knocked on the door, then, noticing the door bell, gave it a tap. Mindy answered. She was baking chocolate chip cookies for her brothers and sisters. She shooed the young ones out in the yard, and they sat around the kitchen table having coffee.

She was a pretty little thing, the kind of girl you wouldn't be afraid to take home to Mom, what with the ruddy cheeks and the earnest Teresa Wright face.

"I'm here about the Ellis murder, Mindy," he said.

"Oh God, you don't think I had anything to do with that, do you? I've been thinking of quitting. I can't go back to that place after what I saw."

"No, no, we have a report that Ellis was bothering you is all. Did you tell anyone about that?"

"Told my boyfriend is all," she said. "I never filed any charges. Mr. Bronson doesn't like people making waves."

"And your boyfriend's name?"

"Oh, don't be getting him into this. He's a teacher at the school, Marshall Preston."

Good old Marshall, sniffing around all the foxy women.

* * *

The nasal recording on Marshall Preston's answering machine said the phys. ed. teacher was at Soldier High.

Dave legged it down the recently-waxed hallway to the gym and the boys' locker room, where he heard the spatter of water on cement. Marshall taking a shower.

At his locker, Marshall dusted himself with talcum powder. "I talked to Ellis about Mindy, " he said. Dave tried not to look. Couldn't hardly help it, though, the guy had a dick like a vacuum cleaner nozzle. "Fran said he was just teasing her, and if she didn't like it, he'd cut it out."

"Yeah, but he didn't cut it out," Dave said. "I saw him ogle her myself the day before he was killed."

"She never said anything to me," Preston said. "Let me ask you something, Deputy. Do you really think I'd need a golf club if I wanted to smack Fran Ellis around?"

Marshall had been doing heavy-duty weights, another reason to hate him.

"I doubt it. Never know, though. If you had to guess, who would you say did this to Ellis?"

"Shit, you've got me. The world's gone crazy. Say, been meaning to ask about Anne Kline. I asked her out. You don't mind, do you?"

"No skin off my nose, Marshall, but does Mindy know about Annie?"

"Do I look stupid to you, Deputy?"

Yeah, you do, Buddy, Dave was thinking, *but I guess they're so desperate for teachers these days that they let anybody into teaching, especially physical education.*

* * *

Bud's was pretty much deserted, except for Pigeon from the Amoco and a few of his buddies who'd been given the go-ahead to form a Crime Watch.

Mingo, Harry, Henderson and Dave took chairs around a table in front of the bar's only window with a view of the traffic on Meade.

Harry, dressed in off-duty attire, a voluminous, pink bowling shirt with "Alley Cats" emblazoned on the back, handed Dave an official-looking letter. "Bronson says you got rough with him the other day during your interrogation."

"You call tossing Olive's pants in his face rough? I'll show him rough." He made a smacking sound, his fist meeting his palm.

Bud, gray thinning hair combed down in a Julius Caesar, came out from behind the bar and stood in front of the table with his arms folded over his apron. "What'll it be, boys?" he said.

"Coffee, Bud," Harry said. "We're all on duty." He winked.

"The usual then," Bud said, chuckling to himself on his way back behind the bar. Irish coffee for Harry. Mingo yelled after him, "I'll take a hamburger with my coffee."

Harry tapped Bronson's letter on the table. "I gotta show it to the commissioners. SOP, you know."

Mingo had that coyote look on his face, probably plotting when would be the best time to move into Dave's office permanent.

"This doesn't have anything to do with the recall petition, does it, Harry?"

"Not hardly. Look, Jenkins, I've been there, you know about what happened with me and the Forman kid. Old McCloskey stood up for me, and I'll stand up for you, so forget it, I'll tell them the man's a chicken hawk. They'll probably want to put him in the stocks. Oh, by the way, Hildegard got the signatures. I'm on the ballot for recall during the November election."

"Sorry to hear that, Harry."

Henderson, formally informal in a black knit shirt, buttoned at the neck and khakis with pleats, cleared his throat, a signal to get on with it. "We talked to that reporter from the press conference," he said, "the one who knew what the murderer sprayed on Egge's back. At first, she wouldn't give us the time of day."

"Yeah, she wouldn't shut up about first amendment rights," Harry said. "Dared me to slap the cuffs on her."

"That was before we promised her an exclusive interview," Henderson said, looking like the cat who swallowed the expensive South American macaw.

"She got an anonymous call is what it was," Harry said. "At first she thought the guy was one of those whackos who like to confess to murders they had nothing to do with. But he had so much detail, and when that other reporter mentioned the spray paint, she thought she'd send out a feeler. Just to see what we'd say."

"How'd the creep know who to call?" Dave said.

"He saw her company car at the motel. He'd even read some of her stuff."

"Bastard must think he's Lex Luther," Dave said.

"Let's hope he keeps it up," Henderson said.

"Any more on the splatballer kid who broke his leg, Mingo?" Dave asked.

"Just a klutz," Mingo said. "None of the combatants from Crookston saw anything either."

Dave brought them up to date on the various interrogations and on what Olive had told him about the threat to Father Mischke.

Bud set the coffee and the food down in front of them, then stood listening in. Nobody told him to kiss off.

"Olive Randall isn't the most reliable person in town," Harry said. He took a swallow of the Irish. "I caught her making out on top of the water tower one night with at least three guys. Did you talk to Father Mischke?"

"Not yet," Dave said.

"Why don't you just go see Harley," Harry said, trying to blow smoke rings. "He just likes to talk tough. His old man is one of our deer hunting regulars."

Dave waved the smoke out of his eyes. "I'll do that," he said. "You can bet I will."

"What's with you and Harley anyway?" Bud said.

"I don't know. I just don't like the guy."

"Let's get back to the murder cases, shall we?" Henderson said. "Would you excuse us, sir?" Bud looked hurt, then turned on his heel and went back behind the bar, where he began kibitzing with the card players.

"Personally I think we should arrest Bronson," Harry said. "Alibi or no alibi. He's got all that motive and now there's Olive Randall as well. If that came out, he wouldn't be able to find a job as a ditchdigger. It's not like he's got a hard alibi." Harry ground out his cigarette.

Dave glanced at his watch. "Shirley showed Mel the murder weapon. He says it's his. He had the handle honed down real thin, hasn't seen it since he was on Egge's junior high team, always thought Lester Krueger took it, but he couldn't prove it."

Somebody put a quarter in the juke box, and Patsy Cline began crooning "Crazy" at four or five decibels.

"Turn that down, will you, Bud?" Harry yelled. "Never liked that boy. Before you came to work for me, he got in some trouble with one of the Oakry girls—they live out there on the farm next to

Krueger. Pretty good spread, at least a section, he raises beef cattle. I don't know what Clay Oakry was thinking when he let his girl go out with that boy. Anyway, he tried to feel her up, she scratched his face, walked home, and spilled the whole thing to her brothers. The brothers tracked Lester down, and he pulled a gun on 'em. They ran off like scared rabbits, but Clay called me about the gun. I went out there and took it away from the boy. Told him to stay away from the Oakry girl. Not that taking that gun away did much good. Miles probably has an arsenal."

The smell of hamburger and onions wafted over their way. Dave bawled out an order. He hadn't eaten since he'd grabbed a slice of bologna from the fridge on his way to the Ellis crime scene.

"Lester looks like a solid suspect to me, Harry," Mingo said. "I had him in for an interview. Talking to him, I got the impression that the old man, Miles, mighta married his sister."

"And where is this Lester Krueger person?" Henderson said.

"I was just out there," Dave said. "Miles says he's job hunting in the Cities."

"You won't see him again," Henderson said.

Mingo was doing something funny with his hamburger. He'd poured the salt into his hand, taken a pinch, salted the burger in a circular motion, and now he was forming an ex within the circle. More hoodoo.

"Lester used to be on our softball team," Dave said, "but he didn't seem quite so off at the time. Wasn't any good, but...And now I can't find the bastard. Anything from forensics?"

"Forensics can't tell us anything about the Ellis letter as compared to the stuff on Egge's back," Henderson said. He shook his head no to Harry's offer of another coffee.

Mingo squinted, then rubbed his eyes. "Freddie Cochran—you know, the gay kid—confessed that he and Olive painted that obscenity on the tower. I don't think he killed Egge though. He just likes to jerk people around." Henderson and Harry grinned. Dave wondered what was so funny.

Henderson rubbed his chin. "What about Egge's wife? She had the insurance policy, and according to Jenkins here, he didn't exactly love his family. Maybe there's a trail there, telephone records and such."

"She's the only other one with a real motive," Dave said. "They're an awfully spooky family, that's for sure."

"I wouldn't dismiss the Cochran kid as of yet," Harry said. "You say he's gay. Maybe he wanted to keep it quiet, and Ellis and Egge knew about it. This isn't exactly San Francisco, you know."

He lit another cigarette. "What a mess. It's been a week, and we're nowhere with this thing. Hildegard says this publicity will ruin everything we're tried to do with the strip mall and Wal-Mart."

"Why do you care what Hildegard thinks?" Dave said, trying to make Harry feel better about the recall.

"I'm still sheriff, Jenkins. And until I'm not, I'm going to care. Hildegard says the Egge and Ellis cases make us look like St. Cloud. I don't think they've ever solved a murder there, have they?"

Harry was ribbing Henderson, who had been involved in the investigation of at least three unsolved murders in the granite city.

* * *

When the other two left, Dave asked Mingo, "That thing you do with the salt, what the hell is that?"

"Back in the old days there was a shortage of salt. You were only allowed a pinch. We Mescaleros don't use salt shakers. It's considered selfish."

"What's with the circle and the ex?"

"Oh, that's a kind of blessing. The sun is circular, the world was created in four days, so we divide the circle in four parts. It also signifies the four seasons, the four directions etc. Kind of like the sign of the cross for you...I mean us...Christians. Wanna know how to hex somebody?"

"Not especially."

"I'll tell you anyway so's the next time we play Harley Barnhouser's team he'll strike out four or five times. What you do is draw a circle counterclockwise."

"You decided to play with us, huh?"

"I guess. You draw the circle clockwise cause the world was created in the east. If you start in the west, or counterclockwise, you witch yourself."

Dave put some money on the table. They waved to the cribbage players and the crime watch. Next stop Shady Brook and Harley Barnhouser's trailer. Dave needed to let Harley know he knew about his threat on the priest.

On their way, over the coughing and sputtering of the Jeep, the Indian declared his admiration for Dave's Shakespeare mentor, the redheaded Debbie Meyer. According to Mingo, she was the incarnation of White Painted Woman, whoever the hell that was.

Barnhouser's wife didn't know where he was. They checked the Legion and Andy's. No Harley.

"I tell you Charlie Bronson bought some strychnine a couple days before the murder?" Dave said, standing on the steps outside Barnhouser's trailer.

"Lucille told me," Mingo said. "Why would he want to kill Hildegard's dogs?"

"Hildegard thinks it's because she fingered Bronson as Egge's murderer. I don't believe any of this shit."

Since it was growing dark, Mingo left to go on duty, and since Dave hadn't tracked down the threatening phone call, he motored toward the rectory, parking to the south on Zouave Road, just behind some shrubbery, but with a clear view of the front door. Harley was a mean drunk. Dave had been to his trailer once or twice because of neighbors' complaints. Dave would watch the rectory for a few hours. Maybe he should go see if the old man was scared. Nah, he wasn't in the mood for another lecture about missing mass.

He could see the old boy reading through the window with a blue dome light overhead and an old cat in his lap. What a lonely existence.

Suddenly he sneezed. Yup, he had a cold all right. Probably got it from Typhoid Mary Bronson. He reached in the glove compartment, came out with a bottle of cough medicine and took a slug, straight out of the bottle, then he took out his penlight and began rereading Egge's desktop files. Mostly Egge wrote about his job, personality conflicts, how lonely it was at the top. Dave already knew about the people Egge mentioned.

Dave glanced up occasionally. Father was still there until around eleven when he shut off his light. Dave checked the doors to the rectory and the church. Some dogs were barking, and across the street, a man and woman were arguing. A baby began to cry, and the woman's voice became even more strident. Was he going to have to go over there and deal with that? The door slammed, the man stalked out to his car and left. Dave went back to his reading. His eyes went to half-mast after a few minutes. He tried to slap himself awake, but eventually he lost it, dropping the journal on the floor.

He was in a cage in a zoo-like place. People were watching him as if he were some strange animal. It was similar to that scene in *2001 Space Odyssey* where the astronaut is being viewed by the aliens in his very own living room, only it was Dave who was being viewed by the people, and he was sitting around a table with his friends during drafting time for the rotisserie league and the audience cackled, guffawed, tittered.

A door slammed and he snapped awake, jumped out of the cruiser, and tried to see his watch. It was pitch black out with no moon, and he couldn't find his flashlight. He raced for the rectory door, tripping on something stiff and furry as he entered the hallway. Switching on the lights, he was confronted with the cat, a belt twisted around its neck. Rosary beads were strewn all over the floor, and a painting of Jesus was propped up against the TV. The Christ's eyes were poked out.

Dave searched the rooms on the bottom floor, then checked the musty-smelling bedrooms above. The priest was not in the rectory. Dave trotted down the creaky stairs, out the back door and toward the church. The door to the sacristy was locked, but as he turned to try the main entrance, a voice said, "I'll call the police if you don't go away."

"It's me, Father, Dave Jenkins."

Father Mischke opened it. "Thank God," he said. The priest was bleeding from his forehead. Dave grasped Father's arm and practically carried him back to the rectory, where they stepped around the cat, and Dave got Father to sit down and take a drink of water.

"I never touch the stuff," Father said. Dave got him a bottle of Scotch from the liquor cabinet and poured him a drink.

Dave went to the kitchen to get a washcloth for the priest's forehead and an ice pack for the lump on his head.

The old priest, his hands pressed between his knees, tried to tell him what had happened. "I heard a noise, kind of like a crowbar opening a packing case, and I looked at my bedside clock. It was midnight. Remembering the phone call, I thought I'd better dial 9-1-1, but there was no dial tone. I got down on my knees and crawled out into the hall where I heard this awful screech, which must have been poor old Pete. Sounded like the hounds of Hell. Mercy, I was so scared. There's a backstairs and a backdoor to the rectory, and I crept that way, trying not to make a sound. The intruder was making an awful racket downstairs. When I was a little boy, our house was struck by a tornado. It sounded like that, crashing sounds, breaking glass. I'm really surprised all that racket didn't wake you up."

Dave had told him that he'd been watching in front of the rectory but had fallen asleep. Maybe he should have followed the directions on that cough medicine bottle.

Father knelt down, trying to clean up some of the mess. Dave lifted him back into the chair, chiding him about interfering with the scene.

"When I got to the back door of the rectory, I opened it and tried to run the hundred yards or so to the church, which has an excellent lock, thanks to the innumerable efforts to rob the poor box. I have arthritis in my knees, so I'm afraid I don't run too well. Twenty years ago I left that church open all night. People sometimes need the most solace at three in the morning. I'd just about made it when I was hit from behind. It felt as though someone had hit me with a pickax.

"I don't know how I got away. You'd think I'd be about the easiest target there is, what with my arthritis and everything. I think the man was drunk, seems like I remember smelling alcohol."

"Could have been drugs." Dave said. "He probably saw three or four of you and picked the wrong one."

Father Mischke managed a grin, poured himself another drink, his hand shaking some. He slopped some of it on his pants leg. "It was pitch dark out. Dark as hell, Thank God. I just managed to roll away and get the door unlocked. I always keep a key on a chain around my neck since I've lost it so often. I tried to slam the door, but the meshuggener got his arm through it just as I tried to slam it. I did the only thing I could do. I bit his hand as hard as I could. He started swearing and withdrew his hand long enough for me to slam the door."

Dave, who had been standing, pulled a hassock up next to Father Mischke and sat down. "Did you notice anything about the man, Father?"

The old priest set the ice pack down, thought for a moment. "Let's see, his hand was very hairy. I think I took quite a hunk out of it. There was an exit light right above the door, so I could see the hand well."

"That's enough for now, Father. I'm going to take you to the hospital. They'll most likely want to keep you overnight. What do you need? I'll get it for you."

Father Mischke rubbed his eyes and looked up. "There's one more thing I need to tell you, David." He looked guilty. "I'm not sure if I should tell you this. Let me just say that I know who hit me. This morning, before mass, a man came to me in the confessional. He confessed that he'd beaten Principal Egge to death. I'm only telling you this because I know what a reckless person you can be sometimes. This man is evil. You need to be more careful."

"Did you get a look at him, Father?"

Father Mischke looked at him as if he were dealing with an ungovernable child. "I can't tell you that," he said.

Dave went into Father's bathroom to collect his toothbrush and razor. So why would Bronson want Fr. Mischke dead? Maybe he'd been watching Olive, and he'd seen her go into the rectory. Olive could implicate him in Egge's death. But if that were the case, why not kill Olive in the first place?

He looked in the mirror. A haggard-looking bastard with bloodshot eyes stared back at him. He ran water in the sink, splashed some of it on his face, shook it off like a wet dog. This murderer was a trickster. He could have wanted Fr. Mischke to live. But why take the chance of Father seeing his face? A big, strong guy should have been able to overpower a sick old priest, even if there *were* three or four of him.

* * *

When Dave returned from the hospital, Henderson, still wearing his pajama tops under his coat, was parading up and down on the sidewalk outside the rectory, pointing out possible evidence to the criminalists.

A crowd was beginning to gather. Some of Henderson's men were trying to get them to disperse.

Dave and Henderson stood on the sidewalk rehashing what the criminalists had found so far.

"The entrance door was wrenched open with a crowbar," Henderson said. "We found it lying in the weeds by the front step. The wound on the priest's head came from a server's cross we found in front of the sacristy door."

"This guy is a real clown," Dave said.

"What do you mean?"

"The sporting motif? First the Louisville Slugger, then the Big Bertha. LaCrosse, get it?

"Yeah sure," Henderson said. "I don't understand how you didn't hear the door being jimmied."

"I haven't been sleeping well lately. When I sleep, I sleep like the dead." Couldn't tell him the truth. Like an animal tranquilizer, it had hit him. He'd never use that stuff again. He'd figured a half bottle would knock that cold right out.

"The boys picked up lots of prints from the belt around the cat's neck," Henderson said. "If he's on file, we'll get him this time."

Henderson lit one of his British cigarettes, offered Dave one. He surprised himself by accepting it. When he inhaled, he grew dizzy. Dave flicked an ash with his index finger. "We need to rap up tonight, Larry. This place is in constant use. The diocese is sending over a substitute priest first thing in the morning." He took another drag. He was growing used to it. He wanted another one after he ground the stub out.

After he left Henderson—no time to sleep—Dave followed the early morning traffic—curiosity seekers and farmers not afraid of any murderer since they'd endured drought, floods, and low prices for years—north to Shady Brook and Harley Barnhouser's lair. The Barnhouser trailer looked as if it had been salvaged from a junk yard, the shades drawn on the windows, the flowers in the trellis long dead. Barnhouser, a homely little cockroach with hair growing out of his ears, proof positive Darwin was right, was hunched on the front step fiddling with a carburetor. When he noticed Dave, he stood, and rolled up his sleeves, revealing a lewd tattoo of a mermaid fornicating with Neptune. Dave wondered how much bug spray it would take to purge this particular pest. Not this time. Despite the hair on Barnhouser's ears, there was none on his hands. No bite marks.

"What you want, fuzzface?" Barnhouser said.

"If I were you, I'd lose that tone, Harley. This is official. Did you make a threatening phone call to Father Mischke yesterday?"

"Don't know nothing about any phone call to Father Mischke. Been in Fargo all day at an American Legion convention. Forgot to tell the wife where I was going. We ain't been getting along. Didn't make it home until three in the morning."

"Gonna need to take your prints, Harley." Dave grinned.

"What the fuck? You can't do that, I got my rights."

"I'll be stopping by here much more regularly to check on Mrs. Barnhouser then."

Harley folded. Dave took his prints with his portable kit, got a phone number from Harley with which he could verify his alibi, then headed back to the office to check long distance telephone records for the previous morning when Olive had said she'd talked to Father Mischke. No one had called the rectory long distance. Harley had been at the Legion convention, but the fellow Dave talked to said he couldn't swear to when he left. Dave thought Harley was lying about the phone call, but if he knew Harley, he was probably too lazy to go out of his way to rough up Father Mischke.

At ten o'clock the BCA report came in, pretty damn amazing for a Saturday morning. When the BCA compared Harley's prints to those on the belt, they came up negative. Bronson's, on the other hand, matched. The prints on the belt left Dave no choice. He'd have to arrest Bronson. He didn't believe Bronson had attacked Father Mischke either. The belt looked like a plant, just like the baseball bat at the Egge murder scene. Damn cough medicine. Had him, and he'd let him get away!

Rather than eat or go home for some rest, Dave hopped in the Jeep and sped toward the intersection of Seminary and Wheat Field where Bronson and the Mrs. had built a large Spanish-style hacienda. Dave needed to check on the man's alibi for the previous night and to tell him about the incriminating evidence.

Bronson answered after the third ring, still in his pajamas, hair mussed like a fright wig, the daggers gone from his eyes. All the bluster he'd had during the first interview in his office had evaporated. The incredible shrinking man, that's who he reminded Dave of. Apparently it had gotten out that Bronson was a suspect and the neighbors were venting their spleen.

The super led the way to the living room, where he directed Dave to a purplish sectional sofa the size of a small state. When Dave sat, he sank into cushions softer than a fat lady's bosom. The super slumped in a matching armchair.

Dave told Bronson about the assault on the priest and the fingerprints.

"I haven't seen that belt in weeks," Bronson said. "I was at home watching a late movie."

"And what movie was that?"

"Casablanca I think. I don't know, I fell asleep."

"Anybody verify that?" Dave said.

"No, I don't know where the wife is. She's filing for divorce. I guess the bad publicity was too much for her. Robbie is at school."

"I suppose next you're gonna tell me some felonious bastard copped the strychnine you bought at Warner's?"

"You know about that?"

"Let me see your hands," Dave said.

Bronson held up his hands. Very hairy, no bite marks, though.

"Would you know of anyone who might be trying to frame you?"

A flicker of fear darted across the man's face. "I have no idea," Bronson said.

Another liar.

"Look, man, why don't you come clean about your relationship with Olive Randall? She could have taken personal items from your house. Have you ever had sex here?"

"I never had anything to do with Olive Randall. Do I look like a fool to you, Deputy? That was one of Jerry Egge's pipe dreams."

Dave fought through the cushions, got up to leave. He'd let Harry make the decision to arrest Bronson. Then he could say "I told you so" when Bronson was proved innocent.

"Those prints should clinch it for the Bureau of Criminal Apprehension, Chuck. A smart man like you, I don't personally think you'd assault a priest. But I'm just a peon. You know where to reach me if you change your mind."

Bronson nodded, showed Dave to the door.

Dave's next stop, Doc Bailey the veterinarian. Bailey ran Soldier's version of the Humane Society. Pigeon Hackett, who doubled as the town dog catcher, brought Doc stray dogs, cats, snakes, ferrets—even a mountain lion once—animals that people thought would make good pets, then reconsidered once they had them. Doc had quite a menagerie, since he'd rather commit hari-kari than put an animal to sleep. He must have had at least fifty dogs and cats. One of the cats was a Persian he called Rain in the Face because of its stoic disposition. It could have been Old St. Pete's brother, and probably was. Dave thought the aristocratic cat would be perfect for Father Mischke.

Chapter 15

The Pink Slip

*"If you want me again look for
me under your boot-soles."*
— Walt Whitman

Dave hadn't been to bed since five the previous morning, when he'd been awakened with the news of the Ellis murder. He was so tired his eyeballs hurt when he looked up, down, or sideways, and he was getting goofy, cruising through stop signs, almost running down a transportation crewman filling in potholes on Peach who'd popped out from behind his truck as Dave drove by. Must've missed him by inches.

He parked his Jeep in front of the sheriff's office, bumping over the curb in the process. When he got out, he left the door open.

Shirley had reached him on his cellular at Doc Bailey's. The FBI report on the names he'd received from Mrs. Szymanski had arrived. He weaved toward the door.

"You look terrible," Shirley said, looking up from her typing. "You really ought to go home and get some sleep." When Shirley got up to get him a cup of coffee, she left a vapor trail, like a jet plane.

"I'm going home now," he said, "but I need to see that report." He tore open the envelope and scanned the xeroxed pages. They were blurred, and he rubbed his eyes for better focus. One hit out of forty possibles. Brad Huntzinger, fifty-two years old, member of the SDS at Berkeley, involved in the bombing of the University of Wisconsin science building.

Berkeley? Hadn't Moe said something about Berkeley? No description, picture, or fingerprints.

When he looked up, Shirley was no more than a foot away, so close they almost bumped heads. She'd changed into a school girl. Her dark hair was pulled back and tied in the back with a big red ribbon, and she wore a fetching beige pants suit with suspenders and little buttons where the clasps would usually be. He felt like resting his head on her breast. If he did, he was sure he'd fall right to sleep.

"Anything interesting?" she said.

"Could be. One of that Ohio principal's students was in the SDS. Remember that? Students for a Democratic Society. He bombed the science building at the University of Wisconsin, on the run ever since. I've got to get home before I fall asleep on the floor. I'll be back around noon."

"Take your time. We'll hold down the fort." She recommenced her typing.

Dave left his Jeep where it was, after slamming the door shut. He'd walk home since he was a menace behind the wheel, and it was only a few blocks to his house. He'd take the shortcut to his house behind the Legion. When he got there, he saw that the fallen tree-bridge over Plum Creek had been washed away. Rather than go the long way around, he shed his shoes and socks and waded across. The frothy river water was so cold it made his teeth ache.

The *Soldier Clarion* was lying on his front steps. He looked down at the front page, the print swimming in and out of focus. The Red River was cresting over flood stage. The people in East Grank Forks were sandbagging in preparation.

When he turned the knob, he saw that the door was ajar. Seems like he'd locked it. Once inside, an odor like brass knuckles jabbed at his nose, a stink so bad the toilet had to have backed up. He tossed his socks in the clothes hamper, dropped his sneakers in the closet, and stepped into the can to check the smell. The toilet was okay, but there were lipstick smears on his bathroom mirror, kiss marks, and a heart with an arrow through it. "Dave and Mary Lou" was scrawled over the heart. Who would know about Mary Lou? Damn small towns.

The hair on his neck stood up. What an awful smell.

He went back out into the living room. Stereo. TV. Everything seemed to be where it was supposed to be.

Maybe Mrs. McKinney had seen something. He loped across Little Round Top and raised his fist to knock. Tillie must have been watching him cross the road because she opened the door before he could knock. The bouffant was so perfect she had to have come directly from Emerson's Beauty Salon. Her daughter Tina stood behind her, looking even more witchy than usual, the hair coal-black and saw-toothed.

"Sorry to bother you, Tillie, but I'm wondering if you saw anyone messing around by my house."

Before Tillie had a chance to say anything, Tina spoke up. "I saw Stormy Guck coming out of there the other day."

Tina moved in front of her mother. He could see her nipples showing through her Black Sabbath T-shirt. Didn't anyone wear a bra anymore?

"You know Stormy is my papergirl, don't you?" he said. Sometimes Stormy would leave his paper on the kitchen table.

"She was in there a long time," Tina said. "I'd check to see you've got everything if I were you." She looked down at his feet. He was getting pneumonia out here.

"I'll do that. Thanks Tina. Thanks for watching the house, Tillie."

The smell was even worse when he returned to the house. He'd have to call a plumber to get it checked out, hoped it wasn't something dead in the walls.

He shrugged off his clothes before he got to the bedroom and was down to his underwear when he opened the door. He gagged on the stink. A huge mound of coffee-colored crap was perfectly centered on his grandmother's patchwork quilt. He did an about-face and slammed the door, hoping somehow the revolting image would go away.

Heard about burglars leaving this sort of present before. It wasn't enough that they'd ruined your sense of security, they had...Damn he was tired.

So this was psychological warfare.

Could he possibly sleep with that in his bedroom? He decided he couldn't. What would he do with it? He'd burn down the house. Nah, Annie and the volunteers would put it out, and in the process they'd see that steaming hill of...

Have to drag the mattress out in the backyard and burn it—no two ways about it.

A half hour later, he'd lugged the mattress down next to the creek, where there were lots of rocks and little vegetation. He poured a gallon of gas on the mess and lit it. Whoosh! He was standing too close to the mattress and the force of the blast singed his eyelids and eyebrows, and the smell of gasoline mixed with filth almost knocked him down.

This had to be the ultimate indignity, eons ahead of Harley Barnhouser sticking his head in a wastebasket full of wet paper towels, fainting smelling of urine. Only miles ahead of all those Mary Lou rejections.

Now he had to get rid of the smell in his bedroom. He had some incense sticks somewhere.

It would be a while before he could sleep in that room again. He'd sleep on the couch.

Once situated on the pullout sofa, with fresh sheets and two goosedown pillows, he found he still couldn't sleep. He was too angry to sleep, and frustrated. Who could have done this? Would Olive and her friends do something like this? Male or female, when he found the bastard who'd done this, he'd eviscerate the son of a bitch and make him eat his own guts.

He got up and put his clothes back on. The phone rang. He picked up the receiver. "Did you know you've got a fire going in your backyard, and it stinks like Gehenna," Moe said.

"What's Gehenna? Never mind, don't tell me—you should have smelled it before I set fire to it."

"Care to fill me in."

"Not now. Can I sleep over there?"

"Still haven't been to bed yet since Father Mischke was attacked? You must be hallucinating. Come on over."

Dave went to his desk drawer and took out his Smith and Wesson. He hadn't been carrying it lately. He hadn't trusted himself since he'd been seeing things.

Out in his backyard, he had several bales of hay stacked on end with a bad guy he called Manfred propped against the straw. He'd made Manfred out of a tattered fart sack. During one of his more creative moods, he'd drawn a face on Manfred, fitting him with an old pair of glasses, tied one of those old wide ties around his neck, and drawn an outline of his body on the sheet.

He emptied the Smith and Wesson into Manfred, reloaded, and emptied it again, his ears ringing from the reports. He'd blown Manfred's head clean off and wrecked his kneecaps and groin. He felt a little better.

When he went back in the house, he picked up the phone, dialed Warner's Hardware. "Nancy, this is Dave Jenkins. Have you got a deadbolt lock? You do? I'll be right down."

After he'd installed the deadbolt, he went to sleep on the bottom rack of Moe's bunkbed, after clearing away the boy's portable library.

*   *   *

Her voice was *low and bluesy*, down there with the eggshells and coffee grounds. "Honey, is there anything else you want?" she said. He turned and licked the rounded part of her shoulder. She tasted like vinegar and dill. Blond underarm hairs protruded from the crack separating her arm and breast. A ticklish sensation rose up the back of his thighs.

He sat bolt upright, as awake as a long-haul truck driver on Benzedrine. Blonde underarm hairs? He'd noticed Olive didn't shave her underarms.

Never been able to get through a whole shower with the water on cold, the needles of ice pelting down on him like sleet, until now. What had Olive said when he'd talked to her in the Jeep outside the church? "If I set my cap for you, you wouldn't stand a chance."

Rather than deal with the situation at his house, he slipped into a pair of not-too-dirty underwear, jeans with one knee out, and a Beethoven sweatshirt Moe had left at the house, and hoofed it the long way back to work, where Hildegard was waiting for him.

His former third-grade teacher was wearing sunglasses since she'd been having trouble with her eyes, and she was carrying a walking stick with one of those chessmen on its top. She was dressed in what looked like a man's suit, set off by a neckerchief. "Hello, David," she said. "I've been out walking the Troops, and I thought I'd stop by for an update on the murder cases."

The Troops were the ambulatory seniors from the Old Folks' home. Hildegard had won an award from a television station in the Cities for community service, primarily for her work with the senior citizens in Soldier.

Hildegard returned to the conversation she'd been having with Shirley. "And how is Howard handling the trauma concerning his father?" she said.

"Sometimes he has dreams," Shirley confessed.

"Dreams heal the soul. Never be too bothered about dreams. I understand Howard is a brilliant boy. It's too bad the district doesn't have better facilities for the gifted."

Dave shuffled his feet. What would she say about the dream he'd just had? He shuddered to think of it.

Shirley offered to fix Hildegard some tea. "If you'd be so kind," she said. "And two cups, David will have some."

Big smile on Shirley's face. He gave her the look, which increased the size of the smile. She saw straight through him.

Hildegard grabbed him by the arm with those eagle's talons and led him back into Harry's office like a little boy who'd been caught throwing rocks on the playground. He could see the Troops through the window, resting on some benches across the street in the park near the church.

"Would you turn down the lights please, David?" she said. "I'm having such difficulty with my eyes lately."

She took a seat behind Harry's desk. This lady knew everything about psychology. She'd chosen the high ground. He sat in the cane chair.

"Shirley tells me you've had another incident. I have a recollection of a similar one involving an African-American basketball person. Is there a Russet, a Bill Russet?"

"You mean Bill Russell," he said, "greatest defensive center to ever play the game. I read that in his biography. His house was burglarized. I just thank my lucky stars he didn't crap in the kitchen sink."

She sat on the edge of the chair with her shoulders back and her chin thrust outward. "Such beastly behavior."

"I just let my guard down, Miss Weiss," he said. "I didn't have my door locked."

She gave him that impatient look, as if he were about to get his knuckles rapped. "It seems to me the man has decided not to wait for you to find him. Do you have a weapon? One of those automatics? Glocks, I think they're called."

"No, just a .38 Smith and Wesson revolver."

"I'm afraid this is just the sort of thing Charles Bronson would do," she said, taking the cup of tea which Shirley handed her. Shirley left on little cat feet. "You're looking ghastly. Haven't you been able to sleep? You should get Dr. Logan to give you something."

Hildegard set the cup down, laced her fingers contentedly. She was a snowplow barging right over parked cars, tree stumps and other assorted impediments. "I won't dillydally, dear. I came over here to encourage you to let Mr. Henderson head up the investigation. This man, if he's a man, won't dare pull anything further once the state police bring their full power to bear.

A knifing pain slashed at his gut.

"Those dark lines under your eyes. I'm afraid you'll drive yourself to the brink if I let you persist."

"But Miss Weiss, Harry—"

"Oh, pish. He's finished. Sheriff Kline has shown you the petition I'm sure. The man has one saving grace, that daughter of his, the one who works with the Little League and the volunteer fire department, Annie I think her name is. Never had the pleasure of teaching her. She reminds me of me when I was her age, always in the thick of it with the boys on the playground. She'd be ideal for you, don't you think? It's time you settled down. I worry some day you'll just pick up and leave us, go off on some, ill-advised adventure in New York City or Los Angeles. You should put down roots."

She'd never been married as far as he knew. All the men he knew were afraid of her.

"Annie and I are just friends, Miss Weiss," he said.

She fixed him with those eagle eyes. He had to look away. "You should know, young man, that if you manage to forge a friendship with a woman, a real friendship, and I'd say from what I've observed that yours is real, you had best take advantage of the opportunity. It will grow into love. Shortly before my time, parents arranged marriages, and they held up. I can assure you that they did." She took up her cup of tea. "I'm wondering what effect this whole unfortunate situation with the Egge murder has had on Superintendent Bronson's marriage."

"I was just over there and she's—"

"You'll arrest him," she said, staring down on him from her eyrie. "The newspapers are beginning to speculate as to why we haven't done so. And now with this new evidence...You'll arrest Bronson, and Mr. Henderson will head up the investigation to find evidence that will tie up the loose ends and determine whether he had any henchmen."

He tried to avoid her eyes, and so he looked at her nose, which was ruler-straight, then down her jawline. In this light, he cold see little hairs jutting out from her chin. "He didn't do it, Miss Weiss. I'm almost positive. The evidence against him is circumstantial, most probably planted."

"Dear David, Mr. Henderson's forensic team should be able to determine that. Bronson certainly had the motive. He was having an affair with Egge's wife, and he was abusing a child. If that ever got out, he'd be finished in his profession."

"I have a feeling the real murderer is aware—"

"You have an eye witness who says Bronson resembles the murderer. Mr. Henderson tells me you have fingerprints and Father Mischke's description of the assailant's hairy hands."

"I checked his hands. There's no bite mark."

"He could have applied make-up. The jury will put two and two together. You can't argue that the man is innocent after what he's done with the Randall girl."

"But Olive won't..."

She flushed just a bit and her nostrils flared. "Mr. Bronson is a very vindictive man. Believe me, I know, the man solicited a candidate to run against me for the school board."

"That doesn't make him—"

"I'm sure I'm right about this, David," she said, standing, preparing to leave. "Felons have been convicted on circumstantial evidence before. Most of the time, as a matter of fact."

"But we found this man in Steubenville—"

"It could do Superintendent Bronson some good to spend some time behind bars, even if he's not guilty. He's rather lacking in humility, don't you think? When I taught in that one-room schoolhouse, I barely saw the so-called superintendent. I don't even remember his name. I was my own janitor, my own disciplinarian, my own accountant, my own office manager, my own carpenter, my own painter, my own curriculum coordinator, *and* my own superintendent. I think I've hit upon the reason for the lack of respect for teachers these days, haven't I, dear?"

She moved toward the door and turned to look up at him. "Oh, I meant to tell you," she said. "I just received a letter from Patrice. I'm sure you'll remember those competitions we had in grade three." She always said grade three instead of third grade. "The girls would compete against the boys to see who could contribute the most money to our foster child. Well, you'd be proud to know that Patrice just got his law degree."

* * *

Dave slept that night, intermittently, with his forehead resting on the windowpane of Moe's second story window, watching his own front door. The incense and the deadbolt lock did not allow him to sleep in his own house, and he had a notion that if he stayed awake he could catch the lunatic the next time he tried something.

Sunday morning, around two o'clock, he was jarred awake by lights down below in his bedroom. He charged down the stairs like the Teddy Roosevelt character in *Arsenic and Old Lace*, but by the time he reached his house, the lights had gone off. He went in and looked around. Nobody was there, but the toilet was gurgling and the house was as cold as a meat locker. The furnace was off. He jogged down to the basement steps, shouldered open the door, and lit the pilot. But, when he tried to leave, he had trouble getting the cellar door back open. When the door finally gave way, after repeated rammings, he went up and brewed himself a pot of coffee. It would help him stay awake. The coffee maker leaked out one cup, then quit. That did it. The place was haunted. Mrs. Macintosh's séance was becoming a necessity.

* * *

Dave arrived at Immaculate Conception church an hour early, hoping to find someone who'd seen the man who'd harassed Father Mischke in the confessional. Some of the elderly usually got there about an hour ahead of time to say the rosary.

Mrs. Walz, an octogenarian who no longer revealed her precise age, remembered a young man acting very peculiarly after mass the previous Friday morning.

The old woman walked with a cane and had a crippling case of osteoporosis. He wasn't sure if she could sit down, but she somehow managed, when they sat together on a bench in the vestibule. Wisps of grayish, white hair escaped from under her kerchief, her cloth coat was frayed at the collar.

"He was standing right next to me, waiting in line," she said. "He leaned against a pew with his one foot crossed over the other and folded his arms. He acted like a little second grader, bored, you know, and he was gawky, ogling all the people. He definitely wasn't working on a firm purpose of amendment, I'll tell you that. He took an awfully long time in the confessional, and when he came out, he barged out of the church without genuflecting. Almost knocked me down."

"Have you seen him before, Mrs. Walz?"

"No, but I don't know many of the younger people. They all act like we older ones have some kind of terrible disease."

What did he look like, Mrs. Walz?"

She thought for a moment, then reached inside her purse, came out with a much used handkerchief, and rubbed her nose. "He was a big man, very handsome and conceited-looking. Stuck on himself, I'd say."

Dave cleared his throat. He felt really out of wack. He had to get his own place. Sleeping at Moe's was like sleeping at the in-laws, not that he had any in-laws. He yawned. "Excuse me. I haven't been getting a lot of sleep. Do you know Charles Bronson, the superintendent of schools, Mrs. Walz?"

"Oh, that's all right. I know your job must be very hard these days what with the press and everything. I know who Mr. Bronson is, but I've never seen him close up. He has that big Spanish house on Seminary. I hear they're not getting along. He's seeing someone else." Her eyes searched his with the intensity of a meat inspector.

"I don't know about that, Mrs. Walz. Could you tell how old the man was?"

"I'm not a good judge of age, but I'd say he was probably in his forties, maybe a little older, about my son's age. You know my son

Jack? He's a certified public accountant. He's a good boy, he helps his mother." She dabbed at her eyes with her little handkerchief.

"Jack does my taxes, Mrs. Walz. He always gets me a nice refund. Do you know Mel Kline, the sheriff's boy?"

"Ach, it wasn't Mel Kline. He lives right next door to me," she said. "He shovels my sidewalk during the winter."

No one who lived next door to Mrs. Walz could possibly do anything wrong.

That day, for the first time since he'd been in the SEALs, Dave sat through an entire mass. He knelt next to Mrs. Walz, who showed him how to follow along in the prayer book. She kicked up an awful fuss when he refused to take communion. She whispered that you didn't need to go to confession any more if you had a firm purpose of amendment. Seemed awfully chicken to Dave. He didn't see any big man among the parishioners, but he felt less tired and curiously sanguine afterwards.

* * *

That Sunday afternoon Dave went with Chief Rain in the Face, the cat he'd picked up at the vet's, to see Father Mischke at the hospital in Crookston. Fifteen stitches, surprisingly chipper. Chief Rain in the Face went to sleep on the old priest's stomach. It was as if St. Peter had never left.

Dave arranged for the nuns at Immaculate Conception convent to take care of the old priest until everything settled down. "We'll be retiring Father Mischke a little early," Bishop Foster said when Dave talked to him on the phone in the lobby of the hospital. "We have a retirement center in Arizona waiting for him. Thank you so much for your concern, Deputy Jenkins. He speaks so highly of you."

From the hospital, Dave went to Mrs. Macintosh's house to pick up Mingo, who would accompany him when he arrested Superintendent Bronson as Harry'd finally given the go-ahead. They sat at the circular table in Mrs. Mac's kitchen drinking Cowboy coffee, a handful of grounds in the bottom of the pot and water, scorched over high heat, the only kind of coffee Mingo would drink. The stuff was so damn strong it took your voice away.

"Can't ignore the fingerprints," he told Mingo. "We've only got Bronson on an assault case, though. I don't see any reason why we shouldn't keep on looking. Did I tell you Henderson is taking over the case?"

"The little dweeb with the Jimmy Johnson hairdo?"

"Who?"

"You know, the former Dallas Cowboys coach?"

"That's the one. What do you think I ought to do?"

"Fuck him."

"My sentiments exactly. Tell you what I'm thinking. We'll get all of those teachers together, and while I'm bullshiting them about why we had to arrest their superintendent and answering their stupid questions, you watch for suspicious behavior. Or else, you bullshit them, and I'll watch."

"Makes sense, I suppose. Two dead pederasts and all."

"That's pedagogues, Dude." Dave stood, looked out at the elaborate treehouse in Mrs. Mac's back yard. "I might as well come clean with you, Mingo. Remember that first day, when I arrived on the scene? Well, I wasn't quite straight with you." Dave sat back down and spewed it out like a drunken fraternity pledge. He told the Indian about all the visions, Egge's pipe, his strange eating habits, the corned beef. And how Mrs. Macintosh said he had two auras, and the Shakespeare incident in Debbie Meyer's class.

Mingo sat there with his chair tipped back, arms crossed, stoically taking it all in, as if Dave were telling him about a planned vacation on the Boundary Waters. Finally he said, "You know I've been trying to have a vision ever since I took a course on Athapascan mythology at Johns Hopkins. I went so far as to go up on Sierra Blanca and starve myself for four days. It was cold up there. Nothing. And you get to have...The Egg Man was a friend of mine, and he picks you. You lucky...Anyway, I can tell you what's happening if you're ready for it now."

"Go ahead, Wovoka."

"You know about Wovoka?"

"Sure, otherwise known as Jack Wilson, the Paiute holy man who started the ghost dancing craze to bring back the buffalo. We're not that far from Wounded Knee, you know."

Mingo gulped his coffee, squinted, cleared his throat. "So I heard. Anyway, we Apaches believe that there's a transition period between death and when a soul can enter the Land of Ever Summer. This is the time the deceased can be glimpsed very briefly or seen or heard through signs, such as a bird call or something out of the ordinary in nature. The Egg Man must 'gather tracks' before he's allowed to enter the land of Ever Summer. He must go to places and look in on people who were important to him during his lifetime. Since the Egg Man was murdered, you want to up the intensity level, which is why you're probably having the visions. As I said before, a ghost medicine ceremony is definitely in order."

Dave rattled the coffee cup in its saucer, spilling some of the tarrish stuff in the process. "I'm going to treat this experience the same way I treat television."

"Television?"

Dave took Egge's pipe out of his windbreaker pocket, pointed the stem at Mingo. "Yeah, I don't understand how it works. I could take a class in television technology and I still wouldn't be able to build a set. But that doesn't mean I won't watch it. You can do that ghost medicine thing if you want, but first we're gonna try a little experiment with Egge's pipe during the faculty meeting. If the pattern holds, we should know if anybody at the school had anything to do with either of the murders."

The Bronson arrest was uneventful as he was passed out on his couch, an empty bottle of Johnny Walker on the floor next to him. He would not wake up.

* * *

Monday provided an opportunity for Dave to reacquaint himself with some of his old high school teachers. He was sitting on a very hard chair, gazing out at eighty noisy teachers and teachers' aides who were gathered in the media center, formerly known as the library. Both the elementary and the high school staff had to be in attendance because the meeting concerned the superintendent. Dave noticed no one sat in the front two rows. The women banded together generally, and the jocks were also confined to one area. You could recognize them because they were the ones with the ugly legs wearing shorts. The faculty was a motley crew, ranging in age from 21-65 or so. Some of the men even had long hair and rings in their ears. He examined the room. No more card index, a computer had taken its place. The clock was an hour behind.

"They don't look too perturbed," Dave said to Mingo, who was trading lovey-dovey faces with Debbie Meyer sitting in third row. "Two murders within their midst and the attempt on Father Mischke, you'd think they'd be going bonkers."

"They're all inveterate TV watchers, just like everybody," Mingo said, "although they'd never admit it. We're all inured to violence." He smiled his coyote smile, then left to chat up Debbie Meyer. Apparently she loved all that stuff about Apache myth and Mingo was teaching her the ceremonies.

Just as Dave was about to chance talking to some of the teachers, the elevator bell went off, three dings, surprisingly loud, unlike the burglar alarm he remembered from his school days, and Larry Merchant, school board chairman, arrived and opened the meeting. The microphone whistled, so Dan Cardwell, whom the kids called 'goat' because he looked like one, played with the controls and got the whistle to go away.

Merchant, whom his friends called T.R., was a square-set man with a brush mustache and very square, horselike teeth. Dave had never especially liked the man, probably because he was a lawyer. That and the fact that Merchant was one of the movers and shakers involved in Hildegard's improvement ventures.

The school board chairman spoke down into the microphone. "I just have a few prefatory remarks before I introduce Deputy Jenkins," he said. "I'm sure you're all worried about what's going to happen with the school system since Mr. Bronson has been arrested. I'll be temporarily assuming Mr. Bronson's job until we can go through the search process. Some of you are aware that we got the go ahead from the MDE to put Mr. White in charge as interim principal since he's almost completed his specialist's degree."

Dave squirmed in his chair. White was the one who'd been up on assault charges for kicking that kid who'd had his legs in the aisle. The good old Peter Principle was in effect once again. The crud rises to the top.

Tuning Merchant out, Dave began to recognize a few faces. Patty Ludwig, the physical education teacher he knew from softball, was rifling through her purse in the fourth row. Her face was too big, she wore blue eyeshadow and blue polish on her fingernails, which were kind of short, probably because of all the volleyballs she had to contend with.

Mrs. Grant was balancing her checkbook.

Somebody sneezed, then took out Kleenex and blew his nose, making a sound like a Bronx cheer. Several people giggled.

Dave touched the pipe. Nothing happened.

Merchant continued unhindered, "We would prefer to leave the decisions regarding education in the hands of the teachers if at all possible, but it's hard. Everyone has their own lobbyist these days." He chuckled, some of the teachers grinned, the cynical ones frowned.

"What about discipline? Conrad can't even handle his own discipline." This was from Dean Schmeck, Dave's old football coach, a little, rotund fellow who looked like he'd never been near a football field but whose team had just won the Class A championship.

Merchant addressed Schmeck's question: "We expect to solicit a discipline committee from each school. You can rest assured, Mr. Schmeck, that the Board will monitor events very closely." Many of the teachers and staff were fanning themselves with their agendas, which had been distributed prior to the meeting. Some of them had been crumpled up and thrown on the floor.

Dave rubbed his fingers over the pipe. Still nothing. Yep, the wires were down all right.

"Get away from the microphone, Larry," Old Barnoff, the biology teacher, said. "We want to hear from the deputy. I wanna know why they haven't arrested Freddie Cochran. Damn it, everybody knows the little fucker killed Ellis." Old Barnoff could get away with this kind of language because he was about seventy years old and didn't care whether he got fired or not. Barnoff looked as though he'd just fallen out of bed on the wrong side. His side hairs stood out from his head like slightly soiled wings, his shirt tails hung over his pants, and one shoe was untied.

"You have no proof of that, Barney," Mrs. Macintosh said. "I wish you'd keep your speculation to yourself. An educator should know better than to generalize." Today her hair was raspberry and she'd lost the befuddled manner.

Merchant grinned a little and said, "Deputy Jenkins, would you like to respond?"

Mingo, the coyote smile in evidence, still sitting in the chair next to Debbie Meyer, could have been a member of the faculty, if it hadn't been for the uniform and the eagle feather.

Dave moved to the podium and bent down awkwardly to speak into the microphone. "We have no evidence that Freddie was involved in either killing or the attack on Father Mischke. I can't discuss any evidence we may or may not have found. I'll just say that we had no choice but to arrest the superintendent."

"Damn it, it's been over a week, and you ain't got nothin'," Barnoff said. "I still think Freddie brained Egge and Ellis. The little shit threw a beaker full of sulfuric acid up against the wall during an experiment. Any kid who'd do that is capable of murder in my mind."

When he'd been in school, Dave had Barnoff for biology. He and his friends had turned on the gas, thrown beakers of water at each other, and counted the number of times Barnoff said "for instance" out loud. He showed movies every other day, and when he did lecture, he spent most of the time talking about his sex life and looking down the dresses of the girls sitting in the front row.

Dave moved closer to the microphone. "I don't think we want to personalize this investigation, Mr. Barnoff."

Barnoff harrumphed and turned away.

Fetching little Debbie Meyer raised her hand and Dave nodded toward her.

"What *can* you tell us?" she asked.

Mingo looked like he was about to burst his buttons.

"Not much," Dave said. "We wouldn't have arrested Mr. Bronson if we didn't have some pretty incriminating evidence. I'm just here today to offer reassurance and to ask if any of you know anything about any of the murders or the assault, that you not hesitate to tell me, in all confidence. No matter how innocuous you feel your potential information is, don't hesitate to tell me about it. That's all I have to say. Thank you."

Dave felt like a fucking politician. He sat back down on the hard chair and looked at the feet of the faculty members out in the audience. Just then, a bug crawled out of Patty Ludwig's purse and ran up her leg. She screamed and slapped at it. Everybody laughed. Cardwell had said the library was notorious for cockroaches and carpet beetles. Cockroaches loved paper according to the librarian.

About this time the teachers got antsy and started talking among themselves. Merchant asked if there were any more questions, but he was generally ignored as the staff went for the doughnuts and coffee, which had been provided by the Boosters.

Dave and Mingo huddled for a moment after the meeting, Mingo raising an eyebrow quizzically. "Best laid plans of mice and men," Dave said. "I never thought I'd squawk about missing out on the boogeyman."

"They don't like to come when they're called, Dude. I shoulda told you. What next?"

"Something I shoulda done a long time ago, sweat Stormy Guck. If the teenagers had something to do with the murders, she's the weak link."

When Dave returned to the office to set his course, he got the shock of his life. Harry had had a heart attack and was at the hospital in Crookston.

* * *

Dave got to the hospital in Crookston at around ten. It took him a while to find Harry's room, wandering through the hospital maze with no sense of direction.

Eventually he was able to find a nice nurse who took him by the hand to Harry's room.

Harry had not been given a private room. The partition was drawn, but anyone on Harry's side of the room could hear everything being said. An old man was complaining about the hospital food and begging to go home.

Considering Harry's large family, the room was packed and claustrophobic. Word had gotten out rapidly, and the room was a veritable greenhouse of floral condolences.

As soon as Dave arrived, everyone was shoved out of the room and a priest, not Father Mischke, went in to administer last rites. Just a precaution, he said. Dave went to the end of the hall, where there was a large window, and stared out into the night.

It was raining, coming down hard, the kind of rain that would render windshield wipers useless. The drops were beading on the window, making pocking sounds—guerrillas trying to penetrate the hospital's perimeter. The parking lot was full out there. Must be lots of sick people.

Someone touched him on the arm. Annie Kline had noiselessly followed him down the corridor. "It's not supposed to be too serious," she said, "unless the surgeon fucks up. He says Daddy needs angioplasty." Dave knew better than to grouse about the bad language. Somewhere along the line she'd had her hair done in kind of a pageboy, probably to impress that asshole Marshall Preston.

"So how'd it happen?" he asked.

Annie reached up and straightened his collar. "Eating breakfast, wouldn't you know? Half a loaf of toast, eight scrambled eggs, a whole box of smokies, what did he expect? Ma tried to get him to eat right."

She let go of his collar, dropped her hands to her side and slouched.

"From what I've heard about angioplasty, he should be back at work in no time," he said.

She moved toward the window. "The doctor says at least a month, but Dad wants to resign because of the murder cases. You should talk him out of it."

"I don't really want to be sheriff, Annie," he said, sitting on the heat register. He was thinking that if Harry was out of the picture, he'd have something to say about whether or not Henderson headed up the investigation.

"So you're going to go ahead and bring Bronson to trial?" she said, her thick eyebrows cast in a frown. "I don't think he did it."

"I don't either. He's not a very happy man and he's got a really bad temper, but then so do I, and I haven't killed anybody lately." He smiled and she smiled back like a mother glorying in her baby.

He glanced around the corridor. A nurse guiding an old man's wheelchair, a couple waiting for the elevator, an orderly pushing a cart stacked with bed linen.

"We found Bronson's fingerprints on a weapon at the Mischke scene," he said. "They were pretty much a clincher. I have some other leads though. Somebody is playing all of us for suckers, getting his rocks off big time."

Annie rested her cheek against his shoulder. She was a lot shorter than he was, one of her appealing characteristics. She looked up at him. "I hope you're not mad at me for dating Marshall Preston."

"He's not the right guy for you, Annie. Thinks he's a real Casonova, that one. Did you know he goes with Mindy Small on the side?"

"I heard that. We only went out a couple times...So have you seen Mary Lou Forman?" she breathed, searching his eyes for a reaction. "She's in town, you know. Preggo and separated from her husband."

"I saw her car," he said.

The orderly was coming back down the corridor, his cart empty. He waved and Dave nodded.

Annie went to the window, and traced a squiggle of rain with her finger.

"You didn't sleep with Marshall, did you Annie?"

She turned and glared at him. "And what makes you think that's any of your business? You went with that saleslady at the radio station for a whole six months—"

She'd slept with him all right.

"Let's get back to the room," he said. Since Annie was so short, he was able to outstride her down the hall on the way back to Harry's room.

She had to practically yell, trotting along trying to keep up with him. "He's been telling those jokes all morning. I think he's gone senile, too."

The priest was finished, and ten heads were focused on the partition, behind which the old man continued his harangue.

"Where is Stormy? I want my Stormy!"

"We can't find her, Dad. She wasn't in her bed this morning. She sneaks out after everybody else is asleep. She was probably out again last night with that gang of teenagers she's always with."

"Find her. I want my Stormy."

Stormy? That girl sure got around.

Harry put an end to the eavesdropping. "Shake it off people. Nobody's dying around here, at least not me anyways. Hey, Jenkins, I didn't know you was here. Yah hear this one? Why doesn't Jesus eat M&M's?"

"They keep falling through the holes in his hands, Harry." Heard that one, too.

Harry wore a euphoric look. Brenda, an older chubbier version of Annie, who was a regular churchgoer, had an expression on her face that forewarned a volcanic eruption, so Dave stopped humoring Harry.

"I hope you don't mind, Harry," Dave said, "but I'm going to continue the investigation, despite the inevitability of a grand jury hearing for Bronson. I think the jury is going to cut Bronson loose with all that circumstantial evidence. I want to hit the ground running."

Harry looked very uncomfortable in that hospital gown. Usually he wore a tie, never loosened. His chest hairs were showing. "You better hire another deputy then, if you're going to be in court and working on the investigation. Somebody needs to handle the other cases, Sheriff. Looks like it's your job now. I wasn't going to run again anyway with my goddamn back."

Although he couldn't believe he was actually doing it, Dave took Harry's hand. It was callused, felt wooden. "You'll change your mind once we catch this sleezeball," he said. "I've told you a million times, I don't want your job."

Harry withdrew his hand, apparently unused to holding hands with a man. "I wish one of the boys would have studied law enforcement."

The five M's shifted their eyes toward the partition, where the old man was still asking for Stormy.

Chapter 16

Thrust and Parry

"There was a little girl
Who had a little curl
Right in the middle of her forehead;
And when she was good
She was very, very good,
But when she was bad she
was horrid."
— Longfellow

In the midst of the maintenance man's hammering and chiseling, Dave toyed with County Commissioner Blayne's letter.

Harry had passed on Bronson's complaint. Either that or Blayne had written to formally notify him about Hildegard's decision to put Henderson in charge of the murder investigations. He put the unopened letter in his back pocket. He could always say the notice got misplaced during all the redecorating.

The maintenance man, Hank Deering, a retired farmer, wrenched the last bolt free, and gently lowered Harry's deerhead to the floor.

Dave settled himself behind Harry's desk and reached for his Bible. He'd inherited the holy book, which he usually kept in the bottom drawer of his desk, from his grandmother. He had to admit that he was still a bit unhinged about the stool specimen that creep had left in his bedroom; he hadn't felt fallible until then.

He flipped through the Bible, stopping to read a few lines here and there. He was still looking for something a bit more palatable than Mrs. Mac's witchery and Mingo's ghost medicine ceremony.

Matthew 6:5-6 drew his attention. It said, *Again, when you pray, you shall not be like the hypocrites, who love to pray standing in the synagogues and at the street corners, in order that they may be seen by men. Amen I say to you, they have received their reward. But when thou prayest, go into thy room, and closing thy door, pray to thy Father in secret; and thy Father, who sees in secret, will reward thee.*

Some plaster from the redecorating project fell on the book. Hank Deering was coming down the stepladder. Dave drew a circle around the quotation he'd just read. That boy Billy Graham was in for some hard time in purgatory if there was any truth in that passage. Dave wondered if there was anything in there about ghosts, ghosts who like corned beef.

Dave put the Bible down on the desk. Had to get moving on finding that new deputy. He'd started carrying his gun again, but he didn't really have anybody full-time to cover his back. Harry had recommended Lucille Robinson, but she was so overweight Dave didn't really have any confidence in her. And would she be willing to cap the loose-boweled son of a bitch if push came to shove?

"I'll try to find somebody who wouldn't blink at bloodshed," he said aloud.

Hank Deering, who was sweeping up, said, "What's that you said?"

"Oh, nice job, Hank. I said 'nice job'. The wall looks much better than it did." Deering looked nonplussed as he still needed to do the painting after it dried. He shrugged, collected his tools, and left.

Dave reached over and dialed the number Mrs. Szymanski had given him. He listened to the dial tone. It rang three times and she picked up. He could barely hear her.

"Hello, Mrs. Szymanski?" He glanced down at his notes, a bunch of squiggly lines that resembled an EKG.

"Deputy Jenkins?" Mrs. Szymanski said. "I was just about to call you. Have you made any further progress?"

He twirled the cord around a finger, cutting off the circulation. Besides the hushed voice there was interference on the line. "I can barely hear you, Mrs. Szymanski. Can you speak up a little? What I'm calling about is that list of names you sent me. One of them is a possible. His name is Brad Huntzinger, and he has a record with the FBI."

Mrs. Szymanski was silent, seemingly taking a moment to reflect. "Oh, I remember him. He was in quite a mess with Felicia Potter, the physical education teacher at the time. Sexual harassment. In those days they believed the teacher. He threatened my husband at the hearing. I really should have remembered, I'm sorry."

Dave swept the remaining plaster from the repair job off Harry's desk onto the floor. "That's all right, Mrs. Szymanski. I'm having trouble with my memory, too, lately. Trouble is the Fibs don't have any fingerprints or mugshots of Mr. Huntzinger. Do you think you could get me a picture?" A snapshot of a teenager was better than nothing. Perhaps the lab boys could age him.

Mrs. Szymanski continued. "Brad was expelled his sophomore year, so there wouldn't be a senior picture, but I should be able to find something in the extracurricular section of the yearbook. How's that?" Dave could hear another voice in the background.

"I really appreciate this, Mrs. Szymanski."

"I'll send it priority mail, Deputy." She paused for a moment as if she were distracted. A next-door neighbor dropping by to ask for a cup of sugar? The UPS man delivering a package? Dave was getting a very clear image of what the old woman's home must look like. "Oh, calm down, Dear," she said. "You'd think you'd want to find the person who tried to run you down. You know, Deputy Jenkins, I always thought that Felicia was responsible for that affair with Brad. She should have known better than to dress so provocatively."

"Uh-huh."

"Bradley was only sixteen and Felicia had to have been at least twenty-five."

"That's quite a difference, all right." Nothing much else Dave could say about that to an elderly woman. "I'll let you know if we make any progress, Mrs. Szymanski." He hung up the phone.

What next? Oh yeah, the new deputy. He'd dial the Moorhead State placement office, run nine or ten criminal justice rookies through the gauntlet, and pick the meanest, ugliest one. But first things first. The slashed tires, the poisoned dogs, the pile of shit—he couldn't subject a woman to that kind of danger. He needed to let Lucille down easy. She was a woman. Grounds for a possible discrimination suit if he didn't give her every chance.

Dave buzzed Shirley and told her to tell Lucille he needed to see her. The girl was as thick as thieves with Annie Kline these days—they lived together at Mrs. Macintosh's boarding house. Another reason to use as much tact as he could muster.

Almost immediately, Lucille stuck her head in the door. "You wanted to see me?"

"Yeah," he said. "Take a seat."

She handed him a note and he glanced down at it. Another complaint from the Miller farm. Some lowlife had snatched a bunch of his prize heifers.

The girl sat in the cane chair. For once he had the high ground. The girl had to weigh at least two hundred pounds, her brownish-blond hair was tied in a knot, and she was wearing those hoop earrings that stretched the earlobes. She wore a mood ring on her right index finger. The girl was smiling, she had dimples—he liked women with dimples—and unusual brown eyes. What was that color, sienna? It looked like Lucille had a pretty face under all that insulation.

"Too bad about Sheriff Kline," she said.

"Yeah it's a real shame. But life must go on as they say." He paused, grasping for a good way to start. He opened her file. "Says here you went to St. Michael's High School in Lead, South Dakota. Is that a Catholic school?"

She nodded.

"I went to a Catholic school from fourth grade on," he said. "The nun in seventh grade, Sister Devine, used to slap the snot out of all of us."

"Not that many nuns left when I went, mostly lay teachers," she said.

"Damn shame. This country needs the discipline. You have to say that for them, they were proactive...Ah, how do you like Soldier?"

"I just love it here. If I can't live in Lead for the rest of my life, I'd pick Soldier. And Annie and Mrs. Macintosh are so nice to me. They make sure I'm always included. Just the other day Martha had a quilting bee and she invited me—she gave me this mood ring for luck. And Annie has me over for Sunday dinner at her mom's. It's just like home over there with that large family."

She shifted in her chair. Must know what was coming.

"Mrs. Macintosh do your horoscope for you?"

"Oh yes," she said. "Isn't it fascinating? I'm a Taurus, that's the bull you know, and Martha says I'm tenacious and faithful and that I'm a very sensual person, which explains a lot, don't you think? She also says I'll have a large family—I was so happy to hear that."

His good angel was whispering in his ear, *Give the kid a break.*

What the hell! He'd brought his basketball hoop from home, stuck it behind Harry's door. Something to do during those boring times when he had to talk to Henderson or that dullard Commissioner Blayne and his cronies. A rebound had destroyed two of Harry's bowling trophies, which he'd had lined up on a filing cabinet. He tossed Lucille the basketball. "Make two out of three and the job is yours," he said.

Lucille gaped at the ball as if she thought it might explode.

"Just a minute before you shoot, Lucille," he said. "Got to make a phone call. Wouldn't want to tempt you to cheat."

He dialed the number, tapped his fingers on the desk top, cleared his throat. "Say, Larry, this is Jenkins. Got a case of cattle rustling. Wouldn't know of anybody around with that MO, would you?"

"Haven't heard of any in years," Henderson said. "Say, Jenkins, about that letter from Commissioner Blayne?"

"Don't know what you're talking about, Larry. Look, I got to go, I'm interviewing a new deputy. Call me if you come up with anything on that rustling thing." He hung up the phone.

Lucille sunk three of three baskets. Dave's jaw dropped. He'd never made that many in a row from this distance.

"I used to play girls' basketball in Lead," Lucille said. "There were only six girls on the team, so I got to play a lot."

The noon-hour whistle blew. It seemed to go on forever, like those civil defense warnings on the radio.

"You trace the clothes the cemetery caretaker found?" he said.

"We tried the shelter in Crookston to see if they'd recognize them. The director, a Mr. Zender, said he thought they belonged to Billy Bum, but he wasn't sure. He hadn't seen Billy since before the Egge funeral. You were kidding about making the baskets, right?" Lucille was playing with the mood ring. You just couldn't put some people at ease.

"Do I look like a kidder, Lucille?" he said. "Just so you understand the danger involved."

"I was the top marksman at school, Mr. Jenkins. And I'm not afraid to shoot. Harry says I can go with when deer hunting..."

"Annie says Sheriff Kline has a minor heart condition. He should be back at work in a few weeks. By then we'll have these murders solved, right?"

"Right, Sheriff Jenkins."

Sheriff Jenkins? It just didn't sound right. Kind of like the day he'd spent at the school, when some of the kids had called him Mr. Jenkins. "It's Deputy Jenkins, Lucille."

Dave had left the door open. He noticed Shirley was listening to the interview. She gave him the thumbs up. If Lucille were going to be a deputy, she'd have to get along with Shirley. He shuffled some papers, closed the folder.

"You ever talk to Mrs. Bronson about that alibi?"

"Sorry, I meant to tell you that night you said you were coming over to review the tipline. She's changed her tune a bit. Says Egge and her husband couldn't stand being in the same room together. And she has no idea where he was the morning Egge was killed."

"Yeah well, they're getting divorced."

"I don't suppose it makes much difference now, what with the attack on Father Mischke?"

"That's that then, I guess. Harry Kline recommends you highly. As does Larry Henderson. I'm the police liaison at the school, and they need me more than ever now that they've lost two principals."

"You'd make a good one."

The girl was really growing on him.

"I'm putting you in charge of this rustling situation out at the Miller farm," he said. "Now you just go on out there and get Shirley to draw up all the papers, and, oh yeah, don't worry about a uniform. Just wear whatever you want."

*   *   *

Moe drove up to Olive's trailer house in Shady Brook, expecting to find a front yard with an old Buick up on blocks, no lawn, and a dozen half-naked kids playing in a dirt front yard. But there was a nice walk with geraniums and shrubs planted in front of the door, and a welcome mat was placed conspicuously on the step.

Putting the car in neutral, he sat there licking his wounds. Every bone in his body ached and he had bandages tied around his hands covering the blisters he'd accumulated helping Rita clean the chicken barn. Never ever wanted to see another farm again.

He was driving his mom's Honda, which was washed, waxed, and polished to a high sheen. He'd recently taken his driver's test for the fourth time, after which, the cop had chewed him out so much, threatening to have him take the drivers' course again, that Moe felt he'd failed again. But he'd scraped by with that 71.

Moe shut off the ignition, gathered up his notebooks, pencil case, and flashcards. The test he was helping Olive study for would be on the Civil War, which he loved. He'd even been to see the battlefields at Gettysburg, Antietam, and Bull Run when his dad had been stationed in Norfolk. He shut the door to the Honda, walked up the short tidy path—the sidewalk edged with neatly mown lawn. He straightened his Beethoven T-shirt, hitched up the sweats he'd worn to hide his skinny legs, and rang the doorbell. The chime was a kind of a Dragnet melody.

Olive opened the door. "Come in here, you handsome little devil," she said. She had her hair down and was dressed in a navy-blue sports bra and shorts, revealing her naval. She had applied very red lipstick and had painted her toenails candy-apple red as well.

He gulped.

As they took chairs around the kitchen table, she tucked her feet under her legs. He ran his damaged palms over the oilcloth with the red checkered pattern and looked out the window into a side yard where Olive's little sisters, Nancy and Patty, were swinging each other on an old inner tube under a giant pin oak.

"What happened to your hands," she said, "you burn yourself?"

"Don't ask," he said. "Another one of my ill-advised projects."

"Oh yeah, Rita told me about that."

"Live and learn I always say," he said.

She opened her history book to the assigned chapters. "I've done the reading," she said, "all one hundred pages, on the causes of the war and the first couple of battles where the North was getting its butt kicked. I don't understand why we have to know this shit. It's ancient history. It doesn't have anything to do with me. I wish you'd explain that to me."

Not exactly the lilting trill one would expect from a sixteen-year-old girl. What did it remind him of? It was the voice of a thirty-five-year old barfly, a voice that made Moe long for the serenity of his monkish room in the converted schoolhouse.

"I'll try," he said.

She pushed a wisp of hair away from her mouth—which revealed that she wasn't such a perfect specimen after all with her bitten fingernails—and rose to go to the refrigerator. She returned with two glasses of lemonade.

"Thanks," he said, took a sip. It was the kind that came in a package. He had to shake the finicky reactions. *And don't even think of asking her anything about the murders yet either, Dufus,* he told himself.

He fiddled with a pencil, erasing an imaginary blot on his tablet. "I think what you said about history is a fair observation. I suppose most teachers would say something like 'those who cannot remember the past are condemned to repeat it,' but for me it's the people. Not necessarily the famous ones like Robert E. Lee or Grant. Bloody Bill Anderson, guys like that. I could talk about Quantrill's Raiders for hours. Don't worry, though, I won't."

"Who's he?" she said, going for the bait. "Wait a minute! I think I know. Ain't he the guy Jesse James rode with?" She raised her eyebrows, tilted at the corners, golden brown.

He was shocked. A girl who knew about Bloody Bill Anderson! Should he propose now?

There was a bowl of Doritos on the table. She took one and offered him the bowl. He hated Doritos. He especially hated salsa, anything with tomatoes in it actually, with the exception of chili and pizza. He pinched himself hard. Kind of hard to do with mummified hands.

"I think I saw that about Bloody Bill Anderson on that biography show on cable," she said.

He took a Dorito, forced it down. "There's something about bad guys," he said. "You know, the Missouri farmers were on Jesse and Frank's side. That's how they stayed at large so long."

Olive put her hand under her chin, took a sip of lemonade. "I know what you mean about bad guys. Jesse and Frank killed that cashier at Northfield, though, didn't they?"

"You know about Northfield?"

"Yeah that was in there, too. Actually I did read some history by accident once. It was about the Middle Ages. I liked the title. It was called *The Distant Mirror*. I thought it was a romance, but then I got hooked almost right away, so I read the whole thing."

Moe hadn't read it. "Speaking of bad guys, my friends in JESSICA think Egge's murderer was an actor. I don't suppose you know the caretaker at the cemetery found some old clothes after Egge's funeral?"

She gave him a look that seemed to say, *How the hell did you know about that?* Instead, she said, "Jessica?"

"That's what we call our chat group. We try to solve unsolved murders like the Jon Benet Ramsay case."

"Oh, I'll bet that's fun."

He looked out the window. Patty and Nancy were laughing at the "Buy America" bumper sticker he'd attached to the bumper. He decided to move things along as the conversation seemed to be lagging. "Look, let's make some flash cards. You can take them along wherever you go and shuffle through them for a few minutes, and before you know it, you'll know the basics. This is a multiple choice test, isn't it?"

While they were talking, Olive's grandmother showed up in her old station wagon and took Nancy and Patty away somewhere. Olive waved at them through the window.

"Yeah, multiple choice," she said, "with one essay question worth fifteen points out of a hundred."

She had the strangest eyes, brownish-black, sloe-eyed detective story writers called that color. Must be an Italian blonde. They were dilated, too, as if an optician were shining a little flashlight in her eyes.

They divided the flash cards into categories: 'generals', 'battles', 'causes', etc., with Olive periodically wandering off for a snack or to turn on the TV or radio.

Back at her task, she wanted to know why Lincoln stuck with this guy McClellan for so long. Moe said he thought it was because the men loved McClellan so much, and he was good at drill. Kind of like a good practice player who can't play in the game. While they were making the flash cards, she got up twice more to wash her hands. Moe knew that wasn't good.

They wound up with a hundred and fifty cards, and Olive had to admit that this would certainly work. She could even fathom "acing the mother," if she could deal with the essay question. Mr. White would have a heart attack. Moe might have to testify for her when she got that "A". He managed to slip one of the notecards into the back of his notebook.

He took another Dorito. "I can probably guess what the essay question will be. Usually something about the strengths and weaknesses of each side, or maybe something about the long-term causes, states rights, that kind of thing."

"Sounds good to me," she said.

"Another thing I do is look for something in the chapter or unit that relates to me," he said. "I'm very religious, see, so the Puritans would be a good example. They wanted to create a 'city on the hill' as an example for everyone else, a kind of utopia, but then that backfired ultimately. They're the reason Americans have so much trouble with sex. Scandinavians teach their kids about sex early on. They go so far as to encourage exploration. 'I'll show you mine if you show me yours'—that sort of thing."

Her eyes lit up. "Now we're in my ballpark," she said. "I think about this subject a lot, as you well know."

Was now the time to spring it on her? She was chewing on the nubs of her fingers. Moe remembered when he used to bite his fingernails. He cured himself by focusing on one nail at a time, telling himself he wouldn't bite his pinky nail, then his ring finger, middle finger and so on.

"I meant to ask you about that, Olive." He could feel the blood rushing to his ears.

"Fire away." She didn't seem at all embarrassed. She took another sip of lemonade.

Might as well just blurt it out. "There's a rumor going around town that you and Superintendent Bronson..."

He couldn't look her in the eye. She lifted his chin and honed in. He was afraid.

"I don't see as that's any of your business, Howard." She made his first name sound like Chauncey, or Heathcote. "I'll bet the deputy sent you over here, didn't he? She paused to let it soak in, and then she smiled. "I'm just teasing, Howard. Everybody in town knows I'm not Bernadette Soubirous."

Damn right she wasn't. That Susan Hayward voice would make the Boston Strangler wince.

"I might as well tell you," she said. "I don't like liars and I'm sure you don't want one for a girlfriend. I've had sex with lots of older guys."

"You don't have to tell me this—" What he wanted to say was: *Olive, if you had sex with Superintendent Bronson, did you take his belt and help plant it at the rectory?*

"I wanna get it off my chest."

"Do you think the superintendent killed Egge?"

"He coulda done it, he thinks he's invulnerable."

"Oh, why do you say that?"

"Charlie thinks the sun rises and sets according to his clock. Lots of older men are like that, guys like my Uncle Bob. He was my mom's boyfriend. He raped me when I was a little girl."

"Your mom's boyfriend?" he said.

"Yeah, Bob. I'm pretty sure he's Nancy and Patty's father." It all came pouring out of her, like flood water through a break in a dike. "I'd been wrestling with Uncle Bob ever since I was a little girl, but then one night, Ma went to the Outdoor with Nancy and Patty, and I stayed home because I didn't like Chuck Norris karate movies. Bob was watching some beauty pageant on TV, Miss Universe I think. I went to the fridge, got some ice water and dumped it down the back of Uncle Bob's shirt. We wrestled again. Only this time he got a hard-on, and he dragged me into the bedroom and did it to me. Uncle Bob had split by the next morning, although I hadn't finked on him. Musta been the blood on the sheets."

"I don't know what to say, Olive."

"Don't say anything. Just listen. After that I got lots of attention from the boys at school because I let them scope the sex manual from my ma's dresser and soon I was giving them an eyeful, too."

"What about your real dad?"

"My own father left when I was a little girl. Wanna see my dad's picture?"

"Sure, why not?" Olive went into the bedroom and began thrashing through a bureau drawer. He stood in the doorway.

She handed him a photo in an oval frame. Rugged-looking guy with a ridgerunner beard, Roman nose, squinty eyes. Didn't look anything like Olive.

"Nice-looking man." They went back to the table. He had to find out about Bronson and the belt. But how?

"Anything like that ever happen to you?" she said.

"Kind of."

"You were raped?"

"My father committed suicide."

"Oh, I guess that's worse. At least I'm still alive. You must be stifling," she said. "You're not self-conscious, are you? Do you have skinny legs or something?"

Moe turned red.

She got up, went to the kitchen sink, and washed her hands. "Oh, he's blushing," she said. "I like that. You're not trying to be macho. I know so many macho guys. It's as if they've got some kind of complex." She sat back down and moved her chair closer to his.

"Let's go for a ride," she said, "there's a good show at the Outdoor." She ran to her bedroom and got this dufflebag that she called a purse, which she filled with cans of Squirt. They didn't have any at the Outdoor.

On the way to the car, he said, "I warn you. I'm not much of a driver." They jumped in the Honda, Moe ground the gears, and they headed out into Meade Street, past the construction going on at the strip mall.

"Wasn't Meade the general at Gettysburg who was slow to follow up on his victory and got fired?" she said.

"Very good, that's called transference. When you refer something you're learning to something in real life. You'll find a lot of Civil War references around here, since the town is named after returning Union soldiers."

He was pretty sure she didn't need any flash cards.

Moving toward Moe's side of the Honda, she said, "Dave Jenkins tells you everything, doesn't he? What's he doing now that Harry Kline is in the hospital?"

He should have known she'd be pumping him for information. Sherlock's smarter brother—that was him all right.

Shifting the five-speed into third, Moe said, "He's acting more like Harry every day. He needs to hire a deputy to help him out. It's kind of funny actually. With affirmative action and all, he's got to interview some women. Oh yeah, he called in Henderson to give Bronson a lie detector test. I guess he flunked."

"That's not surprising."

What was that perfume? It made him feel light-headed. He was having a very hard time paying attention to the road.

Moe came perilously close to a kid in a crosswalk.

"Ah, I think pedestrians have the right of way there, Pleasiac," Olive said, bracing herself against the dash.

He felt the blood rush to his face again. He could kind of see now why those boys were always doing handstands and imitating all-star wrestlers in the lockerbanks. "Sorry, can't get the hang of the clutch and the brake, which is which, you know."

"Maybe I better drive," she said. "My Uncle Bob was a stock car driver. He taught me to drive before I was ten."

He stopped the car and studied her face, remembering their conversation about macho males.

"You really want to? If it were realistic, I'd just as soon stick to my bike."

They switched sides with Olive scootching over his lap, digging him in the groin on the way by. She headed out toward the Outdoor, one of the few remaining in Minnesota.

A cowboy movie he had never heard of was showing. They got some popcorn and drinks from the snack stand. He didn't like Squirt.

About ten minutes into the movie, he got his first kiss, during which she put her tongue in his mouth. It tasted like Squirt. He'd need to read up on it to find out if that was standard practice and if it was sanitary. Olive took his hand and put it on her breast. He began to get an erection.

"Do you like that?" she said. "You can feel them both if you want." She reached up under his sweatshirt and moved over onto his lap.

"I like that a lot," he said, "but we better stop. Father Mischke'll give me a rosary the next time I go to confession."

Olive spit out a mouthful of Squirt.

"Well, I guess I did tell David I'd be a regular little Laura Ingalls," she said. "I lied. We'll take it slow...This is the dumbest movie I've ever seen. That cowboy must have fired that six-shooter fifty times without reloading."

"It's pretty old all right. Look, Olive, something's been bothering me all night. Why didn't you turn that guy in? Your Uncle Bob, I mean?"

"I always thought it was kind of my fault. I was teasing him. And I loved him, you know. That's what men and women do when they're in love. You have any sex yet?"

Damn! the girl was blunt.

"What's the use, you'd never believe me. This is the first date I've ever been on."

"Oh, I thought maybe you cornered some neighbor girl or something." She smiled. "Let's go to your place. That schoolhouse is beyond cool."

Moe thought that was probably all right since his mom was over at her sister's house for dinner.

Past the exit gate of the Drive-in, Olive floored the Honda and laid a patch of rubber. Shifting into third, she said, "Sorry, about that, I didn't think this Jap junk had that much pickup. Say, one thing about that guy that's been offing everybody. If I didn't know better, I'd say it had to be Uncle Bob."

As they neared Bud's Tavern, a truck backed into the street. Instead of braking, Olive hit the accelerator and went around.

"Stupid shit! Bob used to tell us how much he hated priests. God Damn! did he ever hate them. Every time there was a story in the paper about some pederast priest, he'd show it to me and the girls. He said we should never be alone with one."

Mrs. Macintosh was sitting on her front step talking to Debbie Meyer and the Indian as they drove by. They waved and Olive honked.

She turned onto Little Round Top. "And then he had sex with me," she said, "and I haven't seen him since, so I guess it couldn't be him, but you said that Lester Krueger's old man said he was a big guy who looked like a football player, and Bob was really big. Believe me, I should know." Olive pulled into Moe's driveway, knocking a garbage can out of the way.

"Whoops!" she said, shutting off the engine. "Lucky that thing's made out of rubber. Maybe you should've been driving after all."

He unlocked the front door, got Olive settled, and put on a record, Bach's Brandenburg Concerto No. 2. She gave him an incredulous look when he asked her to dance. The house looked different with her in it. The furniture wax glistened, the fluorescent lights gave off a softer hue, the loft window shone like cathedral stained glass, and the carpet felt softer and more buoyant.

"I didn't know you could dance to this shit," she said, checking the place out.

He moved his hand up her back. He hadn't realized skin could feel so good. "I hadn't either," he said. "I've got a little money saved up. You wouldn't want to go on a real date, would you? We

could go to a fancy restaurant in Crookston? Or am I being too tra-
ditional for you?"

She put her hand on the back of his neck, and the hair there
rose to attention. "What the hell, who knows until you try it?" she
said. "I've never been to a fancy restaurant. That Bach guy was
really versatile, wasn't he? What do yah think of Hank Williams? If
he were alive today, he'd make Garth Brooks look like a homeless
person he'd be so rich. I always melt when I hear 'I'm so Lonesome
I Could Cry'." He stepped on her toe, she pretended not to notice.

"I think my mom might have an old Hank Williams album," he
said, resting his cheek against hers.

Later, as they were dancing to "Your Cheating Heart", the
phone rang. It was for Olive.

She took the phone, bit her lower lip, smiled at him. "How did
you know I was here?" she said. He couldn't hear the answer.

He tried to take her back in his arms, but she put her hand on
his chest. "I'm gonna have to go. Freddie needs me." He had the
feeling that they could have been in the midst of coitus, and she'd
have left if Freddie had called.

* * *

When Moe walked Chopin just before bed, he went barefoot,
although once he'd stepped on a piece of glass and had to have five
stitches. He liked to walk down by the dam and the hydroelectric
plant on The Angle, not far from the Forman house.

On this particular night, about two hours after Olive had left,
lots of people had the same idea. There were three cars in the parking slots directly in front of the dam. Any time of the day you could
walk by the dam and find people watching the water. You had to
pay a therapist seventy-five dollars an hour for the same effect.

The temperature had to be in the seventies, and the sky was
very clear with thousands of visible stars. The combination of the
crashing water and the breathtaking view of the stars was almost
too much.

How could his father have taken his own life? There was that
question again, intruding on his good time. He'd pinch himself
hard the next time he began to think about it. Aversion therapy
psychologists called it.

He walked on past the dam, heading toward the water tower.
Maybe tonight was the night he'd garner the courage to climb up
there. *Ha! You're kidding yourself,* he thought. *You're afraid of
heights — you have trouble climbing the slide on the old school playground
behind your house.*

Not tonight.

As he neared the tower, he fingered the pepper spray in his pocket Dave had given him. He hadn't wanted it, but Dave had persuaded him, paranoid schizophrenic that he was, that anything could happen anywhere, even in Soldier, Minnesota. Even he, tough guy Navy SEAL, had been braced by these gang types on State Street in Chicago and had given them money to get rid of them.

Moe glanced at his Mickey Mouse watch, which had been the last Christmas present from his father. It was 10:15, almost time to head back.

A flashing red light was shining on the top of the tower. As he looked up, he was hit in the eye with what felt like bird droppings. He wiped it off, realizing it was saliva. Almost simultaneously, he heard a crash, and these kids started climbing down from the top of the tower. The crash had been a wine bottle, and the kids were Olive and her friends Freddie Cochran, Rita Miller, Lester Krueger—Moe remembered that Dave was looking for him—and that Stormy girl. Olive jumped down and fell into a hedge. She was drunk.

"Hey Mopester, do you know how many blondes it takes to screw in a light bulb?" she said, standing up and dusting herself off. "Don't know, do yah? Two. One to mark the spot and one to run out to the curb, hitch up her skirt, and flag down a truck driver. Hah! hah! hah! Have a little drink with us, why don't yah? We got Chardonnay and Chablis, goes good with everything."

Lester took two quick strides toward Moe, duck hunter's camouflaged hat pulled down over his ravaged face, overdressed in jean jacket, tight jeans and engineer boots. "The pussy don't drink," he said, grabbing Moe by the T-shirt. "He's too good to drink with us. All he ever does is study and kiss up to the deputy. Ain't that right, Pussy?"

Chopin growled, and when Lester wouldn't let go, Chopin began nipping at Lester's ankles. Moe fingered the pepper spray in his pocket, but Lester beat him to it.

"Better call off your goddamn dog," Lester said, waving some sort of handgun, "or I'm gonna have to shoot the mutt."

Freddy grabbed Lester's arm. "Put that fucking thing away before I shove it up your ass," he said.

Moe thought he was taking quite a chance with the possibility of that thing being loaded.

Blam! Moe's ears began to ring.

"Now look what you've done," Olive said, swaying a little bit. "The Indian is gonna be on our asses again. Let's go back up on the water tower. He hates climbing up there."

"Gimme that thing," Freddie said, snatching the pistol out of Lester's hand and hurling it high over the water. It made a ploosh sound, the sound of a penny hitting water in a wishing well. Krueger looked as if he might start something for a moment, but then shrugged and wandered off toward Meade.

"There's no evidence now," Freddie said. "We're just out here havin' a little chat with our friend Howard. Let's walk Howard home, shall we? We'll stash the booze in this hedge and pick it up later."

Freddie looked different tonight. No baseball cap for one thing. And he'd gotten a buzz cut. He was wearing hip-hugging bicycle shorts and no shirt. He had the body of a Greek god, tanned, flat-bellied, and wide in the shoulders.

Olive, on the other hand, could have been an inmate at one of Dorothea Dix's insane asylums, her hair flying every which way, clothes all dirty, eyes glazed.

They made it all the way to Moe's house before Mingo Jones, the night deputy, drove by. Remarkably, the deputy failed to notice Olive, her friends, and Moe flattened up against the side of the house.

"Got anything to drink in there?" Freddie said.

* * *

It was three in the morning, according to his bedside clock, when Moe's mother woke him up, telling him there was this girl on the phone who wanted to speak to him. The girl wouldn't take no for an answer. She'd kept calling back every time she'd hung up on her.

She seemed sober now. "I wanted to warn you to be on the lookout for Lester," she said. "He's hassled kids before. He doesn't have the guts to confront Freddie over chucking his gun, but he needs to blame someone...I had a good time tonight, Howard. Even the studying was fun."

"Thank you, Olive. I'll keep an eye out for Lester. He can't be too overt, Dave is after him. I'll see you in school maybe." He hung up the phone.

It was almost worth getting up at three in the morning to know she was worried about him. He wondered how long it would take to learn karate.

Chapter 17

The Night Deputy

"In all the endless road you tread
There's nothing but the night."
— A.E. Housman

Mingo checked the lock on Warner's Hardware and moved on down the street to Logan's Sports Shop.

It was his favorite time of day—three in the morning. On most nights—for all he knew—he could be the only person awake in town at this hour. He liked that omniscient feeling. He was the only awareness, the protector, the one who never sleeps.

But that was before the two murders and the attack on the old priest. One of the crime watch trucks was out there someplace, driving around in circles.

As he jiggled Logan's doorknob, he thought about his first aborted attempt to free the Egg Man. He'd been hounding Cousin Cecil about procedure for the ghost medicine ritual, but all the old coot would tell him was "observe and learn," and "all Apaches are shamans," and "each holy man must concoct his own method," and when Mingo would make a suggestion, Cecil would say, "Ach, it's all the same thing."

Anyway, finally Mingo had gone out to the murder scene dressed as the Clown in the puberty ceremony for young Apache girls—rolled in ashes, wearing a flannel diaper, a paper sack with eyes cut out, and torn sneakers. As all novice Apache shamans knew, Clowns had the power to open the door between the Shadow World and the Land of Ever Summer. He'd cast some pollen in the four directions, placed some stones around where the Egg Man's body'd been found, starting on the west side, then proceeding south, east, and north, the opposite of what a good Apache would do during a blessing.

Next he'd done some singing, a double dose of power as singers could also open the bridge spanning this world and the next. He faced the east asking for wisdom four times. Then he

245

searched the skies for a sign. An eagle would be good or a dove maybe. Not a bird in the sky. No unusual weather. Not a damn thing. Back to the drawing board.

Mingo spied a pair of boots sticking out of the alley between Logan's and the bank. Pigeon Hackett. Once a week Pigeon got blasted out of his gourd, got lost, and couldn't make it home. Mingo could relate. He had several uncles back in New Mexico just like Pigeon.

Swinging round the corner into the alley, he found Pigeon lying on his back, smacking his lips. "This isn't a good place to pass out, Sport. If Old Man Forman finds you here, he'll have you put away for twenty years." Damn it, Pigeon had thrown up on himself again. One good thing, though, at least he'd changed out of his grungy green Amoco coat and khaki trousers.

Mingo grasped him by the armpits and dragged him out of the alley. Pigeon wasn't such a bad shit when he was sober. Tried to buy his friends, though. Lottery tickets for Olive and her buddies mostly. Mingo could relate to that. He'd gone to a white school in Alamogordo for a while, which is where he'd learned how to play lacrosse. The whites thought all Indians were drunks.

Damn the guy was heavy. He'd have to talk to Bud about this. A truck drove by. Jeremy Gohl, a somewhat more sober member of the crime watch who had the two to four. The truck stopped and backed up. "Need some help?" Gohl said. Gohl and Mingo played darts together at Bud's now and then.

"Nah, I can handle him. Does this about once a week."

The wind picked up, threatening to blow the pick-up into next week.

"Jeez, what was that, straight-line wind?"

Gohl seemed in the mood to talk. The man had hound-dog eyes, made you want to get him a bone.

"Damn Minnesota weather," Mingo said. "Wait five minutes and it'll snow."

"Ain't that the truth." Gohl sighed as if he had the burden of the world on his shoulders. "Yuch, guess it's 'bout time for my relief. Gotta get home to the wife and kiddies. Take it easy, Jones."

Mingo gripped Pigeon by the seat of the pants, gave a mighty heave and boosted him up over the side of the truck, careful not to bang the man's head. By all rights he should take Pigeon in and give him a good reaming. Nah, he'd talk to him at breakfast if he was up. Usually he was. Had to be at the Amoco by seven. Mingo cranked up the 4X4, and coasted toward Pigeon's house, doing no more than twenty miles an hour, so as not to jostle Pigeon too much.

Despite the snail's pace, the truck was idling in front of the Hackett's bungalow before he knew it. Mingo rang the bell and ran for the truck, not exactly thrilled about the possibility of having to help Pigeon get up to bed. Had to wait, though, until he was sure Mrs. Hackett had seen Pigeon. He knew of too many times where a drunk had been dumped in his front yard and choked on his own vomit.

Mrs. Hackett opened the door, grabbed Pigeon by the shirt and hauled away. The door slammed, the sound echoing into the night. An exclamation point on the evening's proceedings, Mingo thought.

Back to work. If he didn't check the bank, sure as hell some asshole would pick this time to tunnel up through the floor and steal twelve million dollars. Scrooge McForman had at least that much in there. *Maybe I'll rob the place,* he told himself. *Teach him for trying to repossess my truck.* He'd just managed to scrape together enough to make a payment, plus the penalty. Have to order the special at Andy's until the eagle shit next.

He drove by the church, parked next to a fire hydrant, and let the truck run. Too bad about that old priest. Could have been worse he supposed. Awfully fishy, though. Bronson wouldn't be dumb enough to leave his prints all over that belt. Usually, you were lucky if you found one useable print. If he were running this investigation, he'd run Olive and her chums in and grill them until their rumps were crackling crisp.

Mingo walked all the way around the bank, checking all the doors, and listening at the front and the back. Nothing. He wished that big mother would try something with him. He'd jam that Louisville Slugger down the fucker's throat.

He got back in his idling truck and steered toward the high school. Harry had said to check the place several times a night, since they had no security, and especially now, because of the murders. Mingo felt the ponies were already out of the barn.

Nothing was happening at the high school. Tomorrow he'd be back over here. What had Debbie said, two-thirty? She'd asked him to do another presentation for her class. He'd tell them about the puberty ceremony, something he hadn't gone into much in his previous talks.

Awfully dead tonight, except for Pigeon and what he'd thought was a gun shot. The town was usually dead. He liked Soldier, though, big cities made him feel as though he were drowning in a giant grain bin. He turned on the radio for a little company. It was the classical station. He'd heard that if you listened to Mozart you got smarter.

He'd check the water tower next—checked that thing fifteen, twenty times a night, ever since Hildegard had chewed him up one side and down the other over the graffiti incident—then the Knob Hill area of Soldier, The Angle, where Blaze Forman and other fat cats lived.

Nothing doing at the water tower either. Days could pass with nothing happening. When it did it was usually only a family disturbance, a car accident, or Olive and her friends breaking curfew.

Mingo shifted down. Maybe he should take Jenkins up on that day shift idea. He'd get to have dinner with Debbie.

He drove all the way down the Angle, made a left on the Climax road, and turned onto Meade at the flashing red light. As he drove by the Merry Widow Laundromat across from the cemetery, a van rounded the corner on Hancock, weaving precariously from one side of the road to the other, sideswiped a streetlight, skidded across the road, and ran head-on into a stop sign. The door popped, and a man rolled out into the street, flat on his back, his arms spread like Christ on the cross.

Mingo got out of his truck and flashed his light on the vehicle. It was one of those hippie vans—more colors than Joseph's technicolor coat. He unfastened his billy—drunks had a habit of playing possum—and moved over to where the man was lying in the street, groaning.

He nudged the drunk with the billy, the man shuddered, then opened his eyes.

"Where'm I?" the man said.

He looked like one of those professional wrestlers Mrs. Mac was so fond of. Big feet, too. Mingo unbuckled his sidearm. "Had a little accident," he said. "Have you been drinking, sir?" *Have you been drinking? Was New Mexico dry?*

The man sat up, shook his head, and said, "Yer an Injin, ain't yah?"

The big fellow fit Miles Krueger's description—what there was of it—to a T. Might be quite a handful if he wasn't so drunk.

The man reached in his back pocket and handed Mingo his billfold. "All yers," he said. "Jes get me back to the motel."

The license was right where most people put them, in that little flap with the see-through window. Robert Haskins, Crookston, Minnesota. Expired over a year. During the few seconds it took for

Mingo to check the license, the drunk kicked out, knocking Mingo on his ass, the billy flying out of his hand.

Mingo found himself lying on his back with a boot heel aimed at his face. He rolled under the van, then kicked out at the back of the drunk's knee, and he went down like a ten pin. Mingo crawled out from under the van, grabbed the drunk's arms and handcuffed him, then he hauled him back to the 4X4, unfastened the tailgate, and tumbled him into the back, where he cuffed him to the tailgate chain.

At the station, the drunk willingly breathed into the boozeameter. Got a .2 reading. Mingo wrote him up for DWI, resisting arrest, assault, and attempting to bribe an officer. He put Haskins into a cell next to Bronson, who woke up and asked, "What's going on, Deputy?"

"Just a drunk," Mingo said.

"Do you have to put him next to me? The guy stinks."

"Should've thought of that before you went and raped a minor," Mingo said. Hated child abusers worse than anything.

"Watch that one close," he told the night jailer.

Back on duty he spied these three kids walking along the street, headed out of town. It was way past the curfew, which was eleven o'clock for anyone under eighteen. He stopped the 4X4 and flashed his light in their faces.

I'll be damned, he thought. Olive Randall, Freddie Cochran and Rita Miller. Drunker than normal. He still hadn't found out who was buying it for them.

"Hey, Chief, caught any outlaws lately?" Freddie said. He took a swig out of the wine bottle he was holding, handed it to Olive, and took a drag off the cigarette he was holding in his other hand.

"Whyn't yah go back to the desert where yah came from?" Rita said. She was wearing a sweater tied around her waist, and since she was slumped over he could see down her shirt. Not that he wanted to.

Olive pushed Rita, causing her to drop the bottle she'd been caressing on the sidewalk. It exploded, sending shards of glass every which way. "Don't you be talkin' to my lover Mingo that way. He's just a big honey bear, ain't you Mingo? Whoops, look what you did." She knelt to pick up the glass, cutting her hands in the process.

Mingo applied emergency first aid, bundled them into the back, careful not to bruise them, and ushered them back to the office.

Had to call the teenagers' parents. He'd argued with Harry that they should spend some time in jail since they were incorrigibles, but Harry didn't like to piss off the voters. Rita's father wouldn't come to get her, and Freddie's mom didn't answer the phone. Olive's mom showed up, with bags under her eyes, half an hour later.

Good-looking woman—child-bearing hips—strong cheek-bones, black, downturned eyes, like an Indian woman. Not too fashion-conscious, rolled up man's flannel shirt, faded jeans, a black beret pulled down over her blondish hair. She couldn't be more than thirty-five.

Mingo asked if he could have a private moment. He let himself into Jenkins's dingy, little office with the master key Harry had given him.

He offered her the straight-backed chair Jenkins kept for suspects and visitors and sat on the edge of Jenkins desk. She slumped down into it almost knocking it over, rubbed her eyes, looked up at him.

"This is the third time this week, Mrs. Randall."

She opened her purse, couldn't find whatever she was looking for, snapped it shut, dabbed at her eyes. Mingo hoped she wouldn't turn on the faucets. It hurt him like a lance through the heart when a woman cried.

"Don't you think I've tried to talk to Olive?" she said. "You see how well I do with her. If you could only see her with Nancy and Patty."

Mingo crossed his arms. "Have you tried counseling, Mrs. Randall?"

She sat up a little straighter, laughed. "I swear I'd make a better counselor than some of those people. At least I've *been* there. I've got to be at the Legion to clean up by nine, Deputy. Can we go now?"

Mingo nodded.

After she left, Mingo tried to pick the brains of the other two, but it was like trying to talk English with a French Canadian. They knew perfectly well what he was talking about, but they wouldn't let on.

He engaged them in a game of 500 for a penny a point. Won three dollars and fifty-six cents. When Harry showed up at seven, Mingo took them home, then had breakfast, and went home to bed.

At two he woke up, took a shower, got dressed in full Mountain Spirit regalia—canvas head covering with slits for eye-holes, headdress, buckskin kilt, red streamers with eagle feathers attached on each arm, bells sewn to the tops of his moccasins—and headed over to the high school for his talk.

There were about thirty goggle-eyed kids—this was the first time he'd gotten all dressed up—in Debbie's class, mostly Anglos, one Korean girl. And lounging in the back of the room, headachy-looking with their bare feet up on the seats of the desks in front of them, Olive, Rita, and Freddie. Despite the crowded room, the other students stayed well away from them, preferring the floor to the desks in front of the outlaws.

"I'd like to introduce you to a friend of mine," Debbie Meyer said. She was wearing a dress today, peach-colored and frilly, with heels. He liked her in heels; usually she wore ugly penny loafers. "Deputy Sheriff Mingo Jones. He'll be speaking to you today about the Mescalero culture. Please give him your full attention."

"Good afternoon," Mingo said. "First off, I'd like to say that Apaches don't believe in the lecture method—"

The class, some of whom had been yawning as it was already rather late in their long day, clapped and whistled. Mingo had them arrange their chairs in a circle as was the custom in Mescalero schoolrooms.

"Thank you, I'll try to keep my prefatory remarks short. Let's start with what I'm wearing, shall we? The feathers represent the eagle, the Creator's representative on earth. As some of you know, all Indians revere animals as they were made first and were meant to protect and aid man, the weakest of all creatures. Originally we all spoke the same language."

"Why aren't you out catching murderers?" Freddie said.

"Freddie! If you don't behave, I'll have to send you down to see Mr. White," Debbie said.

"Fair question," Mingo said. "I just got off duty at seven this morning, as you well know, Fred."

Freddie laughed.

"Let's see now, where was I? Oh yes, my clothes. The beading on my shirt signifies the sun, which is also symbolic of the creator, whom we call Gessen. See these divisions? The circle is divided into four angles which signify the four directions, among other things. The number four is important to the Mescalero because we believe the world was created in four days."

"This costume I'm wearing is the costume of a Mountain Spirit. Usually there are four of them, and they dance during the four-day puberty ceremony for Mescalero girls. These girls are considered holy at that time, and people, Indians and non-Indians alike, can come and be blessed by the girls as they represent White Painted Woman, the first woman in Apache mythology."

He went on to tell them about how during the four-day puberty rites, the girls' parents and relatives gave away food and presents. The reason for this, he said, was because generosity was the most important value in Mescalero society. "The Apache was always on the move as the people believed the ground got dirty if they lived in one place too long. Before we had the horse, we couldn't carry much on the sleds the dogs pulled, so we gave things away." He told them about other traits imbued in Apache girls during the ceremony: strength, pride, and kindness. Among men, bravery was stressed over kindness, as the men were required to protect the family.

"If Indians are so good, what about all those murdering savages we always see in the movies?" Freddie asked.

Debbie moved toward the back of the room. Mingo was just able to catch her on the way by. "Apache warriors warned settlers when they were about to go on the warpath. An arrow along the trail tied with a strip of red cloth meant war. The color red symbolizes man, war, hunting and killing."

He looked at the clock. It was already three o'clock and he'd barely gotten started. "I just want to leave you with what I consider a very valuable insight the Mescalero have learned over the ages. Remember I said the Mountain Spirits dance during the puberty ceremonies? But they're not the most important dancer. The Clown is. He's just the opposite of the sophisticated Mountain Spirits. They're very well dressed and proper. He's dressed like a bum. I think the lesson is one of balance. The Chinese call it ying and yang. With good, there must be evil. With happiness, there must be sadness."

Mingo rubbed his hands. They were sweating, so he rubbed them on his knees. Debbie pointed at the clock as the bell was just about ring. He hadn't even gotten around to telling them about how the Mescalero concept of change, how during the dancing at the puberty ceremony, the Clown would raise questions with signs painted on his chest and back, such as "Nerds Rule" and "Back to the basics", the goal to encourage discussion on whether technology was good for the people.

The bell rang and the students all filed out of the room, some of them looking back.

Olive touched his arm. Her eyes were flecked with slivers of scarlet and she smelled like mouthwash over stale booze. For once the girl had dressed with some restraint, overalls on top of bare skin. But the hair was Barbie Doll hair, sewed on and static.

"I thought that was a great talk," she said. "One of the best we've ever had. Of course, that's not saying much because Debbie here doesn't have all that many speakers."

Debbie smiled. "Thanks, Olive. I appreciate you, too."

"Boy would I like to see that ceremony. Those chicks know when they're expected to be women."

"It's a riveting experience," Mingo said.

"I could maybe hitch out there during the summer. Do they let white people watch?"

Freddie and Rita, hung over, their features sagging and empty, like old photos of the dead Dalton gang after Coffeeville, were slouching in the doorway waiting on Olive. "You coming?" Rita said.

"Be right with you," Olive said.

Freddie wedged his way between Olive and Mingo. "You don't really believe that stuff, do you Chief?"

"If I wore this custom and didn't believe, I'd suffocate. That's how much I believe, Freddie."

Olive looked like she wanted to hang around and talk, but Freddie pulled her by the arm out into the hall. "Gotta go. You let me know if you want some company the next time you go to that puberty ceremony, okay?"

"Will do."

Debbie moved over and tucked her arm in his. "I think you've made a convert."

"She wouldn't be the first brown-eyed blonde...You want to go out to the Egge crime scene?" Something about the drunken man and the hippie van was bothering him. Another look at the quarry road might clarify matters. Besides, he wanted to show off some more.

"Sounds like fun," she said, nuzzling his cheek. "You make any progress with your ghost medicine ceremony?"

"It's coming up boxcars so far. I'm gonna have to give Cousin Cecil another call."

"Maybe what you need is a little female ingenuity."

"Could be." He wasn't about to bring up Cousin Cecil's *religion is a male prerogative* snare.

As they walked out to his 4X4, he told her about the access road behind the quarry and how he'd found some tire tracks back there and two sets of footprints, one set of which the BCA lab had matched to the assailant.

When they arrived at the scene, he had trouble finding the exact place the tracks had been since it had snowed and rained several times since the murder, but then he noticed the little red flag left by one of the criminalists on the grass just to the left of what must have been where the tracks were.

They stooped down to look closer. She smelled like strawberries and looked like all the feisty Irish girls he'd seen in the movies. She had freckles on her nose and green eyes. He never would have believed he'd be interested in a white woman.

He'd been so distracted he almost missed them. Little flecks of paint along where the tracks had been.

"I could kick myself," he said. "Should've noticed those the first time I was here." He'd carried some evidence bags to impress Debbie, so he scooped some of them up and put them in one of them. The flecks were all of a different color, rather like a rainbow.

"Maybe someone slammed the door and these paint flecks fell off," Debbie said. "It was probably an older van, and the paint was eroding." She snapped her fingers. "All those different colors. It's one of those hippie vans. Those hippies painted the vans themselves. The paint would chip easier, wouldn't it?"

"Smart girl. Smart and beautiful. You know, I stopped a van like that. Hauled the fellow in for DWI. Shit. I hope Jenkins hasn't let him out yet."

She looked shocked; he'd never sworn in front of her before.

"Sorry. It's just that I'd bet a month's pay this is the guy. He was a mean-looking galoot. Had the features of one of Belle Starr's boys, and believe me they'd make a brahma bull look like Cinderella. I had my holster unbuckled the whole time I was dealing with him."

* * *

The basketball rimmed out and bounced too far away for Dave to retrieve with his foot. He was talking to Henderson on the phone. "Larry, I'm sending you some paint chips Mingo found at the Egge scene. He thinks they might match up with a van we found."

Chopin waddled after the ball, tried to bite a piece out of it. Moe wrestled it away from him and handed it to Dave.

"I'd like to see you this afternoon sometime, Jenkins," Henderson said. "I'm bringing you a copy of the Commissioner's letter."

"I'll be home. How's six or so? Put a hurry up on those paint chips, Larry. We have this guy in custody and we're gonna have to let him go if we can't tie him to the Egge scene."

It was time to check on the prisoners. They were in the two cells on the basement level. In the anteroom Dave selected a New York Yankees and a Los Angeles Dodgers mug from the rack above Shirley's desk, poured two cups of joe, one without cream, one with, put them on a tray, and handed it to Moe.

* * *

Bronson was watching some talk show, looking awfully bored. He'd been arraigned on an attempted murder charge, as their best evidence against him was what they'd discovered at the rectory. County Attorney Schultz would wait on the murder charge for now. Dave handed Bronson the New York Yankee mug without cream. He said thanks. Bronson hadn't shaved, and his hair was uncombed.

The other fellow was smoking a cigarette and reading a paperback. He took the mug and set it on the floor grunting something. Dave couldn't tell if he said thanks or not.

"Say, Buddy, you can't smoke in here," Dave said.

The fellow glared at Dave, the most malevolent look he'd ever seen on a human being. Hulking brute, wouldn't want to tangle with him. Mean around the eyes, greasy hair, shot with gray, mashed-in nose. Rolled up, cambray shirt, with a darker blue on one arm where a Navy crow had been at one time. Army-Navy surplus stores sold those. Belt buckle with a long-horn steer design. Scuffed work boots, the heels worn down.

"Right, Sheriff," he said and dropped the cigarette on the floor, letting it smolder. The voice had a raspy, drill-sergeant quality.

"Can I get you anything else, Chuck?"

Bronson shook his head no. They stood and watched two people on the talk show discussing a possible cure for AIDS. Terrible disease. Only the first epidemic to come out of the African rainforests, according to the people on the show.

As they ascended the stairs, Moe said, "What did you say that guy's name was?"

"Bob Haskins, according to his drivers license."

"Did you notice the tattoo?"

"Yeah, what about it?"

"It's an eagle, J.W. The man in my dream had a tattoo of an eagle on his forearm."

"Lots of lowlifes have eagles on their forearms. You and Olive have your first *study* session yet?"

"Sure did. And she told me about this guy Uncle Bob. Says he hates priests. She said she knew him a long time ago and that he raped her when she was eleven and her mother drove him off. Awful coincidence, don't you think—Uncle Bob, Bob Haskins?

"And, oh yeah, that kid Lester Krueger—the one you wanted to talk to about the murder weapon—is back in town." They stood near the bulletin board at the top of the stairs, outside the office, the one with the twenty-year-old wanted posters and auction notices. "Did you get the results back from the National Crime Information Center on Mrs. Szymanski's list of troublemakers?"

"One match. Brad Huntzinger, mad bomber for the SDS. No pictures, no prints. I called Mrs. Szymanski. She thinks she can get me a picture."

"Bob Haskins, Brad Huntzinger? Detect any similarity there?" Dave removed a dated auction notice, crumpled it up and put it in his pocket. "JESSICA thinks the murderer is a very smart, idealistic person who doesn't think that he can be caught. Megalomania. Sure sounds like our boy Brad Huntzinger. Did you see the way he looked at you when you told him to put out that cigarette? What else you got?"

"We'll be comparing Haskins's van with some paint chips Mingo found near the quarry where that vehicle was parked."

"Did you notice the cigarette brand the guy was smoking?"

"I've been thinking about letting him go."

"Are you nuts?"

"We got two murders, remember? And we got two sets of footprints at the scene. I'm thinking we let him go, follow him, and maybe find out who killed Ellis, and possibly scoop up his accomplices."

"You're not as dumb as you look. Well, good luck, I've got to make one of my token appearances at the school."

Dave looked at his watch. "I'd say you're a bit late. It's four thirty."

"I gotta see the new guy, Conrad White. He'll probably try to make me go regularly. They all do." Moe reached in his upper pocket, took out a notecard, handed it to Dave. "I thought you might want a sample of Olive's handwriting."

Dave put the card in his pocket. Moe and the dog left.

The Haskins fellow was just too weird not to have something to do with the Egge murder. According to Mingo's report, the van had the motto "Helter Skelter" painted on its side. Had to check his hands for a bite mark, hadn't noticed any bandage.

When he got back to his desk, the phone rang. It was Pete Dickman about a property dispute. Dave said he'd send somebody out. Lucille the new deputy, probably.

* * *

Dave went to the evidence room, signed out the pouch with Bob Haskins's personal effects and took them back to Harry's office.

Thirty-eight bucks. Some change. A Bulova watch. No credit cards. Expired Minnesota driver's license in the name of Bob Haskins. He checked the back of the watch. The inscription read, "To Brad, from Mom."

Had the bastard.

Chapter 18

Out of the Horse's Mouth

"For when is death not within ourselves?
... Living and dead are the same, and
so are awake and asleep, young and old."
— Heraclitus

It was just before quitting time. Dave had cracked the Egge case and was singing "We Are the Champions" and doing a touchdown-scoring, victory dance in front of Shirley's desk.

"You look like you just got lucky with a Dallas Cowboy cheerleader," Shirley said, in the midst of polishing her desktop with furniture wax.

He perched on the edge of Shirley's desk. "I feel like I've had an eight hundred pound gorilla peeled off my back."

"You solved the murder cases?"

"That man in the cell downstairs..."

"Which one, Bronson or the drunk?"

"I better not get ahead of myself, Shirley. I should know for sure when I get that package I'm expecting from Steubenville, Ohio."

"Another one?"

"Yeah, Mrs. Syzmanski is sending me some pictures of that Brad Huntzinger guy, the one who planted those bombs at the U. of Wisconsin."

"No! You think that drunk is—"

The phone buzzed. "Mrs. Macintosh for you," Shirley said.

"I'll take it in Harry's office."

He shut the door, took a seat behind Harry's desk, then grabbed the phone. Women in the background yakking it up. "What's up, Martha?"

"Deputy Jenkins. I was just wondering how the investigation was going. Lucille said you mentioned me."

"I think we've got it licked, Martha. I can't tell you much, for obvious reasons."

259

"Yes, I heard all about the drunken man who ran into the stop sign and the paint flecks that match his van." *Damn blabbermouth Mingo.* "I suppose you searched his van," she said. "I'm wondering if there was any sign of women's clothing?"

"Oh that."

"Yes that. You must remember the man in the baseball uniform."

"How could I forget?"

"I don't think I like your tone, Deputy Jenkins. Do I need to remind you that one of your visions led to the recovery of Colonel Colvill's arm?"

"Yes, that was quite a coincidence, but Olive's always been very high—"

"The point is, the real reason I called, is to arrange for that séance we were talking about the night before Ellis was...I've been in touch with Jerry Egge again, you see. He's had some very interesting things to say about Olive Randall." He could hear glasses clinking, silverware rattling, and furniture being moved.

"I don't see why I need to go through all those shenanigans when I'm pretty sure I've got my man."

"Shenanigans you say? Well then, how about the Ellis matter? And Jerry. One would think you'd be concerned about Jerry. The man needs closure."

"I just don't think it's in the best—"

"You are the most obstinate man. What do I have to do to penetrate that granite layer of incredulity?"

Dave took Harry's letter opener and drew an X on the desktop, found himself reinforcing the mark. He was pretty sure he wasn't going to have any more visions now that he had Egge's killer. "Okay, Mrs. Mac, what does Jerry have to say about Olive?"

"There's a kind of gang—Rita, Stormy, Freddie and Olive. But they all follow Olive's lead. Why don't you come over here, Deputy? I said I wouldn't charge for this one. If you're not concerned with Jerry, you should be about your little friend's father. As I said at the murder scene, he's in stasis, too."

"That's right, you did."

"And you didn't believe me."

"Jeez, I don't know about that séance thing. What about those women in the background? I don't want this to get around."

"Bridge club. Rather pedestrian of me, isn't it? They know everything. Bring Howard Pleasiac with you. Jerry wants him there."

"I have to tell you, Mrs. Mac, I don't believe—"

"But you'll do it for your little friend? His therapy sessions don't seem to be working."

"Can't do it right now, Mrs. Mac. I have an appointment. How about tonight around eightish?"

"Eight is fine. See you then."

"You know what, Mrs. Macintosh, you remind me of my mother."

"I'll take that to mean she wouldn't take no for an answer either."

"Nah, I meant you know how to lay a mean guilt trip on a guy."

* * *

Later on that same day, Henderson of the BCA, wearing a red and white checkered sports shirt under the ever-present BCA windbreaker, pulled up a chair at Dave's kitchen table. He seemed grayer and more haggard. There were red rims around his eyes. Problems with his daughter? Or were his superiors at the BCA after his ass, too?

The kitchen table was the one piece of furniture in the place that wasn't dusty. Dusting the table was the only concession Dave had made to Henderson's presence. He hadn't dressed for the occasion either. Had his feet in a tub of Epsom salts, wearing bermudas with no shirt. He was watching the Twins on his little portable.

Dave got up, wiped his feet on an old T-shirt, got them both a beer. Henderson looked around for a glass. Lots of luck. They were all in the dishwasher, which Dave hadn't turned on. Henderson handed Dave Commissioner Blayne's letter asking Dave to defer to Henderson in the two murder investigations.

"I don't think it matters, Larry," Dave said.

Henderson listened quietly as Dave filled him in on the new developments regarding Haskins/Huntzinger.

"Remember the cigarette butts at the scene? Our suspect smokes the same brand."

Henderson laughed. It was hard to stay upbeat when everywhere you turned, all you got were negative vibes.

"And there's the inscription on Haskins's watch. And the 'SYZ' on Egge's back—Huntzinger had a principal named Szymanski and they hated each other. This is obviously a case of mistaken identity. Mrs. Szymanski had trouble finding a yearbook for that year, but she finally found one in the Steubenville library. She's sending it priority mail."

"So what's the tie between this Huntzinger person and Egge?" Henderson asked, deep craters forming on his brow. Chiseled features Dave guessed you'd call them, if he were trying to describe Henderson in a short story about egomaniacs.

"I don't know yet, Larry. I just know there is one."

Henderson wiped his sleeve across his forehead. "Don't you think you ought to let the FBI in on this?"

"It's been almost thirty years since that bombing," Dave said. "They can wait a little while longer, until we get our cases cleared. Any results on those paint chips yet?"

"I don't think that's going anywhere," Henderson said, "the place is a rendezvous for lovers. Who's to say the vehicle was parked there during the Egge murder? Haskins's lawyer will admit that the van was there, under entirely different circumstances. Bronson has the motive. If your man Haskins was involved at all, he was hired to do Bronson's dirty work."

Dave could have the murder on film, and Henderson would deny Haskins had done it. The man always had to be right.

"The most damning evidence against Bronson is the fingerprints we found at the scene of the assault on Father Mischke," Dave said. "Smells like a plant to me. I'm thinking some kids may be involved."

"What about the lie detector test?" Henderson said. He struck a match on the bottom of his shoe and lit his pipe. Some kind of a cherry concoction he was smoking.

"Oh, I think something else is going on there," Dave said. "In Egge's indictment he accuses Bronson of having sex with an under-age girl. Could be more than one, don't you think?" Henderson raised his eyebrows noncommitally. "Our man Bronson isn't a very noble soul, that's for sure, but why in the world would someone like him attack an old, defenseless priest? Doesn't make any sense."

Henderson took a slug of beer. "You're going to tell me you don't want to go to the grand jury with Bronson. If that's the case, you're going to have to find some forensic evidence to back up your little mistaken identity pipedream."

Dave leaned back in his chair, almost falling over when he realized the wall was nowhere near. "Egge's wife will testify that he was with her at the time of the first murder."

Henderson perked up. "As I said, that doesn't preclude him hiring it done, does it, Deputy?"

"It does not," Dave said.

Henderson was definitely going for the easy out on this. Didn't need any more shit on him. Henderson'd been getting some bad press lately. A rape suspect had been living two doors down from a recent murder victim and no one had pegged the man.

"One good thing about your ineptitude, Jenkins. Bronson's attorney won't be able to argue we didn't consider any other suspects. What about the Ellis murder? Are you saying this crazy man somehow got into the high school with no one noticing?"

"Obviously accidental. No relation to the Egge murder. Ellis got his promotion over several more experienced coaches. Bronson had no motive at all, other than that Ellis was wearing two hats and didn't like it much. But that would be Ellis's motive to kill Bronson and that didn't happen. Then there's the note from the Designated Hitter. Your own handwriting experts say it was most likely written by a woman."

Henderson tapped the ashes from his pipe into a jar lid Dave had provided, took out his pouch, refilled the pipe and relit.

"Any new evidence on Ellis?" Henderson asked.

"Some of the teachers think a student did that one. Whoever did it is guilty of manslaughter, not murder. If it weren't for the fact that a principal's office is so well-traveled, your own forensics would tell you who did that one. Egge's a different story. Haskins drives a van. If you take a look at the original pictures of the quarry scene, you'll be able to pick out the paint chips."

"I don't think they took any. There wasn't any reason..."

"I know this is the guy, Larry."

"Regardless, I want you to search Bronson's house. Should've been done a long time ago."

As Henderson got up to leave, Dave turned back to the ball game, shaking his head.

* * *

Just after Henderson left, Benny Ullman pulled up in his mail truck. Priority mail with the yearbook from Steubenville. Dave tore the package open right in the yard. Mrs. Szymanski had tagged three pictures of Huntzinger. Front row middle of the baseball team. Big kid, visor of his cap obscuring his face, leaning on a fungo bat, curly hair sticking out the back of his cap.

There was also a billfold snap in the sophomore class section. Face much leaner than the man he'd had in jail. His hair was so curly it could have been an unintentional Afro. Crazy even then. Huntzinger was wearing a tooth around his neck. The other picture was one of those feature photos that go with the head shots. Huntzinger and nine or ten other sophomores were shooting baskets. Huntzinger dwarfed the others. Maybe he'd send the pictures to Henderson and see if an artist could age the pictures thirty years or so.

Still planned on letting Haskins go. And if he killed somebody else, with his luck, he'd be the one ducking same-sex marriage at Stillwater.

* * *

It was a crisp night out, the kind of night most people associated with the end of October. Dave was wearing short sleeves, Moe his parka, as they approached Mrs. Mac's boarding house.

"Aren't you cold?" Moe said.

"Aren't you hot?" Dave said. He'd been bitching about Henderson's inflexibility all the way over from Little Round Top, something like four blocks.

Annie Kline was sitting on the porch in one of the rockers, her hands folded across her lap, a bemused smile on her face, a mischievous look in her eyes. "If it isn't ghost busters," she said.

"I have half a mind to turn around and go home," Dave said, smiling. He liked it when Annie got in a playful mood. "Can't your landlady keep anything to herself?"

"She asked me to sit in on the séance," Annie said. "I told her I didn't think you'd appreciate that much. She took out a cigarette, lit it with a paper match.

"Since when did you start smoking?" Dave said.

"I like the look," she said.

"But your dad!"

"You just mind your own business, Mr. Jenkins. Do I get on your case when you get hammered at Bud's?"

"Yeah, all the time."

"I'll go tell her you're here. Lucille and I are going to the movies in Crookston with Marshall."

* * *

All the lights were turned off in the big room where the boarders usually ate. The place was lit with candles, the scented kind you could buy in the grocery store. These particular candles smelled like sandalwood. Mrs. Mac made them sit around a circular table holding hands. The woman was trying to crush the bones in Dave's hand she squeezed so hard. She was dressed in a scarlet kimono, with little mirrors on it, and she had her hair covered with a kerchief, half-moon designs on the kerchief. How corny could you get?

"Jerry liked you both." Mrs. Mac said. "He particularly enjoyed his conversations with young Howard about his college options. And his favorite time of the week was his weekly softball games with the Dogs—although he understood that he wasn't very good. Too old and fat."

Typical cult leader. Butter them up, season them gently, and have them for lunch. Why was he here?

"Ow!" he said. "Did you pinch me?" he said to Moe.

"I never touched you," Moe said. The boy's shoulders were scrunched up, his fingers wrapped around his padded flannel shirt. Still cold, despite the sauna-like heat.

Mrs. Macintosh pressed a switch and the globe in the middle of the table lit up in a kind of cloudy blue.

"It doesn't really do anything. I find that people expect it, though." She paused, established eye contact with both of them, and said, "If there's nothing else I can get you, shall we begin?"

Dave shrugged. Moe smiled enthusiastically.

"I'm sorry we don't have a larger contingent. Annie and Lucille begged off, and my bridge friends were afraid to come when I told them a deputy sheriff would be here."

"The less the merrier," Dave said.

"I guess there's nothing to be done." She adjusted the globe, moving it into a more central position on the table. "Now for Jerry. I feel so bad about that man, that we couldn't come to terms on special education. He knew a little bit about everything, encyclopedic memory. Sure he'd bore the pants off you sometimes, but there was no better companion if you wanted to attend the Guthrie. And he kept up with modern theater as well. Knew all the Mamet plays and Shepherd.

"It's such a shame. He's very unhappy where he is, stuck in a netherland, wants to move on to the next plateau. He's awfully hungry, too, he can only eat vicariously. He wishes you'd improve your diet, Deputy, and he doesn't like beer, especially that Lumberjack swill. He cannot sleep at all, and he's very lonely. But he's growing impatient. Jerry has these certain telekinetic powers and he's afraid he may do something drastic."

"Let's see him move something," Moe said.

"In due time, dear," she said.

She slapped Dave on the arm. "Mr. Egge is very upset with you, Deputy. It takes two to tango, his words, not mine. You need to believe."

"Why don't you tell him to drift over by the jail and see if that Brad Huntzinger is the guy that done him in?"

"He can't do that. I didn't want to say this, Deputy, but this whole incident was intended to be a kind of object lesson for you."

"Me?"

"Yes, as I said before, you need to believe. You knew Jerry's parents' names before you called Silver Bay. Howard here can tell you the chances of that happening are astronomical. You've had all of these visions, visions that your friend Mr. Jones would die for, and what do you do? You sarcastically suggest that Jerry identify Brad Huntzinger as his killer."

"Doesn't seem like such a silly suggestion to me. If all of this is real."

"If Jerry told you who killed him, you wouldn't have any evidence anyway, now would you? Besides, you know all you need to know."

Dave let go of her hand. "I do, huh?"

"You do. Now, may I proceed? Jerry wants to take you back and show you something. I can do that for you.

He wants you to know he doesn't believe the Ellis murder had anything to do with his, no sort of cover-up attempt or anything. He says if Ellis wants his murder solved, he can haunt you himself. The man has retained his sense of humor, I have to say."

Dave rolled his eyes.

"As I said on the phone, he feels Olive was implicated in his murder. He'd discovered, quite by accident, that Charlie was abusing the girl, the underwear in his wastebasket with her name on it that you found. How careless."

"You know about that? Did Mingo...?"

She frowned, her eyes shooting darts. "How many times do I have to prove myself to you?"

"I'll shut up. It's my nature to be skeptical."

"Anyway, Jerry called Olive in to talk to her about what he'd found. He wants to replay that scene for you. He thinks it will help a great deal. Jerry will speak through me."

"Cool," Moe said. "You mean we'll be able to hear Mr. Egge's actual voice? Will you show me how to do this?"

"Certainly. But it takes years of training. Okay, let's all hold hands. Would you turn on the record player there, dear? I find that music helps."

The music was a sort of muted bongo, with occasional animal sounds, the shrieking kind they had in African and South American rain forests.

She did the eyes-rolling-back-in-the-head thing again, and began to speak in a man's voice. Must be tough on the larynx, Dave thought.

"I'm looking out over the football field, a hundred yards or so beneath my office window. I like to sit in the dark and look out the window when I have a tough decision to make. It is about 4 P.M. Mindy has gone home. Nobody else is around."

The voice didn't sound very much like Jerry Egge to Dave. It was more like one of those old radio announcers doing a soap opera. Definitely a man, though.

She continued. "Olive shows up ten minutes late. She's wearing a white T-shirt, braless as usual, and shorts. No offensive saying on the T-shirt for once. The shorts are the baggy Michael Jordan kind. She is barefoot. There's a sneer on her face, which seems to be a natural facial characteristic, not an affectation. I am mesmerized by this girl. Luckily, Olive doesn't know this yet, but I must be careful, she's very perceptive.

"There's an oldies station playing in the background. The Diamonds are singing. I have an odd thought. Maybe I can break through the girl's barrier if I show her how to do the Stroll. I've always thought that dance was the coolest thing about the fifties.

"'What can I do you out of, Scrambled?' she says. The girl has a very low, sexy voice, kind of like Lisa Marie Presley's in that car commercial, the one where she puts her foot down. 'Whatcha doing sitting in the dark?' she says. 'My eyes are tired, and the light hurts them,' I say.

"I reach over and flip on the lights, then sort through the papers in Olive's file. She's looking at me as if I'm some sort of curious species with two heads and multiple eyes. 'I see by your record that you have a 132 IQ, Olive. That's an awful waste.' I close the folder. 'Just exactly what did you plan on doing with your life?' I ask.

"Olive is now sitting on her feet yoga style. 'I thought about mainly doing some modeling. Everybody says I should.' Certainly she'd make an excellent model. The blond hair combed straight back and tied in a bun. The huge, somewhat slanted, dark eyes. The golden, retrousse eyebrows. The charming slightly pugged nose. She was a very distinctive-looking girl."

"But I scoff. 'Have you ever considered that modeling is kind of a passive existence? Actually, this is one of my pet peeves. We call the really expensive models super models, as if they were great actresses or something, when all they do is wear clothes, strut and starve themselves. The designers and the photographers do the real work. Ever think about photography?' I'm talking with my hands. I notice and fold them over my chest."

"Olive turns red. 'Fuck you, Scrambled,' she shouts. 'Do you think being a principal is any better? I know some teachers who would dispute that.' Olive has a blaze in those brownish-black eyes, which is even more of a turn on than her lack of underwear.

"I ignore the disrepect, get up, take a chair opposite Olive. 'This isn't about the usual, Olive,' I say. 'If you want to look like a trollop, that's fine with me. This is about your relationship with Superintendent Bronson. You're only sixteen, you see, and that's statutory rape. Whether it was consensual or not, I need to turn this in to the sheriff.'

"At this point, I go to my file cabinet, draw out an envelope, and place it in her lap. 'I found that in Mr. Bronson's wastebasket,' I say. She opens it and removes the underwear with her name stenciled on the waistband. I sit down, put one loafer on top of the other.

"Olive flares her nostrils defiantly. She's holding the underwear up to the light. She puts the panties back in the envelope, throws it on my desk, then rubs the edge of her nose, looking really bored. 'Get your rocks off sniffing girls underwear, huh?'"

"I'm now standing, looking down on Olive. Trying to keep my voice level, I say, 'I have five years of postgraduate work, and I'd like a measure of respect, young lady.'"

"Her face clears some, and she looks a little cowed. 'I just wish you'd mind your own business. What about you and your wife? Charlie told me about their affair. He was kind of bragging about it. What kind of man would take that?' She looks at her watch, gets up and heads for the door, but I touch her arm and lead her back to the chair.

"Sometimes I can be such a simpleton. Why had I said that about models? 'Let's not make this personal, huh? It's my job,' I say. 'I just want to do what's best for you. You know you can't keep this up with Bronson. What can come of it? You know he could be having sex with other young girls. You say he bragged about my wife.'

"Her face turns red once more. The girl has a hot temper. 'Who do you think you are, God? Let me tell you, there are lots of girls in this school screwing older men, and most of them aren't eighteen either. Ask your daughter?' I clutch my chest. Check and checkmate.

"She tries to get up again, but I hold her down. My hands slip up her thighs. I should be incensed about what she'd said, my hands should be around her throat, but I can't let go. It is as if I have hold of 5,000 volts of electricity.

"Olive pushes my hands away. 'Sex is normal,' she says. 'You're the sicko. I like it. What's so wrong with that? I'd even fuck you.' At that, she reaches out, before I know what's happening, opens my zipper, and drags out my penis. I stand up, despite an increasing erection, tuck myself back in, zip up, and move away from the enchantress.

"'This won't work with me Olive,' I say.

"She crosses her arms. Her breasts jut out like twin footballs. 'Looks like you want to, though, doesn't it?' she says. 'I'll bet you ain't had any in years. You're really missing out. Just watch it, though. Keep your mouth shut about the superintendent and me if you know what's good for you! I ain't going to no damn therapy.' This time Olive makes it to the door, opens it, and slams it behind her.

"I pick up the phone and dial Sheriff Kline's number. I get Mrs. Pleasiac. The sheriff is at some kind of workshop and won't be back until the following Monday, so I make an appointment for 9 o'clock on that day, which I can't keep."

Mrs. Macintosh's eyes lost the Orphan Annie look. She got up, turned on the overhead lights, returned to the table, and blew out the candles.

"Wow," Moe said.

"Why didn't you tell me this was going to be pornographic," Dave said.

"I need to ask you something...," Moe said. "This is hard." He paused. "Can you...Can you talk to my father?"

"Your father is with Mr. Egge, Howard. Mr. Egge is helping him find rapprochement. The old sheriff is with them also. Sheriff McCloskey. He murdered his wife's lover and needs to make amends."

Moe took off his cap, scratched his head, put it back on. "Is that possible...Is it possible for a suicide to...?"

Mrs. Macintosh touched his hand, gave his fingers a squeeze.

* * *

As they left the boarding house, Dave didn't know what to think.

"Well?" Moe said.

A car passed with its bright lights on. Momentarily, Dave thought they were in trouble, but the street lights revealed a metallic-blue van being driven by a man with thick glasses. He checked the back-holster he was wearing to see if the Smith and Wesson was still there.

"She's a spooky lady is what I think," he said.

"No, I mean, are you going to question Olive?"

"Olive told me all this herself. You're the only one who can find out if she was still seeing Haskins. Use your seductive charm. Lure her into bed if you have to."

"You have no moral scruples whatsoever, have you? Why is it wrong for Mr. Bronson to seduce Olive and right for me?"

"Sounds like it was the other way around. I was just kidding. You never recognize irony. I'm just saying you have a better chance of getting her to talk than I do."

"What do you think about Mrs. Macintosh?"

"What am I going to say? You know me; I make the Amazing Randi look like a psychic hotline addict. But I've had more visions than the children at Fatima. I have no choice but to question Mrs. Randall. Find out if she knew a man named Bob Haskins, whether or not he had a grudge against Egge. But if I do that based on some vision I had of her and Haskins at a parent-teacher meeting, she's going to call Harry and tell him his deputy is seriously demented, and he's going to have her call Henderson, who's been looking for a reason to lock me up as a public menace. Do you see my dilemma?"

"Tell her Olive told you about him. I was kind of hoping what Mrs. Mac said about my dad was true, that there's a chance for him, you know."

"I'm sympatico, short stuff, but I can't get too consumed by supernatural claptrap. Tomorrow's a full day. Henderson the Rain King has got me searching Bronson's house for no apparent reason, and after that I've got to police the Founders Day carnival."

"That hasn't been cancelled?"

"Nope, Hildegard says the only way she'd cancel Founder's Day would be in the event of a nuclear disaster."

"I have a possible scenario I'd like to run by you. You know those old clothes the caretaker found?"

"Yeah, they belong to Billy Bum and he took off for points unknown when he sniffed to the fact that he was a suspect."

"I don't think so. I'm thinking Billy and Haskins are one and the same."

"You mean Haskins never really left?"

"Yup. And he hung around Soldier disguised as a shell-shocked Vietnam veteran, so's he could pursue his relationship with Olive. That's why Billy disappeared. I'm going to run this all by JESSICA. I hope you don't mind."

"Most of those people are Star Trek conventioneers, aren't they?"

* * *

Mrs. Randall, her blond hair swept back with a red headache band, was at the end of the bar pre-mixing Tom Collins, the world's worst drink in Dave's scheme of things, glorified sugar water.

"May I have a word with you, Mrs. Randall?" he said.

She grabbed a bar rag, wiped up the spillage. "Olive do something again?" she said.

"Probably, but this isn't about her. Can you take a break?"

"Hey Gene, I need a tenner!" she yelled down at the bartender, Gene Avery, an ex-lifer Marine who managed the Legion and took a shift bartending. The four vets at the bar, who were shaking dice for a drink, looked up as if she were talking to them. Gene nodded.

They went into the little office behind the bar. She lit a Pall Mall, offered him one. He shook his head no, although he sure could have used one. She slouched in the desk chair, kicked off her shoes, massaged her feet. He moved some papers out of the way, sat on the edge of the desk. "What's up?" she said.

"We got a man in jail named Bob Haskins, picked him up on a D.W.I. Word has it you lived with him once."

"Whose word?"

"I won't shit you, Mrs. Randall. Olive dropped the name on a date with Howard Pleasiac."

She rubbed her eyes, kind of dangerous considering the pig-sticker nails painted some kind of purpleish-red.

"Oh Jeez, she'll eat that boy alive."

"Maybe. You know Bob Haskins?"

"I should. Lived with him for six years. He's the father of my two younger girls. He had a good job working on the maintenance crew at UMC, hospitalization, vacation pay. Drank a little, had a terrible temper, but he never hit me or the kids."

Dave picked up her lighter, flicked it on, snuffed it. "He ever say anything about a former principal of his named Szymanski?"

She laughed. "God yes! Practically every day I lived with him. Claimed the man ruined his life. Coulda been a pro athlete, if it hadn't been for the Polack as he called him."

Should have recognized her earlier. She was the woman in the parent-teacher vision. Haskins had to have been the big bruiser who hated having his grammar corrected.

"He ever have anything against Jerry Egge?"

She stubbed out her cigarette. "Seems like he said Egge reminded him of Szymanski after one of our parent-teacher meetings. We went there cause Olive's grades were slipping."

Dave reached for the pack of cigarettes, shook one of the unfiltered coffin nails out, and lit it with Mrs. Randall's Zippo. He was getting used to it, one vision after another coming true. Had Haskins croaked Egge because he reminded him of The Polack? "You seen him lately?" he said.

"Nah, threw him out for messing with Olive."

"Could Olive have been seeing him on the sly?"

"Absolutely not. I called UMC and registered a complaint. They fired his young ass. I made damn sure of that."

Dave bought a pack of cigarettes at the bar on the way out, managed to refrain from having a beer, although the regulars tried to get him to shake. He went through three Pall Malls on his way home, already the smokers cough was back. Haskins knew Egge, but what kind of jury would believe he killed Egge because a former principal had expelled him from school, ruining his chances at a pro career?

Chapter 19

He Called Me Daddy

"So we beat on, boats against the current,
borne back ceaselessly into the past."
— F. Scott Fitzgerald

A ringing sound woke Dave. He just lay there, not sure whether the ringing was in his ears or if it was the phone, then managed to roll over, and slide off the edge of the bed, realizing at the last moment that he was sleeping on the top rack of Moe's bunk bed. Thank God the covers were tucked in and he managed to break his fall, dragging the blankets with him as he sank to the floor. The floor was as cold as a Siberian skating rink. Dave fumbled into his slippers, and a pair of sweat pants, then picked up the cellular where he'd left it on Moe's computer desk on the ninth or tenth ring.

"Sorry to wake you, David, but the FBI is here," Shirley said. "They have a pickup order for Brad Huntzinger."

"I'll be right down, Shirl. Don't let them have him until I get there."

"I won't. I'll give them my ditz act. Hurry up, though."

Not bothering to shave, brush his teeth, or comb his hair, Dave hurried to the office. When he got there, the two agents were gathered around Shirley's desk drinking coffee.

Dave must have looked frantic because the older one, who could've been Jimmy Stewart's twin, stood, put his palm up in stop sign fashion. "I'm Agent Sanderson, Deputy Jenkins." He held out his hand to shake. Dave ignored it. "I realize you're awfully upset about this. I would be too if I were in your shoes. I'd like to put your mind at ease. Bradley Huntzinger will never get out of prison. A co-ed was killed in the bombing he's wanted for. Meanwhile, you'll be able to work on your murder cases at your leisure and he can be tried later, if he's guilty of that one. Larry Henderson doesn't think he is."

"There's nothing you can do anyway," the younger one, an Italian-looking sort with chapped lips, said. "Federal cases have priority, in case you didn't know."

"Now, Dick, we don't want to throw our weight around," Sanderson said.

"Damn right you won't," Dave said. "We're not giving him up."

"Now Deputy Jenkins—"

Dave strode to Shirley's desk, snatched up the phone, punched in Henderson's number in Crookston. The cowardly bastard didn't even have the balls to—

"Henderson here."

"Larry, what the hell did you do?"

"I imagine you're referring to the FBI. I don't see as to how I have to answer to you. Commissioner Blayne gave me the case, now didn't he? You don't seem to realize the clout the FBI has. If they found out we knew about Huntzinger and were waiting to tell them about it until we got our cases cleared, we might as well leave the profession."

"Does Harry know about this?"

"I had no call to tell him. The man is sick. He doesn't need any more stress. Get over there now and do that search on Bronson's house like I told you to."

"You know where you can stick—"

"I'll pretend you didn't say that. Now obey the court order and let them have Huntzinger."

Dave slammed the phone down, picked it up and hurled it at the wall. It hit with a jangling sound, the cord preventing it from smashing into tiny pieces. The two agents looked embarrassed. Shirley stood, took Dave by the arm and led him out of earshot of the other two. She put her hands up against the sides of his face, the way his mother used to do after he'd been in some scrape at school.

"You're like a little brother to me," she said, "so I hope you won't take this the wrong way, but you need to do what Henderson wants."

"But he's letting Haskins get away with murder."

"Let me tell you what quitting your job will get you. My Dan got passed over for promotion, did you know? He retired with nothing to look forward to, except sitting around watching lame talk shows. Quitting leads to depression, since not only did you not get your way, but you wind up penniless and the hunger pangs are worse than your aching pride. And if your boss is a real heel, and Henderson would certainly qualify there, he might even try and blackball you."

Dave kissed her palm. "Who said anything about quitting, Shirl?" No, he'd bide his time, wait for an opportune moment, and then he'd pounce. Like a pit bull on a toy poodle.

He grabbed the keys to Haskins's cell from the hooks behind Shirley's desk, and stalked toward the door leading to the basement cells. The two agents followed along behind. Dave took the steps two at a time, grousing to himself all the way down. If he'd been just a few years younger, he would have walked. Walking never took any tricks, though. Shirley was right about that.

Haskins saw Dave coming, got up from his bunk, looking mildly interested. Dave fought with the keys as he tried to get the cell door open.

When he finally got it open, Sanderson drew a pair of handcuffs out from under his coat, shoved Haskins up against the wall, and locked his left wrist to his right.

"What are you guys, federal dicks?" Haskins said.

* * *

Dave, Lucille, Mingo, and one of Henderson's criminalists took a warrant to Bronson's house. They searched the place for three hours. It looked hopeless until Lucille found a bloody jacket from a rain suit in a garbage bag stuffed behind some paint cans in Bronson's garage. The criminalist went off to match the blood with some samples taken from Egge's body at the original crime scene. He said he'd get back to Dave in a few hours.

After the others left, Dave sat in his Jeep listening to Johnny Cash sing "Five Feet High and Rising." Kind of appropriate considering. If the BCA agent was right about Bronson, he'd have to become a hermit, settle in the upper reaches of Canada, where they didn't have mirrors.

From Bronson's house, Dave went home to put on his uniform, then to the churchyard where the carnival had been set up. He'd volunteered for the baseball dunk, so he had to wear the accursed costume to attract more customers. One good thing—Blaze Forman was the grand marshall of the Founder's Day parade, and Mary Lou would certainly be there.

Dave took a baseball out of the bag lying next to the ticket booth and whanged it up against the target. The trap released and the rock he'd set on the seat splashed into the water. He looked around. The crowd was awfully thin this year, no more than a couple hundred people. The word must not have gotten out yet that they had Egge's murderer and all was right with the world in God's Country, Minnesota, except for the fact that J. Edgar's boys had snatched him away and Soldier would never get its pound of flesh. Damn! He slammed the hockey stick he'd smuggled in to ward off baseballs up against the side of the ticket booth.

He balanced his portable radio up on a two-by-four above where he was sitting on the baseball dunk and tuned it to KSOL, which had recently gone to an oldies format. "Wipe Out" was playing. He hoped that wasn't an omen. Customers already. Annie and her new boyfriend Marshall Preston were first in line.

You got three tosses for a dollar. Dave was on Marshall like shit on stink, taking out his frustration over the FBI incident on the phys. ed. teacher. Besides, it made his gut ache to see Annie with a goddamn two-timer like Preston.

"Hey rubber arm!" Dave bawled. "Bet yah can't get that thing halfway up here." Marshall missed with his first effort, throwing the ball in the dirt. Annie pretended to be talking to her sister Alice.

Dave kept up the pressure. He didn't feel like going for a swim with his clothes on. "*You're* a baseball coach? Yah throw like a girl. Maybe you ought to give Annie a try."

Marshall, completely rattled, was high and wide on his last two efforts. The next several contestants either missed or had the ball swatted away with the hockey stick. Some people wanted their money back, others were yelling, "Cheater! Cheater!" A riot was definitely in the works until Annie sank him on her first throw that he whiffed on with the hockey stick.

Someone else took over on the baseball dunk, and Dave headed for the three-legged race, surrounded by the smell of frying buffalo burgers, the blare of a nasal bingo caller yelling "B-17!" and the throbbing beat of "Walk Don't Run" coming from the beer tent. When he stopped at a concession stand for coffee, a frantic mother caught up with him.

"My Tommy is lost. We've looked everywhere. I just know some child molester has got him."

"Settle down, ma'am. No child molester is going to have the guts to grab a child with all these people around." He sent Mingo, who'd been tracking down kids exploding illegal fireworks, to look for the second grader.

It was time for the three-legged race. In order to prevent ringers, a male name and a female name were drawn from a hat. There would be thirty teams and three heats with the top nine teams racing for a fifty-dollar prize. Entrants had to be at least eighteen because of the monetary prize. Dave had won the race last year. He'd dated the advertising saleswoman from KSOL, with whom he'd won, for a good six months. Until she'd hinted at marriage.

He was the last to draw, and he drew Mary Lou Forman.

Mary Lou touched his arm. She had put her wondrous hair up, fastened with brownish-red tortoiseshell combs. She was wearing a white sweat suit with "Chicago" stenciled in red on her chest. Brand new sneakers with a red stripe along the side. And she was still pregnant.

"You aren't really thinking of running the race in your condition?" he said.

"And why not?" she said. "Women play racquetball, tennis, swim, right up until labor pains set in."

"But you could fall..."

"And I look like I could drop the kid anytime now, right?" She laughed. "I'm just kidding. I bribed the game supervisor, so's you'd be sure to draw my name. I only wanted to talk to you, to remind you of our little agreement."

"Oh, that..."

"Yes, that," she said, hitching up the elastic on her running shorts. "Don't worry, I'll let you off if you're too busy, but I'd heard you have the Egge murderer in jail."

"Not any more we don't," he said, "thanks to Henderson."

"I don't suppose you'd care to tell me about it?"

He shook his head no.

While they were talking, the first heat of the race took off. Mary Lou and Dave turned to watch. About half the contestants fell flat on their faces, some of them hamstrung so bad they never got back in the race. Marshall and Annie, slow and steady, finished first.

That was when Mary Lou's water broke.

Thankfully, Dave had Harry's cruiser with him today. He switched on the siren, blind to the possibility that the blaring whoop! whoop! sound might induce birth, floored the cop car all the way to Crookston, and got there in slightly under ten minutes, a new record for him. His lead-footed effort was partly in response to the possibility of being forced to deliver the baby himself.

A nurse settled Mary Lou into a wheelchair and whisked her off, another muscled Dave into a prep room, where she scrubbed his hands and arms with foul-smelling soap, fitted him with a green paper gown, a cover for his head, and some damn paper booties, then hustled him into the delivery room, where a doctor and nurse were helping Mary Lou into the stirrups on the operating table. She was already dilating some.

"Come over here, Daddy, and hold Mama's hand," the doctor said.

He sidled over and stood next to Mary Lou. She seized his arm like a passing doghouse in a flood. He had no idea what to expect. Certainly, they wouldn't deliver the baby like he'd done on the farm. With a block and tackle.

"Breathe like they showed you during Lamaze training," the nurse told Mary Lou.

She started huffing and puffing like the little engine that could and increased the pressure on his hand. All the color went out of his fingers she was squeezing so hard. Dave was a nervous wreck. He hadn't been through anything like this since Navy SEAL training, when he'd had to swim under a pool of burning oil and stay under water for two minutes.

He never would have believed you could get a whole baby out of such a small opening, but she gradually expanded, and when the doctor said, "Rare back for that high hard one this time, Little Mama," the baby popped out of there like a Jack in the Box. Or Jill in this case, since it was a girl.

The nurse handed him a sponge and he dabbed her forehead. "How do you feel?" he said. Mary Lou didn't look too bad, considering. She had the appearance of someone who'd just gone through a good work out, just a shade of darkness under her eyes, a bit less color in her cheeks.

"So glad it's over. I didn't think it would be that easy. I've heard so many horror stories."

"Me too."

"I'm going to name her Davida," Mary Lou said.

"Oh God," he said, "don't do that to the poor kid."

The nurse cleaned the baby off and handed her to Mary Lou. "She's a big girl," the nurse said. "Eight pounds, three ounces."

The kid was bald and wrinkled-looking with a lop-sided head. She looked rather like a miniature version of Captain Picard on the new Star Trek.

The doctor and the nurse left them alone with the baby.

"Would you like to hold her?" Mary Lou said.

"Oh no," he said. "I might drop her."

"No you won't. Just put your hand behind her head."

When he took the baby, his fingers stung like they did when he forgot to use the oven mit, and his feet felt like he was wearing new sneakers. All bouncy. The little hand caught hold of one of his fingers.

Somehow, he knew, if he had another one of those visions, he wouldn't react quite the same way. Nothing could beat this.

"You better take her back now," he said. "Thanks for letting me hold her."

"Don't mention it," she said. "I owe you one. I suppose now you'll want one of your own."

"Did you hear what that doctor called me?" he said.

"You mean when he called you Daddy?"

"I thought maybe I should tell him..."

"I'm getting a divorce."

"Oh...that's too bad."

"Not really, he was a workaholic. And he had another woman. He won't fight me for custody, believe me."

The nurse came for the baby and Dave looked around, searching for a polite way to take his leave.

"They'll need you back at the Carnival. I heard there's a demolition race."

"Yeah, Annie's in that."

"Is she your girl?"

"We've been out. We're more like friends, though."

The nurse stepped in and said, "There's a phone call for you, Deputy Jenkins."

"I'll be going then," he said. "Congratulations on your new baby."

"You'll call?"

"Do I ring you here? I don't know how long these things take."

"I should be out by tomorrow if everything's right with Davida."

"You're not serious about that!"

She laughed. The tiredness was gone and she had a gleam in her eyes.

* * *

He took the phone at the nurses' station.

"Yeah. Jenkins."

"Mingo Jones here, Indian holy man."

"What's up, Dude?"

"That missing kid, name's Tommy, was playing that game where two sets of kids grapple with each other piggyback, trying to rip the rider out of the saddle. Olive Randall, Freddie Cochran, and their friends were egging the kids on. Tommy had a bloody nose. Let me lock them up. They're incorrigibles. What's next, a hold-up? Extortion of the village burghers? There must have been twenty or thirty of them hooting and hollering, belittling kids who wanted to quit. They were betting on the outcome."

It was hard to tell if he was serious—he probably was.

"Yeah, I need to talk to Olive anyway."

"About Tommy?"

"Nope. Need to see her about the Ellis murder."

Henderson seemed perfectly content to stick Bronson with that one, too. Dave had pretty much decided that Olive had something to do with the Ellis bludgeoning. The note sounded just like her, and one of those graphologists who worked for the BCA said that her handwriting matched the Designated Hitter note. Not that her lawyer couldn't find a dozen other so-called experts who'd swear it *wasn't* her handwriting.

*   *   *

Dave got back to the Founders Day carnival in time for the demoliton derby. Annie Kline had entered an old '55 Ford and won by driving around banging into people in reverse, thus protecting her radiator and other vital parts. Marshall was making a fool out of himself, stomping and whooping it up. Dave thought about giving Mindy Small a call to enlighten her about what her lowlife boyfriend was doing.

A few minutes after the demolition derby, Lucille Robinson returned from the Miller farm, which surprised Dave since he didn't expect her to work during Founder's Day. She looked like a refugee from a depraved costume party with the sunglasses, bandana, Mickey Mouse T-shirt and flip flops she was wearing.

Wiping the sweat out of her eyes, she said, "I found something interesting, out to the pasture where the cows were last seen. I found this old shed that must be somebody's clubhouse. Whoever it is could have seen the rustlers. Apparently the occupants are there at night. There was a lantern and some matches and some marijuana residue. I'm thinking I could watch the place if you want. The daughter looks suspicious, too, although it could just be the cast in one of her eyes."

Dave shut his eyes, pinched his nose. Another one of the visions had come true. Out at Krueger's farm. The man reading *Soul on Ice*, Olive and her friends chanting "Down with the rich."

"Don't worry anymore about the rustler," he said. "We'll talk about it first thing tomorrow morning. Have a good time."

"I need food," she said. "Point me to the buffalo burgers."

*   *   *

When Dave got back to Moe's that night—his bedroom stank too much, despite the incense—he sat in Shirley's rocker looking out the window over at his grandmother's house, thinking about how that little baby felt in his arms and about how he'd reacted when Henderson had said he was letting the FBI have Haskins. Not the kind of thing a grown man should do, even if Henderson was in the wrong. Maybe he'd give Larry a call.

The phone rang. If that was Henderson, he was moving to Canada for sure.

"Yeah," he said.

"It's me, Mingo. I've got some good news and some bad news, or vice versa, depending on your point of view. Our boy Haskins has flown the coop."

"What do you mean he's flown the coop?"

"Sanderson and his partner stopped for coffee, left Haskins chained to the steering wheel in the locked van. When they came back out, they found a broken window, handcuffs and leg chains. Somebody'd slipped Haskins a bolt cutter. So the good news is we've still got a shot at our boy. And besides, I've been doing some checking. According to my snitch, Haskins is very big in drug sales in Crookston and the snitch knows where Sasquatch's crib is at."

"He's probably on his way back to Berkeley, but we'll set up a stake-out just in case. You take the first watch, okay?"

Dave hung up and dialed Henderson.

"Larry, Dave here. You hear what happened with Haskins?"

"You calling to rub it in?"

"Not hardly. That man is dangerous. I was just about to call you before I heard—"

"Why is it whenever I have anything to do with the FBI," Henderson said, "I come out looking like Mortimer Snerd? Remind me, Jenkins, the next time you've got a case, to send Alvarez."

Alvarez was a junior BCA agent who sometimes worked in the Moorhead-Crookston-Thief River Falls area.

"You know, of course, this doesn't change anything in respect to the Egge case. According to the lab tests, the blood on the rain-suit your deputy found was Egge's. Why the hell would anyone keep something like that?"

"Exactly."

"Should be enough, though, for the grand jury. I'll be in touch if we get any word on Haskins."

* * *

That night Dave was lying in the bottom rack of Moe's bunk bed staring at the upper mattress when Moe started talking in his sleep. Sporadic mumbling at first, bedsprings creaking from all the tossing and turning going on up there, a hand flopping over the side of the bed. Dave took that to mean the boy was having that bad dream about his father again. Then Moe said, "Warn him. Warn him about the girls."

A night bird squawked outside the window, and Moe said, "It's harder for a camel to pass through the eye of a needle..."

No chance of getting any more sleep tonight. Dave got up and looked down at his house. Nothing doing down there. He put on his slippers, trotted down the stairs—had to check on the stakeout of Haskins's crib.

He punched in Mingo's cellular number. A grumpy voice answered, "Yeah."

"You weren't sleeping, were you?" he said. "Any sign of him yet?"

"Nope," Mingo said. "Same as two hours ago when you called last."

"I'm wide awake, want me to come on down there and give you a break?"

"I only really come alive at night, Dude. When it gets bright out, I hunt for a coffin."

"Yeah, right. If Haskins shows, don't try to take him by yourself. I'm at the Pleasiac house."

"So you said the last time you called."

Dave hung up. Have to start looking for a night deputy who was a bit more respectful toward his superiors.

Shirley was standing in the doorway to her bedroom. "I heard you talking on the phone," she said. "Is anything wrong?"

She was wearing an old flannel nightgown, her hair slightly mussed from sleep.

"Sorry to wake you, Shirl. Just checking with Mingo. I've been kicking myself for putting you and Moe at risk. This Huntzinger is a real psycho. Who knows what he'll do?"

She came nearer, sat on a kitchen chair, looking up at him. "What are friends for? You'd do the same for us."

"Yeah, but you're not a cop."

"He's probably gone," she said. "Don't you think?" If I were him, I'd steal a car and be on my way to California."

He sat next to her, smoothed a wrinkle on the table cloth. "Seems like a very vindictive man to me if he's the same one who sprayed that message on Mr. Egge's back. He's not going to appreciate the way Mingo handled him. I doubt he's gone anywhere..."

Dave took hold of Shirley's hand.

"Did you think of something?" she said.

"Stolen cars! I should have checked to see if there've been any stolen cars. Sometimes I think I have to be the world's biggest numbnuts."

"You're too hard on yourself. You can't do anything until morning. Want some coffee?"

"Don't go to the trouble. I'm heading back over to the house. It's time I stopped acting like such a baby."

Dave ran back upstairs to get the rest of his clothes. The window was open just a crack, the curtains puffing in and out. The moon shining through the window reflected off Moe's face. He was lying on his back his fingers entwined over his chest. He'd stopped groaning and he had a little smile on his face. It took Dave a while to find his sneakers and socks. In the meantime, Moe woke up.

"What you doing?"

"I'm going home. Say, you remember what you were dreaming?"

"I always remember my dreams. What you do is psych yourself before you go to bed. You say 'I will remember my dreams. I will remember—'"

"Can it, will you Professor Pleasiac? Just tell me what you were dreaming. You were talking in your sleep."

"Some girls were assaulting an old man. My dad, Sheriff McCloskey, and Mr. Egge were watching them do it."

"Sounds like what Mrs. Mac was spouting at that séance thing. She probably put that idea in your head."

"I've had this one a few times. My dad is always in my dreams of late."

"What does 'it's easier for a camel to pass through the eye of a needle' mean?" Dave tied his sneaker and stood up. His eyes were adjusting to the dark, but he couldn't find his cap.

Moe reached over and turned on an overhead lamp. He yawned. "That's from the Bible—"

"I know it's from the Bible. Think I'm stupid or something? Don't answer that. What's the saying got to do with your dream?"

"I don't know. I don't remember that part."

Dave found his hat under the bed, dusted it off and put it on. "You know, I just heard a night bird outside? I think you're a warlock is what it is, and the bird is probably your familiar. You don't want it to get out because you're afraid the villagers will come for you with flaming torches and—"

"Oh, shut up. You just like to pretend that you don't take any of this seriously. Want me to stay with you over there? I'm a very light sleeper. Nobody will be able to sneak up on you if I'm there."

"Nah, you just go back to sleep."

*   *   *

The stars were out and the moon almost full. Dave twirled his keys as he approached his house. As he looked up at the sky, he realized what Moe's dream meant, if it meant anything. "It is easier for a camel to pass through the eye of a needle than for a rich man to go to heaven." Who was the richest man in town? Blaze Forman, Mary Lou's father, was next on the Haskins's agenda, if the murderer was Haskins. He knew Forman was next as sure as he knew his mother's birthday was February 29, and she was only thirteen years old.

Dave dropped his keys, they bounced, and landed on the lawn. He couldn't immediately see them, and knelt down on the sidewalk, feeling around for them.

When he found them, he looked up just in time to see a man in a Frankenstein mask swinging down on him with a tree branch. He blocked the blow with his arm, but he could hear the bone crack, and his arm went numb, stinging pins and needles the only sensation. The tree branch had snapped in two, and Frankenstein reached down for the bigger end. Dave stomped on his hand and Frankenstein let out a yelp, grabbing Dave's foot and trying to wrench it in ways it wasn't intended to bend.

Spittle flew out the mouth opening of the man's mask. "You son of a bitch, I'm gonna cut your heart out for what you did." His eyes were deranged, and he smelled like a goat.

Dave fell down on his back, got one foot under Frankenstein and tried to flip him on his head as he'd done plenty of times doing SEAL training. The prime tenet of SEAL training had always been "use your opponent's strength against him." Only those times he'd had two good arms. Frankenstein bounced back up and was back at him, pounding on his face with what felt like a hammer. Brass knuckles. Dave tried to cover his face with his bad arm, simultaneously reaching for his gun.

"You cocksucker, I'm gonna pound you until your face is fuckin' paste," Frankenstein said.

Dave's lip was split, he'd lost several teeth, and he could taste blood. Before he could raise the gun, Frankenstein kicked it away and went scrambling into the night after it. Dave jumped on the man's back, saw the gun lying about a yard away and began reaching for it, Frankenstein spotting it also. The man bucked him off and Dave landed on top of the gun on his bad side; when he rolled over to retrieve the gun, he was kicked in the face, and the gun flew out of his hand. Frankenstein was at him again, battering his face, and he began to lose consciousness. He tried to call for help, but he'd been hit in the neck and could hardly talk, much less yell. "Please, Jesus," he gasped. "Help me."

His ears were ringing and he was losing his grip. His body felt curiously light and he drifted aloft. He was having one of those out-of-body experiences he'd read about where a person dies on the operating table. He could see Frankenstein down below, banging away at his head with a hobnailed boot.

"Don't you think we ought to do something?" somebody said.

"What can we do?" somebody else said. "Our hands are tied."

"But he took care of my boy," the other voice said.

"You have to return now," a soothing voice not unlike his grandmother's said, and he found himself back inside his body, his broken arm covering his face, warding off blows.

Lights went on across the street and he could hear the whoop! whoop! of a police siren. Frankenstein kicked him in the side, said, "You lucky bastard," and ran off towards the woods.

Tillie McKinney was staring down at him, goggle-eyed, screaming. Moe was standing behind her in his pajamas, as anxious as a mom whose toddler had fallen down a well.

"Let me get some ice for that," Moe said, as he turned and ran for the house. Dave tried to laugh, but it hurt too much.

"Call an ambulance," Lucille said. It must have been she who saved his life. The girl was *really* growing on him.

"Ver are mu keys," Dave said.

Chapter 20

Breaking the Bank

"Gives me some kind of content to remember how painful
it is sometimes to keep money, as well as to get it."
— Samuel Pepys

Harry had observed the doctors push Jenkins's broken nose back in place, bandage it, wrap his forehead in heavy gauze and clamp it in place. The boy's dark hair stuck out at crazy angles, he had two black eyes, his front teeth were chipped, and his left arm was in a cast. With all those bandages, Jenkins could have passed for one of those Egyptian mummies, only not quite that good-looking.

When Jenkins had been awake he'd said his teeth hurt worse than anything, and he had the feeling the docs had missed a broken rib. The docs had strapped him down—he'd been trying to leave ever since they brought him in—and had given him some knockout drops to help him rest. They'd warned Harry not to try to wake him up.

Harry opened his magazine. He was really sick of soap operas and talk shows, so he had taken the candy striper's advice and begun a reading regimen. He was skimming an article in *American Heritage* about the First Minnesota at Gettysburg. All of that stuff that was on Colonel Colvill's statue in Veteran's Park was in there.

Two hundred eighty men facing over a thousand rebels. Eighty-three percent fatality rate. And he'd thought Vietnam was bad.

Harry was feeling much better since the operation. He'd been having chest pains for weeks prior to the heart attack but had rationalized them away as heart burn from too much greasy food. The doctor had already given him a diet and an exercise program. Talk about bland: practically no meat, lots of vegetables, which he hated. Oh well, maybe he'd lose some weight, and his back wouldn't hurt so much.

He'd made friends with that candy striper on her first day when she'd wheeled her magazine cart into the room, crying over some old man who'd told her to "get the fuck out of my room" while he was trying to use the bed pan. Harry never used the bed pan. He'd almost had no choice just after the operation because he'd been so stiff, but he waited until the nurses were gone, unhitched himself from the IV, and crawled into the bathroom on his hands and knees. Anything to avoid the indignity. The nurse had really chewed him out for disconnecting that IV since he couldn't get it back in.

"You better come in here and take it out for me when I need to go then because there's no way I'm going to use that thing," Harry'd said.

Harry had tried to explain to the candy striper that the old man was just sick and that he probably wasn't used to being around that many people. Anyway he'd talked Carrie, that was her name, out of quitting and now she gave him first dibs, as she called it, on the magazines. He was going to get her to bring him something real to eat.

When Harry put the magazine down to rest his eyes—his eyes were really dry from the air conditioning—an old man with a walker was standing in the doorway. Bert McCloud, the biggest liar in the hospital, who claimed he was related to the McCloud who'd been on television. It was no use arguing that McCloud was a fictional character.

Bert inched toward Harry's bed. "How's your friend doing?" he said. "Rumor has it he's got a brain hemorrhage."

The old coot was angling for gossip. Concussion yes, hemorrhage no. Harry turned toward Bert, which was hard since Harry had a stiff neck. "You're not getting anything out of me, Bert," he said.

"Party pooper. How soon they letting you out of here?"

"The doctors said it'll be at least another week. I'm leaving in another couple days, if I can find my clothes."

"I hear they found the one that done the Ellis murder," Bert said.

"Nah, they just got a handwriting match on the note. That don't mean...You old fox, you. I'm going to kick your bony ass if you try that again."

Bert leaned up against Harry's bed, grasping the railing with one hand. "What are you doing about sex, Harry?" he said. "I pinch those cute little candy stripers. I can almost get it up." The old man's hands were shaking so much Harry thought about using his buzzer. He was worried Bert might fall down.

He reached out to steady the old codger. "Better watch it, Bert. You can get in trouble that way these days."

Ordinarily, Bert was a pleasant diversion from hospital routine, but Harry had been wallowing in self pity, and he liked the feeling, so he wished Bert would go away. He looked over at the card he'd gotten from a Green Beret buddy, Chet Hammer. He hadn't seen or heard from him in thirty years. Brenda had most likely found his address from an old Christmas card.

Bert turned and shuffled back toward the door. "You're too smart for me, Harry. I gotta go. Hope you get out of here soon. I'll probably never get out. Feel like a damn yo-yo, going back and forth from the old folks home. It's the diabetes, you know. They cut my toe off."

Harry could hear the slopping of a mop out in the hall. The sound had a definite beat. Some people could fashion a musical instrument out of anything. Behind Bert, an orderly materialized, scrubbing the floor.

"Say, Bert, the floor is wet. Let me get one of those candy stripers to help you."

Carrie came to get Bert and took him to the solarium, a favorite place for Bert where he could flirt with the old ladies who held their hen sessions there.

Harry looked over at Jenkins who was snoring, picked up the magazine, riffled through the pages, set it back down. Wonder if Colvill knows he's got a statue in Veteran's Park in Soldier, Minnesota? he thought. Would he give a rat's ass if he did?

Harry'd been thinking quite a bit what with all the bed rest he'd been getting. Pondering over making his peace, just in case his heart was a lot worse than the doctors were letting on. Could be he didn't have much time. Make it right with your kids, tell your wife you love her, he told himself. Harry had never told Brenda he loved her. It had been her idea to get married, and he'd been twenty-five when she'd asked, so he'd figured, why not? Had to get married sometime and she was the sheriff's daughter. Didn't want to piss him off, and besides, people talked about you if you were pushing thirty and not married.

At four o'clock, his sons showed up. They had an opportunity to open a video store in Soldier, and they wanted Harry's advice. Actually they wanted more than advice; they wanted money. Harry knew the video rental in the new strip mall wasn't doing very well. They just didn't have a very wide selection. Most folks didn't mind driving the twenty miles to Crookston. It gave them a reason to go to the big city. But this was the first time the boys had shown any ambition at all. With proper management, they could make a go of it. They'd have to split the profits four ways, though. Thank God they were all single! Something else to worry about. He agreed to cash in a couple of CD's.

Mel hung around when the others left. He was wearing that watch cap again. If he didn't watch it, he'd wind up bald like Harry. The boy limped over and looked down at Jenkins, who was still out cold, kind of grinned, then said, "I see they've got him strapped in. He try to make a break for it?"

"How'd you guess? The boy reminds me of me when I was his age. I'll bet he left a few marks on the other guy."

Mel frowned as if he'd gotten his feelings hurt. He hadn't meant to...Mel moved back to Harry's bed, fingered his bed clothes. "You really scared the boys. They thought you'd be around forever to take care of us. That's why they want to open the store. You scared me, too. You were right about baseball, I knew I was never that good, but I don't want to open any video store. I want to go back to school and do it the right way. Maybe international business? One of my teammates in the minor leagues was Japanese. He taught me a few words, and it sounded cool, so now I'm taking a course at UMC one night a week. Either that or criminal justice. It didn't seem to hurt you too much."

Tears were welling up in Harry's eyes. This was Mel's way of telling him he loved him. The only other person who'd ever said she'd loved him was Brenda, and he didn't believe her. Harry rubbed his eyes. "I'll pay your way, Mel," he said. "It's only fair if I give the boys the money for the store."

Mel took off his hat, combed his hair with his fingers. "I'd rather work part-time, Dad," he said. "It'll keep me from goofing off. I'll have to budget my time."

After Mel left, Harry felt like he could take on the Hard Boiled Haggerty and Haystack Calhoun. Who could he tell? He hit his buzzer and got Carrie to bring him a card. He'd write his green beret friend Chet Hammer, bragging about his boys. Hadn't written a personal letter since he'd been in the service.

In the midst of writing the card, Mingo and Lucille showed up. What a sorry crew. Mingo had gone native with the headband and knee-length moccasins, probably Jenkins's influence, and Lucille was wearing a Mickey Mouse T-shirt and shades. He'd thought she was fairly stable when he'd hired her.

"We came to tell you what's going down, Harry," Mingo said. "Anybody tell you the FBI let that Haskins guy get away?"

"Jenkins filled me in before they put him under. Could hardly understand a word he said what with all the chipped teeth. They're gonna cap them when the swelling goes down."

"He tell you Lucille saved his life?"

Lucille blushed, looked down at the floor.

"Good girl," Harry said, smiling so wide that it hurt his chapped lips. "I would hope that this will persuade that bullheaded old broad that we can't take Charlie Bronson to the grand jury. I never thought Bronson did this."

"Jenkins tell you I found Haskins's crib?"

Harry was hot, so he opened the flap on his hospital nighty. "Nah. Got somebody watching the place?"

"Henderson came across with some help. Guess he was kind of embarrassed about giving Haskins up to the Feds."

"We'll never let him live that one down. Go see Hildegard again. We have to convince her that the whole town, but especially us, is going to look like horses' asses if we take Bronson to trial."

"There isn't much chance of that since we found the rainsuit in Bronson's garage," Mingo said. "Somebody is doing a nice job on him, you must admit. Could be worse, though, I guess. At least there is no death penalty in Minnesota. Back in the old days a mob would have dragged Bronson out of the jail and hung him up on a streetlight."

Harry tried to sit up, but a pain in his chest knocked him back down. "Something...is really rotten in...Bismarck," he breathed. "What's the SDS doing in Soldier, Minnesota?" He took a deep breath.

Mingo looked concerned. The pain must have shown in his face. Before Harry realized what he was saying, his deathbed resolutions spilled out of him. Must've been because he'd heard that Mingo was some kind of Indian healer.

"My grandfather raked himself over the coals, too, before he died," Mingo said. "Not that *you're* going to die or anything. I think it's just some kind of hormone that kicks in automatically when the old ticker takes a hit." Mingo smiled, the first authentic smile he'd ever seen on the kid.

Jenkins groaned, opened his eyes, struggled to break the straps.

* * *

Blaze Forman hopped and stumbled around his living room, trying to get a foot into his sweat pants. He had to sit down once or twice, he was so out of breath. Doctor Logan had said that if he didn't start exercising and cut down on red meat he'd be dead in five years. His cholesterol was sky high, despite the fact that he was of normal weight for a man his size. About the easiest way he could think of to get in some exercise was bike riding.

Hildegard had strong-armed the town council into building a bike path out past the pond, off the beaten path, so he shouldn't be too much of a laughing stock. He had purchased all the paraphernalia you needed for bike riding, including the helmet, knee pads and elbow pads, plus a ten speed Schwinn, but he didn't want to look too foolish, so he decided to do without the helmet on his first sojourn, although it had been at least fifty years since he'd been on a bike.

When Forman tried the front door, he found he couldn't get it open. Must be the weather. He decided to go out the back door. When he got there, the neighbor's golden retriever was in his path, growling at him. Suddenly, he had one of those premonitions, like when he'd sold his international stock just before the crash. This foreboding told him to wear his helmet, elbow pads and knee pads. When he tried the front door again, it stuck briefly, then opened, causing Forman to bark himself on his knee. He was no longer sure he wanted to go on this bike ride, but remembering the doctor's admonition, he got on the Schwinn and rode away, discovering that, yes, it was true, you never forgot how.

*   *   *

It was late, almost dusk, and Mingo was driving around town patrolling, thinking about death. Harry Kline's confession at the hospital had put him in a blue funk. He hadn't been able to help the Egg Man make it to the Land of Ever Summer and he hadn't been very helpful with the sheriff, telling him that phoney story about a grandfather he never had. His mother's father had died before he was born, and he'd never met his white grandfather. Cousin Cecil was the closest he ever got. When he'd asked Cousin C. what he'd done wrong when he'd tried to hold the ghost medicine ceremony for Egge, he'd gotten the same old "pay attention" malarkey. He was supposed to learn from his mistakes, but who was he supposed to learn from, and how was he supposed to observe something that wasn't there?

Mingo shifted the Jeep into high gear. The banker had repossessed Mingo's truck and he'd been relegated to driving Jenkins's Jeep; one of those bill collectors had stolen his truck right out of the parking lot while he was in visiting Harry Kline.

He'd known he was in for it when he'd seen his latest bank statement. He owed seven hundred fifty-three dollars on the 4X4. Should've figured the interest. Odd numbers were bad luck for a Mescalero. Mingo took the picture of Forman he'd found in a recent edition of the *Soldier Gazette* out of his breast pocket, wet his finger, drew a circle across the man's face with his finger, counterclockwise, and smiled at his reflection in the rearview mirror.

He turned onto Peach Orchard, a street with an overhang of Elm trees, which made him feel especially mellow about Soldier, until he noticed several red X's on some of the trees. Dutch Elm Disease had struck again. The convent was on Peach Orchard, which was where Jenkins'd stashed Fr. Mischke since the assault on his life. Mingo'd heard the nuns were spoiling him so much that there wasn't much chance he'd go for the Bishop's retirement home in Arizona. Mingo had been thinking about going to see the priest about the ghost medicine ceremony. Catholics believed in exorcism.

Mingo cruised through the stop sign leading onto Meade, accelerated the Jeep, which spewed forth oil and gas fumes that would gag a fire-breathing dragon. As he passed the new strip mall, Shirley reached him on his cell phone. "There's been an altercation on the north side of town near the pond," she said. "Lucille is on the scene."

"Check, Shirl. What kind of altercation? Is it those wannabees again?" Mingo did a u-ball and headed back the other way.

"You know I can't say over the phone. Lucille has the situation well in hand."

Mingo floored the old Jeep and was near the Pond in a matter of minutes. He pulled up alongside Harry's cruiser, bubblegum top flashing red. Lucille was ministering to an old man in a bicycle helmet, knee and elbow pads.

Blaze Forman. Mingo did a doubletake, snatched the picture out of his front pocket. This was just too much. That witching stuff was something else. If this worked, the new version of the ceremony he'd been working on to get the Egg Man unstuck should work too.

Mingo got out of the Jeep, slammed the door, bent over to see how badly the old man was hurt.

"He's just scraped up a bit," Lucille said, holding aloft what looked like a gnarled tree branch. "One of them brained him with this shillelagh. Says he was driving down the lane here into this little grove when he was jumped by a gang of girls. Says it was getting dark out, but he thinks the girl who hit him was that Miller girl. He recognized her because she's cross-eyed," Lucille said, imitating the look.

Forman was lying on the grass with his arms folded across his chest, eyes closed, didn't seem to be breathing. Mingo thought he looked exactly like a corpse, except for the bicycling attire.

"What was that you just said?" Mingo said.

"He was attacked by a gang of girls..."

"That's what I thought you said. And one of them was cross-eyed?"

"Yeah, the Miller girl."

He'd been thinking about the Designated Hitter note left at the Ellis murder scene. Mingo opened the cruiser door. "Why don't you take Forman to the hospital in Crookston, just in case? Make sure they keep him overnight until we figure a place to keep him. Maybe we should start up a witness protection program."

Lucille helped Forman into the back seat. "Will do, Mr. Jones," she said. "You don't suppose the nuns would want to keep him, too, do you?"

"He's got lots of money," Mingo said. "He could hire a bodyguard. I need to talk to Andy about something. See you later."

He parked the Jeep at an angle in front of Andy's Diner. Thought he'd check with Andy to see if he knew anything about the attack on Forman. Screenagers liked to hang out at Andy's since he had one of those big juke boxes.

Andy, redheaded, not more than 5' 5" and very touchy about his height, looked up as Mingo entered.

"We've had another incident," Mingo said.

"I know," Andy said. "Pigeon Hackett was driving by on his way home to Mom, saw Harry's cruiser with its flashing lights, and turned right around to tell everybody he could find. Couldn't happen to a nicer guy if you ask me. Forman denied my loan when I opened my business."

"You too, huh?"

Andy was pouring ketchup into those little, red squeeze bottles. "Pigeon says the son of a bitch got attacked by a bunch of girls."

Mingo went behind the counter and filled his thermos from the big Bunn machine. This was going to be another long night. He screwed the cap on his thermos.

Andy put the big jar of ketchup in the frig and came back picking his teeth, red smears of ketchup staining his apron. "Maybe the fellah just hired those girls to mug Forman to throw you off some, huh?"

Mingo put a quarter on the counter and took a piece of beef jerky. "Could be," he said. "I gotta go, Andy. Who knows what's going to happen next around here? You haven't seen Rita Miller tonight, have you? Ray Miller's daughter, out on 185?"

Andy opened the drawer to the till and started counting money. "She the nutty-looking one? He's got a couple of girls. Beats the shit out of them I hear. Did she have something to do with the Forman thing? That fat deputy wouldn't tell Pigeon anything. She's a real piece of work." Andy took a twenty and a five out of the till and put them in his shirt pocket.

"So you haven't seen Rita tonight then?"

Andy shook his head no.

Mingo put another dollar on the counter for the coffee. When he got out to the Jeep, he dialed the Miller farm on his cellular.

"Rita's not here," her mother said. "She went to the Drive-in with some friends. Is she in any trouble?"

"It seems so. Do you own a shillelagh?"

"Oh yes, it's been in the family ever since our people came over from the old country. Has someone been hurt?"

"I can't go into it right now, Mrs. Miller. I'll get back to you."

"I'd appreciate that, Deputy."

On his way to the Outdoor, Mingo noticed black, belching smoke coming from the high school. He braked the Jeep, dialed 911 reporting the fire, then gunned the engine, careening from side to side as he raced toward the school. The front was barred, as was the side door on the south side. He ran around toward the back, where he found the door open. Expecting some kind of connection between the beating and the fire, he drew his Colt and went in through the passageway and around the corner.

Freddie Cochran was swaggering down the hall coming Mingo's way. "Hi, Chief," he said, "I saw the smoke and decided to check it out."

Mingo yelled, "Just put your hands up and don't move," instead of "freeze motherfucker" as he'd wanted to. Freddie ducked into a door off to the side, and Mingo heard a deafening crash.

The volunteer fire department was responding just as he ran out the rear door; he could see Freddie running toward the woods but lost sight of him momentarily as he entered a cluster of trees. This kid wouldn't stand a chance. After all that aerobic exercise playing lacrosse, Mingo would run him down if it took hours. But it didn't take hours since, by the time Mingo got to the grove, Freddie was lying face down, with Lucille's boot on his neck.

"Saw the smoke," she said, "figured I better check it out."

Chapter 21

Trial and Error

*"The Court bows to the lessons of experience and
the force of better reasoning, recognizing that the
process of trial and error, so fruitful in the physical
sciences, is appropriate also in the judicial function."*
— Louis Brandeis

As Mingo guided Jenkins's Jeep past the potholes on the way to the Miller farm, sweat dripped from his nose, rolling down his chin and onto his buckskin shirt. Rita Miller had proven to be an elusive little heifer. She wasn't exactly trying to hide either. Pigeon Hackett had seen her walking down Meade kicking a can; Mrs. Warner had sold her a length of clothesline; she'd been in Andy's playing pinball. Each time the wraith had been gone by the time Mingo or Lucille could get there.

The radiator gauge was dangerously high, and the Jeep was making a funny whistling sound. Mingo still felt blue. Couldn't seem to do anything right lately. Lucille had run down that firebug Freddie, he couldn't find Rita, Debbie's mom was acting anti-Mescaleric around him, and he was homesick for New Mexico. To lift his spirits, he began to sing. "As I walked out in the streets of Laredo, as I walked out in Laredo one day, I spied a poor cowboy wrapped up in white linen, wrapped up in white linen as cold as the day.

"Oh, beat the drum slowly and play the fife lowly, play the dead march as you carry me along, take me to the green valley, there lay the sod o'er me, for I'm a young cowboy and I know I've done wrong."

His favorite song in all the world, always cheered him up, too bad he didn't have the voice to do it justice. "Damn, it must be at least ninety," he said. "Hate the humidity. Dry heat in New Mexico. Hard to believe that it snowed just a few weeks ago. Probably El Niño. South American revenge for the Mexican Cession."

He got to the Miller farm, just as the radiator began to steam. He pulled up next to the sidewalk and shut the Jeep down. It coughed once, twice, then died.

Mrs. Miller, who was sitting on her porch step peeling potatoes into a washtub, brought to mind a white version of Aunt Jemima, the pancake lady, with her hair up in curlers and the bandanna tied around her head.

Mingo tipped his Mountie hat. "Mornin', ma'am," he said. "Deputy Jenkins is in the hospital with some broken ribs, so he sent me out to talk to you about your daughter Rita."

"She ain't here, Deputy. She's over at Olive Randall's house. Ray's out in the field planting corn, if you want to talk to him."

"Mr. Forman says Rita was one of the girls who hit him with that shillelagh I was askin' about on the phone."

"She's an angry girl, Deputy. Ray doesn't help matters either."

"He hit her?"

She nodded, looking down at the washtub. "It's like he hates her."

"And she hates him?"

"Acts like it." She eyed him up and down as if he were an albino buffalo robe she'd spotted at Wall Drug on the way to Mount Rushmore. "You're not from Minnesota, are you?"

"New Mexico, ma'am, but I've got relatives around here. In International Falls."

While they talked, the woman continued to peel spuds. She was an expert with that paring knife; she could peel a potato in one long, spiraling strip. She squinted up at him, not missing a beat. "New Mexico. That's desert country, ain't it?"

"We get snow in the mountains. Mescalero is mountain country."

"Not as cold as Minnesota, I wouldn't suppose?"

"No, not that cold. I'll let you get back to your work. I'll just walk out to the field and talk to Mr. Miller if that's all right."

"Sure thing, Deputy."

The jog would give Jenkins's Jeep a chance to cool. As he walked, he stumbled over ruts and clumps of soil in the field, and the sweat poured off him like water out of a rain spout. The farmer made two passes before Mingo could get him to stop.

Miller put the big green John Deere in neutral. "Heard they got themselves an Indian for that night watchman job," he said. "What's become of Jenkins?"

Mingo knocked the dirt off his moccasins on the trailer hitch. "He had a little fracas with a scofflaw."

"Hurt bad?"

"We think he'll make it."

"Spose you're looking for Rita. The damn dog listens better than that girl. She's goin' to get a whippin' when I see her. Tol' her to stay home and wait for you, and she defied me. I'll bring her in myself, by the hair if I have to."

"Better not do that, Mr. Miller. You can get in deep Dutch for that kind of thing." Miller spit tobacco juice just past Mingo's ear. Mingo flinched, let it pass. "Do you know what Rita may have had against Blaze Forman, Mr. Miller?"

Miller shifted the big wad of tobacco in his cheek to the opposing side. "The girl's so ornery she don't need no reason."

While they were talking, a fine drizzle began to collect on Mingo's shirt, like bacteria on moist bread. Miller had an umbrella attached to the tractor—he didn't offer any shelter.

The rain picked up some and Mingo climbed up on the tractor hitch behind Miller, who scowled at him like one of those Southern bus drivers prior to the civil rights movement. "What about her friends, Ray? Does she know a man named Bob Haskins?"

"You'll have to talk to Ma about that," Miller said. "I don't know nothin' about what the gal does, except that she's got an awful mouth on her."

The tractor was idling and Mingo was having trouble understanding the man, although he could practically smell his breath.

"Ah, Mr. Miller, are you aware that there's a clubhouse at the far end of your pasture? Deputy Robinson found it the other day she was out here investigating your cattle rustling complaint."

The farmer removed the wad of tobacco from his cheek, shucked it off onto the tractor tire. "Don't never go out there. The dog gets the cows. Why feed her otherwise? You make any progress with those rustlers yet?"

"Lucille found some tire tracks from what looked like a U-Haul that we're trying to trace."

This gave Miller a chance to vent about his high taxes and not getting any police protection. Twice he'd been robbed, yatta yatta-ta. Suddenly Miller was a regular orator. Mingo couldn't fathom how the man could wear that felt cap with the ear flaps in this kind of weather?

When Miller let up, Mingo said he'd be in touch when he found Rita and trudged back through the mud and the mist to the farm house where he found Mrs. Miller feeding the chickens. The rain had stopped and the sun was out.

"Back already, Deputy?"

"Yep. Mr. Miller said he didn't know anything about Olive's friends, sent me to talk to you."

"Won't you have a cup of coffee, Deputy? And maybe some leftover birthday cake from my daughter Lucy's party. She just turned eleven. Mother's little helper."

"No thanks, Mrs. Miller." He was standing with the sun at his back and she had to shade her eyes in order to talk to him. "About those friends..."

The black and white dog scuttled over and began licking his shoes. She told it to "get." He knelt down to pet the dog.

"I only know two, Olive Randall and that Freddie boy. She can't seem to make any other friends, but I suppose they're better than nothing. Never had too many friends myself. I was the only kid in the third grade. Until the Welle girl moved in next farm over. We went through eighth grade together. Then I quit to help out on the farm." She put a pail full of yellow kernels of corn down on the ground. "Kids are so strange these days. I'm afraid Rita's been smoking that marijuana. Can you tell me what it smells like?"

He tried to explain. She went to a faucet near the house, ran him a pail of water for the radiator. The Jeep turned over on the first try. As he headed back down the driveway, the black and white dog nipped at his tires all the way down the driveway.

On the way back to town, he was so intent on finding Rita that he hit a pothole, doing a good fifty miles an hour. Jarred all of his fillings and gave him a bad case of whiplash.

* * *

Rita was out in Olive's yard pushing Nancy and Patty on the patched, inner tube swing. She'd been there all morning.

Olive wanted to come along to the station. *Might as well try to bring down two turkey buzzards with one load*, Mingo thought. He needed to quiz Olive about the belt found at the Father Mischke scene, among other things. She usually came clean if you gave her some time to dwell on the matter. The girl seemed to have an innate sense of fairness about her.

Back at the station, he told Olive to wait outside with Shirley, and he and Rita took chairs around the conference table in the Pink Room, where she became absorbed by the Battle of Little Big Horn. He offered her a cup of coffee from the container Shirley brought in. She took a cup, with cream and sugar. He decided to go at the interrogation from an oblique angle. "Rita, does you dad ever hit you?"

The girl had black, curly hair, kind of short, seemed to be watching someone off to the left when she talked to him. She turned the collar up on her white shirt Elvis style, brushed imaginary dust off her faded jeans with the knees out. "The son of a bitch hits me all the time," she said. "He uses a strap, the buckle end."

He took his notebook out of his upper left breast pocket, made a notation about Miller's abuse. "Did you know you could report something like that?" he said.

Rita took a drink of her coffee, grimaced. "I've been telling on people all my life, and it ain't done me no good ever. Boys on the playground, my brothers at home. Lately he ain't been hitting me anyway since after I stuck him with the pitchfork."

Brothers at home? Not another one of those incest cases. The oldtimers on the Rez knew how to handle that. As soon as a boy began to show the urge, the old man would take him to a cathouse. Nothing had stepped up to take the fancy woman's place.

Rita took a pack of Kools out of her shirt pocket and lit one with a wooden kitchen match which she scratched on the wall, leaving a black mark.

He had bigger catfish to fry, so he didn't tell her to put it out.

"Mr. Forman says you went after him with that shillelagh, Rita," he said. "Is that true?"

She blew a perfect smoke ring; the rings rose toward the ceiling where they gradually dissipated. "If it hadn't been for that damn helmet I'd'a killed the bastard," she said. "Old money-grubbing son of a bitch was gonna foreclose on the farm and it's all Ma's got." Rita shook her head as if she couldn't understand it.

Funny, her old man hadn't said anything about foreclosure. He scribbled this information in his notebook. "One of Harry's deputies got killed that way once I heard," he said. He tried to look her in the eyes, but it was impossible.

She ground her cigarette out in the big, yellow, circular ashtray Harry kept in the conference room. An ash escaped the receptacle, flared red briefly, and went out. The ashtray must have weighed about two pounds. He could picture her clunking him over the head with it.

"We started getting letters six months ago," she said. "If I had him here now, I'd bash his brains in with this here ashtray." She lit another cigarette.

He'd heard there was an operation for crossed eyes. All this girl needed was for someone to tell her she was pretty and get her to believe it. Of course, she wasn't pretty...

"Rita, we're thinking this assault may be connected in some way to the attack on Fr. Mischke and the two murders. Do you know anyone named Bob Haskins?"

She ground out the second cigarette. It was only half-smoked. She took out another cigarette, but he put his hand over it before she could light it, pointed at the no smoking sign. He moved the pack of Kools and the yellow ashtray to his side of the table. Needed to get those matches away from her later.

The girl rolled her head around on her shoulders. He could hear the joints pop. "He is...was Olive's old boyfriend," she said. "Actually he was her mom's boyfriend first, until Olive took him away."

This was news to him. Jenkins had said...He scratched his head, took another drink of coffee, toyed with the pack of cigarettes. "Olive says she was raped. You're saying she seduced Bob Haskins?"

Rita pulled on one of her earlobes. "You should know an eleven-year-old girl can't seduce anybody. They call that statutory rape."

"That's true," he said. "So, do you know where this Haskins is right now?"

"You had him—" Rita suddenly looked right at him, as if she'd been to Lourdes and caught the cure. She stood up and glared down at him. "I ain't talking no more, unless I get to talk to Freddie. Either I talk to him, or I want a lawyer." Rita stared at him, as if he were some sort of huge rat who'd just popped out of a sewer grating.

He stood up and moved to her side of the table. "We're going to have to hold you here in jail," he said. "You can have a lawyer if you wish. I'll have to think about whether I'll let you talk to Freddie. Rita, who else was with you when you clobbered Old Man Forman? Was Olive with you?"

She backed away from him, moved to the other side of the table. What was this, musical chairs? "I want to talk to Freddie," she said, crossing her arms over her breasts.

Maybe it wouldn't be such a bad idea letting her talk to Freddie. She'd already admitted attacking Forman. She might be able to loosen Freddie up. What could he lose? Well, for one thing, they could put their heads together and come up with a story that would jibe. No, he didn't think he'd let them anywhere near each other.

Olive was gone when he came out of the interrogation room. "She had to babysit her sisters," Shirley said.

"Oh Christ. Now I gotta track *her* down."

"Sorry. You didn't tell me..."

"My fault, Shirley."

Mingo had Shirley take Rita into the women's bathroom and search her before he put her in the upstairs cell.

Next he dialed Temple, the BCA stake-out in Crookston. "Any sign of our boy?"

"Nothing. I'm so bored I've been reading the manual on my truck. Some stuff in there I never knew."

*   *   *

Dave looked up at the bench, behind which was a portrait of Orville Crookston, the first district judge in Polk County. He was a dour-looking man with a walrus mustache and very heavy, brooding eyebrows. They were so heavy, Dave thought, he must have been a Scottish terrier in a previous life.

He'd finally managed to convince the docs that he was well enough to testify at the grand jury. Maybe it had been the plaintive tone he'd used when he'd said the wrong man would be indicted on a first-degree murder charge if he didn't testify. And so he'd left just after the dentist had capped his teeth.

The real-life judge was already gone, since her only function was to instruct the jury. Dave had to deal with the grand jury foreperson, Emma Boeder, and twenty-two other worthies. Emma was much more amiable than Orville, constantly smiling. Marceled, silver-gray hair, eye glasses with pinkish rims, a neat, blue and white, polka-dot dress, probably had a horde of spoiled grandchildren.

Quite the ritzy place, the courtroom was: chandeliers, plush carpeting, theater-style seating. But the air conditioning was set too high, and his shivering made the pain worse. He'd spent the half hour or so in the witness room in god-awful agony, biting the bullet, fighting the urge to take a pill so's he wouldn't look woozy on the stand.

Dave was first to testify. Schultz, the county attorney, stood at a podium sifting through his notes. The man was dressed in a rather unusual suit with a kind of a tattersall pattern, blue and gray. Dave thought he looked rather like a vaudeville comedian.

"Are you all right, Deputy?" Schultz asked. "We can put off your testimony—"

"Nah, go ahead."

"Deputy Jenkins, would you review for us how you came to suspect Charles Bronson in the murder of Jerry Egge and the assault on Father Mischke?" The county attorney had a very low voice, reminiscent of the announcer who'd done those retrospectives of the Green Bay Packer games when Lombardi'd been the coach.

"I began to suspect Superintendent Bronson when I arrived at the murder scene. I'd heard rumors that he'd been sleeping with Egge's wife."

"Anything else?"

"I was called to the scene of a confrontation at the Super Value between Jerry Egge and Charles Bronson."

"A physical confrontation?"

"Yes. According to one of the bag boys. I didn't actually see the fight myself."

"What other evidence do you have against Superintendent Bronson?"

Dave noticed that one of the ladies on the Grand jury was knitting something. Another woman was apparently sharing pictures of her grandchildren with the juror next to her. Only a few of the sixteen women and seven men were actively taking notes. Mostly senior citizens, several hearing aids in evidence.

He shifted in his seat and crossed his legs. He was in uniform today, and the goddamn starch had the effect of a straitjacket. "An eye witness identified Bronson as resembling a man he'd seen run into the woods just prior to the murder, but the clincher was an indictment written by Jerry Egge accusing Bronson of unseemly conduct."

"And where did you find this?"

"In his den at his home."

"And what sort of conduct was that?" Schultz asked, pacing up and down in front of the witness stand, seemingly thinking up questions as he strolled.

"Specifically the accusation said Bronson had sex with Egge's wife and with one of the students." Dave changed position, shifting his left leg over his right, which gave him a cramp.

Schultz stopped pacing and looked at his yellow legal pad. "Anything else?"

"During the attack on Father Mischke, Father bit a man whose hands were hairy, which fits Bronson. We also found some prints there on a belt the assailant had used to strangle the priest's cat. They matched Charlie Bronson. We're assuming that the Father Mischke assault and the Egge murder are related." He sighed. This was all bullshit. Why couldn't he just tell them what he really thought? Everything was politics.

One of the jurors, a little man with wire-rimmed glasses and no chin, raised his hand. Schultz nodded for him to go ahead. "Ah, Deputy, excuse me, but your report says you are somewhat, shall we say, skeptical regarding the fingerprints. Could you explain why you feel that way?"

"You don't usually find that many usable fingerprints at a crime scene. None of them were smeared. The belt looked like a plant to me."

"Go on," the little fellow said.

"This is just speculation," Dave said. "Do you want me to speculate?"

The little fellow looked at Mrs. Boeder, who indicated that he should go ahead.

"Ask yourself who would have access to Bronson's belt?" Dave said.

"Care to explain, Deputy?" Schultz said, looking totally stymied.

"Well, we know a girl named Olive Randall had sex with Bronson."

"And how do you know this?"

"We found her underwear in an envelope in Egge's safety deposit box."

Several of the jury members snickered. Mrs. Boeder gave them a dirty look. They froze.

"Olive could have taken the belt," he said. "Also, there could be other young girls whom Bronson molested."

"But," Schultz said, "the man Father Mischke saw when he slammed the door on his hand was a big man with curly hair who could have been Charles Bronson?"

"Yeah, all I'm sayin' is that the girl or girls could've got the belt for some other suspect who was tryin' to make it look like Charlie Bronson'd done the deed. Also, it's kind of hard to believe that this wild man was unable to run down an old man with arthritis. And the dead cat, come on now!"

"Let's get back on track shall we?" Schultz said. "Could you tell us what you found when you searched Bronson's house?"

"Later, after we'd gotten a search warrant, we found a bloody raincoat in Bronson's garage. He can't explain where that came from. The blood matches Egge's."

"And isn't it true," Schultz said, "that Bronson voluntarily took a lie detector test and failed?"

Dave admitted that he had. Schultz went on to explain to the grand jury that this couldn't be used during the trial. Nobody asked about Ellis; Dave supposed he would be called to the stand again later.

Never did get a chance to tell the jury there were no bite marks on Bronson's hand or any indication he'd had a door slammed on it.

Since only one witness could be in the courtroom at a time, he returned to the witness room and sat down next to one of the BCA criminalists. She had short hair, almost a crewcut, which didn't go with her ears. He'd noticed there were two kinds of people in the world—those with earlobes and those without. She didn't have any. She looked at him as if he were the monster from the Black Lagoon. Must be the black eyes. That morning he'd tried to pry the one he couldn't see out of open, but the hideous, blood-shot orb was worse than the festering, black and blue bulge.

The criminalist smelled like strawberry yogurt. "Where you from?" he said.

"Duluth," she said.

"You go to UMD?" he asked. UMD had a good hockey team and he figured he could get her talking about the Bulldogs to pass the time.

"St. Scholastica," she said.

"Whatever possessed you to go into law enforcement?" he asked.

She didn't seem offended. "Never could stand a routine existence. There's always something new going down with criminology. It gets me outside."

He asked her if she knew a man named Brad Guild, Mary Lou's ex-husband, who'd gone to UMD. She didn't know him. Perhaps he'd gone by the name Brad Forman-Guild.

No one had shut the door, so he could see and hear the clerk at the Bluebird Inn in Crookston testify that he hadn't seen Bronson from ten o'clock the previous evening until noon the day of Egge's murder. The clerk agreed that Bronson could have easily gone back to Soldier the previous evening, since it was only twenty miles away.

The next witness was a waitress at the Bluebird Inn who'd seen Mrs. Egge at 9 A.M. on the day of Egge's murder, but had not seen Charles Bronson.

Miles Krueger, Lester's dad, testified that he'd seen a man resembling Charles Bronson run into the woods just prior to the murder.

A redheaded jury person who wore her hair in plaits, Indian style, asked Miles where his son was, and Miles said he didn't know. He should have been home by now, since he'd only gone to the Cities for a week to look for a job. Emma Boeder wanted to know how old he thought the man he'd seen was. Miles said he was too far away.

Father Mischke described Bronson's hairy hand. Emma Boeder, playing devil's advocate, asked if there were other men with hairy hands. Father Mischke had to agree that there probably were.

Mrs. Egge, dressed in a blue and yellow sundress, which made her look as if she were on a lake outing, testified that she had been with Bronson the morning of Jerry Egge's murder.

"Are you a heavy sleeper, Mrs. Egge?" Schultz asked, with a sarcastic emphasis on the word "heavy."

"Are you asking if it's possible that Charlie left during the night and made it back before I woke up in the morning?"

"Exactly," Schultz said.

"No, I would have known he was gone."

"Did your husband have a life insurance policy, Mrs. Egge?"

"Yes, two hundred fifty thousand, double indemnity."

"Are you in love with Charles Bronson?"

"Yes, very much so. He could never kill anyone."

"Thank you, Mrs. Egge. You may stand down."

Mrs. Boeder excused Mrs. Egge and asked that Dave be recalled.

She glanced down at what must have been his report, pushed her chair away from the table, and waved a piece of paper at him.

"Deputy, would you care to tell us about your other suspect in the Egge murder case?"

"We're just here to examine the evidence at hand, Mrs. Boeder," Schultz said. "It's not your province—" She gave him a dismissive smile. "You do have another suspect?"

"Yes."

"Care to tell us what led you to this man?"

"It's complicated, so bear with me. At the scene, Egge's body was lying on its back. I found some paint on some of the trees, so I tried to set up a scenario. I thought maybe he'd run into these people out there who were playing war games with those pellet guns they have. Some people don't like that, they think it's a form of vandalism. I thought maybe one of them was a former student...Anyway, when we flipped him over, there was a message painted on his back and legs, the letters 'DYSTH' on his back, and 'SYZ' on one of his legs."

"Any idea what that might mean?"

"We think it means, 'Damn your soul to hell, Szymanski'. I think you have a picture..."

"Oh, yes, it's easy to see. Could you explain how you arrived at the translation?"

Dave told them about the NASSP publication and Moe's code breaking effort.

"Doesn't this imply that the murder was a mistake?"

"It would seem so. We traced the name Szymanski to a former principal living in Steubenville, Ohio. I asked his wife for a list of problematic students. One of them is a former SDS bomber named Brad Huntzinger who may have tried to run Mr. Szymanski over with his car."

"Isn't this a bit farfetched, Deputy?" Mrs. Boeder asked.

"From my limited experience, I've learned that nothing is too farfetched. Have you read *Helter Skelter*, Mrs. Boeder? Charlie Manson killed those people because he wanted to start a race war between the blacks and whites."

"I stand corrected, Deputy," Mrs. Boeder said. "And where does this investigation of Brad Huntzinger stand?"

"We think we may have had him in jail on a DWI and assault charge. We don't have any prints or a picture of Mr. Huntzinger, other than this annual I got from Mrs. Szymanski. The pictures in it were taken thirty years ago."

"And what happened to Mr. Huntzinger?"

"He escaped. Thanks to the FBI."

"Want to explain that, Deputy?"

"As I said, Mr. Huntzinger once belonged to the SDS. He was wanted for a bombing at the University of Wisconsin, during which a co-ed was killed. We were directed to turn him over to the FBI, and he escaped during transference to a federal facility."

"Any idea where Mr. Huntzinger is now?"

"We've staked out a house where Huntzinger had been living according to an informant. And we may have established a relationship between Huntzinger and Olive Randall."

"Very good, Deputy. That would explain the belt and the bloody raincoat." She was silent for a moment. The redheaded woman whispered something in her ear. "Deputy Jenkins, could you explain how you got that cast and the damage to your face?"

"I was assaulted by a man with a club and brass knuckles?"

"And, at this time, Mr. Bronson was in jail?"

"Yes he was."

"Who do you think attacked you?"

"The man was wearing a Halloween mask, the Frankenstein monster."

Schultz looked disgusted. He kept looking up at the ceiling in exasperation.

Dave was getting hot despite the air-conditioning. It seemed as if he'd been on the stand for hours and his bony behind was getting chafed.

"Mr. Schultz," Mrs. Boeder said, "I'm satisfied that Deputy Jenkins is doing his level best to find the person who murdered Principal Egge and attacked Father Mischke, but I don't understand why you're asking for a first-degree murder indictment at this time. It seems to me you have more work to do."

"There's a likelihood of bail for Mr. Bronson on the attempted murder charge. We could lose him."

"I don't think Mr. Bronson is going anywhere, Mr. Schultz. What I am thinking is that you let the press intimidate you into asking for a hasty indictment."

Mrs. Boeder excused Dave, and the grand jury left to decide whether an indictment was called for. Schultz was scowling.

Dave could hear shouting in the deliberation room.

Two hours later, a reluctant Mrs. Boeder reported to Schultz that on the basis of motive, the fingerprints, the lie detector test and the bloody rainsuit, the grand jury had no choice but to return an indictment of first-degree murder against Charles Bronson in the Jerry Egge murder case.

"I want you to know, Mr. Schultz," she said, "that it was a very close vote, 13-10, if you want to know the exact tally. I might add that *some* of the jury members had serious reservations, namely how the teenagers and this mysterious Huntzinger person were involved. I hope that all of this will come clear by the trial date or you could wind up with egg on your face, Mr. Schultz."

Later on in the day, Judge Edwina Alexander set a trial date for Dec. 1. Schultz would not charge Bronson in the Ellis case since there was absolutely no evidence tying Bronson to that murder.

An hour later Dave informed Bronson of the grand jury's decision. He didn't look too unhappy about it, probably because his career was already irretrievably ruined.

All he had to say was, "Can you get that Freddie kid out of here? Either that or tie him up and gag him, he's been badgering me ever since you put him in here."

Dave couldn't sympathize. Neither could the people of Soldier who considered Bronson a Grade A slimeball, guilty or not. His house had been egged, cleaned, and egged again. Mingo had arrested several teenage vandals, who had been released into the custody of their parents, despite Mingo's screaming protests.

Chapter 22

Devoted to the One I Love

"A faithful friend is the medicine of life."
— Ecclesiasticus

Around dinner time that night, Dave chugged up alongside Harry's cruiser and parked in the space in front of it. The neighborhood was post WWII, mostly stuccoed bungalows, a few ranch houses. Weeds were growing in the cracks of what was left of the sidewalks. A block down a combination gas station convenience store, called D*ke's due to a missing letter on the signboard, added to the burnt-out atmosphere.

Dave got out his jug of water, gave Nellybelle a drink, then slipped into the passenger side of Harry's cruiser beside Lucille and Mingo. They were waiting for a BCA criminalist to get there with a warrant. Mingo had scrapped the uniform and was wearing a blue bandanna headband and the knee-high moccasins you see in the pictures of Apaches in history books. Lucille was drinking a can of Pepsi.

Mingo removed his headband and ran his hands through his hair. "I gave the BCA stakeout a couple hours off. I hope you don't mind. Figured it'd take that long to search the place."

"At least," Dave said.

"Lucille here found a tie-in between Rita and Haskins."

"That so, Lucille?"

Lucille swallowed, wiped her mouth with her sleeve. "I checked every U-Haul rental place in the surrounding area. Would you believe there were twenty of them? Anyways, I found a man who signed for a truck as Bill Hoover. The description matched, and he was driving a psychedelic van, according to the manager."

Dave grabbed the Pepsi from Lucille, took a drink. Flat. Lukewarm. "All we gotta do now is catch the blackhearted fuck."

"You know what?" Mingo said. "This guy thinks he's the greatest criminal mind since Professor Moriarty, but he keeps using an alias with the same initials."

311

"You did good, Lucille," Dave said.

"Lucille has been having a very good couple of days," Mingo said, a sly grin flitting across his face. "She's been to the movies with that lady-killer Mel Kline. An R-rated one yet."

"Was not," Lucille said, turning beet red and slapping him on the arm.

"It could've been," Mingo said. "I doubt you were watching the movie."

Lucille hid her face in her hands.

Dave stretched and yawned. His stint on the stand had worn him out. "We can't wait all day, go up there and knock on the door," he said, nodding at Mingo.

Two little kids, a boy and a girl, were playing hopscotch on the sidewalk. Mingo stopped in front of them, apparently waiting for them to finish their game. They stopped playing and let him by, their eyes riveted as if he'd just jumped out of a movie screen.

Mingo was gone a long time. Lucille, trying to make conversation, asked Dave if he had any brothers and sisters.

"Fourteen. Ten boys and four girls." He peeked at her out of the corner of his eye.

"Where do you fit in?" she said. "I'll bet you were the oldest."

"You'd be wrong. Your rebellious child is always the youngest."

"You're funning me, aren't you?"

He winked at her. "We don't pick on anybody we don't like, Lucille." He pulled on a string in the upholstery, and it just kept on coming, like those handkerchiefs in a magician's act. Must have pulled out three yards of the stuff before he cut it with his pocket knife. Lucille was giggling. He gave her his Paul Newman up and down look. She shut up.

Just as the criminalist with the warrant arrived, the door of the bungalow opened, and Mingo loped down the steps of the house with the key to Haskins's private entrance. "Landlady try to mate with Mingo," he said.

Dave checked the warrant, stationed Lucille on one corner of the block and Mingo on the other, so's they wouldn't be surprised if Haskins showed up, and unlocked the apartment.

Haskins's room smelled like wet clothes. The criminalist dusted a water glass he'd spotted on the table next to the bed. A *New Yorker* magazine, a pack of Trojans, a King James Bible, and a suitcase with a bunch of pocket T-shirts and jeans were strewn about the apartment. But a notepad next to the telephone with a definite indentation proved to be the most significant find. Dave asked the fingerprint man for a pencil. He ran the tip sideways across the notepad, revealing an address in Crookston.

Dave went outside and told Lucille to stay put, while he and Mingo went to check out the address.

The neighborhood was just as seedy as the one near Haskins's crib, but it was near a four lane, so there was the extra-added delight of diesel trucks grinding by every ten seconds or so.

They sat and looked at the house. It was grayish-white with an overlay or road grime. Faded awnings on the windows, a rusty railing bordering the front steps. One of the trees in the yard had been struck by lightning.

"What you want to do?" Mingo said. "I could take the back."

"Nah. Let's see if anybody's seen anything suspicious first. That way we'll have some leverage with the guy who lives in the house."

They got out and went to separate sides of the street. Dave knocked on the door next to the dirty little white house. An older woman in a red flannel robe stroking a tabby answered.

"Excuse me ma'am," he said. "My name is Dave Jenkins. Deputy sheriff of Polk County—"

"What happened to you?" she said. "You look like you've just gone ten rounds with Cassius Clay."

"Ma'am, if I might—"

"You here about the hippie van that's always parked in front of that rock singer's house?" she said.

Dave glanced over his shoulder at Mingo on the other side of the street chatting up a young woman. Dave gave him a thumbs up.

"Nothing but drug addicts in that house," the woman said. "A nice family used to live there. The Mortensons. They was killed in a car crash on that Interstate 94 down in the Cities. Not safe for people who ain't used to 'em."

"Sorry to hear that, ma'am. So then, you think the hippie van was selling drugs to people in the white house?"

"I don't stutter. Ain't seen it lately, though. Thought you boys finally did something."

"Thank you, ma'am. You've been very helpful."

Mingo and Dave met on the sidewalk in front of the Jeep. "Sounds like Haskins has been around here, all right," Mingo said. "Want me to call for back-up?"

"Nah, take too long."

They went to the white house and rang the bell.

A long-haired musician-type answered. A radio was playing "Brown Sugar", and Dave could smell dinner being cooked. Liver and onions he thought it was. Suddenly Dave felt dizzy and nauseous and his legs were rubbery. He braced himself on the rickety railing.

"Police," Mingo said, flashing his badge. "We're looking for a man named Bob Haskins. He many be going under an assumed name. Drives one of those hippie vans, painted all kinds of different colors."

"Don't know nobody like that."

"Funny," Dave said, "The lady next door says that van has been parked in front of your place lots of times."

"Must be the folks next door. They're into that sort of thing."

"Mind if we come in and look around?" Mingo said.

"I don't know, the place is kind of a mess."

"We're not looking for drugs," Dave said, "if that's your problem. Mr. Haskins has been involved in a murder. You wouldn't want to be charged as an accessory, now would you?"

"Murder? I don't know nothing about any murder. Sure, you just help yourself. Look all you want."

Dave and Mingo tracked through the house, rummaging through closets, getting Jim Morrison to pull down the ladder that led to the attic. Nothing up there but bat shit. They found a bag of marijuana taped to the back of the refrigerator.

"We'll just keep this," Mingo said. "The lab'll need to analyze it."

"I never saw that before in my life," the guy said. "Must've been here when I moved in. I just rent."

"Then you won't miss it," Dave said.

Back at the Jeep, Dave and Mingo leaned against the fender. "You don't smoke this crap, do you, Dude?" Dave said, tossing the bag in the air.

"Nah, just giving Alice Cooper there some shit."

They drove back to Haskins's former crib, sent Lucille off to check the motels for any customers with names starting with "B.H.", and sat around waiting for Haskins or the BCA stakeout, whichever, to show up.

As long as they had to sit there, Dave thought he'd have some fun with the Indian. "Did you know I'm 1/32 Ojibwa?" Dave said.

Mingo cackled. He had a big smile, reminiscent of the Cleveland Indian logo. Drat! he wasn't buying it.

"The Mescalero consider the Ojibwa spoiled rich kids. They got all that water, you know." Mingo twiddled his thumbs. "I'll bet you a can of Pepsi that the next person to come out of that convenience store is a woman."

Dave looked in his wallet. He had twenty bucks. "If you've got any hair on your ass, you'll make it a twenty," he said.

Mingo didn't bat an eye.

Sure enough, a woman. Dave tried to figure if there was a way Mingo might have known in advance. He couldn't think of one. Wanted to go double or nothing. "Haskins's landlady, her first name. I say it starts with a letter between 'A' and 'M'."

The Indian scratched his face, blew a bubble, popped it, and said, "Are you tryin' to con me? Let's see, her name could be Teresa, Sally, Nancy, Wendy, Rachel. I guess there are just as many names in the second half of the alphabet."

"Okay, let's bet then," Dave said.

"Not so fast, White Eyes. I'll take 'A' through 'M'." Mingo showed his teeth.

The lady's name was Charlotte. Then it hit him. Mingo had gone in there to get the key and the woman had tried to hustle him. The little twerp knew her first name.

Dave was another forty dollars down before the stakeout finally showed.

"Should be able to get the 4X4 out of impound at this rate," Mingo said.

The dizziness and the nausea returned. Dave always felt that way when he lost money, but he figured he better not get behind the wheel anyways. "You better drive, Dude. I don't feel so good."

"A knock on the head'll do that to you."

"The docs said I had a slight concussion. I had one when I played football. Kind of feel like Butkus just mauled me."

Mingo pumped the accelerator on the Jeep and turned the key. She coughed twice, then turned over.

On the road leading to Soldier, Dave said, "I'll fill Henderson in on what we've got."

"I wouldn't tell him anything if I were you. That boy'd find a way to lose holding a royal flush."

"Mine is not to question why..."

Mingo passed a slow-moving pickup. "You have any more of those visions?"

"With a different wrinkle. While Frankenstein was pounding on my face, I kind of drifted up above my body watching him do it."

"You don't say."

"Then I heard some voices."

"Yeah, they claim your relatives and friends who've passed come to help you make the transition. The voices have anything to say?"

"One of them wanted to help me. Said I'd been really good to his boy."

"Well, there's a hint. I heard your little pal Pleasiac's old man committed suicide."

"I've been reading a little bit about this kind of thing. The scientists says it has something to do with endorphins."

"You're hard to convince. I tell you I went to see Father Mischke about the ghost medicine ceremony?"

"You didn't!"

Mingo came up behind an eighteen wheeler, exhaust belching out the tailpipe. A yellow line prevented his passing. "Yeah, Cousin Cecil insisted a white holy man get involved, Egge being a paleface and all. Father Mischke wouldn't do it, but he did suggest that Debbie and I take her class to see a Mescalero puberty ceremony in New Mexico."

"He said that?"

"Yeah, he's worried that Soldier youth don't have a lot of respect for tradition and ritual."

"There's no doubt about that."

"Since most Mescaleros are Catholic, he doesn't see any harm in it. He feels going to the ceremonial might have the same effect as saying a couple novenas for Egge."

"How you gonna pay for it?"

"Mrs. Mac is gonna lay a wager on a horse at Canterbury Park when it opens. She doesn't ordinarily bet, unless it's for a good cause. Says she's never lost."

"As long as it's a sure thing, I can let you have a couple of Benjamins. I just got my income tax return."

The yellow line disappeared and Mingo passed the truck. The words "Crystal Sugar" were scripted on the side in black lettering on a gray background.

"I had another mystical experience when I took Mary Lou to the hospital to have her baby. Never thought I'd go for somebody else's kid."

"Babies'll do that to you."

"She came to see me while I was in the hospital. Said she's going back to Chicago in a few days. She says she can get me a job in a detective agency at twice my present salary. Knows the guy from when she put a tail on her philandering old man."

"The Stinking Cabbage, eh?"

"What's that?"

"That's what Chicago means in Indian."

"That so? Anyway, she called him, told him all about how I found Haskins through that principals' journal. He was impressed, but I need to make up my mind like right now."

"I suppose you want to stick it out until we find Haskins."

"That and the idea of living in a place with a hundred people per square inch. She says she'd never want to live in Soldier. The usual reason, nothing to do here. How about you? I've been noticing you and Debbie Meyer are getting pretty thick. You ever think of...?

Mingo gave him that coyote look again. "I'm not sure she appreciates me for myself. Women think all Indians are wealthy, the casinos you know."

Dave laughed, reached in the refuse between the seats searching for his cellular. Wanted to know if Lucille had found anything.

* * *

While Dave and Mingo were on their way back from Crookston, Mary Lou lounged in a rocking chair at her father's house on The Angle, nursing the baby and watching the sun begin to set.

Sally was fussing and kept clutching at her breast. Mary Lou ignored it. She was thinking about Dave. He'd been so charming at the hospital, but he was such a stubborn man. He'd never consider leaving Soldier.

She ran her hand over the wispy hairs on the baby's head, so fine, like angel hair. The baby smiled up at her and tried to talk. "Ga."

There was a van parked out on The Angle, a blue one with a cracked windshield. A girl was climbing the three tiers of steps leading to the house. As the girl drew closer, Mary Lou realized that one side of the girl's head had been cropped as close as a boy's. She shivered, visualized shaved heads with X's on their foreheads. Young girls swept up in false ideology with pseudo role models. Where had she read that two of those girls were still loyal to Manson after almost thirty years?

She stood, pacing to and fro. The baby, deprived of her sustenance, whimpered. Why am I so paranoid? she thought. Lots of kids wear their hair in that punk look these days.

The girl was almost at the door. Nobody else was home. Her dad was getting the stitches removed from his arm. He'd probably go to the bank after that, couldn't stay away.

A gun. She needed a gun. But she didn't know where to look. Surely her father had one someplace. She'd always hated firearms and wouldn't learn how to shoot one when he'd tried to teach her. "It's for your own protection," he'd said.

The bell rang. The gardener was out there somewhere, seeding and fertilizing. She could see the German shepherd out on the lawn marking his territory in the gladiolus. The bell rang again. Maybe the girl would go away if she pretended nobody was home. But the baby began to cry. Mary Lou put her hand over the baby's mouth, but she only cried harder, and Mary Lou got up to answer.

The girl seemed startled when Mary Lou opened the door. "Hi, there, I'm Olive Randall," she said. "I don't know if David has mentioned me, but I go with his friend Howard Pleasiac. His mom and him live in that old schoolhouse right next to David."

Mary Lou shifted the baby to her other arm. The baby had stopped crying when Mary Lou had opened the door. Sally stared at the girl with her eyes very wide, sucking on one finger. Mary Lou took the finger away, trying to replace it with a pacifier.

"Yes, you know Dave?" she said.

The girl touched Sally's finger. The baby grasped it and wouldn't let go.

"He sent me over here to check on you," the girl said. "He's in Crookston, tracking this guy I told him about who might have something to do with this crime wave we've been having."

The girl wore a Michigan State T-shirt with walking shorts; she rubbed the stubble on the side of her head with the hand the baby hadn't appropriated.

"Olive. You said your name was Olive? I was just on my way..." She looked down at her blouse disheveled from breast-feeding. No, she probably wouldn't believe that.

"Come in," she said, stepping out of the way. Mary Lou didn't want to make the girl angry. Maybe Dave *had* sent Olive to check up on her.

Olive gently extricated herself, stepped inside and looked around. "This is an interesting house you've got here, built into the hillside with all that glass. It's really pretty at night. My mom would always drive us by here when I was a little girl."

The German shepherd was barking now, and he trotted up alongside Olive. She patted him on the head, and he whined. Mary Lou held the baby's head against her cheek.

The girl sat down on the settee near the door. "What a pretty baby," she said. "Dave told me you were expecting. I didn't know that it had arrived. I'll bet it's a girl. What's her name?"

The German shepherd wasn't going to do any good. He licked Olive's hand.

"Sally. Not too many girls are named that anymore, are they?"

"Charlie Brown's sister."

"I hadn't thought of that."

Mary Lou felt the baby's behind. "I need to change her," she said. "Why don't you come into the living room? Sit in the rocker there, and I'll be right back." Mary Lou disappeared into her father's bedroom, where she set the baby on the bed. Through the French doors, she studied the backyard. It extended a hundred yards or so before it dissolved into woods. Could she make it that far before the girl got wise? There was no phone in her father's bedroom, so she couldn't dial 911.

She rifled through the drawers, tossing clothes every which way, searching for any kind of weapon. Why hadn't she tried the kitchen? There were knives in there. She couldn't find anything, but she'd try to get the baby out of the way at least, so she covered her with a blanket, put her in the closet, and went back out to deal with Dave's friend.

Mary Lou pulled up a chair close to the girl, trying to pretend that nothing was wrong. Olive turned toward her with a cheery enough aspect.

"Well, Olive, why don't you tell me about yourself," she said. "That's an interesting hairdo. Is that a new trend or something?" Mary Lou hated herself as soon as she said it. Once again she was reminded of those ominous shaved heads from the Manson news videos.

Olive crossed her ankles. She had a piece of rawhide tied around one ankle. "I woke up one morning, and it was all tangled so I just started cutting, but when I got one side finished, I kind of chickened out, so I left it. It's kind of a statement, you know. You mind my asking how much you spend to keep your hair looking like that?"

Mary Lou was bigger than this girl. If it wasn't for the baby..."I just wash it every day with rainwater, and I use a lot of conditioner. I can cut it myself mostly, just the ends, and, of course, I brush it a lot."

Olive suddenly rose and disappeared into the kitchen. She came back with two cans of Pepsi, giving one to Mary Lou. *Of all the gall!* "I just think that men have this built-in excuse for treating us like ditzes. We spend so much time and money on personal appearance and clothes. It seems so shallow, don't you think?"

"I suppose spending time under the dryer helps some women relax," Mary Lou said. She noticed for the first time that the girl wasn't wearing anything under that Michigan State T-shirt, and she definitely needed *something*.

Olive set her can down on the coffee table. "I shouldn't be so judgmental," she said. "I have this tendency to judge people on first impression. Cheerleaders, for instance. There are cheerleaders and there are cheerleaders. They're not all empty-headed idiots."

Mary Lou chuckled a bit. "I used to cheerlead. You're right, some of them were empty-headed."

Despite the closed door, Mary Lou could hear the baby googling in her basket. She pulled her chair closer to the girl. "So, Olive," she said, "what about your family? Do you have any brothers and sisters?"

Mary Lou noticed a definite change in body language and facial expression. Olive looked almost angelic, despite the shaved side of her head.

The girl drained her Pepsi and crushed the can. Mary Lou flinched a little, despite herself. "Two little sisters. I tried to run away once to Hollywood to become a model," she said. "Pretty stupid, huh? Sheriff Kline brought me back, but I would have run away again if it weren't for my sisters, Nancy and Patty. I don't know what I'd do if I lost them."

Mary Lou took the can from Olive. "Care for another?" If she could only get to the kitchen.

"I've had enough." Olive continued, seemingly addressing her own reflection in the glass behind Mary Lou. "And I have this best friend named Freddie whom I love like family. I can tell him the most horrible stuff about myself, like about the time I got raped, and he'll just say something like 'Shit happens.' You know, like bad stuff happens to everybody, even rich people."

Even rich people? The baby squalled in the bedroom. Mary Lou stood, moved toward the door. "I've got to see to the baby, Olive. It's been nice chatting with you. Tell Dave we'll be all right. The gardener will be around until Dad comes home."

Olive reached inside her purse and pulled out a derringer-like pistol. She got up, moved toward Mary Lou, and pushed the small gun in her ribs. "Remember what I said about Freddie, lady? He's in jail for trying to burn down the school. That prison. Getting us ready to work in a factory is what they're doing. Get to class on time, make sure your assignments are neat, respect authority, conform to the norms."

Mary Lou looked down at the weapon. She could knock it out of the girl's hand easily.

Olive poked her with the gun again. "You and me and the baby are going to get Freddie out. Go and get her now. Hurry. We'll take your car. Gotta make a stop at Stormy's so's she can take a message to David. Then she'll get rid of the van."

Mary Lou didn't move. "What about my father?" she said. "He'll be worried."

Olive brought the gun down on the side of Mary Lou's head. She saw stars, felt nauseous, was afraid she was going to wet herself. Olive reached down and pulled her up. Mary Lou held her head. There was blood.

"I said to hurry, rich bitch!" Olive shouted. "Leave him a note. Tell him you went to visit a friend, and you'll be sleeping over."

Mary Lou staggered toward the bedroom, one hand on her forehead. Where was her father when she needed him?

*   *   *

Stormy Guck cowered outside the sheriff's office, winding Olive's note into a sweaty, indecipherable knot. This was almost as hard as the time she had to plant that bloody rainsuit in Bronson's garage. How come she always got the shit detail?

She was supposed to deliver the note to Deputy Jenkins, but she just couldn't get herself to go in the sheriff's office. She didn't know what to do. And she had to go to the bathroom again. This always happened when she was nervous. And she'd already screwed up. Olive had wanted her to hide the van Bob had stolen, since they couldn't leave it in front of the Forman house, but Stormy didn't know how to drive. She'd gotten the damn thing all the way out to the Krueger farm where she was going to hide it, but when she'd tried to turn off into a little clearing, she'd lost control and hit a tree. Bob was going to kill her. She'd covered the van with some brush and gotten the hell out of there.

"Fuck it," she said, and turned on her heel, headed back toward the serenity of Shady Brook. "It'll wait till morning." She'd watch a little "Wheel of Fortune" on TV.

Stormy hurried down the street, trying to put as much distance between her and the sheriff's office as possible. She hoped no one had seen her standing there. How long had she been there? She had no idea what was in the note. Olive would beat the shit out of her if she read it. The bitch could be so damn mean, especially when they had sex. She liked to pinch Stormy's tits and she liked to bite. If she were a little nicer about it, she'd prefer having sex with Olive than with Lester, who never thought of anyone but himself. Olive really knew how to kiss. Maybe some other boy would be better. She'd only done it with Lester and a couple really old guys, although she'd hinted to some other boys that she was ready and willing.

She'd given out a few blow jobs at the Paramount, but she'd met those boys at the show, they'd never spent any money on her, and they'd never called her afterwards. And then that damn movie usher caught her. God! that was embarrassing. Her grandfather had found out about it. The only adult she could relate to. He was in the hospital with some old age thing. At least she hoped it didn't have anything to do with her.

Stormy looked over her shoulder to see if anyone was gaining on her. She wondered what Bob would do to her when he found out she'd smashed his van.

Grown-ups were so hard to understand, even the so-called responsible ones. They were supposed to be trustworthy, but they never were from her experience. Once she'd been caught breaking into a vending machine at the Value Stop, and she'd done it with the owner so's he'd let her go.

Bob didn't seem to be interested in her sexually.

Superintendent Bronson sure had been, though, and she'd snatched his belt, careful not to get any fingerprints on it, just like Bob had told her to. Bob called her Pickle Tits, the bastard.

She couldn't wait to get older so's she could get some implants like those women in the porno movies Lester was always watching. Nobody would call her Pickle Tits then.

Chapter 23

Death of the SDS

"The Revolution is like Saturn - it eats its own children."
— Georg Buchner

Brad straddled a stump next to the shack on the Miller farm, sharpening his knife on a piece of flint he always carried. He had a can of W-30 oil at his knee. Honing the blade calmed him some, but it didn't stop the pounding in his chest, or ease the stuffy sensation in his head or his extreme sensitivity to sounds.

Szymanski was alive and stalking him. He'd thought he'd killed him twice, but no, he was still kicking, gallivanting around in a Jeep disguised as a deputy sheriff. Brad would have to kill him again, but the only weapon he had was the knife, and he'd have to get in close to use it.

Dusk was settling in, so he lit the lantern. The yellowish light projected grotesque shapes against the side of the shed. The smell of kerosene nauseated him and increased the ticklish sensation in his throat. He placed the lamp on the stump. Pounding his fist into his palm, he paced up and down. Olive was late.

"When I get my hands on that bitch I'm gonna beat her ass so bad..." He kicked out at the side of the old shed; the boards splintered and part of the roof caved in, and he went wild, smashing and hacking, snapping boards over his knee. "Take that you motherhumping, cockeater!" he yelled. "Hyah! Hyah! Hyah!" Then he ran to a rock pile near the shed, squat-lifted a giant bolder up over his head, and shot-putted the thing on top of what was left of the hut. It collapsed with an echoing "whomp".

His head cleared and the ticklish sensation was gone. He always felt so much better after a good pounding.

"Wished I'd had time to do it right when I hammered Szymanski out there in the woods. If it weren't for those idiots with the pellet guns, I'd'a taken his hair. Yeah, scalping him would have thrown a scare into all the moms and pops and their little Shirley Temples."

323

Sapped of emotion, he reached in his pocket for a pill—needed to bring himself back up. Nothing to take with the pill but beer. He unscrewed the cap on his canteen, took a swig. When he swallowed, his vision blurred a bit.

Brad looked up. Somebody was coming down the driveway leading to the Fogel farm.

"Hey, Bob, it's me," the intruder yelled.

Brad reached for his knife. Szymanski? The man hopped down into the ditch, climbed the fence separating pasture from the road, and came closer.

Lester Krueger. Rat-faced, with purplish acne-scars. Pigeon-toed from wearing heavy engineer boots since he first learned to walk. One of Brad's favorite people.

"The Merc quit on me about a mile back. Olive sent me out here to get you."

"You bring any firepower?"

"Nah, the old man took all my guns after I threatened that Pleasiac punk."

"You're about as useless as..."

"What happened to yours?"

"Can't keep one. Olive hates guns."

Lester stooped to pick up one of his *Guns and Ammo* magazines in the rubble from the hut. "What'd you do to the shed?"

He put the magazine in one of the pockets of his faded-green fatigue jacket.

"Kicked the shit out of it, like I'm gonna do to you if you don't shut up. I don't know why I ever got involved with you people. If I'm gonna get that deputy, I'll need a better weapon than this shank."

Who knew the old bastard was gonna be this tough?

Brad lit a doobie, took a long, deep drag.

"Gimme a toke of that, why don't you?"

Brad handed it over. "Careful now, this could lead to a hard-core habit. Next thing you'll be taking it in the ass to make money to buy nose candy. Never should've started using dope myself."

"Yeah, I know, it eats up all the profits."

"Plain old weed isn't so bad, but once I tried some shit that was laced with PCP. Horse tranquilizer. Never knew where I was at or what I was doing. Liked the feeling of complete abandon, though."

"That what you were on the day you wasted Egge?"

"Yeah, didn't think he was going to show up. Olive said the guy was as regular as a morning dump. Just got up to leave when I heard him huffing and puffing up the trail, like a fat stripper doing a fan dance."

"I was there, remember?"

"Can't get over how easily I got away with it. And the coincidence! That superintendent was a born fall guy."

"Don't know why you had to whack the guy with my Louisville Slugger. When that Indian showed me that bat, I thought I was gonna have a shit hemorrhage. You bastard."

Brad held up one finger, signifying *that's once*. "Thought the geek was going to get away there for a minute. Egge reminded me so much of the Polack. I tell you about all those times Szymanski was on my ass?"

"Only a couple hundred times is all," Lester said. "You missed a playoff game because you were flunking math, and your team lost. Then—"

"Fucker thought he was such hot shit cause he fought the Japs in WWII. Szymanski made me work for the janitor the rest of the year that time I pissed in Max Hasselrig's locker. And then there was Felicia. She'd lean over my desk, wearing one of those v-neck sweaters, and give me the bird's eye view. Watch to see if I was checking her out. These days she'd have her ass in a sling, and I'd'a come out smellin' like an American Beauty rose."

"You pissed in a kid's locker?"

"If it weren't for the Polack, I'd'a had a full ride to Ohio State. Women fighting for the privilege of twirling my crank. All I'd need to do was snap my fingers, and they'd lay down for me. I took so many queer jobs when I got kicked out of school. I tell you I once played centerfield for the Rockville Tomboys, a professional girls' team? Got fifty dollars a day for playing in drag. What a hoot!"

"I hear there was some men disguised as women in the Olympics. You got anything to eat? I was in such a hurry to get out here I didn't stop to eat and I been dodging those deputies."

"There're some beans in the pot."

Lester scooped himself a plate of the overdone glop and sat on the stump Brad had vacated, shoveling it in. "Olive says she's staying in town until she figures a way to get Freddie out."

"I'm going to bloody her nose for this."

"I heard the last time you beat her, she waited until you went to sleep and set fire to the mattress."

Brad glowered down at the little weasel. "What else you hear?"

"Just that she's a great piece."

Brad grabbed him by the shirt, lifted him up off the ground. The boy gagged and choked, the phony dog tags he wore digging into his skin. "Look, you little shit, I'm the only one talks about Olive that way. I ever hear you say anything like that again, I'm going to cut your mangy little dick off and jam it down your fuckin' throat."

Lester dropped to the ground, holding his neck. Already reddish welts were showing. "Easy, man," he said. "I thought you didn't care about sex is all, preaching to us about free sex and all that. You know she loves that little fag Cochran more than she does you. Fags made me sick. I don't know why you let him hang with us."

"I don't know why I let *you* hang with us."

"Why do you always shit on me? I'm the only one who'd go to the mat for you."

"There's no way Olive'll ever leave me. She and I been lovers ever since she was in junior high."

Lester stood, dusted himself off. "How 'bout that time she caught you selling dope to grade school kids? And when she finds out about the Nancy—"

"You shut up about Nancy. I don't know for a fact Nancy is my kid. Her mother got around quite a bit before we got together, and, for all I know, she was making it with some other guy while we were shacking up. That Legion is a regular Peyton Place."

"What's Peyton Place?"

"You really are illiterate, aren't you? Olive must have had the mistaken notion that Nancy and Patty were mine, too. She brought them to see me at my place in Crookston. You about done there? You and me are going to take a little walk down to the farm. See if that Miller asshole has any wheels."

"You gonna kill them, too?"

"How many kids did Rita say the Millers have at home?"

"Just the little girl."

"The pigs'll never stop looking for us if we snuff the kid. We won't bother the woman and the brat if they keep quiet. I've creepy-crawled lots of houses. Always left them a little surprise. We'll kick the shit out of old Miller first, like I used to do in Steubenville."

"I'm game for it."

"I'd sneak out of the house in the middle of the night and my buddies and me'd look for homeless people and other dumbasses stupid enough to be out and about at two in the morning."

"Yeah, they call that 'wilding' these days. Bunch of niggers in the park jump some stranger and thump him."

Brad scratched the side of his face. The mosquitoes were slowly eating him up. "All that experience came in handy when I joined the Weathermen. They needed somebody who wasn't afraid to get rough. You hear any more about the deputy?"

"Just that Olive said he was getting a warrant to search your pad, and you were hiding out here until she could think of a place to go. Like I said, she's not going anyplace without Freddie."

"Sometimes I can't believe how stupid those cops are. I almost cracked up at that press conference when I asked that question about the spray paint on Szymanski's back, and they thought nothing of it." Brad rummaged through the rubble from the shed, found the mosquito netting, threw it over his head. He felt even more claustrophobic. "It's getting dark. Let's get going to that farmhouse. Maybe they've got something real to eat."

Brad picked up the lantern and strode toward the Miller barn, a shadowy outline in the distance. Before they got too far, he stepped in a cowpie. Rather than wipe it off on the grass, he kicked his shoe off and couldn't find it in the darkness. The aggravation was building. He'd need another downer before long.

"Better blow out the lamp. With no moon they'd be able to see it easy at the farm."

Brad blew it out. "Smart move," he said, "now I can't see a damn thing."

"Just wait a while. Your eyes will adjust."

They were closing in on a shed close to the barn when Brad tripped over something. A shape moved in the darkness. "MMM-MMAAAAH."

"A fucking cow," Lester said.

"There must be a hundred of them out here lying down on all fours. I heard they slept on their feet someplace."

"Nah, that's horses."

They came to the backdoor of the barn and Brad turned the handle. It was open. When he went in, he practically impaled himself on a three-tined pitchfork leaning up against the side of the door.

"God, the place stinks like a fertilizer factory," Lester said.

"Ten thousand times worse I'd say." Brad heard a buzzing sound. Flies had replaced the mosquitoes. They went right for his eyes as if they were equipped with night vision. As he swatted at them, they got more and more frantic.

Two little pin-points of light were moving along the opposite wall. Brad threw the pitchfork at them, trying to lead them a bit. There was a RRRWWWWW! sound and the lights went out.

"A damn cat," Lester said.

As Brad's eyes adjusted to the darkness, he could see a bull in one of the pens, lying in manure. The ring in its nose was chained to a railing.

"Doesn't that old sodbuster ever clean the place?" Lester said.

"I gotta get out of here," Brad said. I feel like maggots are crawling on me."

They went up some stairs and out the front door. There was a night light over the car shed, and Brad could see a gas tank off to the right. "Let's see if Miller left the keys in his car?" he said.

Before he could put one foot in front of the other, he heard a growling and snarling, and a black and white dog was on him, tearing at one of his pants legs, and he was kicking at it with his other leg unable to get enough balance to do much good. He slammed down at its head with his fist, and now the dog had hold of his wrist, and he swung the dog up against the shed, but it held on as if he were a goddamn T-bone, and he whacked it twice more and the dog finally let go, rolling in the weeds next to the silo. He found his knife and slit the mutt's throat before it could make any more noise.

"Damn it, my wrist and ankle hurt like hell. Why didn't you do something?"

"Keep it down. You're going to wake them up."

"Don't tell me to keep it down, asshole."

Miller's idea of transportation was a rusted-out old bucket of a station wagon. No keys in it.

"You know how to hot-wire a car?"

"Where would I learn that?"

"I don't know, *Hot Rod* magazine in special ed? You tell me. Have to get the keys and a gun from Miller."

They stood there studying the run-down Miller house, barely visible in the poor light coming from the bulb above the car shed, then Brad advanced, and Lester followed along behind like a monkey on a leash.

Brad felt woozy, and blood from the dog bite was dripping all over his pants. Had to have a gun. Had to have a gun, or he wouldn't be able to deal with Szymanski. Almost got him there outside his house. If only he'd used the knife instead of the knuckledusters.

Damn his wrist hurt. He turned the knob on the front door, very carefully. It wouldn't give. The fucking thing was locked. "What kind of farmer locks his doors?" he said. They eased off the front steps and slid around back, hunting for an open window or another door.

Brad was breathing hard and getting nervous again. Had to get that gun, had to get a gun. Had to get a gun now. Had to get Szymanski...had to get Szymanski...before Szymanski got him. But Olive, she didn't approve of guns...no, she didn't approve of guns at all.

He tried a window. It was either locked or stuck. Maybe if he rapped a rock in his coat. Yes, a rock...he needed a rock...a rock as big as a pumpkin. No rocks. He checked his knife, still there, then peeked in a rear window. Couldn't see a damn thing in there. Dark, very dark. Too dark. As dark as ink. Inky, dinky, slinky dark.

"What if Old Man Miller is in there waiting for us?" Lester said. "What if he heard the cat you killed in the barn or the dog when it attacked? We can walk back to town. It's only three miles or so."

"Olive won't know where to find us."

"Fuck Olive."

Brad's head exploded, he bit his tongue hard, then reached for his knife, and drove it upward under Lester's crotch, and kept on driving until he could feel the knife reach lower intestine, then ripped sideways and back the other way. Lester let out an animal-like screech and went down in a heap. Stupid bastard didn't deserve to live. Brad picked him up and dragged him over behind a clump of trees, gave him a kick for good measure. Nobody talked about Olive like that!

Lester's blood had slicked all over Brad's hands, so he caught hold of his shirttails and twisted the knob on the back door. It was locked. He was searching for something to break the lock when the yard light went on.

He hit the ground and tried to flatten out, rolling under a lilac bush next to the back door. Thank God he was wearing his camouflage.

Goddamn! why had he listened to Olive? That Miller geezer probably had a shotgun or a deer rifle if he knew anything about crazy old farmers. They were always threatening him when he hunted on their land without permission. Without permission...without permission.

He won't see me here, he thought. When the old bastard goes by, I'll stick him, take away his rifle, and blow his brains out. Or maybe I'd keep him alive, shoot him in the kneecap, then in the gut, make him beg to die, what I should've done with Szymanski. Szymanski...Szymanski. A delicious shiver went through him.

A light came around the corner of the house. He should attack now, just in case the old bastard got lucky and shined the light into the bushes. Take a chance Miller wouldn't be able to hit him in the dark, be on top of the old plow jockey before he knew what hit him, and he'd cut his throat with his pig sticker...pig sticker...pig sticker. His head hurt so bad it felt like his eyes were going to pop out...pop out.

"Hey, you there! I can see you! Don't move or I'll blow your fuckin' head off! This is my land, and I got a right to shoot any god-damn rustlers I catch. I can see you good so don't you move if you know what's good for you!"

Brad froze. He should have known better than to steal those cows. He'd only gotten a couple of hundred dollars from that meat market. Cost him thirty dollars to rent the trailer...trailer...trailer.

Shit, it was too damn dark to hit anything. He snatched up some dirt and hurled it at the flashlight, simultaneously sprinting for the light. He heard an explosion, and his forehead went numb, his legs gave out, and he crashed to the ground, trying to remember a prayer. "Hail Mary full of grace...grace...grace...blessed aren't thou among women." He needed a priest, but he hated priests. Cornholers, altar boy diddlers, closet winos, stickey-fingered collection-plate swindlers...swindlers...swindlers.

He was dying now. The old geezer was looking down at him shining the flashlight in his eyes...eyes...eyes.

"Get me the priest," he said.

"Ain't no priest going to help you now," the geezer said.

The man favored his old principal—same hair growing out of his nostrils, same aggressive snarl, same wart on his chin—only Szymanski was wearing a feed cap. Why was Szymanski wearing a feed cap...cap...cap?

"You win, Szymanski," he said, as the rest of his body grew numb and the picture faded...faded...faded.

*   *   *

Harry was out of the hospital and in the process of reclaiming his office. Hank Deering was working on the wall behind his desk. The twelve point buck squatted on the floor, watching Hank slaver plaster on the wall. Harry glanced over at his file cabinets, on top of which he had his bowling trophies, which he'd superglued back together. Wasn't too mad at Jenkins for breaking them. After all, he'd told him he was the new sheriff. Should be able to arrange his office anyway he liked, probably thought Harry wasn't coming back. Why worry about bowling trophies? Actually it was kind of pathetic that he took so much pride in them.

He sighed, stared out the widow. It was a beautiful day for early May, the temperature in the 70s. Across the street, he could see Brenda, in her new green dress, and her matron friends parading down the sidewalk from the church, having just completed a bake sale to raise money for floral decorations. An in-line skater passed just in front of them. Those kids were running wild since they'd outlawed corporal punishment.

It was time for another cigarette. He'd ignored the doctor's ultimatum to quit smoking, had switched to Kents instead. However, he was limiting himself to ten per day, had them timed to the minute. He dragged on the Kent, drawing the smoke deep into his lungs. Tasted like laundry soap. It had taken him an entire day to get used to cigarette smoke, and at first, he'd thought he was having another heart attack he was so light-headed.

Harry needed to talk to Lucille and Mingo about the murder cases. Jenkins was over at the school huddling with Conrad White about the fire. A fax from Henderson with fingerprints and a picture of this guy Brad Huntzinger, alias Bob Haskins, had just arrived. The spitting image of Mel.

Since the murders seemed to be solving themselves rather nicely, Harry was having second thoughts about retiring. They had Rita Miller and Freddie Cochran in jail, and there seemed to be a link between them and this Bob Haskins person. Bronson's lawyer was already beginning to make noises about a new hearing. Hildegard would drop the recall petition; maybe from now on she'd listen to him once in a while.

As he was about to buzz Shirley to have the two deputies come in, the phone rang. Shirley said it was Ray Miller. Harry grabbed another cigarette, two hours early. Just having something in his mouth was half the battle. He wouldn't light it.

Harry pulled the lever on his chair, moving it back a notch, put the phone to his ear. "What's up, Ray?"

"Is this Sheriff Kline? I thought you was in the hospital."

"Nope, false alarm. What's this about?"

"That rustler fellah was trying to break into my house. I had to shoot him. Got him and the other one out in the car shed. Dragged them over there on the stone boat. I can tie 'em to the hood of the car if you want and bring them in."

There was some static on the line, a blowing sound as if he had a seashell held to his ear. That and Miller's normal garbled way of talking made it hard for Harry to decipher what the man was saying. "The old woman, she...a noise. I told her to...up and let me sleep. I got to get up at...to milk the cows.

She...me up again a little while later. Said she saw a man...in the..., so I got my deer...out of the cellar closet and went out to...around. Thought it might be that...fellah."

Harry reached over to his desk to get the glass of water he had there. He switched the phone to his other ear.

"Ray, I can't hear you very well. Hang up and I'll call you back."

Miller picked up on the first ring. "That you, Sheriff?" The line was better this time.

"And you shot him where?" Harry asked.

"He was comin' right at me, all crazy-looking. Kind of froze for a minute. Lucky I got off a shot. Shot him in the face, never seen so much blood. I felt sick. I never been to war..."

"Can't be too much left of his face."

"So, you want me to bring 'em in?"

"No, they ain't no deer, Ray."

"Am I gonna get some reward money for this?"

"No, no, Ray, there ain't no reward money."

"You ain't keepin' it for yourself, are you?"

"No, Ray, there is no reward. Why didn't you call me before you went out there?"

"Didn't want him to get away. Worried you'd never catch him."

"Thanks, Ray. Ah, Ray, what does this guy look like? Big guy, with curly black hair?"

"That's him. The bastard killed my dog. I'm puttin' in a claim."

"How bout the other one?"

"It's a kid. I think it's one of the Krueger boys."

"When did this happen, Ray?"

"Never looked at the clock. Around midnight I suppose. He'd've killed us both, but something made me lock the doors and windows. Never done that once since I been living on the farm."

"Strange. You said around midnight, and you're just getting around to calling me now?"

"The wife wanted to, but I needed some sleep, like I told you. Nobody's going to milk the cows for me, and I knew what kind of commotion you fellahs'd raise if I called you. Never would've gotten anything done. I just now got finished."

"You shoulda left the bodies where they were until I got there, Ray."

"Your deputy was telling me about that there hideout they had out to my pasture, thought the Indian and the fat girl was just blowing smoke, trying to get out of finding my rustler, like that other worthless fellah Jenkins. I ain't been out there yet. There's a road out there by the back fence. Want me to take my rifle and look, see if there's any more of 'em?"

"You just wait until I send somebody. Leave the bodies alone now." Harry hung up, lit the cigarette, took a deep drag, then buzzed Shirley. "Shirley, send Lucille and Mingo in here. We got us two more killings."

Harry called Henderson, hard pressed to keep the glee out of his voice. "Larry, you know that fax you sent me, that Haskins guy the FBI let get away? Looks like he's our man. Ray Miller shot him trying to break into his farmhouse."

"We'll have a crime team at the scene in a half hour," Henderson said. "Gimme some directions."

"You hear me, Larry? I said we got the killer."

"Not necessarily. I don't see what this has to do with the Egge murder. Haskins could've been looking for a car."

"The Krueger boy was with him for one thing."

"He dead too?"

"As an eelpout out on the ice. Maybe next time you'll have a bit more respect for the boys in the sticks, eh Larry?" Harry gave Henderson the directions to the Miller farm and hung up the phone—he hadn't felt so good since the first time Brenda had let him unhook her brassiere.

A few minutes later, Harry briefed the deputies about the shooting out at the Miller farm. Mingo and Lucille were slouched in the cane chairs in front of Harry's desk staring up at him. Lucille was eating Cheetos, her fingers coated with orange crumbs. Mingo chewed on a toothpick, looking unconcerned and uninterested, but you could never tell with him.

Harry glanced down at the pad he'd been scribbling on. Had to write everything down these days, or he'd forget what he was going to say. "There's no hurry in getting out to the Miller farm," he said. "It'll take the BCA a while to get there anyway. Mingo, I want you to get me some prints. I mean exclusive of the print guy from the BCA. If they match the ones I got from the feds, I'm going to announce to the newspapers that the Polk County Sheriff's Office has captured the Weatherman bomber and that he appears to be implicated in our unsolved murders. Lucille, you have experience with prints?"

Lucille nodded.

Harry took another sip of water. "Good deal," he said. "I wouldn't know what to look for. Lucille, I want you to help me interrogate Rita and the Cochran boy again. Bring in the video recorder, too. Jenkins is busy at the school, so we'll just handle this ourselves, eh? We'll need to nail down the connection between Haskins and these kids. Haskins bought it at the Miller farm, so Rita knows him, right? The youngsters should fall all over themselves tattling, trying to avoid a murder rap."

After the deputies left, Harry smiled to himself. He'd break those kids and get all the credit for solving the case, and when Jenkins tried to run against him, he'd get zilch for votes.

Just as Harry was leaving his office for the pink room and the interrogation, Shirley handed him an envelope for Dave Jenkins, which had been hand-delivered by a kid from the high school who'd said it was important and that Jenkins should open it right away. Shirley had tried to explain that Jenkins was at the school, but the kid dropped the letter on her desk and ran. Harry figured he'd better open it. It was a note from Olive Randall. She had Mary Lou Forman and her baby, and she would punch their tickets if Jenkins didn't release her friends. This wasn't going to be so easy after all. Harry dropped the letter on his desk and dialed the school.

* * *

Olive snarled into the phone, "Get your ass over here, you little slut."

"Why, where are you?" Stormy said.

"I'm at the pay phone in front of Merry Widow's. We stayed in an empty trailer last night, next to the abandoned garage."

"What you doing there?"

"You little bitch. You didn't deliver the message, did you?"

"I did so. Did just like you told me to do. I had a little accident with Bob's van, though."

"I'll pick you up in five minutes. You be waiting out front."

"But—" Olive slammed the pay phone down.

* * *

Olive rummaged through Mary Lou's purse, looking for something to occupy herself on the trip out to the Miller farm. The blonde was at the wheel of the Acura, just passing the Value Stop coming up on Evergreen Cemetery.

"Wonder what the fuck happened to Lester?" she said to Stormy cowering in the back seat.

"You'll stick up for me with Bob, won't you?" she said.

"That old crate of a Mercury most likely broke down. Bob is probably having a bird by now. I told him I'd be back to pick him up before it got dark last night. And thanks to you I wasn't able to."

"I was scared."

"What was so hard about delivering a little note? Can you imagine what I was thinking when we drove up to the Merry Widow last night expecting to pick up Freddie and he wasn't there?"

Stormy was shivering. All she had on was a pajama top and blue jeans. "I didn't know what the note said."

"It said Dave should take Freddie to the Merry Widow Laundromat by eight and get the hell out or Mary Lou and the baby would get it. That's what it said, you little..."

"I'm sorry, I really am."

"I didn't know what to do. I couldn't very well break Freddie out myself like with Bob and the FBI. Shirley'd never go for the cigarette lighter trick. Who knew how tough she was."

"Pretty tough I'll wager," Stormy said.

"I thought about maybe starting another fire to distract David, but he has those two deputies now. And there was no answer at your house."

"So what are you going to do with them?"

Olive had no idea what to do with the blonde and the baby. Couldn't really follow through on her threat to get rid of them. She'd relied on Bob to do that.

"We'll see what Bob has to say."

The blonde was driving awfully slow, under thirty, and they hadn't even made it to the Outdoor yet. Mary Lou had been pretty damn compliant since she'd cracked her one with the cigarette lighter. Olive had surprised herself when she'd done that. Damn near started crying herself she'd been so freaked.

"I thought you were pissed at Bob over Nancy."

"So I'll kill two birds with one stone. I thought I was doing the right thing by taking the girls to see their father. I'd have wanted to see mine."

"How'd you know this Bob person was their father?" the blonde said.

"Who asked you?" Olive said. "You just drive the car and mind your own business."

"She seen their birth certificates," Stormy said.

Olive scowled at Stormy, then went back to inspecting the purse. The blonde had Huggies for the baby, peppermints, a billfold with a hundred and fifty dollars in cash, and two gold cards, which Olive removed since the blonde would never need them again. She sniffed the baby's hair. The little girl smelled wonderful, kind of like apples and baby powder, and she had such tiny hands and feet with such an adorable, peach-colored woolen cap. Olive was having qualms about the baby, since she brought back memories of when Nancy and Patty were that small. She was such a sober little girl. Olive remembered Nancy and Patty were always crying when they were that age.

The blonde had increased the speed of the Acura to forty miles an hour after she'd passed the double nickle sign on the outskirts of town. Olive could see the brown scab from the crack on the head through the blonde's hair, a mustache on the Mona Lisa. Mary Lou's hands were shaking a bit. Olive guessed hers probably would be, too, if she thought she was going to die.

Olive stroked the baby's hair. Sally. She'd given the blonde some shit about the name being the same as Charlie Brown's sister. It was a whole lot better than being named after Popeye's girlfriend. Olive touched the woman's arm; she could feel a slight stiffening. The blonde had been awfully skittish ever since she'd had to smack her.

She'd make amends. "I'm sorry about hitting you like that," she said. "I just did it cause I didn't know what else to do to get you to behave. Don't worry about your baby. I'd never hurt a little kid. Otherwise, it's a dog-eat-dog world, though. If you don't stand up for yourself, they'll eat you."

Mary Lou smiled. It was that kind of smile that gymnasts used during floor exercise, a Shannon Miller smile. She was now nearing a red-brick farmhouse about a mile from Soldier.

"Your name is Mary Lou Forman-Guild, ain't it?" Stormy said. "The customers at Andy's was talking about you one day."

"What's with the hyphenated last name?" Olive said.

Mary Lou shifted the car back into drive. "Kind of a test actually. I just wanted to see how my husband would react." Mary Lou reached over and straightened Sally's cap.

"I'd never do that," Stormy said.

"Yeah," Olive said, "how could you do that?"

Mary Lou reached down and turned up the air conditioner. "Just a bitch, I guess."

"Me too," Olive said. They both laughed. Olive bit the callus on her thumb, which was bleeding a bit she'd worried it so much. "I would imagine you did it because a lot of other women were doing it. It's hard to maintain one's individuality. See this hair? See this tattoo? Really stupid, huh? I have to give you credit there. You don't see that many women with hair all the way down to their tootsies."

Mary Lou grabbed a tissue out of her purse and wiped the drool from Sally's mouth.

Olive put one of the peppermints she'd found in the purse into her mouth, handed the roll back to Stormy.

The car went over a little bridge where a group of men were working on some kind of repair. One of them was holding a "slow" sign. Olive could see Mary Lou's eyes shift from the man back to her.

"Don't get any stupid ideas," Olive said. "Just keep your eyes on the road like a good girl and I won't have to mess up that pretty face."

The bridge and the men were growing smaller in the rearview mirror. The man with the "slow" sign was watching them drive off. Were the cops looking for the car? Or was he just another horny bastard ogling chicks?

Another half mile down the road, they passed Lester's shabby, green Merc.

"Lester's car!" Stormy said.

"Big surprise," Olive said. She turned back to Mary Lou, whose knuckles were turning white she was holding onto the wheel so tight.

"What were we talking about? Oh yeah, something about our dog-eat-dog existence. Yeah, they'll eat you, or eat at you, you know, kind of chip away at your identity. We killed those bastards because they was phonies. A teacher should be a teacher."

"Olive never killed anybody," Stormy said. "Mr. Ellis was an accident."

"It was the first time I ever saw somebody die. He had blue eyes, and they glowed for a minute, then dimmed. Kind of made me think there might be something to all that shit about an afterlife."

"She didn't have anything to do with Mr. Egge either."

"I don't need you to stick up for me, Squirt. I knew Bob was after Egge, and I'm just as guilty legally as he was. I was supposed to tell."

Mary Lou touched the scab on the side of her head. "I think you may have been expecting too much from your teachers, Olive," she said. "Everybody's human."

They were a good three miles out in the country by now, getting close to the turnoff that led to the clubhouse. Olive was tired.

She'd stayed up last night to make sure Mary Lou didn't try to get away.

"We like to think it's possible for people to be perfect, though, don't we?" Olive tried to tickle the baby, who just looked at her as if she were crazy. "Turn right there. We're going to take the access road to Miller's pasture. It's about a quarter mile ahead. Just before a little bridge."

"What's this book about?" Olive asked, holding a paperback entitled *I Hate You, Don't Ever Leave Me*.

Mary Lou put the car in cruise and looked away from the road. "It's about people who have had a traumatic experience, usually as a child, incest or rape, physical abuse by their parents, that kind of thing. That sort of upset is supposed to cause borderline psychosis. I just picked it up. I haven't really had anything like that happen to me, unless you count divorce." Mary Lou slowed down as they were coming to the bridge.

Olive put the book on the dashboard and said, "Hold it here. Pull over to the side of the road. I need to get my head together before I talk to Bob."

"She's going to have it out with him about her little sister Nancy."

"Shut up, will you? We need to take this private road which leads to the Fogel farm. Part way in we leave the car and walk the rest of the way to the Miller's back gate. It's only a few hundred yards."

Olive picked the book up off the dashboard, paged through it. "Psychosis, huh? Those people are really loony. That's like schizophrenia where you hear voices inside your head."

"I seen that movie *Sybil* about multiple personalities," Stormy said. "Sally Field was in it."

"So I could have that borderline psychosis thing if I was raped when I was young?" Olive said. "Doesn't seem to fit, though, cause me and Bob are still lovers."

* * *

Olive tried to get the baby to take a peppermint, but she wouldn't have anything to do with it.

Mary Lou wanted to slap her hand away. The baby could choke on that peppermint. Maybe she could talk Olive into giving herself up. She wasn't quite as nervous as she'd been driving out here. "Olive, did you know that some of the prisoners in the concentration camps during World War II actually fell in love with the guards? They were dependent on the jailers for everything. The guards actually became father figures."

"Where'd you get that?"

"I don't know, probably some psychology class I took. Everybody has to take psychology their freshman year of college."

No cars were passing on the road, although Mary Lou could hear a tractor in the distance. "Sounds like bullshit to me," Olive said, flipping the book into the back seat, barely missing Stormy. "You must think I'm really stupid. It was just sex. You remind me of that asshole Egge. He was giving me this lecture at the school, the week before Bob iced him, about how the superintendent shouldn't be allowed to do to other girls what he did to me. Bronson didn't do nothing to me. I'm the one decided to hustle him right in his own office."

Olive seemed to want to talk, didn't appear to be in any hurry to get to the clubhouse. If she could just touch her, Mary Lou felt the girl would give it all up. "You're only what, Olive, sixteen?" she said. "Young girls can't make objective decisions about sex. I was twenty-one my first time, and I wasn't ready."

The girl's body language changed. She put the baby on the seat and crossed her arms in front of her. Mary Lou reached out her hand, and Olive slapped it away. "Start the car, lady. It's just over the hill."

Mary Lou knew better than to dawdle this time. She started the car and turned into the Fogel driveway. As she reached the crest of the hill, she could see a cluster of vehicles under a tree a few hundred yards off to the right. One of them was Dave's Jeep.

This was the first time that Olive had looked really shook. "Don't get any stupid ideas. Just keep driving. We'll turn around in the yard and get the hell out of here. Rita must have blabbed."

* * *

Dave, along with Mingo, Lucille and Henderson, were sifting through the remains of what had been Bob Haskins's camp when the black sports car crested the hill. He recognized Mary Lou's car, but he couldn't hurdle the fence and reach the Jeep before the sports car turned around in the Fogel yard and shot by, doing a good sixty miles an hour, too damn fast for a dirt road.

Once at the Jeep, Dave tromped the accelerator and spun the wheels, tearing up tufts of sod, almost rolling the Jeep as he made the turn onto the farm road.

The black sports car was out of sight by the time he got to the county road leading back to Soldier. For a change, he was able to find his cellular without first having to search through all the debris. He dialed up the sheriff's office. "Shirley, Dave here. Tell Harry there's a brand-new, black sports car on its way. An Acura I think it is. Mary Lou Forman's. She's with Olive Randall. Tell him to keep the car in sight, but that I think they're heading for Shady Brook."

It took him about ten minutes to get back into town with the Jeep floored all the way. On the outskirts of town, the radiator gauge started doing three-sixties, and steam boiled out of the hood, but he didn't have time to stop and give Nellybelle water. He'd probably have to shoot her after this.

By the time he got to Shady Brook, the Acura was parked in front of the Randall's trailer, and Harry's cruiser was idling across the road. Harry was sitting straight up in his seat like a sitting duck. Dave parked behind him, crouching down as he approached the passenger side of the cruiser.

He leaned in the window. "Harry, you stupid shit, you better get down. She's probably got a gun in there." Harry wasn't answering. His head had fallen back on the headrest, his mouth hanging open. He was as white as a wedding gown. Dave took his pulse but couldn't find one. He dialed 911 and put Harry down on the seat. Harry would never tell another dirty joke.

* * *

Dave felt bad for Annie, kind of the same as he had when his own dad died. He was never very close to his dad, they hadn't had much in common, a four generation farmer and a town kid in a farm boy's body.

As he thought about his father, getting kind of misty, he noticed the cruiser was on fire. A cigarette was burning a large hole in the seat. He remembered all the times he'd begged Harry not to smoke around him.

"I told you so!" he yelled. Too bad the old goat couldn't hear him. You couldn't tell those old fogies anything. They always knew better. He got out of the cruiser, completely disdaining the possibility Olive had a gun, went to his Jeep, which had steam rolling out from under the hood, and got out his jug of water he'd been using as a stopgap for the defective thermostat. He hurried back to the cruiser and stifled the fire, wetting Harry in the process. He'd tried to be careful, but some of the water rolled down between the poor guy's legs.

After he'd sat staring at Harry for a few minutes, wondering how much a dead body looks like a piece of furniture, the ambulance showed up from Crookston, and he helped the attendants carry Harry's body to the emergency vehicle after they'd first made sure that Harry was really dead.

"The stain between his legs is from the water I used to put out the fire," he said. They gave him the fish eye.

After the ambulance was gone, Dave studied the best way to get Olive out of that trailer. Obviously Olive's mother and her little sisters weren't home, or she never would have come back to the trailer. If he could find Nancy and Patty, he could get them to plead with Olive to give herself up. Nope, couldn't exploit children like that, even if he did have the foggiest idea where they were.

What else? Couldn't use tear gas cause of the baby. He could call her and try to talk her out of there. They got along well. Why not? Because she was obviously nuts, that's why. Haskins was in the SDS—he'd probably convinced her that the world was a pretty shitty place, and that everyone in authority was in it for himself. *Pretty much the same way I feel about things myself*, he thought.

As Lucille and Mingo arrived in Mingo's newly salvaged 4X4, Dave picked up the cellular from the front seat of the Jeep where he'd dropped it and dialed Moe's house, then strolled a little distance away from the others.

"Pleasiac Web Design."

"Hey, guy, glad I caught you," he said. "I'm over at Olive's. We have a situation. She's holding Mary Lou and her baby hostage."

"I told you she was off her nut."

"Why'd you go out with her then?"

"Probably because of your constant nagging about me getting a girlfriend."

"Listen, I haven't got time to argue. Get your ass over here."

"You need me to talk her out?"

"No, I want to use you as a shield."

"Give me ten minutes."

Dave walked back toward the Jeep, where Mingo and Lucille had been standing like movie placards alongside the Jeep while he traded barbs with Moe.

He tossed the cellular in the Jeep. "Don't you two think it might be a good idea to take cover?" he said.

Lucille gaped at the trailer as if she couldn't perceive the problem. Mingo pushed out his lower lip. "We figured if you were walking around out in the open gabbing on the phone, it couldn't be a hostile situation."

Everybody gave him a hard time. Dave moved between the two deputies, took them by the elbows. "Forget that," he said. "Go and get the people out of those trailers. Then block off the entrance to the trailer court. Oh yeah, let Moe Pleasiac in when he comes. He knows the girl."

Mingo got the bullhorn out of the trunk, bawled out, "Please come out of your trailers and keep down!"

It worked, as people streamed from the trailers, running for the exit. If Olive had an automatic weapon in there, most of them would be either dead or wounded.

Dave had a thought. The handwriting on the Designated Hitter letter matched Olive's. It had said she had no need for a gun. He wasn't going to wait for Moe so he could take all the credit.

Before he had a chance to move toward the trailer, he noticed a crumpled pack of Kents and a lighter lying on the ground next to Harry's cruiser, and stooped to pick them up. When he touched the lighter, he could see Harry, clear as the North Star on a cloudless night, and he was saying, "Hey, Jenkins, you hear the one about Buddy Holly?...No?...How did they know Buddy had dandruff?...Don't know, do yah?...They found his head and shoulders in the bushes."

Dave wadded his fists, rubbed his good eye. Apparently he hadn't washed his hands of Harry's jokes after all.

Chapter 24

Blond and Bashful

"When in disgrace with fortune and men's eyes
I all alone beweep my outcast state,
And trouble deaf heaven with my bootless cries."
— Shakespeare, Sonnet 29, l. 1

When Olive peeked out the window, she saw her neighbors, many still wearing bathrobes, streaming from the other trailers, children and pets in tow, rushing toward the entrance of the court. An ambulance, its taillights flashing red, was making the turn onto Meade.

Something else strange was going on, as she could see these peculiar shapes floating along behind David as he approached her door.

She closed her eyes, touched the tips of her fingers to her forehead; it felt a little hot. Could be something she ate. Probably not, though, since her mother was such a fussbudget about washing every little morsel her children consumed, cooking it until all the taste was gone.

Olive opened her eyes. The spooks were still there.

One of them was dressed in a Minnesota Gophers sweatshirt and baseball cap. Mr. Egge always wore that outfit on Grub Day during Homecoming week. The other spook was decked out in a sheriff's uniform. She looked over at the cruiser next to David's Jeep. The driver side door was open. She'd heard Harry Kline had had a heart attack. The ambulance must have been for him.

Closing the chintz curtain, she went back to check if the coffee was perked. She'd been fixing breakfast, and she always liked a cup of joe with her pancakes.

"Look out the window and tell me what you see," she said to Stormy, who was sitting hunched up on the pullout sofa, staring into space, as if at any moment an asteroid would come crashing through the roof.

343

Stormy drew the curtain, came face to face with David. She gave a start and said, "It's the Deputy!"

"Nobody else, nothing unusual?"

"You expectin' somebody else?"

Olive poured a cup, took it over to the window, half believing the spooks would be gone. But no, they were levitating just a bit behind David, who was about to knock on the door. Before David could knock, she opened it, trying to be as cheery as possible. "There ain't no reason to evacuate those people, David," she said. "I don't have any artillery in here. Just this little derringer."

She didn't really expect him to be as gullible as the blonde. Although they could probably pass through walls, she kept the door open a shade longer so the spooks could get in.

If they were real, they could be coming for her, like the grim reaper, only she'd always pictured him wearing a hooded cloak, and faceless, brandishing a sickle. She hadn't thought much about an afterlife. Bob had always said that there was no God, that what you saw was what you got, and if that was the case, why be good?

David took the derringer out of her hand. She didn't fight it. "That's just a cigarette lighter, Olive," he said. "I know you don't really want to hurt anyone, especially a woman and her little baby."

He removed the USS Lake Champlain hat the gang was always on the lookout for. There was a spot of red on his chin where he'd nicked himself shaving. When his eyes met hers, they softened. She remembered the first time he'd arrested her for breaking curfew. He'd called her "Miss." No one had ever called her that before.

"Are you mad at me?" she said, searching his eyes. Never could stand for anybody to be mad at her.

He bent the brim on his cap, even more severely. "We're all worried about you," he said.

All? Could he see them, too? The outlines behind him began to take shape. The overweight sheriff smiled. Mr. Egge moaned, lifted his maroon cap, scratched his head. He hadn't been such a bad sort, for a principal, even if she had threatened to kill him. He got her that job at Andy's during the summer when nobody else would hire her. Could it be she felt guilty about not trying to stop Bob? Was that why she was having hallucinations?

She glanced back at David. "Do you see those...?"

"Those what, Olive?"

"Forget it. You'd never believe me." She still needed to get Freddie out of jail, spooks or no spooks. "If you think you're going to march on in here and take Mary Lou and the baby, you've got another thing coming. Not until you let Freddie out of that jail."

"This isn't the way to go about it," David said.

"I might not have a gun, but I'll claw your eyes out."

David looked down at her hands. "You don't have any finger-nails, Olive."

"Yeah, well I can bite and kick. You'll have to kill me before I let you have the blonde and her brat."

The sheriff and Mr. Egge, still standing near David, shook their heads. Mr. Egge tried to touch her arm. She took a step backward.

"You're not frightened of *me*, are you Olive?" David said.

"That'll be the day. Well, don't just stand there. If you're gonna make a pest of yourself, get on in here. Do you like potato pan-cakes? My sisters and me, we make 'em all the time." She moved over to the stove where she turned up the heat on the frying pan. She flinched from the lard, splattering and popping, stinging her arms.

David followed her over to the stove, turned down the heat. "Where are Mary Lou and the baby, Olive?"

"That's for me to know and you to find out."

"They're in the bedroom," Stormy said. "We didn't hurt them at all."

"You always spoil my fun, Stormy. You having these cakes or not, David?"

"I'd love some," he said. He was holding his cap bill in both hands as if he were afraid he was going to violate some principle of etiquette. She couldn't really blame him for acting so awkward. How are you supposed to act around someone you think is a mur-deress?

Olive picked up the bowl and poured another dollop into the pan. "Take a seat at the kitchen table," she said. "I'll bring you some."

He stepped over to the kitchen table and stood behind a chair as if he were waiting for her to sit.

She added more ingredients to the bowl, picked up the wire whip and beat the batter. "Go on, sit down and we'll talk turkey."

David took a chair, leaning back as he always seemed to do every time she saw him sit. Egge and the sheriff were standing behind him, looking lost. Interesting that they were wearing clothes. She would have expected them to be transparent, like in the movies or in the Saturday morning cartoons. But no, they seemed as real as David, if a bit paler.

She put a finger in her mouth and licked the batter. "Freddie's my best friend in all the world," she said. "I just can't let you put him in Stillwater or St. Cloud Reformatory. You know what happens to homosexuals in places like that." She put several golden pancakes on a plate and handed them to David along with utensils and some syrup. He took up the fork and set to eating.

"It's all my fault really. If I hadn't told Bob about Egge's superior attitude, and that I'd like to kill the dickhead, Freddie would be free as a bird now." She put a hand to her mouth, belatedly realizing that Mr. Egge was right in front of her. He smiled as if she'd been talking about some other Egge.

David stopped chewing, regarded her with that I'm-your-only-friend expression he'd been using ever since he first put foot in the door. "These are great," he said. "I haven't had any since before Desert Storm, out on the farm. Freddie set fire to the school. I can't let him go."

"But he didn't have anything to do with either of the murders."

David wiped his mouth with a napkin. "We may be able to get the charges reduced, if there's some sort of psychological disability."

"You mean like pyromania? He ain't no fire bug!"

"What would you like me to say, Olive?"

Olive got the coffee pot, the kind with the metal filter and the tube that you had to fit into the slot—much better than the automatic kind, despite the coffee grounds at the bottom of the cup—poured him a cup, set it down in front of him. She rubbed the side of her head. Couldn't get used to the bristly feel of it. The spooks were leering covetously at the pancakes.

David wiped up the last of the syrup with a forkful of pancake. "Why don't you tell me what happened from the beginning, Olive? You know you can trust me. We've always gotten along, haven't we?"

Suddenly there was a knock on the door, one of those rat tatta tat tat tats. It had to be Howard, he always did that. She scooted over, flung the door open.

"What the hell do you want?" she said. "Don't you know we've got the Purple Gang in here? We're going to kill all the hostages."

Howard stepped back a few paces and almost fell off of the stoop, tripping over those embarrassing Jesus shoes. Beethoven scowled at her from the face of his T-shirt. She'd never had the chance to dress him right.

Two more spooks came in behind him. One of them, a bug-eyed fat man wearing a fishing hat and an orange Gore-Tex vest, barged past Howard and sat next to Stormy on the slime-green sleeper. The last one was a tall thin man with a shock of brown hair covering one eye who followed the little fat one over to the couch and perched on the arm.

"Dave told me to come on over," Howard said. "He thinks I can help smooth things over."

He needed a haircut. The ends were curling up in the back and he had a funny V back there. "Where'd he get that idea?" she said. "I haven't heard from you since we went to that movie, and we danced to Hank Williams. I'm seriously pissed. Get your ass in here." Olive snatched Beethoven's face and dragged Howard into the trailer.

"'Bout time you got here," David said. He'd finished his pancakes and was slurping down the rest of his coffee.

"Is everybody all right?" Howard said. "Where's Mary Lou and the baby?"

The tall spook's eyes followed Howard as he moved to the kitchen counter and poured himself a cup of coffee. He whispered something in the fat one's ear, and the fat one clapped the tall one on the back. Egge and the sheriff stayed where they were, behind David at the kitchen table.

Olive loosened her apron and put it on the counter. "I'll go get 'em. David was beginning to think I'd already bumped them off." She headed toward the bedroom, giggling as she went, and returned with Mary Lou holding the baby in a bassinet decorated with yellow butterfly appliqués. One of them fell off and clattered to the floor, unbutterfly-like. Howard walked over and picked it up.

Mary Lou's cheeks were colored with red blotches, as if she'd been sleeping face down. If she had been napping, she'd found the time, somehow, to do the hundred strokes. The tresses were as lustrous and free of snarls as ever.

"Hello David and Howard," Mary Lou said. "Olive was just making some pancakes for us. We were talking about the best way to deal with this unpleasant situation." She took the butterfly from Howard but couldn't seem to get it back on the bassinet.

Olive stepped over to the TV, pushed the "on" button. "The Young and the Damned," her favorite soap, was on. It was about these sisters, Amanda and Terri, who'd lost their parents in their preteens and been separated, both in love with the same corporate pirate. She hadn't seen it in a while.

"That's a good one," Mary Lou said, patting the baby on the back.

"Both of them are sluts," Olive said.

"I think Amanda is prettier," Stormy said. "And she dresses better."

Olive slumped on the slime-green couch, next to the tall drink of water with the hair in his eyes, and put her feet up on the coffee table, something her mother always forbade. "I'm gonna stop watching that smut. Let's get on with this then, huh?"

"Why don't you tell us about the Ellis murder?" David said.

"Rita killed that phony geek when he tried to feel me up."

"That Rita's a mean bitch," Stormy said. "Once she held my head under water and wouldn't let me up."

"Will you shut up, Stormy? This is my story. Where was I now? Oh yeah—we got called in for a parental conference, Rita and me, 'cause of that dress code nonsense, when he started scoping me out again as if he'd never seen tits. It was about six o'clock and every-body was gone. Rita and me never told our parents to show since this guy was just acting principal, you know, and we thought we could handle the creep."

The bug-eyed spook with the fishing hat broke up in hysterics. The tall one, who could have been a double for Hawkeye Pierce, shushed him.

"He was practicing his putting," Olive said, "and he offered to show me how. I knew he was gonna try something since it was so late, and everybody was gone. I guess he didn't expect Rita to show up, it wouldn't have been the first time. Anyway, I thought I could flirt with him some, maybe give him a little feel, and get him to for-get about the six months of detention we already had. Guys gotta get their rocks off. I couldn't blame him with that hogger he had for a wife. Rita gets jealous, though, and she nailed him behind the ear with his driver."

"What about the letter?" David said.

"Yeah, that was pretty stupid, wasn't it? We just sat around staring at the body for a while, then we busted up the office and wrote that Jack the Ripper letter." She sat up a little straighter, met David's eyes. "I'll bet you were wondering how we knew all that stuff."

Stormy jumped in again. "I overheard you and Mel Kline when you were talking at Andy's."

"Yeah, and she snoops around in your stuff when she delivers your paper. She's the one who slit the tires on your Jeep."

"I didn't want to," Stormy whined. "Bob made me."

Olive shifted from the couch to the kitchen table opposite David, entwined her fingers behind her head, massaging her neck.

David got up and poured another cup of coffee. Black, no sugar. "What about Father Mischke?" he said.

Mary Lou seemed awfully quiet. Olive glanced over at her. She was curled up in an armchair by the door nursing the baby in front of God and everybody. She never would have pegged her for the nursing-in-public kind.

Olive turned back to David. "Bob hates priests," she said. "I told you, didn't I, Howard? He said the priest could identify him. I don't know how. I told you about him 'cause I was afraid he was gonna try something with Nancy. Bob's dead, ain't he? He told me he was going to off the old priest, which is kinda why I went to see Father Mischke that time he told me about the threatening phone call."

"I can vouch for that," Stormy said.

"Freddie and me tried to save him, and we did, didn't we? That should count for something. If Freddie were just a crazed pyro, he wouldn't even care about an old priest." Olive stared past David at Egge and the sheriff who were frowning and nodding. "Does anybody besides me see those two guys back there?" Olive pointed toward the wall behind David.

The room grew quiet, so noiseless Olive could hear Howard's asthmatic breathing. David gazed at Howard and then over at Mary Lou and the kid. He didn't seem too surprised that she was nursing the baby.

One of the ghosts, the tall one with the unruly hair, had drifted over to stand beside Howard. He had one arm around Howard's shoulder, although Howard didn't seem to notice.

Howard was the first to speak. "What do you see, Olive? Describe them in exact detail and don't leave anything out."

"They look like people."

"Is one of them tall and lanky with a cowlick?"

"Yeah, he's standing right next to you."

David picked up the derringer, lit the flame, seemed to hold it over his palm, then snuffed it. The baby gurgled. "We really should get on—"

"It's my dad!" Howard said.

"It's too much booze and drugs!" David said.

"My dream encyclopedia says that the spirit world coexists with this world," Howard said, "separated by a differing rate of vibration. You raise your vibration rate, the spirit lowers his, and shazam! you got spirits."

"Knock it off, Moe," David said. "Olive has gone through a very traumatic experience."

"You think I'm crazy don't you?" Olive said. "The two behind you favor Sheriff Kline and Mr. Egge. There's another one, a little fat guy with bug eyes, sitting on the sofa. They're making me feel all shivery." She massaged her arms as if she'd just come in from a howling blizzard.

"I believe you, Olive," Howard said.

David put his chin in his hand, gave Howard a pleading look, then turned back to Olive. "What about the fire?"

Olive pushed a wisp of hair out of her eyes. "Freddie's not a pyro, he was only trying to cover for Rita. He's a very loyal guy, let me tell you. But Rita's too stupid to handle something like that. If I hadn't been there when Ellis croaked, she wouldn't have known whether to shit or go blind."

David wrote something in his ever-present notebook.

"Who knew that old buzzard Forman would be wearing a helmet?" Stormy said. "If anybody deserved to die—"

"Sorry, Mary Lou, but it's true. Rita was so clueless! You either nix the plan, or you take him out some other way. You can't leave a witness." She was rather surprised at herself, since she was about as violent as the batter in the pancake bowl.

Howard put the coffee cup on the counter, grabbed a chair and pulled it over to where Olive was sitting. "What about Bronson's fingerprints, and the bloody rain suit found in his garage?" he asked, searching her face.

She reached over and brushed a hair off of his shoulder. "Bronson was fucking Stormy, too," she said.

Moe's face reddened. She reached over, stroked his cheek. "I'm sorry, but you wouldn't call it making love now, would you? That's why Charlie wouldn't say anything in court. Once was an indiscretion, twice is perversion."

"You cow," Stormy said, hiding her face in her hands. "Wait till I tell them about you."

The corners of Howard's mouth turned down. "Stormy can't be more than thirteen!"

"Almost fourteen," Stormy said. "Half the seventh grade class is already doing it. It ain't just me!"

Olive would have to make sure her little sisters had proper values by the time they got to be Stormy's age.

"I don't understand how you could condone—"

Olive gave Howard her *aren't-you-wet-behind-the-ears* look. "Easy for you to talk. Some women already had babies at that age during the Middle Ages. And the aristocrats could go to a peasant cottage and just take any young girl they wanted. I read that in *The Distant Mirror*. Things haven't changed much."

"One more thing," Dave said, "before we head over to the office. How about Uncle Bob? I know he killed Egge and went after Father Mischke. What about motive? I can't believe he murdered Egge because *you* were upset with him."

This was harder to explain. It sounded so juvenile. She cleared her throat, found she couldn't talk, cleared it again. "Bob remembered Egge. He'd been to a parent-teacher conference with my mother once. 'A pissant high school principal correcting a college instructor's grammar' was how he put it. Kept calling Egge 'Szymanski'."

This time David's face flushed. He surveyed the room as if he were really trying to see the spooks. "Hold still, Olive," he said. "Let me get this straight. Huntzinger killed Mr. Egge because he'd corrected his grammar?"

"You got it. We never really split up after my mom threw him out. Kind of cool how he managed it, really, with my mom on the lookout for him and everything. Disguised himself as a burned-out vet, used to brag about how naive Harry Kline was."

David slapped the table. "I knew it! Why the hell didn't I keep my eyes on the bastard?"

"Anyway, Bob and me just kept on doing it. He turned me on to cocaine, even sold some for him. And he taught me, Rita, Freddie, Lester Krueger and some of the other girls all about the protest movement."

"He said that communism is the only fair system of government cause everything gets divvied up equal," Stormy said.

Olive gave the girl her *will-you-get-your-own-story?* stare. "Bob thought it was obscene that someone like Bill Gates could have billions of dollars, and children in Appalachia didn't get enough to eat."

"Tell us about the clubhouse on the Miller farm," Howard said.

"That's where he used to do his preaching," Stormy said, "out there on the Miller farm."

"I was coming to get him when you spotted me. Bob used to be in the SDS when he was going to Berkeley."

"Hear that about Berkeley?" Howard said to David. "Maybe now you'll listen when I try to tell you about dream symbolism."

"Let the girl talk," David said.

"Bob said even Henry David Thoreau and Thomas Jefferson believed in civil disobedience. Everything was going so rotten that it was our duty to strike back. He really lost it when the air went out of communism. He couldn't see any hope for the world after that, started using even more heavily. He stole Ray Miller's cows cause he was losing all of his drug customers. Even they thought he was too weird to be around. Freddie wanted to turn him in when we found out about Egge, but I wouldn't let him. I changed my mind when Bob started ogling and touching Nancy."

The spirits behind David were shaking their heads in disbelief. Olive scanned the room. She'd lived here all of her life, and she knew she only had a few minutes left before she'd be leaving for good. She focused on the curio stand where her mother kept family pictures. Olive and the girls on their first communions. Getting on the bus on the first day of school. Blowing out the candles on birthday cakes.

"I still don't get it," Howard said. "Egge dissed your Uncle Bob at that parent conference, Egge lectured you about Bronson and you told Bob about it, but why did he spray that curse on Egge's back?"

Her head was getting so heavy. "Pay attention why don't yah? I said he got Egge and Szymanski confused. He was pretty wired up on drugs, and he's hated teachers, especially administrators, ever since he got kicked out of high school. I didn't really believe he'd do it. Most of the time he was kind of full of shit, you know what I mean? Said he was a former college professor. I knew he was never no professor. He had all these ideas for making money that never came to nothin'. Once, he even made plans to hold up the bank. I talked him out of that one."

"The other tracks out at the Egge murder scene?" David said.

Olive slumped down on a hassock. "Lester went along with Bob the morning he killed Egge. He was waiting in the clearing beyond the quarries with the van. Just like a mongrel dog, Bob could kick the shit out of him and Lester'd come back for more."

"Anything else?"

"Nah, that's about it. I'll go peaceful if you promise you'll do everything you can to help Freddie."

David nodded.

"I maybe coulda stopped Rita, but I was preoccupied with Nancy." Olive ducked her head. More strands of hair were hanging in her eyes. She didn't have the energy to sweep them back.

"Olive," David said, "would you get up and put your hands on top of the counter there? I've got to cuff you. It's the law."

This gave Olive a surge of adrenalin. She couldn't believe he was that much of a cowboy. She couldn't let him cuff her until she could hide her razor blade in her secret place. She'd built up some pretty good callus from going barefoot and from waitressing during the summers and on weekends during the school year. She'd read that Houdini got out of all those chains by hiding a key in a slit between the callus on his feet and the skin. Nobody would ever think to look there.

"I need to use the bathroom before we go," she said. "Okay? I promise I won't try anything."

"I can't let you go alone, Olive. If you did anything to yourself, I'd look pretty foolish, now wouldn't I?"

"I'll go with her," Mary Lou said.

Thank God for the blonde; she was so gullible.

Olive took down her pants and sat on the commode. Mary Lou averted her eyes, tried to find something to occupy herself with. Olive grinned.

"I got chigger bites all over my ankles when I was out swinging Nancy and Patty on the oak tree, and I can't keep from scratching. Would you check the medicine cabinet for some calamine lotion?" Her mom didn't have any calamine lotion, so Olive knew that would keep Mary Lou occupied with the door to the chest obscuring her vision. While she was peeing, Mary Lou would keep her eyes averted and keep searching for that calamine lotion until Olive said quit.

Olive cut, with one hand bracing her wrist, careful not to hurt herself, a dead giveaway. The blade slid in the slot as if it were meant to be there. She'd have to walk on the balls of her feet like a dancer. Shouldn't be a problem. Freddie had said she was very light on her feet—that time they'd crashed the Prom and Egge'd had a bird cause freshman, they'd been freshman then, weren't allowed.

Did David really think she was stupid enough to try to cut herself right in front of him? All they'd have to do was put a tourniquet on her, and the doctor could sew her up good as new.

When she returned from the can, David was still following procedure. "I need to read you your rights, okay Olive?"

She got up and did what she was told as he placed a hand on one of her shoulders, snapping the cuff shut with the other. She imagined what it would be like with him. Kind of like it had been with Freddie at first, up in a hayloft in the country, just holding each other, kissing some and taking their time. Until he'd realized he preferred guys. Seemed like ages ago, before sugarless gum, before rock and roll music, before female orgasms.

Chapter 25

Everybody Wants to Be James Dean

"Thou wilt be condemned into everlasting redemption for this."
— Shakespeare, *Much Ado About Nothing*, IV, ii, 60

Dave stood on the top step of the dugout, looking out toward center field, where some boys were teetering on the rickety scaffolding in front of the scoreboard. The Climax team still used clumsy signboards to keep score, and the boys were in charge. One of them dropped a card onto the field and was promptly pushed off the scaffolding. When he tried to climb back up, the others stepped on his fingers.

Mingo clapped him on the shoulder. "I'm bummed, Dude."

"Couldn't come up with enough money for your Mescalero field trip, huh?"

"Nope, that's coming along fine. It's my dad."

"What about your dad?"

"He says, ordinarily he'd love to see me, but he's got these three kids, my half brothers and sisters, and he never told them about his first marriage."

"That's the pits, Dude."

"I don't know if I'll be much good today, man."

"You've always got your Cousin Cecil."

"That's true."

"From what you've said, Cecil's ten times the stud your real old man is."

"Kind of short, but otherwise he chews nails."

Dave pointed to a section of the grandstand where Charlie Bronson and Sue Egge were sitting behind the backstop off to one side, near the port-a-potty. You couldn't mistake that five o'clock shadow. Hardly anyone else in that part of the grandstand. Some townsfolk didn't approve of his dalliance with another man's wife, and they'd heard rumors about young girls. "Kind of surprised to see him here," Dave said.

"Probably just rubbing it in."

355

"Heard he was moving to Minneapolis to take a job as an executive with some investment outfit."

"No shit."

"Bronson's a very versatile human being," Dave said. "In order to do his job, you need to be a leader, a diplomat, a public relations expert, a business manager, a psychologist, a mediator, a negotiator, an architect, and a curriculum expert. At least that's what he said during this school board meeting I was at when someone asked him to justify his eighty thousand dollar salary."

"You forgot one," Mingo said.

"What, that he's a horse's ass?"

"Close enough."

"If there was any justice, that man would be standing trial for statutory rape on at least two counts. But neither Olive nor Stormy will cooperate."

"Fuck it. Let's get out there and tear these Sex Pistols a new asshole."

"Yeah, let's win one for Jerry." They slapped palms, and Mingo sprinted to his spot at the hot corner to take fielding practice.

Dave ambled out to the mound—he had to pitch since he hadn't found a replacement for Egge—and turned to survey the outfield. Albertson Plumbing, Old Dutch Potato Chips, Blatz Beer, Winston Cigarettes, and Ford Motor Company had all long ago purchased billboard space on the outfield fence. The signs were fading.

The third base foul line looked like a used car lot. Mostly older model Chevys, Fords and Volkswagens, some of them gunning their engines, all candidates for a cracked windshield. Elmer Frick strolled from car to car taking tickets. Fifty cents for a single, a maximum of two dollars a car. The Bloomer twins were smooching with their boyfriends of the moment on the hood of a cherry '55 Ford. A group of younger boys were crouched on the grass taking lessons. One of the older boys noticed and swore at them.

Dave felt a drop of rain on his arm. Ominous clouds were drifting overhead—the radio had said there was a fifty percent chance of rain. He scooped up a handful of dirt and began rubbing up the ball. Dave hated pitching. Something happened to your batting average when you pitched. He turned back toward the Bloomer twins. His own love life was in a state of flux. He'd fallen back into bed with Annie Kline. The one date he'd had with Mary Lou had been a total disaster. Wouldn't stop talking about her ex, spent an hour and a half looking for casual shoes prior to their dinner reservation, kept hinting about him taking a job in Chicago. No fucking way.

Annie Kline, taking fielding practice at short, snagged a dribbler and fired, the ball thudding into her brother Mel's mitt at first base. What an arm. She was more Dave's type—the kind of girl you could watch the Super Bowl with.

After Dave had rubbed up the ball, he began mutilating the spheroid with a razor blade so he could at least get the thing to flutter some, hopefully causing the ball to dip or dart just before it got to the hitter. Gamesmanship, they called it—nothing wrong with it. Like in football, where the center moved the pigskin ahead before he snapped it.

Sam Frobisher called "Play ball!" and motioned for the first batter to step into the box. Sam was a retired shoe repairman who took himself very seriously when it came to umping softball games. He would not abide any swearing because there were ladies present and had thrown many a player out of the game for much less.

Dave checked the crowd again. Mary Lou sat in the first row behind the backstop teaching Sally to wave. Off to her right, under a red and white canopy, Moe, along with Mrs. Mac who had recently retired from slow pitch, was hawking brats for the school band. Moe had been coming to see Olive at the jail regularly. If the laughter coming from her cell was any indication, Moe had been doing a good job cheering her up, he and the dog Chopin.

Dave got the first hitter to ground out to Annie at short, walked the second batter, and got the third to waft a weak fly ball to Lucille in left. Harley Barnhouser was up.

"You're going down, Meatface!" Dave screamed.

"I'm taking you deep, Needledick," Barnhouser yelled. Barnhouser's stentorian breathing was so loud Lucille could probably hear him out in left. Barnhouser inched forward in the batter's box, waving the bat in a tight circle. The more Dave waited the more likely the hyper little turd would get himself out. If only this were baseball, he could dust the dirtbag off, put him on his ass in the mud, but all he had was this stupid oversized nerf ball. He turned his back and grooved a deeper slice out of the cover.

Just as he released the pitch, the man on first took off for second, and Barnhouser punched the pill just over Johnny Logan's head into short right field where it nestled in the bluish-green sod, twenty feet from Logan's grasp. The runner scored easily. Over at first, Barnhouser jumped up and down on the bag like a monkey on a trampoline.

In the third Dave bunted his way on, and Lucille launched one into the cornfield behind the leftfield fence. He kissed her on the mouth when she crossed home plate.

Barnhouser came to bat in the fifth with the bases loaded and the score still two to one. Harley nailed one just to Annie's right, seemingly out of reach, but Annie dove, came up with the ball in the webbing, and rifled it to first, just nipping the sliding Barnhouser. Anybody knows you don't slide into first base; you run through it, according to Joe Morgan on ESPN. Joe should know, he was the second baseman on the Big Red Machine and considered by some to be the greatest second baseman of all time. Barnhouser thought he was safe, the language got a little blue, and Frobisher threw him out. Dave motioned for Mingo to take his place on the mound. He didn't care any more. The devil had been exorcised.

* * *

The American Legion honor guard's firing of the twenty-one gun salute caught Dave completely by surprise, causing him to nudge Moe, who was standing too close to Harry Kline's freshly dug grave.

"Watch it, will you?" Moe said, as the smell of cordite drifted out over the mass of Legionnaire hats.

"Stupid clowns," Dave said. "The Klines aren't even here yet."

"I wonder what's keeping them?" Moe said, goggling down at the grave he'd barely avoided falling into. Could've smudged his blue-striped dress shirt with the red bowtie and suspenders and brand-new sneakers.

Dave adjusted his mountie hat, which had come askew. "Probably still trying to scrape the mud off. The Kline boys and I spent all morning digging that there grave. Or I should say, they dug and I watched, cause of the cast."

"Haven't the Klines ever heard of a backhoe?"

Dave pulled him back a bit, away from the cavernous hole. "Annie saw this feature story on the news about a cemetery in the South where they don't use backhoes to dig graves. The town's people take turns. I went along to supervise."

"You're a true friend."

"I am. I even helped Annie pick out an inscription for Harry's headstone. 'Forgive O Lord, my little jokes on thee and I'll forgive the great big one on me.' Isn't that perfect? That's from a poem by Robert Frost."

"Cool."

"Did you do something to your hair?" Dave said, ruffling Moe's moptop. "You look more like a Beatle today than a Stooge."

Moe slapped Dave's hand away. "Don't do that. It took me an hour to get it styled. Moe is dead. I want to be called Howard from now on. I'm going to take advantage of the college option program next year, and Moe doesn't sound like a theoretical physicist."

"Excuse me Stephen J. Hawkings." Dave kicked at the mound of fudge-like soil next to the grave. The stuff smelled like a mulch pile.

"I'll worry about you when I'm gone. Have you decided whether you're going to run for sheriff, or tie the knot and take over the bank?" Moe took one of those rattailed combs out of his back pocket and ran it through his hair.

"Mary Lou and I are quits."

Moe staggered, as if he'd just been hit with a shovel. "What happened? I thought she was your dream girl."

"Pick a reason. The woman was the Imelda Marcos of the Midwest. She's money, I'm burnt toast. She wants to live in the Stinking Cabbage."

"It's your life I guess. I've always felt you and Annie were a better match anyway."

"That's what she thinks. Just last night Annie said something about how I reminded her of Harry. I was just drifting off to sleep around midnight, when she poked me in the ribs. 'You know what?' she said. 'I've always known the kind of man I wanted: a big, dumb, humble guy who worked in a gas station and played with the kids, a small town type who hated big cities and would never even think of moving, even for more money. You fit the bill, Phil.'"

"A big, dumb, humble guy, huh?" Moe said. "I don't know about that last part."

"You'll pay. Anyway Annie was so appreciative when I went to the house to tell the family personally about Harry's death that she dumped Marshall Preston on the spot. I got a little misty thinking about my own dad, and Annie must have thought I was teary-eyed over Harry, which I was a little."

"Everybody needs a foil—bosses are always good for that. Now that you're acting sheriff, you may find Mingo and Lucille have changed their opinion of you."

"I'm changing *my* opinion of them. Mingo was pretty stupid with that bullhorn, and Lucille's junk food habit is beginning to annoy me."

Dave squinted up at the sun. Not a cloud in the sky. As blue as a pair of faded Levis. "Nicer day today than Egge's funeral. I was just over there checking out his grave before you got here. I haven't had any little messages since before I went in to coax Olive out of that trailer."

"You could have been more supportive of Olive, considering what you'd been through."

"Just doing my job, son."

Moe sat on the top of one of the gravestones, dangling his legs. "I meant to tell you I talked to Egge the day before he died. Sometimes I'd get a little bored practicing the piano, so I'd go up to his office and shoot the breeze. He apologized for not doing better by me. I told him the teachers helped me quite a bit, by showing me what to read and that. I was trying to make him feel better, you know."

"What's a little white lie?"

"He asked me where I get my inquisitiveness. I said most likely it was in the genes. I guess he thought that if he could find out what made me want to learn, he could pass it on to the other kids."

Dave sat next to Moe. "I could have told him what prevents kids from wanting to learn. Everybody on God's green earth wants to be James Dean."

"Why James Dean?"

"Not him so much, but somebody like him. You want to be like Mike, and you buy his hundred dollar tennies, or you want to be Elvis Presley, so you comb your hair in a ducktail and sneer a lot. The girls want to be Farah Fawcett, and they get their hair fixed like hers."

"I doubt that anybody remembers who Farah Fawcett is."

"These days they all want to be Courtney Love and they get their bodies pierced and tattooed. In other words, everybody wants to be cool. Kids act up in class because they want to be with it. They jump from the second floor railing because they want to prove that they're just as bitchin' as Batman."

Moe smirked. "You ought to write that down, I'm sure Hildegard would love it."

"Should be some crow sandwich on her menu."

"I wouldn't say that if I were you, if you want to be the next sheriff. I must say you look *marvelous* in that uniform."

While Moe and Dave were talking, the hearse arrived, and the Kline boys emerged and filed toward the rear door. The funeral director turned this crank-like thing, positioning the coffin so that the pallbearers could carry it to the grave site. The Klines were dressed in their Sunday best, dark suits with open-throated shirts, with the exception of Marv, the clothes horse, who was decked out in a wine-colored blazer and two-toned oxfords.

"I wonder if he made it out?" Dave said.

"Are you talking about Egge? You're not telling me you're actually coming over to Mrs. Mac's way of thinking?"

Dave crossed an ankle over his knee. More people were beginning to arrive for the funeral. He hadn't realized Harry had so many friends. "Not much chance of that happening, but I did go to church Sunday for the first time since I was in the SEALs, not counting the time I went cause of the attack on Father Mischke. You know what? It wasn't boring, I didn't ogle the girls, I didn't daydream, and I followed right along in the prayer book. I felt uplifted when I left Immaculate Conception. I'm going back next Sunday, and I might even go during the week."

"Well, shut my mouth. I'd have sworn you'd join Madalyn O'Hara before you ever dipped your hand in holy water again."

Resembling the Green Bay Packer front four, minus helmets and shoulder pads, the Kline boys hoisted the casket up on their shoulders and marched toward Harry's final resting place.

"I noticed *you* fell for it hook line and sinker," Dave said. "Somebody with your scientific bent..."

"You mean what Olive said about the ghosts?"

"Yeah that and the séance."

Moe adjusted his suspenders. "I've been going to see Olive, you know. Doing a little metaphysical research. She's quite a messed up girl, but that doesn't mean I still don't like her. Anyway, after you handcuffed her at the trailer, she said Mr. Egge forgave her for what happened with Bob Haskins."

"I think you were ready to believe it because of what she said about the spook with the forelock."

"I'm wondering why he wouldn't let *me* see him. Anyway, I feel a lot better about my dad's suicide."

"If you say so."

Moe knocked on Dave's temple. "Do I need to remind you that you knew where Colonel Colvill's arm was, that you were aware of Egge's parents first names before you called Silver Bay? How many of those visions did you have anyway?"

"A few. I don't want it to get out that I've been basing my murder investigations on a rust stain on the side of a barn. Officially, this office does not recognize the existence of any para-psychological evidence."

"You really are going to run for sheriff, aren't you?"

The Kline boys, their faces slicked with sweat, their breathing labored—Harry had approached three hundred pounds prior to his death—placed the coffin on the elevator which would lower the body. Dave got up off the gravestone and stretched. He lit a cigarette. Moe scowled, waved the smoke away from his face.

Father Mischke said some prayers, the funeral director levered the coffin down below, and it was time for Dave to help fill in Harry's grave.

Annie cried as she cast the first shovelfull down where Harry's face would have been if it hadn't been for the coffin. Dave tossed the cigarette aside, choked down on the shovel one-handed, and pitched a load of clay down on Harry, thinking about how close he'd come to being the one gettin' dumped on. What if Lucille had been a tad late when the Frankenstein monster had rearranged his face? He'd been about to cash in his chips. What would have happened to his *Show me, I'm from Missouri* soul?

Dave took his cap off and wiped his forehead with his sleeve. There was hair on his sleeve when he looked at it; he was winded, too, putting on a lot of weight lately.

He handed the shovel to Mel and stepped back to join Moe. Some people laughed at their relationship. A grown man in an official capacity who spent most of his time with a kid. They probably thought there was something sexual about it. The bastids.

Speaking of sex. "I meant to tell you," he said, turning to Moe. "Annie wants you to come over Sunday for dinner. Her little sister Aimee has a crush on you, I guess."

This shoveling bit was not ceremonial. It was Dave's turn again. He took the shovel and tossed another load of reddish-brown muck on Harry. A shiver went up his spine, as if he were the one down there having the dirt thrown on him.

Moe's face puckered up like he'd just swallowed a dose of castor oil. "Aimee Kline has a crush on me? She's never said more than two words to me." He was getting a little loud, attracting questioning glances from the other Klines. Thankfully, Aimee was sitting in the hearse with her mother and didn't hear the conversation.

Dave tried to shush him. "When you have a face like yours, rather reminiscent of the elephant boy, you have to take what you can get. Just remember how put off you were by the beautiful, aggressive Olive, how you ran and hid just cause she made one, little overture."

"You sure do have a poor memory. The world's biggest chauvinist. I don't suppose you remember telling me never to make the first move, that no relationship is ever equal and that one personality is always stronger. 'One partner is always wondering when the shoe will drop. Never let a woman know you're serious about her until she mentions the 'L' word first. And always hunt for a humorous way to say it when you finally do, if you ever do at all' is what you said."

"You know me, sometimes I talk like a man with a paper asshole. Anyway, you should be glad Aimee is quiet, most women literally can't shut up. I understand Aimee's musical, too. Spells her name kind of funny, though. You two should have lots in common. God knows I couldn't see the forest for the trees with Annie." Dave handed the shovel to Mel Kline.

"You know what I think?"

"This isn't going to be another one of your soliloquies, is it?"

"It was the play Annie made on Harley Barnhouser's grounder. That and the fact that you two could be twins. It's been scientifically proven that we all tend to seek out our own mirror image when we select a mate."

"I hadn't noticed we looked anything alike."

The grave was full. They would leave the cemetery custodian to put on the final touches. Dave shook hands with the Kline boys and made for his Jeep with Moe fast on his heels.

"I know you!" Moe said, a little out of breath. "You never forgave Mary Lou for dissing you in high school. You were just looking for a chance to get even."

Dave increased his stride. "The woman's got bad genes. Blaze Forman is her father."

"You're crazy."

"That sounds strange coming from one who takes three showers a day."

"At least I take showers. Most people realize the Saturday night bath is anachronistic."

Dave decided to let him win this round. He'd sneak over there sometime, listen for the shower, and flush the toilet. He reached the Jeep and turned to look back at the grave. Just off to the left there were two motorcycles, real hogs, decked out to the max, albeit with sidecars. A tall, odd-shaped man, wearing a Minnesota Gopher baseball cap, was crouched in one of the sidecars. He waved at Dave. The other man, a spitting image of Harry—bald, overweight, smoking a cigarette, saluted. A little round fellow in a fisherman's hat, and a tall mope with a bad cowlick sat astride the other hog. The pompadoured driver of the first machine, decked out in rap-around sunglasses, jeans, and jean jacket, could have passed for the original Rebel Without a Cause, the torment of high school principals across the land.

Suddenly the driver kick-started the engine, and the motorcycles wound their way out of the cemetery onto Co. Road 185, and began to ascend the hill heading toward the Miller Farm. Dave took his eyes off them momentarily to check whether Moe saw them, too, and when he turned back, they were gone.

Moe got in on the passenger side of the Jeep, Dave fired her up, and they drove off toward Meade Street and the supplementary rotisserie draft at Andy's Diner.